RODEO REBEL

JOANNE ROCK

THE INHERITANCE TEST

ANNE MARSH

MILLS & BOON

First Published in Great Britain 2023
by Mills & Boon, an imprint of HarperCollins*Publishers* Ltd
1 London Bridge Street, London, SE1 9GF

www.harpercollins.co.uk

HarperCollins*Publishers*
Macken House, 39/40 Mayor Street Upper,
Dublin 1, D01 C9W8, Ireland

Rodeo Rebel © 2023 Joanne Rock
The Inheritance Test © 2023 Anne Marsh

ISBN: 978-0-263-31752-7

0123

MIX
Paper | Supporting
responsible forestry
FSC™ C007454

This book is produced from independently certified FSC™ paper
to ensure responsible forest management.

For more information visit: www.harpercollins.co.uk/green

Printed and Bound in Spain using 100% Renewable electricity at
CPI Black Print, Barcelona

RODEO REBEL

JOANNE ROCK

For my three amazing sons,
Taylor, Camden and Maxim.
I could not be more proud of you.

Prologue

Gavin Kingsley couldn't pack his bags fast enough.

"You knew about this all along, and yet you said nothing to me." He stalked around the built-in dresser inside his spacious closet while he fumed aloud for the benefit of his oldest half brother, Levi Kingsley, currently on the other end of their teleconference.

Even now, Levi's face was framed in the tablet screen perched on a shelf between a display case of watches and the charging station for Gavin's electronics. He'd lived in this custom-built house for all of two years after agreeing to purchase land next door to the western Montana–based Kingsland Ranch, where he'd been raised. Somehow, his half brothers had convinced him to oversee the growing stud program at Kingsland, even though their father—Duke Kingsley—had never viewed Gavin as favorably as his sons by Duke's first wife.

Foolishly, Gavin had allowed himself to believe his estrangement from his father would be temporary. That Duke would welcome him back into the fold, and they'd smooth over past differences so that working together and living next door to Kingsland all made sense.

Only to be disinherited by his father's surprise will.

The memory of that moment—of the realization that he'd been an interloper in his own life, that his own father hadn't thought he deserved the Kingsley name—threatened to rip another hole through him.

Levi's voice cut through the maelstrom. "Gavin, I had no idea Dad intended to leave Kingsland Ranch solely to Quinton and me."

Not interested in his brother's explanations, Gavin swept out a drawerful of T-shirts and shoved them into a duffel bag. He'd sell the house as soon as possible. For now, he needed to catch the first flight out of Montana.

Far from Kingsland Ranch.

"I call bullshit." He yanked open a drawer of workout gear and grabbed a handful of items to add to his going-away collection of clothes. "You're a trustee of the estate. Obviously, you had to know in order to be named in the living trust—"

"Just because I'm the trustee doesn't mean I knew Dad's directives until the lawyer read them to us this afternoon," Levi shot back, his deeply olive skin showing a tinge of red as he got more fired up. He sat in his home office at the Kingsland main house, the same home where Duke had died of a heart attack two weeks before. Behind Levi, Gavin could still see the wooden sign with interlocking horseshoes that made up the ranch's logo. "The only reason he created that trust was so the estate could avoid probate and we could maintain day-to-day operations without any gap in management."

Gavin pulled out a garment bag to hold his dress shirts and suits.

"I find that tough to believe, given all the closed-door

meetings you and Dad had about the trust and his plans for Kingsland." Bad enough that his brother had lied to him by omission all these years, allowing Gavin to believe he'd have part ownership of the ranch and a say in the daily operations. But his own father hadn't thought Gavin warranted a footnote in his will.

But then, Duke had long looked at Gavin as less than worthy. Duke's two sons, Levi and Quinton, had been born of a love match between Duke and Adele Boudreaux, the daughter of one of the most successful horse breeders in Texas. After Adele's sudden death in a riding accident, Duke had married for convenience's sake, turning to his housekeeper, Isla Mitchell, as a temporary nanny for the boys. Gavin's mother had never escaped the taint of that domestic situation in her wealthy husband's eyes. After their divorce five years later, Gavin continued to have privileges at the ranch, but he'd spent a considerable part of his youth attempting to gain his dad's approval. Tough to do when he hadn't lived at Kingsland full-time. He and his mother had a downgraded lifestyle, where Gavin felt more like a visitor in his father's home than a son. Later, in his bull-riding days, he'd quit striving for approval and indulged his wild side, content to stir Duke's anger in a classic case of "some attention is better than no attention." But Gavin had cleaned up his act years ago and assumed he'd be included in the family business eventually.

Hell, he'd had faith in that idea so completely he'd allowed Levi to talk him into building his home next door to the Kingsley acreage.

"Well, believe it," Levi fired back, shoving a hand through dark hair that favored his French Creole mother. "And you can't leave now when we're about to launch the stud program. We can't do this without you—"

"Excellent. I can't deny I'm pleased to hear that," Gavin retorted. "Considering the blow I've been dealt this morn-

ing—to say nothing of Dad's illegitimate son, who got
screwed over even more than me—I like the idea of the
new business failing spectacularly without me."

Even though he'd worked his ass off to assemble all the
right pieces and the right horses to launch the Kingsland
breeding program. He hadn't thought twice about pooling
his resources with his brothers', assuming they would all
benefit from Kingsland's success. Now he wished like hell
he were launching the stud services under his own ranch's
name. He needed to consult a lawyer to figure out how to
untwine his finances from his family's.

"Gav, the kickoff event is just a few weeks away. And
we already promised Lauryn Hamilton that Kingsland
would sponsor the bachelor auction to benefit her horse rescue since the timing coincides with our launch." Levi leveled a scowl at him. "Do you mean to tell me you're going
to let her down after all the hoops she jumped through to
pitch this thing to us?"

Gavin's hand paused on the zipper of the garment bag
as he envisioned Lauryn's disappointed—gorgeous—face
if the Kingsley family backed out of the fundraiser she'd
worked tirelessly to pull together. He'd been the point person for Kingsland and had even promised her he'd go on-
stage to offer himself as a bachelor.

Something he wouldn't have done for anyone but her,
a woman who'd intrigued him for years yet had previously kept him at arm's length because of the reputation
he'd earned during those hell-raising days of his bull-riding career.

Part of that may have been because Gavin had run afoul
of her adoptive father, who also happened to be the local
sheriff. There'd been a long-standing enmity between him
and Sheriff Hamilton after Gavin had torn through his
newly planted cornfield on four-wheelers at midnight with
some buddies when he'd been all of fifteen. Clearly, the

man didn't believe in character redemption, even though Gavin had personally replanted the field. The sheriff had continued to hound him for the slightest misstep for years.

But her dad might not have been the only reason for the distance Lauryn kept between them. After college, she'd spent two years in Duke Kingsley's employ, working as his administrative assistant while she saved money to start her horse rescue since she was a passionate champion of providing homes for animals that had been neglected or abandoned.

Lauryn's rescue, Hooves and Hearts, now operated just a few miles down the road from Kingsland in the small town of Silent Spring, Montana. But given that she'd worked closely with Gavin's father for two years, he had to wonder if part of her refusal to give him the time of day—apart from this new fundraiser, Studs for Sale—was because Duke's view of Gavin had further tainted her own.

Making him wonder…as Duke's administrative assistant, had Lauryn been privy to the will that left Gavin with nothing?

Gritting his teeth, he shouldered the duffel bag and tried to collect himself before answering more calmly. "It's not me who let Lauryn down. If the event doesn't happen, it's your father's doing, not mine."

If it had been just a matter of money, Gavin wouldn't have even cared. He could make his own fortune, Kingsley wealth be damned.

But he'd been denied the ranch. His home. His livelihood. Something he'd assumed was his birthright as a Kingsley. A fresh wave of fury threatened to drag him under again, and he had to shake himself to ward off the anger.

Levi launched into another argument, but Gavin switched off the device to end the connection. He was too angry to field questions about his decisions right now. The hurt was too raw. The resentment all-consuming. His dad hadn't even bothered to explain the omission of his other sons in the will. Gavin and Clayton Reynolds—a son by a mistress—hadn't warranted even that much.

Gavin needed some time to get his head around what had happened so he could forge a new course for himself. One that didn't have anything to do with Kingsland Ranch.

Rationally, he knew he would miss working with Quinton and Levi. It hadn't been their fault Gavin had been disinherited. And he would miss their help with the stud program he'd taken so much pride in developing.

But he wasn't about to just hand over all his hard work to his brothers now. The breeding business couldn't launch with the Kingsland name on it—not when Gavin was no longer in the Kingsley fold. They'd need to draw up a division of assets.

A divorce from his own family.

Yet—as he stalked through the living area of the massive home he'd built to overlook the Madison River, which snaked past Kingsland's grazing pastures and created a boundary between his holding and his family's—Gavin was surprised to realize that despite all the hell that had rained down on his head today, his thoughts still circled around the fact that he'd have to disappoint Lauryn Hamilton. But not even the lure of her mysterious hazel eyes or her deep, throaty laugh that always sounded like she was thinking something slightly wicked could make him stay where his contributions weren't acknowledged or appreciated.

He'd kept Lauryn safely in his personal fantasies for years. For now, she'd just have to stay there since the last thing he needed was any attachment to this godforsaken place.

One

Fit to be tied, Lauryn Hamilton steered her pickup truck along the Madison River, past the well-known Montana ranch where she'd worked for two years. But Kingsland, with its interlocking-horseshoes logo and endless acreage, wasn't her destination today.

The road was paved and smooth, making it impossible to kick up a cloud of dust and gravel the way she would have preferred as she drove toward the man who had stood her up this afternoon. Because this level of anger required some kind of physical outlet. If not dust clouds and gravel, then throwing her meeting notes in Gavin Kingsley's face would have to suffice.

She stomped harder on the accelerator, beyond ready to confront the charismatic bad boy of Silent Spring. He'd made a big deal about chasing her for years—behaving as though he wanted her even as he gladly dated every woman in her age bracket for miles around. Then, the one time when she'd actually needed the flirtatious rancher to show up for her—to help her get the Studs for Sale event off the ground—he hadn't bothered to put in an appearance.

Even though he'd chosen the time and date for the planning meeting weeks ago. He'd agreed to sponsor the auction that would be held at Kingsland Ranch. Had even seemed excited about it. Didn't he have any sense of responsibility?

The main ranch house came into view a moment later, but Lauryn bypassed the mammoth two-story family compound to seek out Gavin's place. She'd never visited it personally, but she'd heard all about the home's construction two years ago since the former bull rider had always been a subject for gossip among Silent Spring locals. His good looks and bad boy reputation had made it impossible to avoid talk of his escapades ever since she'd moved here, back when her parents had adopted her at twelve years old after the most traumatic month of her life.

Rubbing a hand over one shoulder where the scars of that time had left her with a visible reminder of old hurts, Lauryn could still recall hearing about Gavin for the first time, when he'd driven through her dad's fields at midnight. At first, she'd envisioned a boy similar to her— someone in a foster home, who'd had a rough start to life—when she'd imagined what the late-night intruder might be like. When she'd learned that he was the son of the wealthiest man in town, an overindulged Kingsley son, her curiosity about him had vanished.

They'd always been worlds apart, from their very different beginnings to the way Gavin thumbed his nose at the world while she strove to make people like her. But when Gavin had agreed to help her with the Studs for Sale event, she'd believed—briefly—that he'd changed.

The more fool her.

Moments later, the newly constructed cedar home came into view. Smaller than the main residence but impressive nevertheless, the two-story building was L-shaped around a wide redbrick driveway with darker pavers laid out in the pattern of the Kingsland horseshoe logo. Lauryn parked her truck right in the middle of the emblem and jumped down to the ground, her boots striking the stone pavers with determined steps.

Checking her watch, she noted the time was half past noon before she stepped onto the porch and raised her fist to knock on the door.

"Gavin." She called his name as she rapped quickly on the wooden barrier. "It's Lauryn. I need to speak with you."

No answer came.

Not by word or deed. The door remained shut, the house remained quiet and her call went unanswered.

Where could he be? He knew how important the Studs for Sale event was to her. Her horse rescue desperately needed the infusion of capital the bachelor auction would bring since she was expanding the rescue into an equine-therapy program—an effort close to her heart, considering how much it had helped her recover from the trauma she'd experienced as a child.

Knowing that Hooves and Hearts would benefit from the auction, she'd done all the preplanning work herself to make certain that her sponsors could make a difference simply by writing a check. But Gavin had wanted to take on a bigger role since her event coincided with the launch of Kingsland's breeding service. Her Studs for Sale bachelor auction would naturally bring a lot of spotlight to Kingsland. It made no sense for Gavin to abandon the project now.

Peering around the quiet front courtyard, she spied empty wooden benches beside manicured dwarf trees, chokecherry bushes full of white blooms and pink bitterroot flowers climbing over low rocks. Everything well tended.

But no Gavin. She'd already left two disgruntled messages for him, so she didn't see any point in calling again.

Lifting her phone, she opened the screen this time to text Quinton, Gavin's brother, who'd agreed to be one of the bachelors auctioned off for Studs for Sale. His tech business had brought him a different kind of visibility than his siblings and—she hoped—his fame in the digital community would attract all the more attendees to the auction.

But her big draw remained Gavin. His bull-riding fame had brought him a huge following that would welcome the opportunity to bid on an evening with him. She walked over to one of the benches near the chokecherry bush and took a seat in the spring sunlight to type.

Do you know where Gavin is? He missed a meeting on the bachelor auction.

She glanced up from the phone, still hoping to see some sign of Gavin. Returning from the fields on a tractor, maybe. Or riding up on horseback. But the only sound in the stillness was her phone chiming with an incoming text.

Haven't heard from him since he took off after our father's will reading. The old man cut Gavin out of everything.

The statement took her a moment to absorb. Lauryn knew Duke Kingsley had died two weeks prior. She'd once worked for the man, but they'd never been close. To show her respects, she had attended the wake with her mom and had offered condolences to the three Kingsley sons who'd attended. But she hadn't heard anything about the family patriarch's will.

Gavin "took off"? Her stomach knotted at what that might mean for her event.

Her fingers hovered over her phone since she had no

idea how to respond. Before she could decide, another text from Quinton appeared.

Not sure about Kingsland sponsoring the bachelor auction now, Lauryn, since we can't run the breeding business without Gav. But you're still welcome to hold the event at Kingsland.

Things went from bad to worse. The gala was just three weeks away. She thanked Quinton for the information and told him she'd get back to him about the auction.

Distress over the event and her frustration with Gavin were certainly tempered by the news that he'd been cut out of his father's will completely. He must be devastated. And no matter how much Gavin had gotten under her skin over the years, she hated to think of his dad pulling the rug out from under him that way.

She walked toward her pickup truck as she debated her options, ducking away from a honeybee buzzing nearby. And in the quiet that followed, just as she reached for the door handle of her vehicle, she heard the rumble of an engine in the distance.

A sound that grew louder, as if coming closer.

The ranch road wound past Gavin's house and continued on to the lower pastures. Conceivably, a ranch hand could be driving out to work on fences or check on animals in those fields.

Yet some sense tickled the back of her neck like a premonition.

A sense confirmed a moment later when a familiar oversize black pickup came into view.

Gavin's truck.

Her heart pounded faster as he drove closer, the outline of his face becoming visible as he neared. Stetson in place, he locked eyes with her through the windshield, his brown gaze like a laser beam as he held her in his sights.

Inexplicably, her pulse stuttered and then quickened.

The black sheep of Kingsland Ranch had returned.

So much for returning to Silent Spring without anyone noticing.

Gavin met the challenging hazel gaze of the town's sexiest woman as he drove toward his house. Lauryn Hamilton stood in the middle of his driveway, arms crossed, chin tilted up. She was dressed for business in a figure-hugging short-sleeved navy blue dress that buttoned all the way up the front, the hem brushing the tops of her high-heeled chocolate brown boots. Long chestnut-colored waves rested on her shoulders, her full lips pursed in a moue of displeasure.

Today hadn't been the first time he'd seen that expression on her face when she looked his way, so it shouldn't bug him so much now. Especially when that pout of hers was so sexy it ought to be NSFW. But Gavin couldn't enjoy the sight of those plump pink lips quite as much now, knowing he was only going to disappoint her further when he told her he was backing out of the bachelor auction.

Behind him on the jump seat, the thump, thump, thump of his Rottweiler's tail reminded Gavin that he wasn't the only one who'd spotted their guest.

"Maybe you can put a smile on her face, Rocco. I've got my work cut out for me otherwise," he observed as he parked his truck alongside hers. "I could use the backup."

Gavin cracked open the door and stepped down to the brick driveway before opening the rear cab door and unhooking the carabiner from the pup's harness. While Rocco bounded out of the truck, Gavin pasted on a polite smile, having learned from past experience that behavior trending toward charming or flirtatious would only earn scorn from the horse-rescue owner.

"Hello, Lauryn. To what do I owe the pleasure?" He reached in to remove an empty trunk from the cargo bed while Rocco approached Lauryn with a butt-wiggling tail wag.

At least Rocco was able to get some love from her. Lauryn scratched behind his ears, assuring the Rottwei-ler- husky mix that he was a very good boy.

A sentiment he guessed she wouldn't be sharing with him.

While Rocco soaked up the attention, Gavin slid the trunk onto the driveway, well aware of his mission to pack up more clothes while he figured out his next move.

Seven days on a beach in Mexico—some more sober than others—hadn't been enough to help him cool off about being disinherited. But now that he'd mourned the loss of the life he'd thought he was going to lead, he was ready to make a new plan that didn't include the Kingsleys.

"The pleasure?" Straightening from where she'd been petting the dog, Lauryn followed him toward the house as he carried his trunk to the front porch while Rocco trot-ted off to the barns. "It is not a pleasure for me, Gavin, because I wasted the whole morning waiting around for you to begin a planning meeting for the bachelor auction. Needless to say, you never showed up."

Ah, damn.

He paused in the middle of entering his security code for the front door, regret slamming him for the oversight.

"Was that today? I should have messaged you." He'd thought about it a few times during his week of drinking away the past, his father and all the hopes he'd had for a life in Montana working beside his brothers. But when-ever a thought of the Studs for Sale event crossed his mind, urging him to call Lauryn, he either hadn't had his phone handy, hadn't been able to get good reception or had ended up thinking about Lauryn in ways that weren't at all businesslike…

"I would have appreciated a heads-up," she agreed, stopping at the edge of his porch as if there was an invisible line there she wouldn't follow him across. "Better yet, you could have been there with us since Kingsland is the biggest sponsor. I specifically arranged the best time for you so you could ensure the event showcased the ranch." Her tone stopped short of being chastising, no doubt because of the clout and capital at stake while she believed him to represent Kingsland's interests.

How fast would that change once she found out he was backing out of the event?

He knew she'd always been wary around him. That her father's opinions of him—and her own dad's familiarity with the scrapes he'd gotten into as a younger man—had colored her view of him. Her cool demeanor ever since she'd arrived in Silent Spring as the sheriff's adopted daughter had told Gavin that she didn't think much of him. But in their two previous meetings about Studs for Sale, he'd had reason to believe maybe he was changing her mind about him.

Not that he needed her good opinion, damn it.

His head pounded with the stress of coming up with a solution on the fly. He should have been thinking about this kind of thing for the last week, but simply getting through the days with the knowledge that his own father had thought him unworthy of the family legacy had been hellish.

Stabbing the rest of the code into the buttons on the security pad, Gavin disarmed the system and opened the door to settle his trunk in the foyer. Then he stepped outside again to finish their conversation.

"I'm sorry, Lauryn." Restless and edgy about a topic he

didn't want to have with anyone, let alone a woman whose view of him had always been biased, he rocked back on his heels while he measured his words. "I've been reeling this week since learning my father cut me out of Kingsland Ranch in his will."

He studied her reaction carefully, searching for the slightest hint that she'd had previous intelligence of his father's intentions during the years she'd been Duke's assistant.

And, lo and behold, a nervous swipe of her tongue along her upper lip was her only visible response. She didn't seem surprised by the news. Only...uneasy?

His suspicion about her connection to his father grew. Not just because she might know more than she was saying. But also because she could have tainted his father's opinion of him.

"It's my turn to apologize, Gavin." Her gaze flicked to the ground, where she shifted her feet before meeting his again. She shaded her eyes to look at him in the strong afternoon sunlight, her tone softening. "I heard the news about the will from Quinton when I called him a little while ago, and I can't imagine how upsetting the last few weeks have been since your dad's passing."

A conversation with his brother would explain why the news about being disinherited hadn't surprised her. Yet her cool composure still gave him misgivings about how much she knew and when she'd learned of it. Sun beating down on his shoulders, he pointed toward the shaded area at the end of the house and gestured for her to follow him as he answered.

"'Upsetting' would be an understatement. More like someone cut me off at the knees." Hating the way that could be construed as self-pitying, he halted just inside the shaded overhang with a view of the Madison River. Pivoting to face her, he cut to the chase. "That's why today's meeting completely slipped my mind. I've been thinking about next steps, and all that really remains clear to me right now is I can't stay here."

Lauryn had been following close behind him, but she took a step back now, grazing a rocking chair with her knee. She reached long, manicured fingers blindly out to one side to steady herself on the back of the chair.

"What do you mean? You can't stay at the house anymore?" Her dark eyebrows knit in confusion. "Quinton mentioned you've been gone—"

"As in, I can't live in a house next to Kingsland anymore. I don't even plan to stay in Montana. And unfortunately, I won't be able to represent Kingsland at the bachelor auction, so I'm not going to participate."

At her gasp, he hastened to add, "I'll donation match, of course. Just let me know what you think an average bid for a bachelor might have been, and I'll write a check."

Two

Heaven help her.

Even after being disinherited, Gavin Kingsley assumed he could fix every problem by writing a check.

As if he hadn't just swung a sledgehammer through an event she'd spent months preparing.

Lauryn stared at him as he tugged off his Stetson and set it on the patio table nearby, his faded jeans hugging lean hips while he turned. An olive green Henley shirt showcased his strong arms and shoulders, his build taller than many of the most successful bull riders. And yet he'd made a name for himself in the years he'd competed, earning prizes and recognition that even his cynical father had grudgingly noticed. Not that he'd been impressed. Duke Kingsley had told Lauryn that Gavin only sought out the rodeo to avoid real work.

A sentiment her dad would have surely echoed if she'd ever asked his opinion. Certainly her father had weighed in enough times in the past weeks about her decision to approach Gavin to do the bachelor auction in the first place. Logically, she understood that Sheriff Caleb Hamilton couldn't help but view the black sheep Kingsley with a jaundiced eye. Silent Spring's local lawman had had plenty of opportunities to field phone calls when a younger Gavin would slip into local pastures to practice bull riding on the neighboring ranches' rankest bulls. Or when he'd organize drag races near the river on summer weekends, risking his neck to push a car as hard as it could go.

Or so she'd heard.

She had friends who'd attended those races and spoke with breathless admiration about Gavin's daring and control as he beat out the field with his prowess behind the wheel. Yet she'd never actually attended one of those underground meets.

But it had been years since he'd done things like that. A change tracked roughly to when he'd quit the pro bull-riding circuit so he could help his brothers with Kingsland. Lauryn had been too busy starting up her equine rescue at the time to take much notice of his return to town, but he'd certainly turned the heads of all her friends. And while he'd maintained his devil-may-care approach to dating, his work ethic had seemed admirable. Up until today's missed meeting, in fact, Lauryn had been impressed by his commitment to her fundraiser event. He hadn't tried to lay on the charm with her or make sly remarks when she'd suggested the Studs for Sale name. If anything, he'd been readily supportive of the rescue, offering suggestions to make the evening flow smoothly and connecting her with two other eligible bachelors who promised to excite lots of bidding.

She'd thought that he'd turned a corner from his old ways.

But today, he'd stood her up at an important meeting and offered to buy his way out of a commitment.

Now Gavin ran a hand through his longish brown hair, tucking a few shorter strands behind his ear. The stubble around his jaw and mouth was several days past shaving, the effect only adding to his rugged sex appeal.

Or it would be, if she were a woman who sought out bad boys, which she most decidedly was not. Gavin Kingsley might be going through a truly rough time in his life right now, but that didn't mean she would let down her guard around a man who—for most of his life—had played fast and loose with rules.

And women.

The reminder made her stuff down the urge to console him. To tell him she understood how losing a parent could make someone feel adrift and alone.

"Gavin." His name sounded too intimate on her lips. Was it because of the thoughts she'd been having about him? She dragged in a breath scented with heather and catmint from the flower bed surrounding the patio. "I'm grateful for the offer of a donation, but what this event really needs is *you*. Your contacts, your participation."

"You mean *Kingsley* contacts." His lip curled. But then his dog trotted toward them again, the black face with tan points appearing suddenly from behind a thicket near the river's edge, and Gavin's expression eased. He whistled for his pet, causing the Rottweiler mix to kick it into a higher gear as he headed toward the porch. "Maybe Levi or Quinton will—"

"No, I need *you*." She said it with emphasis, and as soon as the words were out there, she heard how personal that sounded. Her cheeks warmed, and she was glad for a reason to turn her face away from Gavin as Rocco reached them. She scratched the dog's ears, having gotten to know the handsome Rotty well during the years she worked for Duke since Gavin had visited the main house frequently. "That is, you bring something different to the table than your brothers. You're…" She struggled to find a tactful way to say that women from halfway across the state had told Lauryn they were attending the event to bid on a date with the sought-after bachelor rancher. "…very popular."

"So I'll find someone to take my place." He raised his arms in exasperation, making Rocco whine a sympathetic chorus even as the dog left Lauryn to sit beside his owner. "Lauryn, I can't be a part of this. I'm done with Kingsland for good."

Anxiety balled in her gut as she realized how serious he was about this. Could he really bail on her this late in the game?

His face was on the event website. A popular internet blog devoted to cowgirl life had planned a feature. Two national horse publications were covering the fundraiser, a fact that had appealed to Gavin when the launch of Kingsland's stud program was set to coincide with the bachelor auction.

"So participate under your own ranch name. Don't go as Kingsland. Go to represent Broken Spur." She pointed to the wooden sign on the vintage silo close to the river.

Unlike the sleekly stylized horseshoes logo of Kingsland, the Broken Spur sign used an actual rusty spur sticking out of the wooden placard at an awkward angle.

"Seriously? I didn't even pick the name. I just inherited it when I bought the place." Bending to scoop up a rope chew toy that lay nearby, Gavin waved it in front of Rocco before winging it out onto lawn, sending the dog running. "It's not like I'm planning to do business here—"

"So you're going to just hand over the stud program to your brothers?" She'd edged closer to make her point.

Pushing at his pride.

Pushing her agenda because her rescue deserved her best efforts. She'd invested too much time with Studs for Sale to let the event fall short of all it could accomplish.

She recalled with perfect clarity the moment a piece of her soul had begun to heal because of equine therapy. She owed her ability to move forward in life to horses, and she planned to pay that gift forward to other people wandering the world, feeling hollow inside.

"Hell no." Emotion flashed in his brown eyes when he turned her way. Anger. Resentment. "But I don't have a plan yet to launch the business when I need to untwine my financial interests from theirs."

They stood entirely too near. Breathing each other's air in a silent moment that stretched out between them.

The musk and leather scent of him made her want to step closer still. Then his gaze flicked lower, raking over her mouth. Lingering. A shiver rolled through her, skin prickling with awareness. But then, reminding herself who she was talking to and how much she didn't want to be just another woman who fell under his spell, Lauryn edged back again.

"What will it take to make you reconsider?" Needing some space between them, a distraction from the pull he exerted over her, Lauryn bent to take the chew toy Rocco had proudly returned to them.

When she flung it as far onto the lawn as possible, she could feel Gavin's eyes on her.

"My presence is that important to you?" The timbre of his voice, smoky and soft, tripped up her spine in a peculiar way.

She shook off the sensation, admonishing herself that this talk had to be all business.

Hooves and Hearts needed the income from this event too much for her to get caught up in whatever games Gavin liked to play with women.

Games she suspected he excelled at.

"The invitations have gone out," she explained, chasing the image of sensual playtime from her brain. Where had that come from? She wished his conscience would just kick in and explain to him that a responsible adult would make good on his word to be a part of the fundraiser. "Guests have RSVP'd. They all think you're going to be there."

His jaw worked, flexing and tensing, as he seemed to chew over the idea. Once more, his attention dipped lower, taking her in from boots to breasts.

Or maybe her breasts just noticed his attention more than the rest of her. Her face flamed hot, and she found herself sliding one hand beneath her hair to lift the mass that felt too warm against her neck.

Catching herself in the act, she released it once more, yanking her arms to her side as she realized his gaze was calmly fixed on her face again, his expression masked.

"If I do this for you, I wouldn't be going for the sake of the guests." Something about his words made her wary even as hope reignited.

"Meaning you might attend after all?" She searched his brown eyes, looking for the catch.

"On one condition." His chin ticked up.

She sensed a challenge coming, but she needed his participation too much to care.

"Name it."

Between them, Rocco's furry body brushed against her, the dog's panting audible as he waited for another round of fetch. But she didn't dare look away from Gavin as she mentally urged him to follow through with the auction.

As if she could impose her will on him if she stared hard enough.

"Go on a date with me."

He couldn't have surprised her more if he'd asked her to drag race him.

In the silence that ensued, she heard a tractor at work in the distance, a sign of the Broken Spur's fields being worked nearby. The engine hummed in chorus with the warning bells jangling in her brain.

"Excuse me?" She'd heard him clearly enough. But she had to be missing something since he'd never made an overture toward her.

She'd assumed the occasional hot looks that he sent her way were a knee-jerk reaction, an automatic facet of being a ladies' man. They'd had little to do with her personally.

No doubt he flirted with everyone that way.

"It's a simple request, Lauryn. I'd like—just once— to take you on a date." Never looking away from her, he gave a soothing scratch to Rocco's head and somehow released the dog from the game with some kind of nonverbal command.

Or so she guessed since Rocco took his toy onto a rug near the back door, where he lay down and put his head between his paws with a long doggy huff.

Rocco seemed to comprehend the man in front of her far better than she ever would.

"I don't understand. Why would you want to do that?" She already knew she would agree. Of course she would say yes for the good of the charity event.

The man was a sought-after bachelor for a reason, not the least of which were his good looks and magnetic charm. Women threw themselves at him. And while he'd always moved on quickly from them, Lauryn had never heard any complaints other than that they were sad when their time with him came to an end.

There was an implied compliment in that.

But she wanted to know why Gavin would request such a thing when he could have dozens of women lining up to be his very willing partner for any given night.

A ghost of his old, careless grin crossed his face.

"No need to sound so surprised." He leaned a square shoulder against the wooden post at the edge of the patio, as if settling in for a casual conversation when his words had thrown her into a whirlwind of confused anxiety. "I don't think you need for me to tell you you're a very compelling woman."

Flustered, she shook her head.

"Don't be ridiculous. I'm not fishing for compliments, Gavin. I just can't fathom how a date with me will make it any more bearable for you to participate in an event you're obviously now dreading." An awful thought occurred to her. "Is this about my father? A way to tick off the sheriff?"

Any hint of a smile vanished.

"How little you think of me," he observed wryly, shaking his head. "Although, oddly enough, even as you offend me, you manage to tap into a reason that I want this date."

Impatience stiffened her spine. Tension tightened in her shoulders.

"You're talking in riddles. Can you please just be straight with me?"

"Of course." He arched a light brown eyebrow at her, as if she were the one playing word games. "I don't appreciate that you think the worst of me. And given the way my own father just erased me from his life, it gets under my skin that people are determined to write me off."

The accusation hit home with pinpoint accuracy.

No matter that she believed Gavin had well-earned his reputation, a part of her still felt the sting of his allegation. She pursed her lips, unsure how to respond.

But he saved her from replying when he continued speaking a moment later, "So, if we're going to work together on this bachelor auction, I'd appreciate it if you'd take the time to get to know me. Go on a date with me, Lauryn." That trademark smile returned at full wattage, a potent weapon in his seductive arsenal, as he lowered his voice a notch. "Find out for yourself if I'm as bad as everyone says."

Three

Gavin knew Lauryn wouldn't refuse.

Yet having the ice queen of Silent Spring over a barrel didn't give him the satisfaction it might have at one time. Maybe because he had every reason to suspect she'd played a role in depriving him of the family legacy, a concern that left him feeling more bitter than vengeful since he couldn't do anything to change the fact that Duke Kingsley had gone to his grave assuming the worst of his son.

"Fine. It's a deal." Lauryn thrust her hand toward him to seal the bargain. "One date in exchange for your participation in the bachelor auction—both as a bachelor and as a sponsor."

He noted she was careful to spell that out.

Smart businesswoman.

And yet the gesture provided all the more proof that she thought him less than honorable. Making him doubly glad he'd come up with the date scheme as a way to learn more about her and how much she'd known about his disinheritance.

"We're in agreement," he assured her, taking her soft, slender fingers in his to seal the deal.

Beneath his thumb, in the tender vee of her palm, he felt the warm throb of her pulse beneath her skin. A rhythmic beat that jumped faster when he gave it a small, tentative stroke.

For a moment, Lauryn's hazel gaze flashed with startled awareness.

Right before she drew her hand free.

"Then let's agree to a time to go over the meeting notes I had ready for this morning," she murmured, folding her arms across her chest in a way that made her breasts all the more enticing.

Not that he let his gaze linger.

He wasn't about to push a seduction agenda with a woman whose good will he required if he was going to draw her out about her relationship with his father. Although somewhere along the way, he wouldn't mind hearing Lauryn Hamilton acknowledge that the chemistry between them wasn't all one sided.

"How about the day after tomorrow?" He'd need to rearrange his schedule since he'd already agreed to meet a Realtor the next day to view ranch properties in Wyoming.

Now Gavin would need to cool his heels in Montana for at least a few more weeks until the bachelor auction.

"It will have to be after noon," she answered without even consulting a schedule. "I'm driving out to Twin Bridges that morning to deliver a four-year-old mare to a family who fell in love with her after visiting the rescue last month."

The warmth in her voice, the glow in her face at the mention of the animals in her care, told everything about her commitment to her cause. No matter what Gavin learned about his father from her—or not—he could hardly begrudge the time and investment in someone so dedicated to equine rescue.

"That's fine," he assured her, gesturing toward the walkway back toward the front of the house where her pickup waited beside his so he could escort her out. He had new plans to make for his remaining days in Silent Spring. "If you're running late that day, just shoot me a text. I can meet later, if necessary."

As they moved out of the covered-patio area, Rocco rose to follow, tail wagging sleepily after his doze. To keep his attention off the enticing sway of Lauryn's hips as they walked, Gavin allowed his attention to move to the custom-built ranch house he'd spent so long designing to his exact specifications—from the detached garage with separate kitchen and suite for guests to the hand-hewn timber used in the living area and the spectacular river views. He would miss the place when he left, but this work with Lauryn would keep him here a little while longer.

"Thank you." Lauryn shifted her hair to the opposite shoulder as they walked, a few silky waves brushing his arm. "But I don't anticipate any problems. The adopter is an experienced horseman buying the mare for his teenage daughter. I know he's got the stable and pasture ready, and he's paid in advance for a year's worth of hay."

"Sounds like your ideal customer," Gavin observed as they reached her truck. "Where would you like to meet?"

She nibbled her lip as she thought, and Gavin distracted himself from her mouth by reaching for the handle on the driver's-side door.

"Would you mind if we worked here? Your place is on the way back from Twin Bridges."

The thought of having her all to himself again sent a surge of red-hot desire through him. He tried to ignore it, grateful he'd have a couple of days to come up with a plan for their time together.

Because he would swear that the chemistry between them had grown more potent this afternoon. While he'd always felt the draw just beneath the surface of their interactions, he'd seen a hint of her reaction to him today, and that had amped up the heat far beyond anything the mild spring sun dished out.

"Of course. And if you send me the meeting notes ahead of time, I'll be all the more prepared." He made the offer mostly so he could devote more of their time together to conversation about her. He needed to find casual ways to get her talking about those years in his father's employment.

Yet to see the obvious pleasure she took in the gesture, he almost felt guilty for the ulterior motive.

"That would be fantastic." Her eyes lit up as she looked at him. "I'll shoot them your way once I get home."

Holding the door for her while she stepped up on the running board of her sporty red pickup truck, Gavin couldn't help but see a flash of her bare legs as her navy sheath dress hiked up away from the tops of her suede boots.

Rocco chose that moment to bark, looking back and forth between them.

A friendly goodbye to their guest? Or a reminder to Gavin to put his eyes back in his head?

He gritted his teeth, guessing it was the latter, while Lauryn's gaze shifted to the dog before she laughed with pleasure.

"It was good to see you, too, Rocco," she said sweetly, reaching down to scratch the dog's head before she tucked her dress more securely around her legs. "I'll be back at the Broken Spur before you know it."

Gavin told himself it was stupid to envy his pet, but

the big fur-beast was damned lucky to have Lauryn's long fingers stroke him. No wonder the tail-wagging recommenced with renewed enthusiasm.

"See you then," Gavin managed over a dry throat as he shut the door behind her.

Stepping back with a wave, he watched her pull out of the driveway.

And no matter that he'd gotten out of the meeting exactly what he wanted—an opportunity to find out how much Lauryn had known about his father's plans to disinherit him and what role she might have played in the decision—Gavin couldn't help but think he'd signed on for a whole lot more than he bargained for.

Two days later, Lauryn folded her arms on the four-rail fence behind her client's spacious home in Twin Bridges.

In the pasture in front of her, she watched Toffee, the bay mare, explore her new surroundings. The horse nosed a pile of clean straw behind her brand-new stable, then walked slowly toward a black spruce tree that would provide good shade in the summer.

"She seems right at home, doesn't she?" a familiar feminine voice said behind her.

Turning, Lauryn met the kind eyes of her former foster mother, Ellen Crawford. The older woman looked exactly the same as Lauryn remembered her from her brief stay with the Crawfords before the Hamiltons adopted her when she was twelve years old. Maybe a few strands of the blond ponytail that hung over the shoulder of her red flannel shirt were grayer, but the keen blue eyes were just as warm, the walk just as full of vigor. Ellen and her husband, Chip, had fostered children right up until a few months ago, when they adopted their last foster daughter, Zara, now the lucky recipient of the bay mare they'd taken in from Lauryn's rescue.

"Toffee is going to love this place." Opening her arms for a hug, Lauryn gave the tall, spare woman a quick squeeze, the earthy scent of herbs clinging to her from her work in the greenhouse next door, where the Crawfords sold plants and trees. "But then, you have a knack for making everyone feel at home here."

Ellen smiled her pleasure as she joined Lauryn at the rail. "She'll be good company for Zara. I remember how horses helped you come back to life after you moved here."

Memories crowded her thoughts, the sudden intrusion of the past uncomfortable, even though she'd worked through the worst of it a long time ago. Ellen Crawford was the only person in Lauryn's life who could speak so openly about the horror she'd faced in her previous foster home.

Not that she'd been mistreated. Her then-family had been kind enough, if a little overwhelmed by the number of children under their roof at the time. Their home had been an aging farmhouse, and there'd been plenty of room for them all and fun places to explore. An attic. A basement. Barns and outbuildings. Much of it hadn't been in use at the time, but Lauryn and her favorite foster sister, thirteen-year-old Jamie, hadn't heeded their parents' warnings about staying out of the older structures. They'd grown comfortable in their "hideouts," sneaking books into their best-loved haunts to escape chores or avoid their brothers.

Not that they needed a reason. Both had been caught up in the joys of having a real sister and best friend, a first for each of them. They'd been glad just to spend time together, sharing every secret while they braided one another's hair and dreamed of living next door to each other once they were old enough to leave the foster home.

A dream that had never happened for Jamie.

After the accident, Lauryn didn't recall much until she'd arrived at the Crawfords' home and her new foster mom, Ellen, introduced her to equine therapy. Over the next several months, Lauryn found a new best friend in the understanding brown eyes of a Champagne quarter horse gelding.

"Champy was a godsend," Lauryn admitted, her voice thick with the memory of the bond they'd formed. A downside of her adoption by the Hamiltons had been their insistence that she not visit her quarter horse friend anymore—or anyone from her past—believing a fresh start would be best. She hadn't complained about it, sensing that, as a twelve-year-old with a traumatic history, she'd been fortunate to find a forever family at all.

"I'd forgotten his name." Ellen chuckled softly in her easy way as they watched Toffee snuffle around the black spruce needles before snorting in disapproval at the scent and backing away. "Champy. What a good horse."

For a moment, they remembered the gelding in companionable silence. That ability to sit with uncomfortable things—sadness, memories—was one of the reasons Lauryn had sought Ellen out after college. As much as Lauryn adored her adoptive parents, they'd had a tough time talking about the past, and they certainly hadn't wanted her to either. No one in Silent Spring knew her real personal story because the Hamiltons had told their friends they were adopting a relative's child.

Lauryn's past had been swept under a rug.

But Jamie—like Champy—deserved remembering.

A moment later, Ellen's voice called her back to the present. "We received your invitation to Studs for Sale. It sounds like quite the event you've put together."

Nearby, Chip stepped out of the stable and into the pasture, giving them a wave as he walked toward Toffee, brandishing an apple.

Lauryn was grateful for the extra moment to gather her thoughts about the auction. Her planning meeting with Gavin was only an hour away, and visions of seeing him again had occupied far too much space in her mind the last two days.

"I hope so. It's been a lot of work, but it will be worth it if it raises enough money to take my plans for the equine-therapy facility to the next level." She'd dreamed of this for years.

She would have never guessed what a big role Gavin would play in bringing the equine-therapy center to life.

"I was surprised to see Gavin Kingsley on the list of available bachelors." Ellen's tone was teasing as she slanted a sly look Lauryn's way. "I thought he was the last man in Silent Spring you wanted anything to do with."

"Have I said that before?" Straightening from the fence, Lauryn picked at a string from around the button of her flannel work shirt.

It sounded like something she'd thought, certainly, but she couldn't recall venting about Gavin to Ellen.

"Long ago, when you first went to work for Duke Kingsley," Ellen reminded her more gently. "I remarked that it was a job with good contacts, considering that even then you hoped to work with horses. But you made it clear Gavin was not anyone you thought very highly of."

That she'd spouted off so openly about him gave her a little more understanding into why Gavin had insisted she get to know him.

"There's a chance I rushed to judgment about him when I was younger," she admitted, pulling back her shoulders. If she wanted people to bid on Silent Spring's resident bad boy, she shouldn't speak negatively about him, of course. That didn't mean she'd changed her opinion. "He might have more redeeming qualities than I realized now that he's an adult."

Ellen nodded as she escorted Lauryn toward the truck and horse trailer backed partially on the lawn. Chip had wanted her to unload Toffee as close to the pasture as possible in case she was spooked by the new surroundings.

"The sheriff definitely doesn't think so." Withdrawing a pair of work gloves from the back pocket of her jeans, Ellen smoothed out the crumpled fingers before putting them on, her brow furrowed. "I remember blowing by Gavin's truck one day last year when I was in a rush to get to an appointment. Then, in the rearview mirror, I saw your dad tear out from a speed trap to pull Gavin over."

The story made Lauryn a little uneasy since she'd heard from friends that her father had it "in" for Gavin. But then, Lauryn had the advantage of knowing her dad's side of things. All the old pranks. All the history.

"They definitely don't get along," she acknowledged, hoping they would be civil at the Studs for Sale event. She felt sure her parents would attend to support her, although she hadn't received their RSVP yet.

"The funny part is, Gavin hadn't been speeding. I felt so guilty, I even called the police station to let them know they must have caught the wrong vehicle on radar and it had been *me* driving hell for leather through there. But your dad was adamant he had a reason for pulling over Gavin."

Defensiveness for her father rose.

"And I'm sure he did." She attempted to say it with levity, but the comment fell flat as she met Ellen's troubled blue gaze.

In the awkward moment that followed, she gestured toward her truck and continued, "But I should get underway now. I'm so grateful to you and Chip for making this transition easy for Toffee."

Ellen's face cleared as she gave a nod.

"Our pleasure. And I'm excited to break out my dancing shoes for the evening of the bachelor auction. That band you hired is one of Chip's favorites."

After a few more pleasantries exchanged, Lauryn was

in her truck again and driving to her meeting with Gavin at the Broken Spur Ranch.

Heading south through the scenic beauty that came with this stretch of 287, Lauryn heard her former foster mom's words circling around in her head.

Not just *what* she'd said. But *how* she'd said it. Because Ellen Crawford wasn't a woman to mince words, or to share a story just for the sake of shooting the breeze.

Clearly, the incident she'd witnessed with Lauryn's father pulling over Gavin had bothered her enough to relate it. Almost as if she felt defensive of Gavin. Which stirred Lauryn's uncertain feelings about him all the more. During the years she'd lived in foster homes, she'd grown accustomed to reading the room quickly, trying to get a take on people in a way that even now made her prone to overanalyzing.

Maybe she was doing that now, picking at stray threads that didn't need unraveling.

The elevation increased before it decreased again, her truck feeling the incline more with the heavy horse trailer in tow. Still, she checked the time on her dashboard and saw she would arrive punctually enough.

No need to text Gavin in advance.

Even as she thought it, her truck's Bluetooth chimed with a notification from her phone, the connection informing her she had an incoming message from Gavin Kingsley. The system was even polite enough to ask her if she wanted the message read to her so her eyes could remain on the road.

Curiosity hummed through her, even as she felt a zing of kismet that he'd apparently been thinking of her at the same moment she'd been thinking of him. Foolish, really, given they had a meeting scheduled shortly. She should be relieved he'd remembered it this time.

Then the disembodied voice of her messaging app sounded over the truck's speakers, reading aloud to her.

"Hey, this is Gavin. Just checking in to make sure we're still on for this afternoon. I'll be in all day, so don't rush if your delivery runs long."

Lauryn's pulse thrummed faster, remembering the way Gavin had touched her the day before when they'd shaken hands on the deal they made. There'd been a moment—an infinitesimal shift of his thumb along the back of her hand—when heat had spiked all through her. A charged instant between them she hadn't been able to forget.

Now she would see him again so they could work together in close proximity on her event. Her stomach flipped.

Was that unease she was feeling? Anxiety?

It had all been her idea to ask him to be a part of the bachelor auction, so she only had herself to blame now, if the thought of being next to him for hours sent a sensual shiver through her. She could blame Gavin for other things, but roping him into this event had been all her idea because she'd known that the man would corral feminine interest for miles around.

Had she thought all her father's stories about him or all Duke Kingsley's disparaging remarks about his son would prevent her from feeling the influence of Gavin's charisma?

Just one touch yesterday had shattered any illusion of the kind.

Licking her dry lips, Lauryn reminded herself she had the very best of reasons for going forward with her plan: both to have Gavin in the bachelor auction and to maintain his help in organizing the event. He was a people person. A party person. While she was definitely not. His participation was crucial on so many levels.

No matter that they'd never been overly friendly toward

one another in the past; he'd proven in their early meetings that he knew a lot about charity fundraisers and black-tie events since he'd been born into the Kingsley wealth. The fact that his father had disinherited him didn't suddenly void out the skills Gavin had honed over a lifetime.

He was good at this, and she needed him.

Clearing her throat, Lauryn spoke to the voice-messaging system through her Bluetooth microphone. "Send a message to Gavin Kingsley," she requested, waiting for the beep that indicated she could begin talking.

"The meeting is still on for this afternoon. I'm on my way now."

After the notification was read back to her, she confirmed the text and asked for the note to send, ignoring the sensation in her belly that felt sort of like butterflies.

It was only nerves, of course.

And since the therapy center she was dedicating in memory of her foster sister was riding on the outcome of Studs for Sale, Lauryn would do everything in her power to ignore the draw of the most notorious stud around.

Four

This isn't a date.

Gavin repeated the words to himself as he adjusted the place settings he'd arranged on the patio table built into his dock. He'd gone to some trouble to ensure the place for their meeting looked appealing, and he'd even ordered lunch in case Lauryn hadn't eaten. But as he reviewed the location of the table under a pergola, surrounded by container plants and shaded by ivy growing between the overhead wooden slats, he wondered if the sheriff's no-nonsense daughter might think it all a bit too much.

Especially since this meeting wasn't a date, damn it.

But he wanted to make her comfortable, and after he'd reviewed the meeting notes she sent him the night before, he knew they had a lot of ground to cover to work out the flow of the event. Then, afterward, he had a plan for drawing out the conversation. Maybe weave the talk around to the time she'd worked for his dad.

Something he wouldn't be able to do if she disappeared as soon as their business concluded.

He didn't have any longer to wonder about the setup, however, as a moment later, a dust cloud on the road leading to the driveway alerted him to Lauryn's arrival. Gavin jogged away from the dock to meet her, tempering his thoughts with reminders that he was only spending time with her to find out what she knew about his disinheritance.

And if she'd contributed to it in any way with her skewed view of him.

Yet as he rounded the corner of the detached garage to see Lauryn step out of her pickup truck in snug-fitting black jeans and work boots, a pink-and-gray flannel shirt tucked in on one side to reveal the narrow waist beneath it, Gavin struggled to recall those good intentions. Didn't matter that she was dressed for ranch work after the horse delivery, her face free of makeup and her chestnut waves bound into a ponytail. Or that she carried a binder that was surely full of tasks for them to accomplish. Gavin could only think she looked good enough to eat.

Preferably in slow, savoring mouthfuls.

"Hello, Gavin." Greeting him with a wave, she paused near the hitch for her horse trailer to rewrap a length of excess security chain that had come unhooked. "I'm surprised Rocco didn't come out to say hello too."

"If he was here, I'm positive he would have beaten me to you." He gestured for her to walk with him toward the trout pond, and she kept pace beside him. "But the foreman lured him out to help drive the horses to the summer pasture. The broodmares are all even-tempered and easy to move, but Rocco likes to keep up his skills."

"This must be a busy time for the breeding program," she observed, her step stalling as her hazel eyes fixed on their destination. "Will we be working outside?"

"That was the plan." The spring had been mild, and he'd assumed that—like him—she probably worked out of doors often enough to be accustomed to the temperatures. "But we can relocate easily enough—"

"No need. This is perfect." A smile hitched at the corner of her lips as she recommenced moving toward the dock perched at the edge of his trout pond. "I just wasn't expecting anything so charming. What an ideal backyard."

"I spent a lot of time making sure this place was exactly the way I wanted it." He felt the tide of bitterness rising at the thought of leaving Silent Spring, the home and grounds personalized in every way. But since he didn't want to talk about that yet, he quickly switched topics. "So this morning's adoption went well? I know sometimes it can take a horse a while to settle down after a trailer ride."

He waved her ahead of him as they reached the cobblestone path that wound around a firepit and then up to the bi-level dock over the pond. The patio table under the pergola had been built closer to a storage shed where he kept fishing gear and lawn equipment, while the lower deck held two Adirondack chairs positioned side by side, looking out over the pond and the river beyond.

"Toffee couldn't be happier," she reported as she trailed one palm along the blooming clematis vine that wound up one of the pergola posts. Her touch released the soft fragrance of the pale pink flowers. "She managed the trip like a trooper, and she's in good hands in her new home."

When they arrived at the table, where he'd arranged place settings at two of the four chairs, he withdrew one of the seats on the bare side of the table for her.

"How's this? I thought we could dive into the meeting agenda and then, if we're not finished within the hour, we can at least take a working lunch."

For a moment, he studied her face as she took in the details—the linen napkins and simple white china on tan straw mats, the crystal water goblets but no wine glasses, the pewter jug of sunflowers in the middle of the cast-iron table. At least he'd had the forethought to leave his tablet and a notepad out, too, in an effort to show her he was serious about helping her with the event.

He knew he walked a tightrope with her, balancing his need to draw her out with her desire to nail down the details of the event.

When her gaze flipped back to his, her expression was guarded. Her tone even, if a little stiff.

"That's thoughtful of you. Thank you." Taking a seat in the chair he'd indicated, Lauryn set the manila folder she carried in front of her as she tucked closer to the table. "If we stay focused, I'm sure we can plow through this at a good clip so I'm not taking too much of your time."

Dropping into the seat beside her, he switched on the tablet, more than ready to finish up the work ahead of them, though for entirely different reasons. Lauryn might be plotting a quick departure from Broken Spur Ranch.

As for Gavin?

He already had a plan for luring her to stay.

This is just business.

Lauryn reminded herself as she reached for a raspberry on the small dessert charcuterie board one of Gavin's household staffers had brought them after a light lunch. The food had been delivered after they'd worked for about ninety minutes. She'd debated stealing away without accepting the lunch invitation, but that seemed unnecessarily rude when Gavin had offered so much of his time and expertise to help finalize the plans for the event day.

So she'd made quick work of a delectable chicken-salad sandwich from the tray of choices Gavin's housekeeper had offered half an hour ago, thinking she'd leave afterward. But by the time the small dessert board was delivered a few moments ago—laden with bite-size fruits, chocolates, macaroons and a salted-caramel dipping sauce—Lauryn worried she'd ventured into too-friendly terrain with a man she needed to be on her guard around.

Popping the raspberry in her mouth, she savored the burst of sweetness while she tried to gauge his next move. "This is so decadent. If this is how you conduct business meetings, I can only imagine how on point your dating game must be."

Gavin arched an eyebrow at her as he dragged a square of dark chocolate through the caramel sauce. "Spoken like a woman who is angling for hints about our upcoming date."

"Hardly." She bristled, face warm, as she snagged a macaroon. "Just observing that it's no surprise women line up to date you when you are such an attentive…er, host."

"Not you, though, Lauryn. You've been careful to avoid me for as long as I've known you." Leaning back in his chair, Gavin crossed his long legs at the ankles as he observed her. "I don't think you're won over by things like that."

"Maybe I go for substance over style," she teased, her skin prickling with awareness wherever his brown eyes lingered.

And while she would like to blame a cool spring breeze for the shiver that danced down her spine, she knew it had more to do with Gavin's heated regard. Somehow, digging into the macaroon didn't ease the renewed hunger she was feeling either.

"I think there's more to it than that," he argued, selecting a strawberry from the small pile on the board between them. "You've been opposed to me from your first day in Silent Spring."

A low-flying—noisy—crop duster overhead gave her an extra moment to consider his words.

"Now that's just not true," she said after a moment. She hadn't known anything about Gavin for months after the Hamiltons had taken her in.

"Isn't it?" An amused expression carved a dimple in his cheek while a mischievous glint shone in his eyes. "How else would you explain the way you sprinted out of that 4-H meeting the first time you came to town?"

A humming sound started in the back of her brain at the mention of 4-H. She'd had a bad experience there the one and only time she'd gone.

Not that it was any fault of the organization.

She'd been visiting the Hamiltons before her adoption had been finalized, and Mrs. Hamilton had been a local group leader, so Lauryn had gone with her for the day.

"Lauryn?" Gavin straightened in his seat, his expression clouding. "What's wrong?"

He reached out to her, laying a hand on her arm.

The humming in her ears grew louder. She stared down at the place where Gavin's fingers curved around her wrist. It was the only place on her body that didn't suddenly feel chilled.

"Nothing." Shaking her head, she didn't want to remember that time in her life. "I'm fine."

"You're white as a sheet. Should I call someone? A physician or—"

"No." She laid her free hand over his where he touched her. Gripped his fingers hard in hers. "It's really nothing."

And yet she knew the more she refused to acknowledge what was happening to her, the worse it would be. She hadn't experienced a full-on panic attack in years, but she recalled how terrifying they were. How it felt like having a heart attack.

Even now, the noise in her ears had cranked up to full volume, drowning out whatever Gavin was saying to her.

She watched his lips move. Understood he was worried for her.

Something about the concern in his eyes touched her. Anchored her, even.

So, keeping her gaze locked on his, she tried to remember the steps her old therapist had taught her. *Don't fight the attack. Ride it out. Try to remain in the situation.*

If she didn't give herself a chance to confront her fear, she'd never get over it.

Just thinking about the advice that had helped her in the past started to ease the vise on her chest.

"It's just a panic attack," she managed, becoming aware of the warm, strong palm between hers.

"How can I help?" He shifted even closer, squatting beside her chair so he could wrap his other arm around her shoulders.

The warmth of that touch permeated her flannel shirt, banishing more of the chill that had taken hold.

Comforted her.

"You are helping," she insisted between long, deep breaths. In her mind, she counted down the inhalations to make sure they lasted long enough. Then counted down the exhales too.

In another few moments, the sound in her head quieted. Her heart rate slowed down a bit. She became aware of Gavin's hand lightly rubbing her shoulder. It shouldn't feel so good.

But she didn't have the wherewithal to fight relief from the panic, no matter the source.

"Are you any steadier?" he asked a moment later, his brown gaze intent as he watched her. "Your color is a little better now."

"It's easing up now," she assured him, fighting the urge to lean into him more. To breathe in the strength and warmth of him. To take shelter in those strong arms. "Maybe I should have a drink of water."

If nothing else, it would distract her from how much she enjoyed his touch.

Gavin refilled her glass from a stainless steel pitcher on the table; then he passed her the tumbler.

"Here you go." He returned to his seat, though he'd pulled his chair so close to hers their knees still touched as he faced her. "I sure as hell hope I wasn't the cause of whatever brought that on."

How to tell him?

She remembered the advice about confronting her fears. It had worked well for her in the past, so she wasn't about to start hiding from the things that upset her now. Even if that meant sharing this part of her history with Gavin.

"You couldn't have known," she insisted, her thoughts returning to that long-ago incident she'd buried deep in her subconscious. The memory of it had only just surfaced, a forgotten relic of a time she'd tried so hard to forget. "I didn't remember that it was you with me in the tent that day."

Gavin's eyes widened. "Are you kidding me? All this time, I thought I'd offended you somehow—"

She shook her head vigorously, snatches of the episode returning one piece at a time as her mind's eye cleared. Vaguely, she was aware of the spring breeze on her face, lifting locks of her sweat-dampened hair from her temple. And Gavin seated across from her, his fingers still clutching hers while the small fountain in the middle of the trout pond continued to spray water in all directions, the soft swishing lulling her to remember a moment almost thirteen years in the past.

"That was my first panic attack," she said finally, forcing herself to meet his eyes. To speak the words that she once would have found impossible to confess. "I didn't know it at the time. I just felt this crushing weight on my chest and started running."

She couldn't even recall where she'd gone. But she did remember being back in a bed at the Hamiltons' house afterward, terrified they wouldn't adopt her after learning she was a girl prone to bouts of anxiety.

But they'd tucked her into bed with quiet words that it would be okay. That she was safe.

"I don't understand." Gavin cupped her chin with his free hand, tilting her face as if he could somehow read her if he could find the best angle. "If I didn't upset you, what went wrong? One minute, we were plotting the composition of a soil sample in order to determine forage yield in a cow pasture. And the next minute, you were tearing at the walls of that tent to find the exit."

Lauryn's pulse quickened again at the visceral memory of feeling trapped. Her airway clogged. Unable to escape.

But this time, she breathed through it, reminding herself she was safe. Free.

"We did a 4-H exercise that night," she recalled aloud, knowing she had to walk herself through the event that had triggered the first panic attack in years. And while she understood that Gavin was curious about what happened, her first priority had to be soothing herself. Only then could she explain any of it to him. "The junior and senior members worked together since the senior leader was absent."

"Right." He nodded slowly, confirming her memory of the incident, as his hand fell away from her cheek. "That year, we were still meeting at the main lodge of the old scouts' campground next to Twin Lakes."

"I remember cabins." She closed her eyes, seeing it all again. The small alpine lake in the Greenhorn Mountain Range. A fallen sign over the entrance to the camp. A handful of rustic cabins. A few tents pitched by the senior members as part of an exercise they'd completed earlier that week. "There was a big green tent that one of the boys said was the sturdiest one around."

Gavin laughed. "That would have been me. Bragging to impress the new girl."

Lauryn couldn't believe she'd forgotten the whole thing.

Her first time meeting kids she'd later gone to school with, and yet no one had brought it up to her for all these years? Then again, the 4-H group had been comprised mostly of students in the next school district over since both she and Gavin had lived on the fringes of their district. Maybe the club hadn't consisted of that many people who'd been in her life after her adoption.

"We ended up working in that tent," she recalled, a vision of sitting cross-legged under the center dome of the canvas roof returning to her mind. "Until a bunch of boys started shaking the posts."

An involuntary shudder ran through her at the memory. She'd been terrified from that point forward, her mind seized with panic that the canvas would collapse and she'd be trapped.

The way Jamie had been trapped the night Lauryn tried to save her sister. Another bolt of panic speared her insides.

Or was it grief this time?

Her hand went to her belly, clutching her abdomen. As if she could hold her feelings inside.

"Some of my friends decided to test the theory that it was the sturdiest tent around so they could show me up." Gavin's voice remained low and even, his hand still around hers. "They were determined to make me look bad in front of you."

Lauryn heard his words, the scenario making sense, even as she continued to see it unfold through her own terrified eyes.

"The roof looked ready to cave in on us," she said, her throat dry with remembered fear. "I don't recall anything after that. Not until much later, when I was back at the Hamiltons' house."

"You don't?" Gavin's dark eyebrows crinkled in confusion before his expression cleared again. "Do you want me to tell you what happened after that?"

"Yes, please." She forced herself to nod, even though she didn't really want to know. Sometimes it was easier not to dwell on the confusing and scary parts of the past.

"You looked straight at me." Gavin's steady voice anchored her as much as his touch. "And your face went as white as it did today. Your lips moved, but no sound came out. I moved toward you because I was worried, but then you spun out of my reach and tore out of the tent. For a moment, you battled with the flap near the door, catching your foot on it before scrambling away."

His forehead crumpled as he related the story, as if the remembered worry was still cause for concern.

"I figured you hated me," he continued when she didn't reply. "From that moment on. Later, when you moved into Silent Spring permanently, those same friends that were with us that day egged me into driving over to your place one night to see if you really did think I was the devil incarnate."

She swung on him then, putting the pieces together. "The night you rode four-wheelers through Dad's fields?"

He rolled his eyes. "Yeah. Well. That part was unintentional, but that was the level of smarts we had at fifteen."

Lauryn struggled to make sense of the events through Gavin's eyes, reseeing their history in a completely different light. Not that it mattered much. Gavin remained a ladies' man and a player, a guy used to having people fall at his feet no matter what he did. She was still a woman struggling to make people like her, to do the right thing. To be a good person and deserve her parents' love.

To make up for not saving her sister.

"Lauryn?" Gavin's voice interrupted her musings, his tone gentle and intimate somehow.

His hand still holding hers with a tenderness that undermined all her good intentions where he was concerned. Because now that the panic had subsided, she couldn't help but notice the way his calloused hands enveloped hers. Nor could she stop herself from imagining those work-roughened palms skimming over more of her body. Her hips. Her thighs.

"I should go." She rose to her feet, tugging her hand free of his before gathering her notebook and pen. Her breathing coming too fast again but for entirely different reasons. "Lunch was nice, and I appreciate your help—truly, I do—but I really need to get going."

"So soon?" Gavin stood too. "Are you sure you're okay to drive?"

When her knuckles brushed her water glass, he caught it in time before it spilled.

Get it together.

"I'm fine, really." She knew her behavior probably seemed as erratic to him as it had over a decade ago when she'd run from that tent. But today had been rough enough without reliving the worst of her nightmares to him. Without her libido waking up and seeing Gavin in a too-sexy light. "We'll talk soon. I'll tell you about it another time, okay?"

Backing up a step, she bumped into her chair before she righted herself and edged sideways.

"You don't owe me any explanations, Lauryn. But I don't think you should drive while you're upset—"

"I'm not upset," she assured him, running an impatient hand through her hair. Everything she'd thought she'd understood about Gavin Kingsley had been disrupted by today's revelation. She needed to figure out what it meant. To decide if it had any bearing on the kind of person he was or if his character remained fixed in the category where she'd always placed him. As for the attraction? She'd find a way to put the lid back on that somehow. "I just need some space to get my thoughts together. I'll text you."

"I'm at least walking you to your truck," he informed her crossly, his hand steadying her at the elbow as she missed a step going up the flagstone path away from the trout pond. "You can allow me to do the gentlemanly thing there, I hope."

"Of course," she murmured to herself even as the warmth of his touch aroused more feelings she didn't want to experience toward Gavin. "I don't mean to be rude. I'm just—" She didn't know what she was about to say. But when she arrived at the door of her pickup truck, she felt saved from trying to make any more sense. "Thank you for all the help today."

His brown eyes saw deeply into hers. Full of concern.

And something more. Something she couldn't quite define.

"Text me when you arrive home, or I will worry." His voice was stern. Uncompromising.

She might have bristled if she hadn't appreciated the interest he took in her well-being.

"I will." She opened the truck door before he had the chance to do it for her. "Bye, Gavin."

Moments later, she was heading for home, recounting every moment of the new memory about a time she'd thought was well buried in her subconscious.

She hadn't expected to deal with memories like that today. And when combined with the need to be on her guard around Gavin, all her defenses had just sort of... caved in on themselves.

Not unlike that long-ago accident that had claimed the person she loved most in the world.

Pressing harder on the accelerator, she knew she

couldn't outrun her demons. But just this once, she could put some distance between her and the newest threat to her peace of mind. Because even though it had been an old memory that had upset her today, it had been Gavin Kingsley who had talked her through it.

Gavin who had stroked her arm and brought her back to firm, stable reality.

Gavin who had wanted to know she was okay.

Her chest felt tight when she thought about how easily he'd slid into the role of protector.

Next time, she wouldn't fall apart so readily. When they saw one another again, she would be armed with the knowledge that he wasn't concerned about her so much as he was trying to work a seductive angle. Right?

Taking a deep breath, she let out a long, slow exhale as she felt the world right itself again. She probably wasn't the first woman in distress Gavin had comforted, and she wouldn't be the last. With the pieces of her perspective slotting back into place—her world making sense once more—Lauryn thrust all thoughts of Gavin to the back of her mind.

Five

Three days after his meeting gone wrong with Lauryn, Gavin backed his horse trailer toward the Kingsland Ranch's newest stables and braced himself for another potential failed mission—retrieving the highly ranked sorrel stallion he'd obtained for the Kingsland stud program.

A top-ten barrel horse sire for two years running, Streaking Saint was slated to be the cornerstone of the stallion battery. An athletic horse with impressive pedigree and an enviable disposition, Streaking promised to make Kingsland a small fortune.

Or he would have.

Except that Gavin had researched all the stallions himself, and he'd been the one to find Streaking at a good deal. He wasn't about to walk away from the horse he'd purchased just because his father had decided he wasn't worthy of the family legacy. He had spent too many years tying himself in knots trying to earn his father's approval.

Then, he'd overcorrected that mistake, turning to bull riding and hell raising for a rebellious few years.

He couldn't allow his father to take up any more space in his head.

But considering how many ranch hands were on-site this afternoon, Gavin didn't hold much hope he would be able to load his stallion without someone alerting his brother. Quinton wouldn't care since he seemed genuinely angry about their father's shifty maneuverings with the will. Levi was another story, however.

As the oldest, Levi took his responsibility as family leader seriously. And he'd made it clear he wanted to keep the Kingsley family united under the Kingsland Ranch banner.

Something that stood a snowball's chance in hell of happening.

Satisfied with the trailer's proximity to the barn doors, Gavin threw on the brakes and switched off the ignition before stepping down from the truck. And while, yes, he'd readied himself for the possibility of running into trouble this evening, no potential confrontation with his siblings would be worse than how quickly things had deteriorated with Lauryn during their last meeting.

After sliding the big barn door open wider, Gavin unfastened the safety latch on his horse trailer and lowered the ramp, all the while thinking of the cryptic conversation that had gone in a far different direction than he'd imagined.

Had she really not recalled their first interaction at a 4-H club meeting so many years ago?

For years, he'd assumed that he personally had done something to upset her, something that turned her against him for good. Even though only a few years separated them in school, and Silent Spring was a small town, they'd never been friends. She'd always been distant toward him.

One of his theories had been that she was claustrophobic and blamed him for the tent almost caving in on them. Or she viewed him as a bully who somehow coerced his friends into freaking her out. Who knew? They'd been kids.

I didn't remember that it was you with me in the tent that day.

Her words had turned all his memories on their ear, upending the little he'd thought he'd known about Lauryn Hamilton. As for the plan he'd had to draw her out about his father…well, that hadn't gone as he'd hoped either. Next time he saw her, he'd have to work harder to drive the conversation and find the answers he needed.

Even though a part of him just wanted to get to know her better. Unravel the sexy mystery that was Lauryn. Because damn, but it had been difficult to pull his hands away from her once he'd started touching her. What started out as comfort had stirred a deeper awareness. He'd held her hand, and she'd peered at him with big hazel eyes full of gratitude, almost as if she saw something more in him.

Something meaningful that others didn't see. Especially not his father.

But that was probably just his imagination talking. Lauryn had looked at him like that strictly because he'd helped her through a panic attack and not for any other reason. He needed to remember that.

Now he cursed himself for spending his time daydreaming about touching Lauryn's soft skin and wrapping his arms around her. He had a job to do here, and the sooner he got what he came for, the better.

Walking into the trailer, he popped open the roof vents and straightened a heavy horse blanket on the bar that would help keep the stallion comfortable on the ride home. Then he retrieved a halter and lead rope before heading into the Kingsland barn.

The sweet scent of clean hay drifted toward him, the

barn quiet since most of the animals remained outside in
the pleasant spring weather. But deeper in the barn, in the
last stall on the left, Gavin spotted Streaking Saint already
stabled for the night. In an effort to help him transition to
the new grasses in the Kingsland pasture, the staff had
agreed to bring him into the barn at dinnertime and keep
him there until morning to limit how much he grazed until
he got more used to a different diet.

"Hey, buddy," Gavin greeted the horse softly, reaching
to stroke the sorrel's neck. "How do you feel about taking
a ride tonight, just you and me?"

At fifteen and a half hands, the stallion was sleek but
well muscled, with the bearing of a show horse and the fire
of a competitor. Even now, he tossed his head and whin-
nied as if to remind Gavin he was made for better things
than standing in a stable all night.

Chuckling to himself at the animal's antics, Gavin
opened the stable door to step inside so he had more room
to slide on the halter. He slipped the nose band in place,
then secured the strap behind the ears, making sure to
leave enough room to keep the horse comfortable for the
short trip.

He opened the stall door again and led Streaking out
into the aisle just as a tall figure appeared at the entrance
of the barn.

"Going somewhere?"

Levi glared at him, staring him down in his Stetson like
an old-time gunslinger angling for a fight at the saloon.

A gusty sigh heaved from Gavin's lungs. He was so
done arguing with his family.

"What does it look like?" He kept his tone light and
tried to ensure his touch remained easy on the lead rope.

He didn't want to upset Streaking, who was still adjusting to a new barn and new routine.

"It looks like you're a damned horse thief, Gav, but

I know even you wouldn't do something so rash." Levi strolled toward them, tipping the brim of his hat higher as he took in the sights around them.

The open horse trailer. The lead rope in the hands of the disgraced half brother.

"Leave it to you to take up the misguided-patriarch vacancy as soon as it came open," Gavin shot back, ticked off now and unable to hide it, even for the animal's sake. "But if you've conveniently forgotten who did all the legwork to find this horse and purchase him, then it's no wonder you consider yourself ill-used."

Beside him, Streaking danced sideways, tensing along with the man who held his lead.

"I remember who did the legwork," Levi insisted, his voice low as he came to a stop a few feet away. "Maybe you don't recall who paid fifty percent of the sale price?"

Close up, Gavin could see the dark circles under Levi's eyes. His jeans and work shirt were more rumpled than they'd normally be after a day on the ranch, his whole bearing weary.

Had Levi been losing sleep about the inheritance drama? For a moment, Gavin felt the tug of empathy. Of all his half siblings, he would have credited the oldest with the most scruples about fairness. Even as a kid, Levi had been the one to make sure Gavin got his fair share of Kingsley assets.

He'd sent Gavin back to his mother's house with extra toys those first two Christmases after Duke divorced his mom, asserting that Gavin deserved more presents since he didn't get to live with them full-time anymore.

The memory eased some of the starch in his spine.

"We went in halves on at least five other horses," he reminded his sibling. "But I'm only taking this one. That's more than fair."

Levi reached out to stroke Streaking's nose, soothing

the horse's agitation. "And I'd appreciate that opportunity to hammer out the details of what's an equitable solution with you, brother, but we need to do that in the attorney's office. Why haven't you returned any of the lawyer's calls about setting up a meeting?"

The reminder of the messages and letters from the law office only served to rile him all over again.

"I'm not interested in padding a lawyer's pockets to work out something you and I can agree on with a handshake." It ticked him off to think Levi and Quinton didn't trust him. "If you don't think I'll follow through on an agreement—"

"It's not that simple." Backing away from the stallion, Levi lifted both arms in exasperation. "How are we going to come to an agreement if we don't make time to talk through all the angles—"

"What angles?" Gavin asked through gritted teeth. "The only thing that's changed is that I'm not a part of Kingsland anymore. Simple as that. So offer me a financial settlement for what I've invested in the family business, and let's all move on."

He'd suggested as much on that first awful day when he'd found out he wouldn't be receiving a share of his father's estate. Before he'd walked out of the room, he'd told Quinton and Levi that he would expect to be reimbursed for every cent he'd invested in the stud program.

"And what about the rest of the assets? We just divide things three ways between you, Quinton and me?" Folding his arms, Levi seemed to size him up.

"That's your business, not mine."

"Well I can't do that since there are four of us who are entitled to Kingsland, Gav. Not three. How can we come up with an equitable settlement of the estate when we don't even know where Clayton is living, let alone how to get him back here to work with us?"

Swearing beneath his breath, Gavin felt the guilt rise up, rattling him at the knees. How could he forget about his own brother, albeit one who'd been in his life for all of a couple of summers? And of course, since Gavin hadn't lived at the ranch full-time after his parents divorced, he hadn't been around Kingsland very often during those summers when Clayton Reynolds had visited.

Quinton had been quick to mention their sibling right after the reading of Duke Kingsley's will, but Gavin had been so upset for himself, he hadn't paid much attention to the ways Clayton had been shortchanged too. To Gavin's mind, at least Clayton had the good sense not to mix up his finances with his father's estate, proving himself far smarter than Gavin.

"You're right, of course." Gavin laid a hand on Streaking's neck, taking more comfort from the animal than he was giving. "I thought Quinton was going to hire a private investigator to locate him."

"He did. And he found a last-known address at a little town in the Aleutian Islands, but we're not sure about our next steps." Levi broke off his explanation to nod toward the sorrel stallion. "You want help getting him loaded?"

Surprised Levi wasn't going to argue anymore about the horse, Gavin nodded. "I'd appreciate that." He made a soft sound of encouragement to the animal before leading him out of the barn. Once the steady clip-clop of hooves moved toward the trailer, Gavin picked up their discussion. "Can't the PI let Clayton know we need to contact him? Settle the estate?"

"We could." Levi swung himself up into the side bay of the two-horse trailer ahead of Gavin and Streaking. Once there, he withdrew a box of raisins from the breast pocket of his canvas work coat, giving the box a shake to rattle the dried fruit inside. On cue, Streaking's ears pricked forward, his attention on the treat as he walked straight into the opposite bay. "But since Clayton made it clear five years ago that he doesn't want anything more to do with Dad, we didn't know if that was the best approach. If the investigator doesn't handle the meeting well, Clayton could go off-grid completely, and we'd never find him."

Levi shared the treat with Streaking while Gavin began securing breakaway ties to keep the stallion steady for transport.

"And we still don't know what happened between Clayton and…" He couldn't bring himself to call Duke Kingsley *Dad* these days. "…your father?"

Levi tucked the raisin package back in his pocket before emerging from the trailer to help Gavin close the ramp and back door.

"Only Clayton knows." Levi settled his Stetson more securely on his head while Gavin slid the bolt closed on the doors. "Quint is leaning toward going up there himself to talk to him."

"All the way to the Aleutian Islands?" He didn't hide his surprise at the idea of Quinton setting everything else aside at Kingsland Ranch to personally hunt down the half brother who'd turned his back on the rest of the family. "Seems like a long way to go only to find out the guy wants nothing to do with us."

"He's still family, and family is too important to just walk away from without a fight." Levi's tone was firm. And more than a little pointed. "Besides, Quint wants answers about Dad and his reasons for trying to cut us out of one another's lives. He thinks maybe Clayton can shed some light on that."

Maybe.

But maybe Lauryn could tell them more about their father's motives too. She was a whole lot closer by than the Aleutian Islands; and in spite of his old suspicions about her, Gavin couldn't deny that he was eager to see her again.

Their last visit had altered some of his previous perceptions of her, making him less sure that she'd had an axe to grind with him from the very beginning of her days in Silent Spring.

"We all want answers," Gavin agreed, ready to be underway now that he had Streaking in his possession. In the barn behind them, he could hear the ranch hands bringing in some of the other animals for the night, and Gavin didn't want to answer any questions about his plans. "But I doubt Clayton Reynolds will have the first clue as to why Duke disinherited *me*. I feel certain that I wasn't involved in whatever went down between the two of them."

He dug in his pocket for the keys to the truck while Levi walked with him toward the cab door.

"Maybe not. But in the meantime, will you call the attorney back? At least bring their office up to speed on what you've invested at Kingsland so we can be sure we work out something equitable if I can't convince you to stay on board?"

"I'll give the lawyer a call." Levering open the door, he was already thinking about the call he'd make first, however. He needed to talk to Lauryn again. To press her for the answers she'd been unwilling to provide last time about their first meeting. Because even though he had a whole other set of questions about her time working for his father, none of that mattered until he figured out what had turned her against him. If not that first encounter when she'd had a panic attack—and hadn't even remembered he'd been there—then what was it that had made her wary of him all these years? Something she'd shared with Duke Kingsley?

"Thanks, Gav. It means a lot—"

"But there's no way I'm staying on at Kingsland." After slamming his door, Gavin fired up the truck engine while he spoke through the open window to his brother. "Once the bachelor auction is over, I'm leaving Montana, and I won't be back."

Breathing in the spring scents of a meadow in the hills above her horse rescue, Lauryn relaxed into spending time with one of the new mares she'd acquired the week before.

"What do you think, Marigold?" she asked the four-year-old palomino she was leading into the meadow for some hand-grazing time. "Is this a good spot?"

Marigold was already dipping her nose into the clover, her white tail swishing gently to keep a few deerflies at bay.

Easing her grip on the lead rope, Lauryn laid a hand on the animal's shoulder, remembering how much she'd enjoyed this exercise during her own years as a patient of equine therapy. They'd been encouraged to gravitate toward the individual animals that felt "right" to them; then they'd learned more about their horses by grooming them and paying attention to what brushes and touches the animals liked best. In later sessions, they were allowed to spend time getting to know their horses, often leading them into quiet pastures for hand-grazing moments like the one she was recreating with Marigold today.

She still found the activity therapeutic when her spirit was unsettled, the way it had been ever since her lunch with Gavin that had stirred a forgotten memory.

Now she'd promised to share more with him about why she'd had the panic attacks, but how much did she want to confide in a man she was wildly attracted to but wasn't certain she trusted? Yes, he'd been kind to her when the icy grip of heart-racing anxiety had taken hold. Had helped her through it in a way that touched her to recall.

But was that kindness to women just a reflex for him?

She couldn't lose sight of the fact that she'd wanted him to go on the auction block for the bachelor event precisely because he was a notorious charmer.

"How much should I tell him, Marigold?" she asked the grazing palomino while she twined her fingers in the animal's white mane.

Birds chirped and squawked in the quiet following her question. The only answer Marigold made was the gentle tearing of grass as she ate.

Lauryn tipped her head to the animal's flank, feeling the sun-warmed coat on her temple as she soaked up the peace of the meadow and the moment. She hadn't known how much she needed this time until she felt some of the week's stress ease off her shoulders.

Besides the episode with Gavin, her father had messaged her twice in the last three days, asking her to remove Gavin from the bachelor docket at Studs for Sale. She'd been too annoyed to answer with the manners and respect the reply warranted, but she'd have to craft an answer soon.

Even as she thought it, her phone vibrated in her back pocket. Not the quick pulse of a message, but the longer rumble of an incoming call.

Tugging it free, she glanced at the caller ID.

Gavin Kingsley's name filled the screen and instantly, her breath caught. Her heart rate quickened.

After a stroke of her hand along the horse's back, she pushed the button to connect the call, knowing she needed to speak to him soon.

"Hello, Gavin." She kept Marigold's lead rope in her free hand, unsure if she could trust the mare if she ground-tied her.

The horse seemed docile enough, and had had some training somewhere along the way, but she'd been taken from an older woman with more animals than she could properly care for. Lauryn felt sure Marigold hadn't been overtly abused, but she'd certainly been underfed and ill tended.

A condition Lauryn recalled well from her three years in the group home where she'd met Jamie.

"Lauryn, I'm glad you picked up." His voice, deep and resonant, had an immediate effect on her. Warm and smooth against her ears.

She remembered how he spoke to her softly when she'd been troubled and in the grip of the past.

"Of course," she said as mildly as possible, unwilling to reveal the way she shivered just hearing him. She leaned into Marigold again, soaking up the comforting presence of the horse. Remembering that she was talking to Gavin so that she could save more horses. Expand her rescue into equine-therapy efforts that would help more people. "I'm glad you stayed in town for my bachelor auction, so we're even."

"I called about that, in fact." He kept his tone light too.

Maybe he'd picked up on her vibe. Her desperation to keep their relationship professional and casual.

"I'm listening."

"I have an idea for promoting Studs for Sale on social media to reach more people and elicit more write-in bids. Do you have time to meet tomorrow so we can go over the specifics?"

She would love more promotion.

And more write-in bids for higher donations was music to her ears.

So even if seeing him turned her insides into knots, she needed to say yes.

"Of course. Where should we meet this time?" She wasn't sure about inviting him to the rescue. Her mother and father lived only a few miles from her.

She didn't need the added pressure of having her father show up in the middle of a meeting with Gavin.

"Would you be able to meet at Kingsland Ranch?"

She almost dropped her phone in surprise. The suggestion shocked her, given how adamantly opposed he was to doing business with his family anymore.

But she knew the ranch well, having worked there for two years.

"That's not a problem. Whereabouts?" The ranch was huge, with multiple homes on the acreage, plus the office headquarters.

Her heartbeat kicked up pace.

"I'll meet you at the entrance. I have a spot in mind, but I don't think it's anywhere you would have seen while you worked there."

"You're full of surprises. But I'm game. Can we do later in the day? I've got a meeting with a potential builder for the new therapy center at noon." She wanted bids ready so she could make an informed decision about the structure she'd need on her property once she raised the necessary funds from the charity event. "Will three o'clock work?"

"Perfectly. I'll see you then." He was all business as they said goodbye.

Lauryn knew she couldn't have asked for a better follow-up call to their awkward last meeting. Gavin hadn't mentioned the incident, and he hadn't pretended they had any sort of new intimacy based on the shared personal moments.

That was excellent news.

Yet long after she disconnected the conversation, she couldn't help but feel she was walking into trouble with him tomorrow. Because the more time she spent with Gavin Kingsley, the more he defied her expectations. The more he showed her he was someone other than the man she'd thought she understood.

And even worse?

In spite of everything she knew—or thought she knew—about Gavin, she couldn't stop thinking about touching him again.

Six

Today, he would stick to the game plan.

Gavin needed the reminder tattooed across the insides of his eyelids, apparently, because the moment he spotted Lauryn's truck heading toward him for their appointed meeting, he was already envisioning how she would look today. What she would be wearing. How she would smell.

Thoughts that ran counter to the damn game plan, which was to draw her out about the time she'd spent working at Kingsland Ranch. He couldn't afford to get distracted by how she wore her hair or by imagining how those chestnut waves would feel sliding through his fingers. Or draped across his bare chest.

And yet he'd been battling thoughts like those—and far more explicit images—for days.

By the time she pulled off onto the grassy shoulder near the ranch sign and parked her red pickup truck next to his, Gavin had himself under control. Although his eyes still took in the fact that she wore her hair loose and wavy over her shoulders as she stepped out of her truck. And yes, he may have noticed that her black jeans and gray button-down with the Hooves and Hearts logo showed off her lean feminine form to delectable effect; yet Gavin didn't let himself dwell on any of that.

"Thank you for meeting me here." He'd only been waiting for her for a few minutes, but he'd taken a seat on the tailgate so he could greet her when she arrived. Now he dropped to his feet and gestured toward the cab of his truck. "Are you comfortable riding with me? Your vehicle won't be disturbed here, if you don't mind leaving it."

"Sounds good." She hit a button on her key fob as she strode closer. Her vehicle made an electronic chime, the running lights flashing once. "It's all locked up."

He walked to the passenger side of his truck a step ahead of her to pull open the door. As she murmured a thank-you and stepped up to slide her boot on the running board, Gavin got his first hint of her scent. Orange blossoms, maybe. And something spicier too. He caught himself before he leaned closer to take a deeper breath.

Lauryn's fragrance would have to remain a mystery because he was sticking to the game plan. Once he was sure she was settled inside the cab, he shut the door and rounded the vehicle. When he climbed into the driver's seat, she was already buckled in, her legs crossed so that one black ankle boot bounced a silent rhythm in the space between them.

Was she nervous?

The thought cooled his heated thoughts more effectively than any mental pep talk he could have given himself.

"You said you had an idea for promoting the auction on social media?" she prompted him, glancing his way expectantly as he steered the truck back onto the Kingsland Ranch entrance road.

He supposed he should be grateful she wanted to keep things businesslike right now when he was battling memories of how she'd felt the day he'd tucked her under his arm and comforted her. She'd been in his thoughts ever since, desire for her a persistent ache. Yet, when combined with the niggling sense that she was feeling anxious, he couldn't just take the conversational lead she offered. He needed to check in with her first, given the way their last meeting had ended. Lauryn had had a full-blown panic attack, and she'd left before he even understood why.

He didn't want to risk treading into uncomfortable terrain for her.

"I do. But first, tell me how you're doing. Is everything okay?" He glanced over at her before turning down a dirt road just past the hay barn.

Her eyes widened at the question, but her foot was still bouncing double time like her toes were conducting an invisible orchestra.

"I'm fine. Ready to work." Her tone was off, though. A little high and not quite steady. Perhaps she heard it, too, because she pasted on a wide smile before trying again, "Just really intrigued by your cryptic invitation today."

"I'm ready to work too," he assured her, giving a brief wave to the equipment manager repairing a tractor in the shade of an elm behind the barn. "But I wanted to make sure you're not anxious about anything."

As he spoke, he laid his palm on her ankle just above her boot. Her foot abruptly stilled.

His gaze flicked briefly toward her face.

"Oh, right." Her hazel eyes darted from his, her cheeks flushing a pale pink as the truck trundled over a pothole. "Possibly, I'm remembering the awkward way we parted last time. I hope what happened isn't going to…interfere with what we're trying to accomplish?"

Relief eased the tension in his shoulders. At least she hadn't been nervous to be around *him*. He could alleviate this particular disquiet.

"As far as I'm concerned, we don't need to discuss whatever spurred the anxiety attack again if it makes you uncomfortable." He told himself to move his hand away from her ankle, where it still rested. A dictate he would follow just as soon as he wrapped his fingers around her lower calf to give her a reassuring squeeze.

The soft gasp she quickly smothered sent a bolt of heat through him. His chest pounded with the need to follow up that sound. To explore what other ways he could make her gasp with pleasure. To feel that rapid breath rush from her lips to warm his skin…

"I appreciate that." Her words sent his hot thoughts scattering, reminding him he needed to stick to the plan. Her voice cracked a little as she continued, "So. Um. Tell me about your idea to promote the event?"

This time, Gavin knew better than to ignore the conversational escape from the images flooding his brain. As they continued the short drive to the mountain overlook he wanted to show her, he tamped down his feelings to focus on work.

"I think we should do a big social media campaign," he began, ready to outline every last detail until his pulse stopped hammering in his ears. "We spotlight one bachelor every three days leading up to the event…"

As he spoke, he sensed Lauryn relaxing into her seat while she listened. No doubt she was just as eager as him to ignore the chemistry between them.

He just wished his game plan to ask her about her time working for his father didn't rely so heavily on personal conversation. Developing a rapport.

Because he could already tell the effort to learn more about her was going to mean battling this attraction that grew more potent every moment he spent with her.

Two hours later, Lauryn reviewed the notes on her phone. She'd opened a spreadsheet to compile a content-management calendar for the auction's social media properties, and with Gavin's help, she'd already scheduled the first bachelor to spotlight for the auction.

Now, seated on a wooden bench overlooking the western face of the Madison Range, she couldn't deny that he'd been a huge help today. When she'd first arrived, something in the way he looked at her made her wonder if his idea of a promotional opportunity had just been an excuse to see her. Her pulse had leapt at that look, and the attraction had simmered even hotter when she'd sat beside him in his truck on the way to the scenic lookout where they'd been working for the last two hours.

Then, when he'd touched her, she'd felt that brush of his hand everywhere...

Yet he'd only meant to reassure her. She'd been moved to learn he was concerned for her after her anxiety attack. The thoughtfulness had melted her defenses a bit, showing her that unexpected side of him.

Now, with her content calendar created—and with Gavin's hard work getting in touch with all the participating bachelors to schedule their features on the Studs for Sale website—she couldn't be more pleased with what they'd accomplished.

"This is brilliant," she announced, watching the Hooves and Hearts Instagram page explode with positive feedback after her post about the "Stud Spotlights" beginning the next day. Each of the bachelors had agreed to repost their spotlight material on their own social media properties, which would increase her reach exponentially. "I can't thank you enough for sharing the idea, and helping me organize it so quickly too."

Shutting down her phone, she sighed contentedly as she gazed out over the mountains under the cloudless spring sky. The view here was one of a kind, and Gavin was correct that she'd never visited this corner of Kingsland Ranch before. It had made for a perfect spot for working, even though they'd had to employ a Wi-Fi hot spot in order to stay connected to a network for scheduling posts online.

"My pleasure," Gavin returned, his head still bent over his phone, where he tapped in a few final notes on the page of questions he was sending to all the bachelors to answer. Each bachelor had been assigned a day on the auction website and was responsible for answering the questions in time to post them for a spotlight. "I sat on a charity board for a children's hospital last year, and they did something like this, featuring a few of the kids in their program. It really helped personalize the charity."

"You did?" Lauryn pulled her attention from the mountain range back to the man seated beside her, trying to envision him taking time away from ranching and his reputedly busy personal life to donate time to such a worthy cause. Then, as he lifted his head from his phone to arch an eyebrow at her, she felt embarrassed to have judged him so quickly. "That is, I didn't know you were involved in other charities. I know volunteering that way requires a lot of time, and I certainly appreciate all you've done for Hooves and Hearts."

Shaking his head, Gavin went back to tapping in a few final words on his phone's screen. "Contrary to popular belief, I don't spend all my waking hours chasing women and ticking off the local sheriff."

His jab was well-placed, so she could hardly be offended.

Though it did make her wonder how he'd come by his reputation.

"In that case, I hope the bachelor auction will help people get to know you better," she said finally, wondering how he would answer the ten questions they were sending to all the participants in Studs for Sale.

What more might she learn about this man with hidden layers?

"Somehow I doubt it." Finishing his work on his phone, he set the device on the far side of the bench. Then he tugged off his Stetson and laid that aside too. He combed his fingers through his light brown hair for a moment, letting the breeze play with the strands. "In my experience, people seldom change their minds about their neighbors once they've formed an opinion."

"That seems like a cynical view." Did he believe that she'd underestimated him? Pigeonholed him into the same slot as always?

"Does it?" He folded his arms across his chest while he peered out over the green valley that lay between them and the mountain range. Behind them, the rap-rap-rap of a woodpecker knocked on the big aspen tree that shaded the bench. "My father viewed my mom as an interloper in his world, even five years into their marriage. He never could see her as more than a domestic. An underling."

The bitterness in his voice caught her off guard.

She'd expected him to point out how frequently his own character had been misjudged—by her; by her dad; by his father, even. That he was more defensive of his mother than himself spoke well of him in her eyes.

"I'm sure it must be painful losing your dad before you were able to resolve those feelings." She remembered that Duke Kingsley had been a hardheaded man with a mercurial temper.

"He certainly seemed resolved on his end." Gavin shook his head as he dug one bootheel into the gravel that had been laid around the bench. "He rejected my mom long ago. Rejecting me now... It shouldn't come as a surprise."

"I'm sorry." Her throat tightened for the emotions he must be feeling. The hurt that had to come with the shock of the disinheritance. Every instinct inside her urged her to cover his hand with hers. To offer her touch the way he'd given his to her during her panic attack.

But given how much she'd been thinking about touching him this week, she didn't want to risk acting out of desire.

She tucked her hands under her knees, keeping them to herself.

"He was judgmental. Too proud," Gavin conceded. "But there were still things about him I used to admire." The shared confidence made her feel closer to Gavin.

Again, she felt pulled toward him. Wanting to offer more.

Instead of giving in to the urge to touch, she shared a piece of her past that she'd rarely shown anyone else. "I was too young to remember much about my birth parents. They left me in a Billings-area homeless shelter to be taken in by the foster system. But I knew friends in my foster homes who experienced the loss of problematic relationships. I remember how they struggled with regrets over the things left unsaid."

In the quiet that followed her admission, she glanced over at him to find him studying her in that intent, see-right-through-her way that he had.

"I never knew that about you. That you'd been in foster care." Frowning, he sat up straighter on the bench. "When you came to Silent Spring, the sheriff told everyone they adopted a relative's child. I thought you were his niece, maybe—"

"No." She cut him off, unwilling to remember how adamant her adoptive father had been that she not reveal anything of her personal history with the friends she'd made in Silent Spring. "He felt it would be best for me to have a fresh start here. I know he meant well, hoping that if we all pretended my past didn't exist, I would somehow forget that it happened."

She'd kept her story to herself long enough, however. Perhaps that was why she sometimes felt called to visit Ellen and Chip Crawford in Twin Bridges. To be known for herself. To have her history acknowledged.

Yet even now, having revealed this much of herself to Gavin, she didn't plan to tell him about Jamie. The loss of her foster sister was a deep wound, and she could still appreciate the wisdom of not having that part of her story shared unless she chose to relate it.

"How has that been?" Gavin asked, calling her from her thoughts while the woodpecker behind them took up its rap-rap-rapping up the tree again. "Do you think the fresh start helped? Or did it feel like the sheriff was trying to mold you into someone you weren't?"

She heard an edge in his voice that made her wonder if he really wanted to know or if he was simply searching for more reasons to dislike her father.

"He's not a bad person." Rising to her feet, Lauryn moved away from the bench to take in more of the scenery around them now that they'd finished their work for the day.

Besides, the conversation was making her uncomfortable. Her parents had been good to her. A lifeline to her future, where she could help others who'd been through traumas with the horse rescue and equine therapy.

"I'm not suggesting he is," Gavin continued more softly, standing to close the distance between them. "I just can't help but identify with having a father who is only interested in an airbrushed version of his progeny."

The spring breeze stirred the branches of the aspen tree nearby, a few fuzzy catkins brushing against the shoulder of her gray Hooves and Hearts button-down. Overhead, the leaves fluttered in the wind, filling the silence between them.

All the while, tension coiled in her belly as Gavin drew

nearer. His broad shoulders stretched the cotton of a well-worn blue T-shirt, the sight of his strong arms calling to mind how it had felt to have one slung around her the last time they were together.

"That's not fair, Gavin." Stepping closer to make her point, she laid a hand on his forearm. "Not to your father, and not to mine either."

"Isn't it?" He nodded toward a path branching off to one side of the clearing where they'd been seated. The grass was more trampled there, the dirt trail leading slightly down a hill. "Come this way." He took her lightly by the elbow, turning her toward the trail. "I haven't shown you the real reason I chose this for a meeting place yet."

Curious, she accompanied him, her skin still hyper-aware where he'd touched her. The air grew cooler as they briefly entered deep shade to head down a set of woodland steps made from flat rocks toward another sunny clearing ahead.

"My dad just wanted what was best for me," she explained, hoping it was true. Sometimes she wondered why he wasn't as fully on board with the horse rescue as she'd once hoped he'd be.

Why hadn't her parents RSVP'd for the bachelor auction yet?

"What about my father? You worked for Duke Kingsley for two years. Do you really believe he thought well of me?" Reaching the last of the flat stone steps, Gavin pivoted to look back at her while she made her way down the rest of them.

His question was pointed.

And full of land mines she'd rather not pick her way through.

"That's not for me to say," she hedged, recalling her employer's tirades about his rodeo rebel son. "I was just an assistant, so we had a business relationship—"

Too late, she noticed how carefully he scrutinized her. How he gauged her expression.

"You don't have to cover for him, Lauryn. You wouldn't be the first person he made sure knew that I was a disappointment to him."

Her cheeks warmed uncomfortably, but she wasn't ready to deny his statement outright.

She hovered on the last of the stone stairs, not stepping down to the tall grass below because Gavin remained there, giving her no ground. Demanding an answer?

Frustration rose.

"Your relationship with him was obviously complicated—"

Gavin acknowledged as much with a scornful laugh.

She ignored it to continue speaking, her temper beginning to simmer. "—but you still have good relationships with your half brothers. And in my opinion, family is too important to just turn your back on them when times are hard."

What she wouldn't give to have her foster sister with her today. Did he have any idea how fortunate he was to have so many blood relations around him?

Although she didn't say that last part aloud, maybe he read the gravity in her eyes because he backed up, opening her path to stand beside him in another sunny clearing.

Her focus remained on him for long moments afterward. She saw the tension working in his jaw, the deep furrow of his brow as he weighed her words—or perhaps thought of his retort since he was hell-bent on leaving Silent Spring and Kingsland behind him.

Clearly, the idea of family didn't have the same hold over him that it did for her.

"My mother is my family too," he said finally, his expression easing as he exhaled a long breath. "And I guess it feels like, in slighting me, my father has slighted her all over again."

Understanding dawned. Or at least, more than she'd had before. As she thought about that—Gavin's fierce defense of his mom—he indicated the land ahead of them where they stood shoulder to shoulder.

"This is Mom's garden, by the way." He made a sweeping gesture to encompass everything in front of them, his other hand resting at the small of her back to lead her nearer to the spot. "She loved to sit up here for the view of the mountain range when she was still married to my father. She planted the garden the year before they divorced, and the perennials still continue to flower year after year."

As he spoke, Lauryn tried not to think about the intimacy of his hand at her waist, attempting instead to focus on the explosion of spring colors some five yards ahead. A cloud of blue and yellow butterflies hovered over an assortment of blooms in pinks, blues, reds and whites. The stone steps had led them into a clearing with a completely unexpected rock garden in the middle of nowhere.

Even at this distance, she could detect the tiny flowers of white lilies of the valley around the perimeter. Blue and violet strains of rock cress filled in gaps between the rocks and other plants. Dark blue columbines grew side by side with magenta anemones. Here and there, the surprise yellows of a flower she thought might be called baskets of gold broke up the pinks and blues.

"This is so beautiful," she said with soft reverence, her every nerve ending alive from being close to him while she savored the sensation of stumbling into an enchanted place. "Someone must care for it still?"

Her pulse sped with awareness of him. His touch. His warmth. Six-foot plus of potent masculinity.

Spying a dirt path lined with smooth stones, she moved

toward the entrance, knowing she needed to break the contact with him so she could collect her thoughts. Steady herself after the sparks of attraction had lit her up inside. Besides, she was eager to see the blooms up close.

"I do," he admitted, keeping pace with her as a hummingbird zipped past her ear. "Or at least, I did. I'm not sure what will become of it once I'm gone."

At the edge of the garden, one foot already on the path, she pivoted toward him. Confused. Surprised.

Only to find him standing very close to her. His chest was mere inches from her. She had to tilt her head to meet his gaze. Her senses were all on high alert.

"You'd really leave this behind after lavishing hours—years—of care to keep the garden thriving?"

He stared down at her for one long heartbeat. Then another.

Her mouth went dry at his silent regard. Her breath hitched as a hint of his scent—balsam and spice—teased her nose.

"It's still just a plot of earth," he answered at last, his jaw flexing again. "And one that no longer belongs to me."

Lauryn detected the pain in his voice.

Oh, he hid it beneath the bitterness in his tone. But she was beginning to understand him a little better. Starting to see hints of the man behind the charming mask he normally wore.

Resisting the impulse to lay her hand on his chest, she reminded herself to think before she acted. Instead, she turned to walk one of the twisting paths through the garden. Here and there, boulders served as sculptural accents. Shrub rosebushes hugged some of the stone paths. She could only imagine how beautiful the floral oasis would be by midsummer.

"Thank you for showing me." Running her fingers along a fractured gray rock that played host to hundreds of tiny purple rock cress blooms, Lauryn breathed in the mingled scents of the assorted flowers. "I can see why your mother loved this spot."

A hint of a smile tugged at the corners of his lips while a robin sang a cheerful tune from a nearby tree branch. Gavin idly pulled a weed from the flowers close to where her hand rested on the rock.

"After how things went the last time we got together, I thought it would be a good idea to meet in the most tranquil place I know."

Memories of their meeting at his house, when she'd spiraled into a panic attack and taken comfort from his presence, crowded her mind. Reminded her how his hand had felt on her.

Even now, his elbow brushed hers as he tossed the weed aside, the warmth of his arm lighting up all her nerve endings from just that accidental graze.

"Thank you for that." A breeze made a lock of her hair tickle her chin as Gavin's attention moved to her face.

His brown eyes dipped to her jaw for a moment before his fingers reached to slide the hair away from chin. When his thumb just barely skimmed her lower lip, Lauryn felt her heartbeat trip.

Restart faster.

She told herself yet again to back away.

To think carefully before she did something she might regret later. Something she couldn't take back.

Yet her toes were already flexing inside her boots, lifting her higher to meet his mouth as it descended toward hers. The moment spun out slowly. So slowly.

He gave her all the time in the world to change her mind while his focus narrowed to her lips. Yet with her heart drumming out of control, her skin tingling everywhere and her breath quickening, she couldn't have possibly walked away from just one taste of Gavin Kingsley.

So in the end, it was her who pulled him closer. Eyelids falling shut, telling herself it was just this once, Lauryn kissed him.

Seven

Lauryn's kiss was like nothing he'd ever tasted.

Soft. Sweet.

But underneath the tentative brush of her lips over his? A wealth of passion and sensuality just waiting to be explored.

Still, it was a wonder that Gavin could concentrate on kissing her at all when his head shouted at him that this was happening too soon. That Lauryn expected him to be a ladies' man and dole out charm and kisses like a major player. Hadn't he wanted her to get to know him better? To understand he wasn't the bad guy people thought?

He hoped this wasn't some kind of test to see how fast he could cave to his baser instincts.

Even as the thought crossed his mind—troubling as hell—she made a sexy little sound, half breathy gasp and half throaty moan, that shut down everything else in his head. Because in spite of everything, he recognized that sound for what it was.

A hot and needy demand.

One he would be damned if he could ignore.

Especially with her fingers scrabbling at his T-shirt, the curve of her breasts flattening against his chest. Gavin banded his arm around her back, drawing her against him.

Hard.

Just this once he needed to feel her, to know the shape and give of her body when fitted to his. He lifted her slightly, bending her back over his arm. He groaned when her hips met his, the sound mingling with Lauryn's hungry murmur of approval.

Wasn't it? Approval?

Remembering they were in the middle of his mother's garden and that he was supposed to be showing her his honorable side, all while figuring out what she knew about his father's plans to disinherit him, Gavin forced himself to break the kiss.

He wrenched his eyes open in time to see her lashes flutter more slowly, like a dreamer awakened.

Her damp lips were swollen and pink, her cheeks flushed as her gaze sought his. He employed every ounce of his restraint not to sink right back into that kiss.

"What is it? Why did you stop?" Confusion clouded her hazel gaze.

There had been a time in his life when seeing a woman look at him that way, combined with words that urged him on, Gavin would have indulged them both without a second thought. But Lauryn wasn't just any woman.

And after a lifetime of having his character underestimated, Gavin wasn't the same man he used to be. Gritting his teeth with the effort, he lowered Lauryn's feet back to the ground and released her.

"Was that a test?" His tone was harsher than he'd intended.

But he'd already taxed his restraint enough for this afternoon. He didn't have any tact left for his words.

"Excuse me?" Her eyes flashed with a different kind of fire than what he'd seen there earlier.

"You know I'm hoping to show you another side of myself." He shoved a hand through his hair, trying to recall how he'd failed at the game plan once again. "Did you kiss me to see if my status as a reprobate still applies?"

Her mouth opened in a surprised O for a moment before she snapped her jaw shut again. Her eyes narrowed.

"I don't play games like that," she informed him stiffly. She folded her arms as she backed away a step.

Retreating. Regrouping, maybe.

Making him feel like an ass for thinking there'd been more to her motives. But if the kiss hadn't been a way to prove to him that he was as much a player as ever...

Did that mean she'd been acting on the chemistry he'd always known was there?

His heart thumped hard in his chest. Too bad he'd just alienated her big-time with his question.

"Lauryn—"

"If it's just the same to you, I'd appreciate a ride back to my truck." She moved toward the rock steps built into the hillside that led up to the lookout bench. "Now."

Ah, damn.

He'd misread things with her. Probably doomed himself from ever tasting her lips again.

As he followed her back through the second clearing, picking up his phone and hat on the way, Gavin realized that the idea of never kissing her again bothered him even more than failing at his one mission today.

Finding out what she'd known about his father's plans to cut him out of his will.

Fortunately for him, he still had the promise of a date with her in his back pocket. It could be his last opportunity to learn why his dad wanted to erase him from the Kingsley legacy.

Worse? It might also be his last chance to smooth things over with a woman whose kiss he feared would remain on his mind longer than any full-blown intimate encounter he'd ever had.

Two days later, Lauryn pulled into the driveway at her parents' house for Sunday dinner and willed all thoughts of Gavin Kingsley to the back of her mind.

She would have banished them from her head completely, but after two days of trying, she knew that wasn't possible.

Yet.

Parking in front of the second garage bay, where her mother's little-used compact car normally rested, Lauryn shut off the engine and checked her reflection in the rearview mirror. As she smoothed away a trace of flour on her cheek from the biscuits she'd made to contribute to the meal, she reminded herself that Gavin Kingsley would be out of her life for good after the bachelor auction.

She hoped the memory of that kiss that had scorched her insides would leave with him. Because it mortified her to know a fusing of mouths that had turned her world upside down had meant so little to him that he thought she'd merely been testing his bad boy status.

Swearing under her breath, she scooped up her purse and her covered plate of biscuits, then opened the door. Already, her father was stepping out onto the porch to greet her.

She steeled herself for an evening with him. Because while she loved her dad, she couldn't understand his complete lack of support on the bachelor-auction fundraiser. Bad enough he hadn't submitted the reply card assuring her of his attendance. But for his only response to be messages asking her not to include Gavin? That hurt.

She felt a little nervous about it. And yes, a bit hurt too. Those feelings, combined with her concerns raised from Ellen Crawford's story about the sheriff's treatment of Gavin, plus the recent panic attack about events she hadn't recalled before Gavin's reminder of it, made this Sunday meal seem more emotionally loaded than usual.

She had questions about all of it.

"You're just in time." Sheriff Caleb Hamilton was a big, burly man who'd served as an elected official in Silent Spring since before Lauryn's arrival. Even without his uniform, he carried himself with authority, his stern glances enough to make the kids in town straighten up and the drivers on Main Street slow down. "Let me give you a hand."

He met her at the bottom of the porch steps of the small stone ranch house, taking the biscuits from her as he kissed her on the cheek.

"Thank you. And why am I 'just in time'?" She followed him into the house.

The scent of a roast chicken filtered in from the kitchen. Along with another, harsher scent of something burning. And the sounds of pans banging while her mother loudly berated her oven.

"A cooking mishap, I think." Her father raised a brow as he stopped short of entering the kitchen. "I was afraid to ask."

Laughing, Lauryn took the biscuit plate back from him before he could steal one before dinner.

"Because Mom is so intimidating," she teased. "Just make sure the table is set, and I'll handle the rest."

Her dad saluted her before leaving her to her own devices, his playful gesture so reminiscent of her girlhood days that she felt renewed hope for the conversation she'd been putting off with her parents. Namely, were they attending her fundraiser or not?

"Hey, Mom, how can I help?" Lauryn wound around a kitchen cart that served as a makeshift island.

Violet Hamilton glanced up from where she knelt in front of her open oven, her short dark hair frizzy from the heat. "Oh, thank goodness you're here."

Setting aside the biscuits, Lauryn leaned closer to assess the damage in the form of bubbling black goo on the bottom of the oven.

"Apple-pie spillover?" she guessed, seeing a pie already cooling on the open windowsill. She grabbed a metal spatula to scrape away the worst of the damage from the oven floor. "I can clean up if you want to finish the chicken."

"That's a deal," her mother said, smiling gratefully as she rose from her spot on the floor.

Lauryn set to work, not minding the chore itself but regretting that her mom's frantic movements around the kitchen prevented any predinner questioning about her father's state of mind regarding the auction. Violet was the soft touch in the household—the good cop to the sheriff's sterner approach.

Because even though Lauryn wasn't a kid anymore to stress about her dad's input on her life, she was also mindful of all he'd done for her over the years. Choosing to adopt her when she'd been an admittedly troubled kid after losing her closest friend in such a traumatic way. Later, he'd stood by her when she'd had panic attacks, traveling ninety minutes each way every week to take her to equine therapy. Then, more recently, he'd helped her to purchase the land for her rescue, allowing her to pay him back at a ridiculously low interest rate.

So the idea of disappointing either of her parents weighed on her heart, and she couldn't imagine ever outgrowing that feeling.

A few minutes later, the three of them took their usual seats around a weathered old farm table that had been one of the original pieces of furniture to survive the fundraising efforts of long ago.

After Lauryn laid her napkin across her lap and made quick work of passing dishes around the table, she debated how to tactfully seek answers to the questions that had been building up in her mind all week.

Before she could begin—actually, before she even cut into her chicken—her father spoke first.

"Lauryn, your mother and I were troubled to hear you've been meeting with Gavin Kingsley recently," he began, still loading his plate with mashed potatoes.

Her gaze flicked across the table toward her mother, who kept her own eyes on her meal. A signal she didn't wish to be involved. And, Lauryn guessed from her long experience in wading through family dynamics, a sign that while Violet hadn't given Caleb her approval for roping her into the "we're troubled" comment, she also wouldn't gainsay him.

Meaning Lauryn was on her own.

She didn't bother asking where he came by his information. Silent Spring was a small town, and her dad made sure to pick up his morning coffee every day from Red Barn Roasters, the best spot to hear all the local gossip.

Taking a sip of water while she considered her response, she decided to parry with a counterattack.

"Gavin has been helping me organize the fundraising event for Hooves and Hearts," she answered, slicing into her chicken. "Which reminds me that I haven't received your RSVP yet. You *are* attending, I hope?"

Her mother shot a quick glance at her father.

Something about the look on her mom's face made Lauryn suspect Violet was as interested in the answer as she was. And just like that, her stress ratcheted up a notch. It hadn't been her imagination that her parents were deliberately not replying to their invitation.

"We were waiting to speak to you about it first." Her dad gave her the same flinty look he used at traffic stops, his blue eyes cool. "I'm hoping you'll change your mind about including Kingsley in your list of so-called 'eligible bachelors.' You won't be doing the young women in attendance any favors by letting them bid on that piece of work."

Defensiveness for Gavin surged as she recalled his words to her.

In my experience, people seldom change their minds about their neighbors once they've formed an opinion.

No wonder he'd taken such a cynical view when her father spoke about him that way. Still, she knew a reasoned argument was the only way forward with her dad, so she waited while she took another bite of her chicken, willing away her frustration.

"I have two of the Kingsley brothers signed on for the auction," she said finally, meeting his gaze from where he sat at the head of the table. "Which one are you objecting to?"

Her mother made a choked sound that might have started as a laugh before she turned it into a cough. It was tough to tell when her father dropped a frustrated fist on the table, making the silverware jump.

"The only one with a police record," he shot back. "Lauryn, you know Gavin Kingsley was a teenage delinquent and has done nothing with his life but drag race and make trouble since then."

The anger in her dad's voice surprised her. She'd known he had problems with Gavin dating back to that time Gavin had driven into their fields, but she hadn't realized the enmity ran so deep.

"Half this town drag races at the canyon, including plenty of your friends, Dad, and I've noticed you don't mind looking the other way when they race." She'd been to the event once when she was younger and a bunch of her friends were going. The races didn't happen often since they definitely skirted the law, but they were always well attended. "You can't hold it against Gavin that he wins. And I'm not sure it's fair to say he has a record when he trespassed here when he was just fifteen years old—"

"Are you seeing him?" Her father's voice cut right through her words.

Even her mother looked up from her plate at the question, a strain of worry in her eyes.

Lauryn felt her face warm. Which was ludicrous since she was a grown woman who'd worked hard to build a life she could be proud of. One she would have hoped they'd be proud of too.

She didn't want them to worry, but she also couldn't help feeling cornered.

"You are, aren't you?" her father pressed when she didn't answer immediately. "I thought you were smarter than that—"

She dropped her fork, letting it clatter back to the plate.

"Excuse me?" She felt cold inside at her father's thoughtless remark.

She'd worked hard to overcome a lot in her life.

The nightmares that had followed losing her foster sister. The panic attacks. But also the insecurity of being behind her peers in school for the first eighteen months she'd been in Silent Spring. Her wounds from the accident with Jamie had put her in the hospital for weeks.

Afterward, the emotional recovery and therapy had taken even more time away from academics. So for this man, of all people, to question her intelligence…

"I have to leave." Lauryn rose from the table, unwilling to sit through a meal seasoned with insults. "Mom, I'm sorry."

"Honey, I didn't mean that." Her father rose, too, but she was already hurrying out of the dining room to retrieve her purse. "Lauryn, wait. We're just worried about you. That young man's own father didn't trust him enough to leave him anything. That ought to tell you something."

She could hear his heavier footsteps behind her as the sound of his accusations grew louder. Closer.

Plucking her handbag off the counter, she swung around to confront the big, bluff man she loved but who was as stubborn as anyone she'd ever met. And, as his most recent words replayed in her head, an awful thought occurred to her.

"Did you have anything to do with his father's will?" she asked, anger making her speak this time without bothering to weigh her words. "Did you help poison Duke Kingsley against his own son?"

Her dad stopped in his tracks. "Duke didn't need my help to see that one was a bad apple. And I don't plan to support any fundraiser that makes some kind of hero out of Gavin Kingsley."

He said the name like he had a bad taste in his mouth.

And even though Lauryn had known her father could be bullheaded, she was still caught completely off guard that he could be so adamant about this. There had to be something she didn't know about her father's history with Gavin. Some piece she was missing. Because his reaction was over the top. Uncalled for.

Cruel, even, since it was beginning to sound like her father hated Gavin more than he loved her.

"So you won't attend Studs for Sale even if it's *my* fundraiser? For a cause close to my heart?" She searched her dad's blue eyes, looking for the love she'd seen earlier when she'd walked into the house.

How many other times had she felt this way? Like she

had to earn love because it was never just a given for someone like her, a foster child with problems. With a past.

Behind her father, she could hear her mother's murmur, as if urging the sheriff to a softer stance. But to no effect.

Her dad's arms folded across his barrel chest in a gesture easily recognizable. He was drawing his line in the sand here. If she had Gavin in the bachelor auction, she wouldn't be seeing her father at the event she'd worked tirelessly to organize.

And given the way her dad had always been the stronger voice in their parents' marriage, she guessed that meant her mother wouldn't be putting in an appearance either.

In that moment, she knew her choice, and it was an easy one. Not because she believed so strongly in Gavin, although she certainly had begun to see him as a much different person than her father and even Duke Kingsley would have had her believe in the past.

No. She knew what she needed to do, because she wasn't going to knuckle under to emotional extortion anymore. If her father didn't love her enough to overlook his own prejudices for one evening, then she'd rather not have his support.

"Good night, Dad." Tucking the strap of her handbag onto her shoulder, she pivoted fast and walked out the door and into the early evening.

Once she arrived at her truck, she gave herself a moment to lean against the fender. Closing her eyes, she tried to catch her breath after the confrontation.

All the while, wanting nothing more than to run back into Gavin's arms, consequences be damned.

But since that definitely wasn't an option after the way their kiss had ended, Lauryn pulled her cell phone from her bag and did something she rarely indulged.

Opening a message box for a group chat, she prepared to type an SOS to her girlfriends. She'd maintained some friendships from high school. Not everyone had stayed in Silent Spring since graduation, but a couple of them had returned after college to build a life in the town where they'd grown up.

It's been a day here. Anyone up for a drink?

Within seconds, she saw the text bubble dots that indicated someone was responding. A moment later her phone chimed.

Is this a not-so-veiled request for girlfriend talk therapy?

Lauryn welcomed the laugh that came with her friend's reply.

Possibly. Care to discuss after a margarita?

Five minutes later, she had a plan to meet with two of her friends at a bar on the edge of town. Sliding into the driver's seat of her truck, she backed out of her parents' driveway and headed south, not allowing herself to think too long about the fact that she was heading to a bar owned by Levi Kingsley.

One that his brother, Gavin, had been known to frequent.

Eight

Tipping back a longneck bottle of his brother's latest craft beer, Gavin welcomed the citrusy tang of the IPA as he took in the lack of business at the Stockyard.

A couple of young ranch hands from Kingsland sat at the opposite end of the old-fashioned mahogany bar from him. Gavin had stationed himself close to the doors leading to the back office. A bartender kept himself busy cleaning already-spotless glasses since there wasn't much else to do. The place was empty except for a few bikers and two tables in the back where some people Gavin didn't recognize— out-of-towners, for sure—kept up a lively game of darts.

The jukebox played a country rock song that couldn't quite hide the desolate feel of a joint that was usually hopping at this hour, even on Sundays.

A moment later, the door from the back office opened and Levi stepped into view, rocking his usual threads: a low-key suit with no tie that still seemed way too formal for a Montana bar on the wrong side of the closest incorporated town line. Everyone else in the place wore jeans and boots.

A funny thing, too, considering Levi was the most important rancher in town. But then, Levi had always gravitated to the business side of things, managing their father's wealth and diversifying the Kingsley assets. Hence the Stockyard, which he'd bought three years earlier.

Levi didn't look quite as much like his usual power-executive self today, though. In spite of the suit and an heirloom Breitling watch that rarely left his wrist, the guy had circles around his eyes that suggested he hadn't slept well in a long time.

Gavin understood the feeling well. Sleep was an elusive beast in the wake of their father's death.

"I'm liking the IPA," Gavin offered by way of greeting, raising his bottle as Levi moved around the bar to take the seat beside him. "Good job on this one."

"Thanks, brother." Levi nodded at the bartender, who was already bringing over a glass of water for the owner. Levi's preferred beverage when he was working. "Wish there was an occasional patron around to drink it."

"Right. What gives?" Gavin picked at the label on his brew, tearing into the face of the logo for Gargoyle King. The image was dark and gothic and had never been what he'd expected from his older brother. "Why is the place so empty?"

"Bad press from Dad's will is spilling over into all corners of the business." Levi downed half the glass of water, then spun on the saddleback barstool to look out over the vacant tables.

Gavin set aside his drink, trying to make sense of his brother's words. "Not possible. Who would give a rat's ass about what Dad—*your* dad—did with his money?"

He recalled there'd been a couple of mentions of the family's fortunes in local news outlets after Duke passed, but the coverage had been limited because they'd avoided probate. Everything had already been in trust for Levi and Quinton.

"Plenty of people," his brother muttered darkly. "You forget what a huge following you had as a bull rider—how much support around the whole state. There's been a lot of backlash against Kingsland businesses among people who see you as the injured party in the inheritance drama."

Gavin shook his head. Disbelieving. "Injured by Duke Kingsley, maybe. Not by you."

The party in the back cheered a bull's-eye shot as Levi shrugged.

"Your fans have actively called for a boycott of Kingsland businesses. Like it or not, they're trying to rally around you the best way they know how." Levi glanced his way briefly before adding, "The female fans, in particular."

Gavin cursed under his breath. He'd put that part of his life behind him when he returned to Silent Spring full-time, agreeing to help his brothers launch the stud service at Kingsland Ranch. But there had been a time when he'd been a fan favorite on the rodeo circuit, his popularity helped by a *Men of Rodeo* calendar he'd done for charity. And, truth be told, his interviews about winning had struck a chord with some people.

He'd made no bones about needing to prove himself as the underdog in a powerful family. Something he wouldn't have done now, with the benefit of more maturity behind him. But back then, he'd still been stinging from his father's criticisms of rodeo, insisting Gavin should have been doing something "more productive" with his life.

Which, in Duke Kingsley's mind, meant making bucketfuls of money for the Kingsland coffers by working for the family business.

"I had no idea." Gavin ran a hand over his bristly jaw, hating that his former supporters had made trouble for his brothers. "I haven't been on social media much this week, but I can log on tonight and tell people that boycotting you sure as hell isn't helping me."

Maybe he hadn't noticed the storm brewing online because he'd been too busy this week helping Lauryn plan her bachelor auction. Too preoccupied with sending out the questionnaires to the other bachelors and sharing ideas for promoting Studs for Sale.

Ah, hell, who was he kidding?

For two days straight, he'd been consumed solely by thoughts of Lauryn and the kiss he couldn't get out of his head.

"I'd rather you just sit down with Quinton and me—and Clayton, when we find him—to legally accept your quarter of the estate. We could put out a press release and assure everyone we've addressed the injustices of Dad's will and divided things evenly among us."

Levi's head swiveled toward the bar's front entrance as it swung wide, the last shafts of daylight slanting through before a new arrival.

Gavin took the opportunity to return to his beer while he considered his reply. He wasn't going back into the Kingsland realm again. His father hadn't wanted him to have any of it, after all, and he refused to ignore that final judgment from the family patriarch.

His dad had accused him often enough of not respecting authority. He would damn well respect the old man's final wish, and then he wouldn't have to waste another minute of his life feeling like he'd stolen a legacy not intended for him.

But how to make Levi understand when his brother had never stepped a toe out of line and only wanted to right their father's wrongs?

Just as Gavin set down his beer again, his brother elbowed him. "Gav, look who's here."

Levi's low voice should have been a warning. But Gavin took an extra moment to hand his empty longneck bottle back to the bartender before ordering another.

So the sound of a woman's full, throaty laugh from inside the bar caught him unaware. That sudden burst of mirth tripped over his skin, nimble as a tongue, both sexy and familiar.

The hairs at the back of his neck straightened. Awareness warming his flesh even before he turned around.

Knowing who he'd see.

Still, the sight of Lauryn Hamilton at a table near the front windows with two of her friends sucked the air out of his lungs. The last glow of daylight was filtered by a gray shade on the long pane overlooking the parking lot, but the dulled rays still managed to pick out the burnished highlights in her chestnut hair as she smiled over something her girlfriend said.

Lauryn wore a blue-and-white-print dress, demure and pretty, but the vee cut of the front gave him a mouthwatering view of cleavage as she leaned forward at the table. The high-top gave him an excellent glimpse of her lower body as well. Neutral-colored spiky heels made her calf muscles flex where she crossed her legs, one she braced on the barstool while the other tapped in rhythm to the country rock song on the jukebox.

"Damn, but she looks great," his brother observed from beside him.

Gavin spun on him. Tension snapped his shoulders straight. "What did you just say?"

Levi's focus narrowed on the table with every bit as much intensity as Gavin's had a moment before. Then, as if he sensed Gavin's regard, Levi dragged his gaze from the women.

"Kendra Davies," Levi noted more blandly, turning

back to the bar for his water glass. "Just surprised to see her in town again after she relocated to Denver."

Relief coursed through him.

His brother hadn't been talking about Lauryn.

Now Gavin did a double take, noticing the other two women at Lauryn's table. On her right sat petite, dark-haired Hope Alvarez, dressed in jeans and a pink Henley with her new veterinary business logo printed on the pocket. She'd just set up shop in the next town over. She'd made a house call recently for one of Gavin's mares, and he'd noticed her ease and skill with the animal even though she'd only been in business on her own for a few months.

On Lauryn's left sat Kendra Davies, a statuesque blonde wearing a fitted navy suit and staring at the phone in her hand. Gavin remembered her from school, though she'd been closer to Levi's age than his. He didn't think he would have recognized her if Levi hadn't been practically gawking at her.

He was about to inquire about that. Or, more likely, hassle his brother about it. But then two things happened at the same time.

First, Lauryn's gaze snapped up from her friends and locked with his. Almost as if she'd felt his attention on her.

That instant of connection, even if it was only a long look across the room, set the heat inside him flaring again.

But simultaneously, one of the dudes from the dart game in the back of the bar made his way toward the table. His intentions were clear from the look on his mug, which was somehow both lascivious and too confident at the same time.

Gavin didn't even bother to excuse himself from his conversation. One moment, he was seated beside his brother. The next, he was charging across the bar, having no other plan other than to intercept the would-be hassler before he got anywhere near Lauryn.

Lauryn couldn't imagine what had prompted Gavin to stride toward her with a look on his face like he was going to throw her over his shoulder and carry her back to his man cave, but something about that expression made her body tingle head to toe.

Lingering at the most delicious places in between.

"Incoming," her friend Kendra muttered, setting aside her phone. "But no one leaves this table until we finish what we came here for. Agreed?"

On her other side, Lauryn sensed her friend Hope nodding emphatically. "Absolutely."

Forcing her attention away from Gavin, Lauryn wished her heart would quit knocking around so hard in her chest. "Um. Sure. Okay."

"Girl," Kendra warned in her most severe tone, raising one perfectly arched eyebrow to glare at her. "*You* called this meeting. Stick to the plan."

She nodded, knowing her public relations–expert friend had a valid point. Beside her, Hope's eyes darted to something behind Lauryn's shoulder, just before an oily, unfamiliar voice sounded from that direction.

"Hello, ladies." The greeting came from a cloud of cologne, heavy on the musk, at the same time a hairy elbow planted itself on the table between Hope and Lauryn. "What are we drinking tonight?"

A young man's face followed the elbow as the guy settled a narrow chin in one hand to leer at Lauryn. Her first thought was that this was why Gavin had charged across the bar toward her.

Her second was a moment of dismay to realize Gavin only had that caveman expression on his face because he wanted to intercede and not because he planned to bring her back to his lair and have his way with her.

Which shouldn't be such a letdown.

"No touching," Kendra barked at the newcomer. "Respect our personal space, please."

"We're good, thanks," Lauryn assured the guy as she edged away from him.

Only to find herself leaning into Gavin, who'd rounded the table to slide an arm around her on her opposite side. The warmth and strength of him—from his hand gently squeezing to the weight of his limb draped along her shoulders—sent a shiver through her.

"Sir," Gavin addressed Hairy Arm respectfully, even if he flexed his muscles like a junkyard dog's hackles. "The bartender has your tab ready for you and your party. You can settle it up front."

Hairy Arm straightened, taking some of the cologne cloud—mercifully—with him. "We're not leaving—"

"You will be if you don't allow these ladies to enjoy their evening in peace," Gavin warned, his arm still wrapped possessively around her.

The touch was for a good cause, of course.

He was helping her send the interloper packing, and probably doing a faster job than they could have managed on their own. Even Kendra, with her big-city street sense and willingness to go toe-to-toe with anyone, couldn't have ousted him as quickly as Gavin. Because even now, Hairy Arm huffed his way back to his own table, muttering curses.

Sadly, no matter how many strides the sisterhood made forward, some misogynist creeps only paid attention when a fellow Y-chromosome carrier did the talking.

A moment later, the bartender arrived with an icy bucket of six longnecks from the craft brewery owned by the Kingsley family. Lauryn recognized the Gargoyle

King labels as cocktail napkins and frosted mugs were passed around.

"Courtesy of Mr. Kingsley," the barkeep announced as he straightened from the task and nodded to Levi just before the owner disappeared into the back office. "Let me know if you'd like anything else."

Distracted by the free drinks, and curious about the way Kendra's harrumphed how "some people were too proud to come over to the table to say hello," Lauryn missed the moment when Gavin gave her shoulder one final squeeze and vanished again.

A new party had entered the bar, too, so maybe Gavin had stepped outside when the door was open.

She hadn't even had a chance to say thank you.

Or tell him she needed to talk to him. Not that she would have shared the conversation she'd had with her dad this evening. At least, she didn't think she would have. Maybe she just wanted to apologize for being one of those people who'd made up their minds about someone before gathering all the facts...

"Which do you want?" Hope was waving a beer bottle under her nose, her pink Henley sleeves rolled up enough to show off the colorful ink of the animals scrolling around one forearm. "The lager or the IPA?"

"Lager," Lauryn decided, attempting to shake off thoughts of Gavin to focus on her girlfriends.

If anything, her hormones racing out of control tonight was more reason than ever to seek advice.

"So..." Kendra cast a speculative look her way. "You and Gavin Kingsley?"

"Definitely not." How many times had she told herself she shouldn't get attached to the town's bad boy billionaire? Even without his father's inheritance, he was a wealthy man in his own right. She'd read his bio for the bachelor auction. She knew about his personal investments in his brother's start-ups. And his own business—the stud program—already had a staggering net worth, assuming he untangled it from the Kingsley family to keep a portion of it.

Streaking Saint alone would make him a very rich man.

Hope exchanged a wry look with Kendra across the table while the jukebox switched to an old country romance ballad. Then Hope pointed her beer at Lauryn and said, "Yet he just draped himself all over you a minute ago, and you didn't even blink."

Sighing, Lauryn remembered this was why she came. She needed the help and advice of friends. Especially this week, when she was already feeling the annual melancholy that came with the impending anniversary of her foster sister's death in another two weeks.

After making sure Gavin was nowhere within hearing distance, Lauryn's gaze snagged on an older couple who'd moved onto the Stockyard's small dance floor to twirl a slow two-step, their eyes locked on one another as if they were all alone. A hollow pang filled her chest.

Then she bent her head closer to her friends and told them everything. The panic attack, the kiss, the unexpected side of Gavin she'd uncovered and—toughest of all—her fear that her father had carried an old, baseless grudge too far.

What she didn't understand was why.

When she finished her story, Kendra gave a low whistle. Hope chewed her lip.

"Well, what do you think?" she prompted them, reaching for a second beer. She would only have a few sips. But the tale had taken more out of her than she'd realized. "I should ignore the hot looks, shouldn't I? Run for cover? I keep reminding myself that he has female admirers chasing him from here to Kalamazoo."

Hope laughed as she scraped her dark curls into a ponytail and tugged a scrunchie off one wrist to tie it. "Maybe so, but that doesn't mean he's chasing them back. You can't really hold it against a man for being charming and attractive."

"Can't you?" Kendra asked, though her attention was fixed behind the bar, where Levi Kingsley was deep in conversation with an older woman in a fringed jean jacket and black Stetson. "The Kingsley men all seemed to inherit their father's sense of entitlement."

Lauryn frowned, thinking about Gavin's determination to leave town and not take a cent from his brothers for the legacy that should have been his. "I'm not sure I agree—"

Kendra whipped back around to face her, setting her bottle on the table with a too-hard thud. "Sorry. You're right, and I'm off topic. What I don't understand is why you don't just go for it with Gavin? You want him, and from the hot, possessive looks he was giving you tonight, it's clear he wants you too." She shrugged, her expensive-looking navy blazer hugging her figure as she moved. "You already know there's a chance he's a player, so just go into things with eyes wide open. Enjoy some fun while it lasts."

Lauryn hadn't expected a green light. She'd thought maybe her friends would share what they knew about Gavin. Or help her scour his social media for clues about the real him. Or—actually, she'd had no idea what to expect.

Then again, she'd only just begun trying to knit together a serious friend group in the last year, as part of her ongoing path to healing from losing her closest friend ever. This kind of thing—drinks with the girls on a Sunday— was new to her.

As was advice on her romantic life since, so far, the guys she'd dated had been safe choices. Sheriff-approved.

"Hope?" Lauryn turned to her other friend. Hope Alvarez was as down-to-earth as they came. Before she'd gone away to veterinary school, she'd raised her own sheep and goats. Even now, she bred award-winning sheep in her spare time. "What do you think? Am I crazy to consider this? Especially with Dad giving me hassle for reasons known only to him?"

A smile curved one side of Hope's lips as she spun her empty beer bottle in circles on the table. "Gavin is great with horses, so he can't be all bad in my book. Sorry if that's a weird metric for applying to guys."

"No. I appreciate that insight, actually." Lauryn's equine-therapy days had taught her that horses were discriminating judges of character. "I just hate that my parents have turned my friendship with Gavin into a reason not to attend Studs for Sale."

She hadn't realized until she said the words aloud how wrong that felt. How much it hurt. Or how much she'd counted on the support of her family. She'd worked hard to be someone they could be proud of.

Hope covered her hand, her silver rings a cool weight on Lauryn's fingers. "Your dad can be a good man and still wrong about this. It's okay to trust your own instincts."

The advice settled around her, resonating.

"I guess you're right." She squeezed Hope's hand. Then reached for Kendra's and squeezed hers too. "Thanks, you guys."

Some of the tension that had been riding her ever since the argument with her father seeped out of her now. The fun of the night out, and the soft guitar strains of another romantic country ballad, soothed her insides.

Just in time too. Because a moment later, she spotted Gavin heading her way again, his brown eyes locked on her.

Stirring her senses.

"Incoming," Kendra whispered again, only this time it wasn't a warning so much as an invitation.

A possibility.

Releasing her friend's hands, Lauryn licked her lips. Ready for whatever happened next. Because as long as she kept her eyes open and her heart on lockdown, she looked forward to everything tonight had in store for her.

Nine

As Gavin made his way toward Lauryn's table once more, he assured himself his intentions were good.

Honorable, even.

He'd given her time to catch up with her friends, refusing to descend on her the moment she set foot in the bar like the jerkoff who'd hit on her earlier. But something about the posture of her friends told him they'd finished the intense discussion they'd seemed to be having earlier. The veterinarian was now pointing out some of the ink on her arm to the suit-clad publicist across the table while Lauryn swayed her shoulders in time to a country love song, her gaze stuck on an older couple who'd hit the dance floor for every slow tune in the past hour.

As far as Gavin could tell, he wouldn't be interrupting. And he really did just want to apologize for the way he'd reacted when they'd kissed.

Stopping just short of her chair, Gavin rested one arm

along the back of the stool while he extended his other hand to her. "May I have this dance?"

Okay, so his good, honorable intentions were easier to accomplish if they could speak privately. If it meant having Lauryn in his arms at the same time because they were in a bar and she'd been swaying to the music, that was just a happy coincidence.

"I'd like that." Her breathy words were a soft huff against his cheek where he leaned in to hear her.

She slipped her fingers in his palm as she slid off the barstool, her pretty dress hugging her curves as she moved. When her hazel eyes locked on his, he felt the spark that always ignited when she was near. Only now, it felt hotter.

Because she didn't break her gaze? Or was it because of the sexy little grin she gave him before she sashayed ahead of him toward the dance floor?

Whatever it was, he couldn't ignore the subtle twitch of her hips as she moved, the hem of her dress caressing her thighs as the fabric swished. His heart thumped harder while he scavenged around his brain for those good intentions.

She spun toward him once she reached the wooden dance floor his brother had built near a small stage that featured live acts on Fridays and Saturdays. Tonight, the jukebox and the older couple were their only company as Gavin embraced her, dropping any pretense of two-stepping his way through this conversation.

Lauryn looped her arms around his neck in return, her body drawing closer to his like she wanted to be there. She felt soft beneath the thin material of the dress, her skin warm right through the silky fabric.

"Are you enjoying yourself this evening?" Gavin asked, knowing he wouldn't be able to focus on the apology he wanted to make if he kept letting his thoughts wander down the dangerous terrain of how Lauryn felt against him.

"Yes, it's good to spend time with friends. I haven't made enough space for that in my life." Her fingers played idly with the hair at the back of his neck, and he wondered if she realized the effect she was having on him. "Thank you for the help ousting our visitor earlier. We could have handled it—"

"Of course you could have. But you shouldn't have to put up with being hassled in the first place." Sensation streaked down his spine from the featherlight touches of her fingers. "Especially when—as you said—you're out to catch up with friends you don't see often enough."

"You're right." Her smile unfurled, the sign of her happiness making him feel like he'd won something more significant than any rodeo buckle. "I appreciate not having to waste our energy chasing off some presumptuous stranger. It gave us more of our evening to talk."

He was curious about what that conversation had involved. He'd noticed—in the handful of times his attention had found itself fixed to her throughout the evening—that she'd been doing most of the speaking. Was something troubling her?

The idea worried him as they shuffled slow steps around the dance floor. The older guy winked at them as he and his partner twirled past.

Gavin's grip tightened on Lauryn's waist. He didn't want to be another presumptuous guy trying too hard to get close to her, so he didn't think it was right to ask her about her conversation with her friends. Instead, he reminded himself what he'd wanted to discuss with her in the first place.

"I owe you an apology." He couldn't stop his thumbs from grazing light circles where they rested just above her hips. "That's half the reason I asked you to dance."

"An apology? What for?" Her head tipped to one side as she gazed up at him, her full lips looking incredibly kissable.

The memory of her taste flooded his senses, the need for a repeat of that kiss urging him to pull her closer. Press all of her to him while he tested the soft give of her mouth once more.

"For ever suggesting you'd kiss me to prove some kind of point." He shook his head, still disgusted with himself about that. "If I'd been thinking straight, I would have known that's not something you would do—"

A ghost of her earlier smile returned. "Why weren't you thinking straight?"

The coy look in her eyes was a teasing aspect he hadn't ever seen on her before. He liked it.

Tremendously.

"Are you flirting with me, Lauryn? Right in the middle of my heartfelt apology?" Everything about the bar faded away, his senses narrowing to only her.

"Maybe. Is it working?" Her hazel eyes blinked up at him.

"Too well." He couldn't resist reaching up to trace a touch along her cheek. Tease his fingers along the line of her jaw. "Well enough, in fact, that I'm going to feel severely disappointed if it's the alcohol talking."

She laughed, her legs brushing against his. "Considering I only had one sip of a second beer, I seriously doubt that."

Desire for her surged. He had to remind himself where they were. That tonight wasn't his date night with her. He couldn't just act on the hunger she stirred simply by being in his arms.

What had changed between them to make her feel comfortable with him this way? Enough to kiss him? Flirt with him?

He knew she'd avoided him because of his reputation in the past. Had she really begun to see beyond the hearsay of a few people who had it in for him? Namely the sheriff and his own father? He'd wanted her to get to know him before the bachelor auction. Maybe she really had.

Gavin bent to speak into her ear through the veil of silky chestnut waves. "You can't begin to imagine how much I'd like to take you home with me tonight and show you how thoroughly you're affecting me."

The shiver that went through her trembled through him too.

When her eyes found his again, the green depths glowed brighter. Hotter.

"Maybe we should go out on that date I promised you," she suggested, her steps slowing to a stop.

He hadn't realized the music ended until that moment, his thoughts too crowded with images of her in his bed. Beneath him. Over him. Shouting his name on a hoarse cry as he teased her release free...

"A date." He repeated the words that sounded entirely too tame for what he wanted with her. He couldn't seem to let her go even though the jukebox switched to a fast-tempo country rock song. "That's a good idea. We'll talk through exactly what's happening between us. Figure it all out."

Her lips parted. Her breath came faster. She stood so close he could see the pulse pounding faster in her neck.

"Sounds like a plan." Giving him a jerky nod, she slipped by him to walk back to her table.

Gavin followed a step behind, wishing he had the right to kiss her goodnight.

But he couldn't lose sight of why he'd remained in Silent Spring in the first place. As much as being around Lauryn Hamilton tempted and tantalized him, he needed to figure out what role she'd played, if any, in him being disinherited.

And if she hadn't done anything to taint him in his father's eyes, Gavin still wondered if she'd known for years that he would be losing his place in the family legacy. Because that would hurt too. He'd spent so long trying to prove himself to people.

He didn't think Lauryn was playing games with him—he'd meant what he said when he'd apologized for assuming her kiss was a test. Yet something had shifted her opinion of him, and he wanted to know what that might be.

"I'll call you tomorrow," he assured her as he delivered her back to the table with her girlfriends, both of whom were now on their phones, heads bent together as they scrolled through their screens. He lowered his voice for Lauryn's ears only. "So you can make good on that promised date."

"Do that." She laid a hand on his chest, steadying herself to arch higher on her toes so she could speak close to his ear as well. "And you can make good on some of those things you mentioned to me too."

If there'd been any doubt in his mind about her intentions for this date, they were gone now. A fire blazed over his skin where she'd been touching him a moment ago, her words replaying in his head.

He'd wanted this damned date so she could get to know him better. To show her there was more to him than the heartbreaker reputation.

But right now, he couldn't imagine any scenario with Lauryn that didn't lead them into bed so they could excise the attraction still scorching him from the inside out.

Anticipation shivered over Lauryn's skin as she neared the small airfield where her outing with Gavin was set to begin.

Seated in the back of the big black SUV he'd sent to pick her up, Lauryn kept her eyes trained out the window, looking for her first sight of him. Or of the glider plane he'd promised to take her on today.

I think we're almost there, she texted to him now, remembering how nervous she'd been about the date at first when he'd changed the day two times. At first, he hadn't revealed why the days had switched, and she'd been nervous that he was having second thoughts about being with her. Then, when she'd pressed him about it, he'd admitted that he wanted to take her on a glider plane but that he needed the weather to cooperate for the best ride possible.

Once she'd understood the plan, the day swapping had all made sense. She'd agreed to meet him at the airfield since he had to transport his glider from the ranch, where he sometimes used it, to an airstrip. There he would meet a pilot friend of his to help him launch it so Lauryn and Gavin could land at a surprise destination.

Lauryn knew dinner was included at the other end. Since she'd never been on such an elaborately planned date before, she couldn't deny being excited. And that was before taking into account that she would be spending the rest of the day—and quite possibly the night—with Gavin Kingsley.

Besides, since the conversation with her girlfriends at the bar, she'd experienced a new need to embrace life. Not just with Gavin. But by taking chances. Seeing friends. Not trying so hard to please everyone—her parents especially—that she dimmed her own light. For years, the trauma of losing her foster sister had sent her down a path of caution. Safety. But maybe she owed Jamie better than that. Survivor's guilt never went away fully, but she could honor Jamie's life by living hers more robustly.

Her phone vibrated with an incoming message.

I see the SUV. Look out the passenger side window.

Scooting across the seat to the opposite side of the vehicle, Lauryn glimpsed the long body of a white fixed-wing plane, the nose painted bright red where it sat on a dark green field of grass. Two men stood talking beside the aircraft, one tall with broad shoulders who lifted his arm to wave. The other guy was shorter and wiry, with a pair of dark shades concealing his eyes.

A second, larger prop plane idled in front of the glider. The prop plane would act as their tow plane since the glider had no engine. Once the tow aircraft got them airborne, the prop plane would disconnect and fly back home while the glider simply…soared. She'd read up about it online and was excited to find out what gliding felt like.

Moments later, the SUV wove its way onto the small field, stopping near the prop plane to let her out. Gavin was at the door almost immediately, opening it wide to greet her.

"Are you ready to fly?" He held out a hand for her while a fresh spring breeze blew over her face, the sound of the plane engine rumbling softly.

"I'm ready." Slipping her hand into his, she realized how much she'd grown to trust him in a short space of time. From the way he'd comforted her after her anxiety attack to all the hours he'd volunteered for her fundraiser event to his defensiveness of her at the bar.

Minutes later, she was settled in the back seat of the glider, staring up at Gavin as he finished his rundown of safety essentials. She knew where to find a parachute, though Gavin had assured her she wouldn't be needing one. And apparently she didn't need a headset either. He had a microphone and cockpit speaker, but those, too, he said shouldn't be necessary.

The pilot for the prop plane—Heath—was already seated in his aircraft, waiting for Gavin's signal that they were ready for takeoff.

"Here's your most important piece of equipment." Reaching into the back pocket of his jeans, Gavin shook out a brimmed white hat like a fisherman would wear. "Some extra sun protection."

Taking it, she noticed he also wore a brimmed hat, though his was a ballcap with the name of a small-town rodeo. The shadow it cast on his handsome face didn't begin to detract from how appealing he looked today as he double-checked her seat belt.

"Thank you." She fitted the hat to her head, tugging down her ponytail so the cap sat more comfortably in place. "Good thinking."

Her pulse throbbed faster, excitement building for the new experience.

"You're not nervous, are you?" Gavin asked, his brown eyes full of concern. "I want this to be fun for you, not anything to cause anxiety."

She shook her head, understanding why he wanted to be careful. She never had explained the panic attack she'd had at that first lunch meeting with him.

Reaching for his hand, she laid her palm on top of it. "On the contrary, I'm really looking forward to this. I recently decided I need to be a little more adventurous, so this comes at a perfect time."

A smile wreathed Gavin's face, and she could see how much he'd been looking forward to this day too. The spark of awareness was there in his eyes, reminding her she had so much to look forward to even after they landed.

"Excellent." He lifted her hand to his lips and kissed it before letting go again. "You're in good hands, Lauryn. I promise."

Her heartbeat was still jolting from the brush of his lips on her skin when he jumped into the pilot's seat and gave a thumbs-up to Heath in the prop plane.

At first, she only noticed the increase in volume of the plane's engine as it surged forward, the line between the prop plane and the glider stretching longer. Going taut.

A thrill shot through her once the glider lurched forward, bumping lightly along the grassy field as the prop plane rolled forward. Faster. Faster. Exciting. The flight… and the man.

"You're going to have the best view you've ever seen of Granite Peak," Gavin called back to her from his seat just ahead of her. All the while, their speed increased, the trees lining the airstrip seeming to blur before her eyes. "And it will quiet down for us to talk more easily once the prop plane lets us go."

She could hardly process what he was saying as the two planes lifted into the air, one behind the other.

Her squeal of delight split the air as they went airborne, the glider sliding slightly to the left of the prop plane as it pulled them high above the ground.

At first, she saw the tops of the trees just beneath them. But minutes later, they were well atop the pines, the view of the mountains and the Absaroka-Beartooth Wilderness enough to take her breath away.

"Wow, Gavin, you were right." She reached forward to lay her hand on his shoulder, feeling the warmth of him through his long-sleeved flannel and the cotton T-shirt layered beneath. The flex of his muscle under her palm sent a thrill of another kind through her. "This is incredible."

"Just wait until we separate and start soaring on our own. We're almost at two thousand feet now." Even now, he steered the rudder to guide them to the right of the tow plane. "Riding the wind currents is like nothing I've ever experienced before."

Considering Gavin had been a professional bull rider and a winning amateur drag racer, his endorsement of soaring as a unique sensation meant all the more. Giving her the sense that he was sharing something special with her. She was too caught up in watching him maneuver the glider, however, to comment on it now. She felt like she needed to store up all the sensations and take them all in.

"Here we go," Gavin warned her, reaching for the tow-release lever, something he'd pointed out to her in his overview of the craft. "We'll be separating now, and it will be just us and the wind currents."

Lauryn didn't feel anything different, but she knew the propylene line that had secured them to the tow plane no longer held them because the prop aircraft drifted down and to the left before circling back the way they'd come. The glider, in the meantime, continued in the same direction, the long wings tilting ever so slightly as Gavin tucked into a current.

The sky turned quiet as the other plane's engine moved out of hearing. Soon there was no sound other than her heartbeat and the air moving past them, no louder than a windy day.

Below them, she could see the imposing dark gray mountain peaks, some ridges still bearing snow. Between them, bright blue alpine lakes twinkled up at her like gems dotting the rugged terrain. And all the while, the glider tilted and swayed, silently cutting through currents she would have never known were there if Gavin hadn't explained how he would make the ride last. Apparently, he could stay aloft for hours when the weather was favorable for soaring.

"I can't believe how easily you move around the mountains," she called up to him, her voice slightly raised but no more than if she was sitting in the back seat of a car and talking to the driver.

"Keep in mind I've flown around this area many times. The ridges create really interesting airflow. But if I were going to take the glider to a new range, I'd research the currents carefully until I grew familiar with them." He steered the glider along a peak she didn't recognize, high enough that she didn't feel nervous about their proximity to the ground but near enough to the land that she could see some bighorn sheep scrambling along a rocky outcropping.

The view was spectacular. And soaring felt freeing. She was shocked at the time when Gavin turned to ask her if she was ready to land. Checking her watch, she saw almost two hours had passed. The sun had slid lower on the horizon, although it wouldn't be dark for another hour at least.

"I'm ready." She knew she would treasure this experience.

He'd given her so much more than just a date.

"Good. Because I'm excited to share your next surprise." He tipped one glider wing lower, steering them to the right.

Stirring anticipation.

She knew dinner awaited them somewhere. And afterward?

Her mouth went dry at the thought of staying with him for the night. But after the glider ride, she was more certain than ever that the day wouldn't be complete until she'd lived it to the fullest—in Gavin's arms.

Ten

Gavin couldn't have scripted a better day.

He'd hated having to reschedule his date with Lauryn two times, but with the perfect wind currents today, he'd been able to land the glider precisely where he needed, a feat he could have only been certain of with optimal weather.

Now, hearing her happy laughter as he brought the aircraft down on a grassy meadow beside a mountain-lake retreat house, he knew he'd planned well. Satisfaction swelled in his chest as the plane skidded along the grass, as flawless a landing as he'd ever performed.

"I can't believe you!" she exclaimed from the seat behind him as he peeled off his cap and sunglasses before stepping out onto the grass. "You flew us so close to the surface of the water I thought I could reach down and touch a wave."

He hadn't been quite that close. But he recognized the exhilaration in her voice. Remembered feeling the same way plenty of times when he'd flown. And yet none of those past outings were as fulfilling as providing the experience for her.

"I take it you're a fan of flying?" he asked, extending his palm to help her out of the craft.

She still wore the fisherman's hat he'd given her, the wavy brim shading her hazel eyes as she looked up at him, the green depths glowing in the violet rays of the setting sun as it dipped behind a mountain peak. Her black jeans and fitted quilted jacket were the sorts of items he'd suggested for the plane ride since it tended to get cool above the mountains. When her hand slipped into his, he closed his palm around it and hoped he wouldn't be letting go of her for hours.

"I think I'm addicted. That was amazing." Stepping from the glider, she peeled off her hat and placed it beside his on the cockpit seat. "I can't thank you enough for sharing this with me."

With high pink color in her cheeks and her ponytail clasp slipping lower on her thick mane of hair, she looked deliciously tousled. He fought the urge to dishevel her further, not wanting to assume anything about the evening ahead of them when she'd only signed on for dinner. Besides, he'd planned one hell of a meal.

But it nearly killed him to see her full lips glistening where she flicked her tongue along them.

He swallowed hard, still gripping her hand as they stood in the grassy meadow.

"It was a pleasure." His voice sounded lower than normal, his thoughts straying to how much he wanted her. Clearing his throat, he forced his attention away from her mouth and turned them both toward the lake house he'd rented for their meal. "I've never flown with anyone else."

"I'd never guess that. You're so good at it." She peered up at the three-story stone-and-wood cabin perched on a narrow strip of land overlooking the private lake. "Why haven't you taken anyone else with you before?"

"I like the sensation of flying so much I guess I came to think of it as a way to unwind. It's always been a private thing for me." He paused at the base of the stairs leading to an outdoor deck. Glancing over at her, he squeezed her hand lightly. "But after our dance the other night, some instinct told me you might like the adventure."

"You were correct." Her pupils widened a fraction. She swayed closer. "It was exactly what I needed."

His heart thudded harder. Pulse ratcheting faster.

He couldn't fight the urge to touch more of her. Untwining his fingers from hers, he skimmed his palms along her hips. Drew her closer.

"Not true." He stared into her eyes, refusing to look away. "Exactly what we both need is waiting for us inside." He nodded fractionally to indicate the three-story mountain retreat.

"Point taken." She bobbed her head in agreement, her breath turning thready and uneven. "Let's go explore that. Right now. No more delays, no more waiting."

Her meaning was clear.

Thank goodness.

He had so many plans for this woman he hardly knew where to begin. Logic told him the faster he got her indoors, the sooner he could make good on every last one of them. But the way she looked up at him now, her hazel eyes dipping to his mouth, practically *willing* him to kiss her, he couldn't move just yet.

Just one taste.

Because he owed her a kiss to make up for that last one when everything went wrong afterward.

Banding his arms around her, he lifted her against him, bringing their bodies flush, her lips aligning with his. The soft cry she made at the contact echoed everything he was feeling inside. And yet nothing was going to distract him from kissing her the way he'd been dreaming about.

This time, when he covered her lips, it was more than a kiss. It was a claim.

One he'd wanted to make for a very long time. Longer than he'd ever admit to himself. The lush give of her mouth welcomed him, her lips parting. Welcoming. And he took everything she offered. More. His tongue explored greedily, memorizing the silky textures, the mint-and-cinnamon taste, the quickening of her breathing when he stroked his free hand up her spine to cup the base of her head.

For long moments, he teased and played, mouths mating. Then, wanting more, he drew back to nip her lower lip, dragging it slowly between his teeth. Sucking.

He couldn't get enough of this woman. When his kisses trailed lower along her jaw and beneath her ear, he savored her soft pleas of "more" and "hurry," her breath warm against his neck where her head lolled to one side.

Only then did he realize how her fingers worked the buttons on his flannel, her hands shoving at the placket as it opened.

"Too many layers," she muttered impatiently, her touch slipping beneath his T-shirt to the bare skin. "I want to feel all of you."

Forcing his lips away from her skin, he edged back to look at her. "I want that too." Then, lowering her to her feet, he guided her up the outdoor stairs with him toward the deck and entrance. "Come on."

"Where are we exactly? Is this one of your homes?" she asked as she kept pace beside him, hurrying up the steps with her hand hooked lightly around his upper arm.

When they reached the wide wraparound porch overlooking the small alpine lake, he keyed in the door code.

"No. I just rented it for the weekend. I figured it might be easier for us to spend time together without the speculation from all of Silent Spring." He knew her father kept tabs on him, and he suspected the sheriff was even more vigilant about keeping a watchful eye over his daughter.

"You're right about that." She sounded concerned, but when he turned to look at her over his shoulder, she seemed to shake off whatever her momentary worry had been. "And the view from this place is beautiful. It's like we're all alone in the world up here."

Still clasping his hand, she paused after he opened the front door of the house, her eyes roaming the clear blue water that lapped the rocky shore near the house foundation below. Beyond the lake, a dark gray mountain loomed, the side dotted with green pines in some places and snow fields in others even though the weather was almost sixty degrees where they stood.

"We *are* all alone," he assured her, grateful to leave Kingsland and the complicated family dynamics behind him, along with too many people who'd judged him unfairly. "For as long as you want to stay here."

Lauryn turned toward him again, her gaze colliding with his. "Lead the way."

When the door to the oversize mountain cabin closed behind them, Lauryn didn't waste a second.

With the adrenaline from the glider ride still buzzing in her veins, she threw herself into Gavin's arms before they even left the massive foyer. There would be time to explore later. She'd seen enough of the gorgeous view. The walls all around them now were dominated by huge windows overlooking that same perspective so that even indoors she felt like she was still perched above that clear blue lake carved by glaciers. Surrounded by the scents of pine and cedar.

Only now, she had Gavin's strong arms to anchor her, his hands roving everywhere, arousing every inch of her with his touch. The sensations he stirred felt so good, so dizzying and sweet, that her legs trembled beneath her.

"I haven't stopped thinking about you since that night at the bar," she confided, her hands picking up where they'd left off outside, gliding along his abs just beneath the hem of his T-shirt.

"I haven't quit thinking of you since that kiss in the garden." His voice was a low growl in her ear as he captured her wandering hands in his. "Which means I've had plenty of sleepless nights to consider just how I want to do this."

A shiver vibrated through her at the sensual promise inherent in those words. Or maybe it was from the way his fingers gently restrained her wrists.

"A man with a plan," she mused, unable to keep herself from canting closer, stepping between his thighs so their legs brushed. Her belly grazed the impressive length of his erection on the other side of his zipper, the contact making her blood sizzle. "Care to share?"

"Since I only have the promise of one date with you, one night, I can't rush. I won't hurry. Not when I need you to remember this for a long, long time afterward."

Her knees turned liquid as they faltered beneath her.

Not just from the rush of pure longing for whatever he had in store for her. But also from the jolt of a sudden fear that once would never be enough to satiate everything she wanted from him.

For a moment, she wondered if she should renegotiate terms. Suggest they not worry about a time limit for this. But she'd only made up her mind to enjoy the connection. Seeing him again this way in the future would make it more difficult to tell where the fun ended and a relationship began.

Something she wasn't ready for.

"But I want you," she told him simply. Honestly. "It's not rushing if we spend all night indulging each other. And we could start right here." Glancing around to get her bearings, she saw they were mere steps away from a sunken living area. Leather couches rested at angles to one another, positioned to take in the best views. "On the sofa."

"I want you too." He hooked a finger in the waistband of her jeans, tugging lightly. Making the denim move against her in a maddening caress when she craved his hands. His mouth. "But if we start tearing one another's clothes off on that couch, I'm going to forget all about my good intentions for you. And I refuse to lose focus."

She might have replied, but he chose that moment to slide his fingers along the front of the waistband to the snap of her jeans. Flicking it open, he lowered it slowly, his knuckles grazing her in ways that made her waver on her feet.

"Ooohh." She couldn't possibly articulate an answer when his brown eyes seared hers so that she couldn't look away. "Gavin."

His deliberate touches torched her thoughts along with her argument, until all she wanted was to put herself in his hands. See where this night would take them.

His forehead tipped to hers, the warmth of his skin stirring her, along with the flat of his palm where he laid it over the black lace of her underwear.

"Will you come with me to the bedroom?" He whispered the question lightly through her hair, just above one ear. "Let me undress you and take my time pleasuring you."

Another shiver tripped down her spine. She'd wanted this. To quit trying to please everyone else all the time and embrace life. Experience. Joy.

"Yes, please." Her words were a rasp of air along her dry throat. "But, Gavin, it can't all be about me. I want you to feel good too."

"Every single thing about this is going to make me feel

good," he promised, his brown eyes serious as he took her hand and drew her toward the back of the luxury cabin.

Anticipation sending her heart slugging against her rib cage, she followed him along the gray-stone floor through the sleek chef's kitchen, the dark quartz countertops and light wood cabinets mimicking the colors outside the tall windows, where daylight was quickly fading. A bowl of clear blue stones decorated a natural-slab dining table.

Every moment's delay, every second making her way through the large vacation home, had her aching for more. Wishing they'd stopped at the sofa after all.

Then, beyond the kitchen lay a main floor suite, its open double doors beckoning them toward a king-size bed that dominated the room. A stone fireplace took up one wall, while two sets of French doors with lake views filled a whole other side of the room. Here, too, the view was stunning, the lake still visible in the violet dusk. But as soon as they crossed the threshold, Gavin pressed a button on a wall remote to shutter the doors, blinds in the glass blocking views in or out.

Sealing the two of them into their own private haven.

With the press of another button, flames lit the gas fireplace, the orange blaze flickering to life to cast a moody glow over the gray-and-white quilt.

Anticipation sparked along with it, especially as she watched Gavin shrug out of his flannel shirt. Then he reached for the hem of his tee and raked that up and off his body, revealing a male physique so mouthwatering she remembered why he'd been a *Men of Rodeo* calendar staple every year he was on the bull-riding circuit.

But when she reached to touch him, he captured her hands. Kissed the knuckles.

"Now you," he prompted her, guiding her hands back down to her sides. "I'm dying to see more of you, Lauryn."

Was he? The idea tantalized her as he lowered the zipper on her black quilted jacket, peeling it off and tossing it on a leather ottoman nearby. Then, returning his gaze to her, he slid his hands beneath the long-sleeved shirt she'd wore, bunching it higher. Higher. Lifting it over her head to join the jacket.

This time, his eyes never wavered from her body, still clad in a black lace bra that matched the underwear now visible through the open zipper of her jeans where he'd touched her earlier. She didn't own much lace, and she hadn't worn this set before. But the effort she'd made was well worth it as his focus narrowed to her breasts, his pupils so wide she could only see a hint of the brown iris ring before his head bent to kiss her through the lace bra cup.

Back arching, she fed herself to him shamelessly, needing more. Aching everywhere. His arms banded around her, her hips meeting his and teasing forth another ache, hot and urgent.

She twisted against him, pleading without words. He only answered by switching to her other breast, kissing and licking at her through the lace of her bra until she shrugged and wriggled her shoulders free of the straps. She didn't want him looking too closely at the back of her shoulder anyway, where a network of old scars lingered. The dim room and her hair kept them hidden for now.

"You're so beautiful," he said against her skin as he unfastened the hooks at her back. "Everything about you makes me want you more."

When he'd freed her from the bra cups, the lace fell free, exposing taut pink nipples damp from his kisses.

"I like looking at you too," she reminded him, hooking her fingers in the waist of his jeans. "It's only fair."

The hot skin of his abs twitched under her touch, and she had to fight the urge to stroke him through his jeans. Now that she'd made the decision to embrace this time with him, she found it hard to go slow. Especially with

her heart drumming triple time and Gavin's sensual attention making all her nerve endings prickle with awareness.

"You first," he reminded her as his hands slid into the
gap in her open jeans. "Remember? That's going to be my
mantra tonight. Lauryn goes first."

He cupped her hips in his broad palms, igniting more
shivers as he worked her jeans down her legs. When they
stalled at her boots, he bent to remove first one and then
the other.

She balanced herself with one hand splayed on his
broad, naked back, marveling at the fact that this was
happening. She was going to be with Gavin Kingsley.

And he wanted her to go first.

By the time her jeans came off, leaving her in nothing
but her panties, she trembled everywhere.

Straightening, Gavin's eyes were molten until he noticed the way she shook.

"Hey." His hand cupped her cheek as he pulled her
against him. "Is everything okay?"

"More than okay." She nodded fast. "I'm just…so ready.
I haven't done this in so long and—"

He kissed her again, quieting the words that were awkward for her. Only when she forgot what she'd been saying
did he pause enough to speak against her lips. "I didn't
know. Let me take care of you."

She wanted to tell him that he didn't need to worry
about it. That orgasms weren't a big deal for her and it
would only stress her out to put too much emphasis on
having one since hers were about as common as unicorn
sightings.

Especially when she was with a partner.

But then he was kissing her again. Lifting her against
him to carry her toward the bed. She wrapped her arms
around his neck. And with his body rubbing against hers
as he walked…she lost herself in the way he made her feel.

Aching. Hungry.

Wet.

When he lowered her to the mattress, she kept her hold on him, liking the way his stubble—a few days' growth, at least, shadowed his jaw—raked lightly over her skin. She arched into him as he lay over her, wanting more contact.

Instead, his heavy thigh pinned hers, leaving himself room to touch her through her panties. Circling. Rubbing.

Stars lit up behind her eyelids, it felt so good. So exactly right. And when he slid aside the damp lace to touch her slick heat, she felt waves of pleasure like an electric shock.

This man wasn't guessing or fumbling. He knew exactly where she needed his touch.

Her face heated. Her whole body heated as Gavin crooned in her ear, telling her how beautiful she was. How sexy. How much he wanted her. How very much he enjoyed watching her.

And a moment later, her potential release twisted and coiled, tightening her to the breaking point. Her breath caught. Held. Then, unbelievably, the release just…unleashed.

Pleasure flooded through her hard and fast. Over and over.

Her body undulated against his hand as he wrung every last ounce of her orgasm from her body.

Breathless, panting, she wanted to tell him what a miracle that had been for her. But when she opened her eyes, she saw the desire in his. The need. Sweat popped along his brow. Tendons stood out at his neck as he reached for a condom from somewhere. His jeans, maybe.

He left the condom on the mattress beside her while he raked his jeans off. She swallowed hard to catch her breath, wanting with her whole being to make him feel as good as he'd made her feel.

"It's your turn," she reminded him, reaching down to wriggle out of her panties.

His teeth were already on the condom packet.

A moment later, he had it rolled into place.

When he nudged his way inside her—inch by inch, to let her adjust to him—she wanted to weep from the pleasure. Everything about being with him felt so good. So right.

She knew part of that was from the hormones and the orgasm. But, oh God, having him inside her was amazing.

Once he was seated fully, she tilted her hips. His gasp thrilled her. So she did it again. And again. Soon, they moved together in sync, driving each other higher.

Rolling over to take turns being in control. At some point, he felt the scars on her shoulder and went still. He looked questioningly at her, but she placed a finger over his lips, silently asking him to leave it for now.

She wanted this night to be about pleasure. Living to the fullest.

Only when her legs were aching pleasantly did he flip her to her back again, his lips sucking at her neck. Gently biting. Sensation tripped down her spine as he held there, his movements faster. More intent.

When she wrapped her legs around his waist, he reached between her legs to touch her the way he had earlier, his fingers sure as he stroked her again. Coaxing her body once more into that trick that no other man had managed.

"Gavin." She wanted to tell him it couldn't happen again.

Except the first waves of it were already stealing her breath. Her body clamped around his. Tight. Tighter. And then he was shouting her name while she thrummed with her own release, his body following hers into that blissful oblivion.

His chest heaved against hers. Her pulse hammered in

her ears, the aftermath making her skin tingle and buzz. For long moments, she just lay there beneath him. Overwhelmed by her senses and the magic that had just happened.

She didn't think that was overstating it either. No one had ever wrung so much pleasure from her body before. Herself included.

A dozen slugging heartbeats later, Gavin rolled away from her, kissing her on the temple before he stood to clean up. Which gave her a little time to watch him as he moved around the bedroom, his bare skin bronzed in the firelight.

Her mouth went dry just looking at him. Thinking about what had happened between them tonight. What did it mean? What came next?

Questions—worries—piled up in her brain, one after another. She had no exit strategy for this. No clue how to "be" when he returned to bed. She'd spent so much time this week imagining what it would be like to live a little, but she hadn't really plotted out what would come afterward.

Her heart beat harder as he returned to her, holding a glass of water in one hand for her.

She melted a little more inside, her defenses nowhere in sight. Tomorrow, she would worry about how to be. He knew it was temporary, after all, and he'd done this kind of thing before, hadn't he? She'd just follow his lead.

For tonight, she had hours and hours in front of her to make the most of her one night with Gavin.

Eleven

Gavin cracked open one eye at a sound in the kitchen. The electronic beep of a coffeepot, maybe. He could smell the scent of java in the air.

It took a moment to orient himself since the sun hadn't yet risen after his night with Lauryn at the mountain-house retreat. Dark hung heavy in the bedroom suite. He'd shut off the gas fireplace at some point, so he couldn't see much now. Still, the cold half of the bed told him that Lauryn was no longer beside him. Her scent still clung to the sheets.

Memories from their evening together bombarded him. After that first time making love on the bed, they'd devoured the offerings delivered by a local catering company. The champagne and caprese salads were easy enough to open and serve themselves, but they'd decided to steam the king crab legs. They'd worked side by side in the kitchen, him preparing the shellfish while she warmed up the side dishes. Then they'd spread a blanket on the living floor to eat a picnic in front of the fireplace.

Only to shower together and repeat all the fun of their first time together and more.

Which made him wonder where she'd found the energy to be up at this hour. They'd been awake half the night exploring all the ways they could give and take pleasure from each other.

Now, after peeling off the covers and tugging on his jeans, Gavin brushed his teeth before following the scent of coffee into the kitchen of the three-story cabin. He saw her by the light over the range, her pretty face illuminated in profile as she lifted a steaming cup of coffee to her lips.

Was she already second-guessing their time together? He feared that might happen, especially when they hadn't discussed anything before they'd launched into one another's arms. He understood Lauryn wasn't the kind of woman to enter into a physical relationship lightly. He'd heard she'd dated in college, but there hadn't been anyone in her life in Silent Spring—serious or otherwise—as far as he knew.

And the rumor mill in a small town was relentless, so if there'd been other men locally, he would have heard something.

He dragged a counter stool toward him to take a seat, alerting her to his presence. "You're awake early."

A thin smile curved her lips briefly. "Sorry if I woke you. I was having trouble sleeping."

"It seems too early for morning-after regrets," he observed lightly, trying to get a read on her. "At least, I hope it is."

She was shaking her head before he even finished speaking. "Nothing like that." Taking a step toward him, she halted again. "Do you want a cup of coffee?"

"No thanks, I'm good." He pulled out the stool beside him so she could take a seat on the gray leather chair. "Is anything wrong?"

Rounding the island, she padded closer on bare feet. Her brown waves were gathered in a loose knot, secured by a pencil. She wore the jeans and long-sleeved black shirt from the day before.

"I've been rehashing an argument I had with my dad last week before I saw you at the Stockyard." Sliding into the seat beside him, her arm brushed against his, calling to mind all the ways they'd touched the night before.

Even after acting out their feelings for one another over and over again, just that graze of her body still stirred arousal. Sharp. Fierce.

"You had a disagreement with the sheriff?"

She raised a brow, giving him the side-eye. "You say that like my father is an easy person to get along with."

"Sorry. I just meant that it seems as if the two of you have such a solid relationship. He's so protective of you. He obviously loves you a great deal."

Lauryn fitted her fingers around her mug, as if trying to absorb as much warmth from the steaming cup as possible. "Thank you. It's good for me to remember that being overprotective is his way of showing love."

"Then why the argument?" he prompted, genuinely curious about her.

He didn't know when he'd stopped trying to pry free information about his own father from her, but he acknowledged to himself that Lauryn didn't seem like she'd had any kind of vendetta against him. No reason to share negative stories about him to his father in the years they'd worked together. The woman he'd come to know wouldn't have done something like that.

"We disagreed about you, actually." Lifting her eyes to his face, she studied him for a moment before raising the cup to her lips again. Sipping. "He and my mother are refusing to attend Studs for Sale because I've asked you to be one of the bachelors."

Disappointment weighted his shoulders. And yeah, maybe even a little embarrassment, which was crazy. He was long past the age of needing a father's approval to see his daughter. Still, the sheriff's disapproval stung. "I can't say I'm surprised. Your father has never made a secret of his dislike for me since that day with the four-wheeler."

"But why?" Lauryn shrugged, the loose topknot on her head slipping sideways. "He has encountered teenage hijinks without holding a grudge before. Why go out of his way to give you a hard time for years?"

He had insights about that, but before he could answer, she continued.

"For that matter, my former foster mother told me that she saw Dad pull you over before when you weren't speeding or doing anything wrong." Her speech quickened, her brow furrowing as she related the story that had troubled her. "Ellen even phoned the station to let them know they got the wrong person because it was her who was speeding that day, and her car was close to yours. But she said no one seemed to care."

Gavin covered her knee with his hand, squeezing lightly. "It's okay. Your father and I have a long history, Lauryn. But there's more to it than you might realize."

"I don't understand." She frowned. "How so?"

In that moment, her goodness—her belief in people—put him to shame. She genuinely didn't know what he was about to tell her. And seeing that made him regret that he'd ever thought she could have swayed his father against him. Or knowingly withheld information about the disinheritance.

"Duke Kingsley paid your dad to hassle me in an effort to steer me straight. Or, depending what day Duke told the story, he might say that he was simply paying to have me watched and protected. My dad wanted to be the first to know if I was making trouble." He rubbed the ache that started in the back of his neck, the frustration and anger with his father residing there in a tense tangle. "Although sometimes I think he only requested that information to justify why he always made me feel like an outsider in my own family."

Lauryn remained quiet for a long moment. Coffee temporarily forgotten, she had swiveled her stool to face him fully. Her eyes were wide. Disbelieving?

"Are you suggesting…" One hand went to her temple. Massaged. "I can't believe this. You're saying my father took bribes from your dad to give you a hard time?"

"No, that's not what I meant," he rushed to reassure her, not wanting to paint her father in a harsh light. Gavin knew how much she loved and respected her parents. "I don't think it was any different than your dad moonlighting a security job to make extra cash. Plenty of police officers do that."

"Not during the same hours that they're collecting a paycheck from the municipality where they work." Her fist clenched on the dark quartz counter. Squeezing. Pounding. "That would be completely unethical to use his uniform that way."

Had it been a mistake to tell her?

"I'm sorry, Lauryn. I thought you knew about their arrangement."

"How?" She slid off the counter stool to pace around the kitchen. "How would I have known that? I thought Dad gave you a hard time because he was bitter about his cornfield all these years."

His stupid, misguided effort to visit Lauryn that first time had resulted in him driving over newly planted fields with his friends.

"That's when it started." Gavin knew because his father had been practically giddy to tell him that he'd better watch his step going forward. "And I'm sure your dad was an easy sell for the job because he was righteously pissed about the cornfield. With good reason."

He wasn't sure how he'd become the defender of Caleb Hamilton all of a sudden, but he knew it wouldn't do him any good to be the one to come between Lauryn and her father.

Blinking rapidly, she looked from him to the floor-to-ceiling window where the very first rays of dawn brought a rosy glow to the sky and the water reflected it.

Then back to him again. This time, her face was a mask. But her eyes were clear. Determination glinting in their depths.

And a distance that signaled their night of intimacy was over.

"I think I'd like to go home now." She brushed a touch along his upper arm. "I know we need to talk about what happened last night, but right now I'm too upset to think straight. I really need to talk to my father."

His gut clenched. That wouldn't go over well with the sheriff. Especially when he learned the source of Lauryn's information. Maybe it would be better to stick with her a while longer.

"I'll drive you." He'd left a truck here in preparation for their trip. And he'd need it later to disassemble the glider enough to transport it back to the airfield. "But if it's any consolation, now that Duke has passed, your father won't have any reason to keep tabs on me anymore."

The sheriff's payday had stopped when Duke died.

"Except he's still refusing to attend my event because you'll be there, so maybe there's more to his enmity than you know." Anger simmered in her words. Picking up her coffee mug, she walked it over to the sink and dumped the contents down the drain before switching off the machine. "Either way, I need to talk to him."

Gavin understood she wanted to leave sooner rather

than later. But he regretted that they hadn't had a chance to sort out where things stood between them. With the bachelor auction around the corner, he would be leaving Silent Spring soon. Tomorrow, he had an appointment with a Realtor in Wyoming to look at potential ranches so he could start over without the long shadow of the Kingsland legacy hanging over him.

Part of him longed to remind her of that; once he was gone, she needn't worry about what her dad thought of him.

But another part of Gavin already knew it would be tougher walking away from this town after last night. Whether Lauryn wanted to face it or not, things had changed between them.

And he understood that the kind of chemistry they shared wasn't the sort of thing either of them would be able to forget.

Seated on the back deck of her parents' house with a cold drink and her laptop that evening, Lauryn waited for her father to get home from work.

She'd seen her mother just long enough to exchange hugs, but her mom had plans with her book club friends and had rushed out the door. Now, trying to use her time wisely while she waited to confront her dad, Lauryn double-checked the scheduled content on the Hooves and Hearts social media properties to make sure the bachelor spotlights were ready for the next couple of days.

She also needed to fill the hours of her days now as the anniversary of Jamie's death approached. For years, she'd had to pretend the date was just like any other so as not to upset her parents, who'd asked her to make a fresh start. Since moving out on her own, she'd tried to remember her foster sister in meaningful ways, but the day was never an easy one.

Scrolling through the posts now while a few hopeful

robins hopped around the back lawn, she realized today had been Gavin's profile day. The number of comments on his photo and Q and A were higher than for any of the other bachelors.

Some sixth sense told her not to linger overlong on the comments. Reaching to take a sip of her water from one of her mother's World's Fair drinking glasses, she reminded herself that she'd invited Gavin to take part in the auction because he was popular. A charmer. He had a huge fan following from his rodeo days, and even an underground drag racing following from his appearances at races around the state. Yet the wealth of fire emojis—with lips, kisses and hearts coming in tied for second place—she couldn't quite look away from the reader reactions to the profile.

Gavin, I love you! I would bid everything I own for a night with you!

That was a common theme.

There were other, more graphic comments that, as the owner of the page, she needed to delete. Which was frustrating when she didn't want to wade through all the responses. Deleting quickly, she tried to speedread her way through the rest, just to make sure everything else was page-appropriate.

Her eye snagged on a commenter's name.

Camille7, with a white flower beside the moniker. Her senses tingled a moment before recalling that Gavin had dated Camille Jorgensen, the wealthy daughter of a British polo player who'd retired to a sport ranch nearby. Camille also happened to be an up-and-coming attorney, so she'd had dealings with the Sheriff's Department. Hence, her father.

Camille's comment read, *Gavin, I have good news for you! Can't wait to share when I see you at the auction. Get ready for a date you won't forget when I win.*

Lauryn's skin crawled, and she had to glance up from

the laptop to remind herself she was just sitting outside on her parents' back deck. The robins were singing and hopping around playfully. An aspen tree fluttered in the breeze.

Anyone else would be thrilled to see Gavin had raised so much interest and potential money for Hooves and Hearts. That's what Lauryn had wanted. Wasn't it?

A sound from the house behind her startled her from her thoughts. A moment later, a shadow appeared at the door before her father opened the screen and stepped outside, his expression one of pleased surprise. He still wore his uniform—khaki from head to foot, a gold star on his chest. His head was bare, however. He must have dropped his hat in the kitchen on his way outside.

"Lauryn, it's good to see you." He clapped a hand on her shoulder where she sat, squeezing lightly over the place where her scars intersected. "I felt badly how we left things last time."

Her stomach sank. It ran counter to all her natural instincts to argue with her father. The man who'd given her a permanent, safe and loving home. Yet she couldn't forget what she'd learned about him. And she had to know if it was true.

"Dad, I have something I need to ask you," she began, closing her laptop and setting it aside.

"I hope it's not about the auction, sweetheart," he said as he took the Adirondack chair next to hers, the wood creaking with his weight. "I can make a donation, if you like—"

"Did Duke Kingsley hire you to keep tabs on Gavin?" she blurted, her nerves strung too tight to wait another minute.

The look on her dad's face answered for him: A slackness in the jaw that was normally a chiseled square. A shift in the blue eyes that usually looked right through a person. Then there was the long pause.

Her hand went to her lips, covering her mouth and the gasp of surprise. Not until that moment did she realize how much she was counting on him to deny it.

"Now, listen—" he began, but she shook her head, unwilling to hear a rationalization.

"Is that even ethical?" she asked. "Ellen Crawford saw you pull him over once when he hadn't been doing anything."

The chiseled jaw went granite solid again. "I suppose you heard this from the man himself?"

"Why do you dislike him so much? I've never understood—"

"I'll tell you why." Her dad sat forward in the chair so he could turn more fully toward her. "Because he plays fast and loose with people's feelings, Lauryn. Breaking one heart after another. I've seen him do it, just the way his mother did before him."

She felt her eyes go wide. "His mother?"

"Isla Mitchell was the same way before she married Kingsley. Playing with hearts and not caring—" He stopped himself, his face coloring in a way she'd never seen before.

Understanding dawned.

"You dated Gavin's mother?" She wondered if Gavin knew. Clearly, he'd known about her father's deal with his dad and had been aware of it for some time. How much more did he know about her family than she did?

"Yes, and she thought nothing of moving on when a better opportunity came along. Like mother, like son." The bitterness in her dad's voice was unmistakable.

Her heart felt a pang of sadness for her mom that her dad would still harbor such strong feelings about another woman.

"So you've paid him back by hassling him since he was a teenager." Gathering up her laptop, she rose from her seat, not sure she could hear anymore today. "I came here to learn the truth, Dad, but I think I've had more than I can take today."

Especially when her father's image of Gavin as a player fell so closely on the heels of all those social media posts she'd just read—including Camille's assurance she would win him and share good news on their date. Not to mention, she was shaken to think her parents' marriage might not be as solid as she'd once believed. Had her mother been a rebound relationship rather than true love?

Her stomach knotted as her dad rose to argue with her, but perhaps he recognized the expression on her face as that of a woman who had all she could take today, because he huffed a heavy sigh and nodded.

"Gavin Kingsley will be leaving town soon enough anyhow." Her dad folded his arms over his barrel chest as he watched her walk down the steps of the porch. "Then he won't be our problem anymore."

Shock and disillusionment chilled her.

When she reached the grass, she turned to glare back up at him. "Did you have anything to do with getting him disinherited?"

Caleb Hamilton's bushy eyebrows shot up, the sun glinting off his sheriff's star. "Of course not. But I'll bet I know who did."

She waited. Curious. She might be angry with him for a lot of things, but there was no denying her father had his ear to the ground for happenings around Silent Spring. "Who?"

"Duke's other son, Clayton Reynolds, had a huge blowup with him before he left town for good," her dad explained, leaning his elbows on the deck railing as he looked down at her. "I heard from more than one person that Clayton said he and Gavin would get even with their old man one day when they destroyed the legacy he'd groomed for his other two sons."

Frowning, she tried to make sense of that. "And you think Duke wrote Clayton and Gavin out of the will to ensure that didn't happen?"

Her dad shrugged, scrubbing a hand along the back of his neck. "He probably figured it would be better not to chance it than to leave his estate to a pair of hooligans who were only out to wreck it."

Indignation fired through her. "Gavin Kingsley is not a 'hooligan.' He's a good person, Dad, and I'm disappointed that you were too busy holding an old grudge to see that."

Her father opened his mouth as if to refute her or make excuses, none of which she had the least interest in hearing. Not when she didn't know how she could trust a word he said. So she held up her hand, shook her head.

Pivoting fast, she stalked away, ignoring the sound of him calling out her name, because she didn't want to argue anymore today. Learning what she had about her father hurt.

That's what she felt foremost.

And yet, as she slid into the driver's seat of her truck and contemplated everything else that had come to light today, she couldn't deny a tiny worry about Gavin. Or, more to the point, about her feelings for Gavin.

Their night together had been nothing short of epic.

Not just because the sex had been blow-your-mind amazing.

But because she'd woken in the middle of the night to all kinds of feels. He'd taken her for a glider ride. He'd wanted to show her the garden his mother made. He'd held her during an anxiety attack and hadn't demanded explanations later.

He'd even felt the scars on her shoulder and hadn't

pressed, giving her time to share her story when she was ready.

Gavin had become special to her.

While that was exciting and gave her all kinds of butterflies, she also remembered that her father's distorted vision of him was based on at least a few shreds of evidence. Gavin had dated widely. He had a reputation for thrill seeking—both in life and love.

And no matter how much Lauryn had loved every minute of their night together, a part of her worried about Camille Jorgensen and all the other women who couldn't wait to bid on him at Studs for Sale. Her faith in her own judgment right now was shaky at best, considering what she'd just learned about her dad.

Gavin would be leaving town soon, as her father pointed out. So if she had feelings for him that needed resolving, she needed to do it soon because the bachelor auction was coming fast—just five days away now. And then Gavin would leave Silent Spring forever to start over somewhere else.

A thought that turned the butterfly feeling into a lead ball in her gut.

Twelve

Driving home from Wyoming after a day spent walking potential ranch properties, Gavin steered his truck toward the Hooves and Hearts Horse Rescue and the woman who had been on his mind nonstop since their passionate night together.

Since dropping her off at her house the day before, he'd tried to give her space. She'd been agitated after discovering the news about her father, so they hadn't spoken about where things stood between the two of them. Had it been wrong of him to share what he had about the sheriff?

The thought troubled him, along with the fear that he'd let things spiral out of control between them too quickly. As much as he'd wanted her—craved her—he'd known that acting on impulse when it came to their chemistry could have negative consequences, given their past.

He'd wanted that date with her to show her another side of himself. Instead, they'd ended up in bed together, and he worried that he'd proven all her original concerns about him. That he was a player and a ladies' man, a reputation from his bull-riding days that he hadn't done a damn thing to squash even though it was vastly overrated, since he'd been hell-bent to get under his father's skin.

Shortsighted of him now that he'd met a woman whose opinion really mattered.

She really mattered.

And that was the other thing that troubled him. What did he do about the growing feelings for Lauryn when he wasn't going to remain in Silent Spring even one day after that bachelor auction? The war with his father had died along with Duke Kingsley, but that didn't mean Gavin wanted any part of the complex network of businesses tied to the family name, let alone Kingsland Ranch.

At least he'd been able to share his point of view about that with his followers when he'd scheduled his spotlight post for the bachelor auction. He hadn't seen the reaction online yet, but he hoped once his fans knew it was his decision to part ways with the family businesses, they would halt the boycott efforts of Kingsley holdings. He'd hated seeing the Stockyard so empty, especially when Levi had started the place on his own.

Now, turning onto the back road that led to Lauryn's horse rescue, he admired the obvious hard work she'd put into the place. He recalled the property from years before, when it had been a hobby ranch for a family who fell on hard times. Gavin had been friends with the younger son, and could remember how overgrown it had been at the time.

Today, the access road had been paved and widened, brush cleared from both sides and symmetrical rows of ornamental trees planted. The effect was welcoming, and he had no doubt the horses entering the rescue appreciated the smoother ride to their new home.

Farther ahead, he could see the arched sign reading Hooves and Hearts. Six-foot brick columns held the wooden fence posts, wrought iron lamps on either side illuminating his way. Seeing what she was doing here, especially once he reached the spacious new stables she'd built, made him glad she'd talked him into staying through the bachelor auction. Her cause was a good one, and she would put the funds raised to truly worthwhile use.

He admired her work ethic, especially knowing that life had come easier for him, given his father's wealth. Even though he wanted to forge his own future going forward, he was still launching from a platform of support.

Pulling up to the stone ranch house with wide wooden porches, he parked in the driveway. He half wished he'd brought Rocco with him, as his dog adored Lauryn, and the Rottweiler would have fun exploring this place. But it wouldn't have been fair to the animal to be cooped up in the truck for the three-and-a-half-hour drive each way to view prospective ranches.

As he opened the truck door and stepped down to the driveway, Lauryn appeared, silhouetted in the front entrance way.

His heart rate kicked up just seeing her.

Until, as he walked closer, the expression on her face became clearer. Her eyes were glistening. Her lower lip trembled.

Worry for her filled his chest as he quickened his step.

"Lauryn, what's wrong? Are you all right?" He slid a protective arm around her shoulders, feeling her warmth through the long gray sweater she wore over a Hooves and Hearts–logo T-shirt and black leggings.

A tiger-striped cat curled figure eights around her legs, offering feline comfort as they stood on the welcome mat under the glow of the porch light.

"I'm okay." She sniffed, swiping the sleeve of her sweater beneath her eyes. "The past few days have been a lot, after learning the truth about my dad and some other things he told me. And now today—"

A long, shaky sigh eased free as he held her.

"What about today?" he prompted, regretting that he'd shared something causing her pain.

She bit her lip for a long moment. Then, seeming to come to a decision, she nodded toward the porch swing swaying gently in the evening breeze.

"Let's sit," she suggested, sniffling once more, her eyes puffy. "I owed you an explanation anyway."

Confused, he moved with her toward the swing, holding the cedar bench seat steady for her while she took a seat on the thick blue cushion. Then he settled into the spot beside her.

"You don't need to share anything unless you want to," he reminded her, unwilling to pry even though he was curious.

Mostly, he just wanted to offer whatever comfort he could.

"But I told you that I would explain the anxiety attack, and I never did." Taking a deep breath, she relaxed against the planked seat, tipping her head onto his shoulder. "Today I want to share the story. I need to."

"Of course," he reassured her, stroking a stray strand of hair from her cheek. "I'm listening."

Around them, the evening grew cooler, so he pulled a spare fleece blanket from the back of the swing to drape over her legs. The scents of hay and earth from the stables and paddock nearby permeated the air. Every now and then, a whinny or a soft snort came from the barn area. The tiger-striped cat jumped onto the swing to take a seat on Lauryn's other side.

"I told you that, before the Hamiltons adopted me, I was in foster homes," she began, smoothing the blanket over her lap. "But I didn't tell you about the best friend I made in a group home where I lived for a couple of years. Jamie."

The careful way she said the name, with a wealth of emotion behind the word, made his gut clench for fear of where the story would end. He tucked her closer to his side, letting her speak without interrupting.

"She was a year older than me," Lauryn continued, her breath warm against his shirt where she rested against him. "Jamie liked all the same books I did, and we were happy kindred spirits in a house full of hard-luck kids. The farmhouse was old and not well maintained, but our foster parents made some of the outer buildings off-limits to keep us safe."

He felt colder by the minute as she spoke, so he couldn't begin to imagine what the story was doing to her. Tension clawed up the back of his neck, but he tried not let it affect the way he held her.

Pausing, she placed a hand on his chest and levered herself up a little so she could face him before she continued. "But I was really drawn to one of them—a dilapidated potting shed with a small porch—just a step, really, and two columns in front of it." Her eyes closed briefly as she dragged in a shuddering breath. "And I talked Jamie into going in there with me one day even though she thought it looked…unsafe." She bit her lip. "She went in with me anyhow, and we started reading *A Separate Peace*." Her voice failed her. She swallowed hard. "There was a terrible cracking sound. Like a tree falling. I looked up at her for a fraction of an instant before the structure collapsed."

"Lauryn." Her name erupted from his lips on a pained sound he hadn't meant to make. But he couldn't imagine how awful that had been for her. "How badly were you hurt?"

She shook her head impatiently. "It's not a story about

me. You felt the scars on my shoulder. What happened to me was nothing. I tried to get Jamie out, but—"

He waited, wishing she didn't have to say the next words. But only because he hated that she'd lived them.

"—she didn't make it," Lauryn finished, exhaling a long, slow breath. "She died because I convinced her to be somewhere we shouldn't have been in the first place. If I'd listened to her—"

His stomach dropped as he reached for her, sick in his gut for what Lauryn had been through. She couldn't have been more than twelve at that time, and she'd had to grapple with something horrific all on her own.

"It wasn't your fault, Lauryn." He hugged her to him. Stroked a hand over her back. "You were a child. Both of you were. And you both deserved people looking out for your welfare."

"Logically, I know you're right," she admitted softly, her voice muffled against his shirt. "But it took a lot of years to let go of the guilt. And even now…it's an effort to remember that I shouldn't blame myself."

She pulled back from him, peering up into his eyes.

"I'm so sorry you went through that." He cupped her shoulders in his hands, rubbing along her arms. "So, so damned sorry. And I can't even imagine how much it upset you when those kids shook the tent poles in 4-H that day."

He hated that he'd been a part of that. Not that he'd done the shaking, but he'd been there when she'd turned and run. That day must have been an awful reminder for her.

"I didn't even remember the 4-H incident until you brought it up. It's odd that I blocked that episode out of my mind, but all these years later, I still remember exactly where we were in *A Separate Peace*."

"I would have never let them touch that tent pole if I'd known." It was a useless thing to say about a moment long past when she'd gone through something so much worse.

But it was the only thing he'd had any control of in that time of her life.

"I know." A wobbly smile brightened her face briefly. "And living without her has been hard, but I've done it, year after year. It's just always tougher on this date, the anniversary of her death."

"Today?"

At her nod of confirmation, he pulled her into his arms, holding her tight. He'd read somewhere once that a hug helped someone hurt or grieving because it gave a boundary to pain, enclosing it. He didn't know if that was true for how Lauryn felt now, but he hoped so.

He'd do anything to ease her hurt. Needed to do more for this woman who gave so much of herself to help others.

Which gave him an idea.

Easing away from her, he tipped her chin up so he could see into her eyes. "We could have a bonfire." He'd noticed a firepit when he'd dropped her off here before. "And make it like a memorial in her honor."

Something shifted in her gaze. Something that looked almost...hopeful.

Straightening, he warmed to the idea, remembering a similar gesture his mother had made for him a long time ago, when they'd said a formal goodbye to their old life as full-time residents of Kingsland Ranch. "I don't know if it would help, but you could even write a letter to her—"

"—and let the fire carry the ashes of my words to her." Lauryn finished the sentence her own way, already nodding. "Yes, Gavin. I would really like that."

An hour later, Lauryn sat beside Gavin at the roaring blaze he'd built to commemorate Jamie.

He'd pulled over a patio bench from her back deck so they could sit beside each other while she penned her letter on a notepad lit by the orange flames inside the stone-rimmed pit. Her legs were curled beneath her as she worked. She'd put her cat, Festus, in the house earlier so she wouldn't have to try finding him in the dark. Night birds called to one another, their whistles and songs audible over the crackling of the logs and hiss of sparks that made their way onto the cool, damp grass.

Even the act of writing the letter felt therapeutic, reminding her of the days at equine therapy. Gavin had been wise to suggest the exercise. And the fire itself.

Both comforted her in a way she'd really needed today.

For now, she'd put aside the other worries about her father, about her parents' marriage. About Gavin himself and what would happen after the bachelor auction. She simply concentrated on her lost foster sister, the grief and the love still overflowing her heart.

"I'm finished with my letter now." She stared down at the pages on her legal pad. The reminiscences about stories they'd shared—those they'd read and those they'd told one another about their lives. Details she hadn't shared with another soul since.

"Your hands must be cold," he observed, his brown eyes full of concern and tenderness.

She appreciated him being here so much.

"They're fine." Still, she pressed the back of her knuckles to her cheek to warm them. "And I'm glad I wrote it all out."

He withdrew a folded sheet of paper from the pocket of his jacket. All this time, he'd been dressed in a gray suit and dark blue dress shirt. She knew he'd been touring ranch properties across the border today, and he looked every inch the high-powered rancher.

"I hope you don't mind if I—" He closed his hand again. Crumpling the paper a bit. He cleared his throat and began once more. "I wrote my own goodbye just now. This one is a bit overdue as well."

His father? If it was Duke Kingsley he had in mind, that seemed like a good thing. She recognized Gavin had been deeply hurt by the disinheritance and hoped maybe this would help give him closure.

She took his free hand in hers and squeezed it tight. "Of course I don't mind."

They stood shoulder to shoulder for a long moment, staring into the yellow and red flames flickering upward.

"Are you ready?" Gavin held out his paper toward the pit, the firelight casting shadows over his handsome face.

"I am." Folding the pages of her letter, she kissed the missive and tossed it into the hungry inferno.

She watched as the paper curled and turned black. Shrinking and then disintegrating. Sending a few white ashes out into the spring wind.

Beside her, she felt Gavin pitch his letter into the fire a moment afterward. She closed her eyes, letting the moment wash over her. The grief and the goodbye, the love and the remembering. Her heart felt full, but in a good way. Or at least, a better way.

"Thank you for this." Her voice sounded scratchy from the emotions in her throat.

"I'm glad I could be here with you today."

Turning toward him, seeing the strength and warmth of his big body beside her, she felt a rush of hunger for him. Need.

He reached toward her, thumbing aside a tear she hadn't realized was on her cheek. His touch sent a shiver through her.

Not questioning the impulse, she captured his wrist and held his hand to her face, kissing his palm.

"I'm glad you were here, too, because I'm not done needing you tonight." She stepped closer until they were chest to chest, breathing one another's air. "If I put out this blaze, will you come in the house and start another one with me?"

"I want that. So much, Lauryn, I want that." In spite of his words, he didn't move. He remained very, very still. "But I don't want to take advantage of a vulnerable time—"

"You won't be," she urged him, laying both hands on his chest. Smoothing her way down his shirt front. "How is it taking advantage of me when I'm doing the asking? I just want to lose myself. Forget about everything else."

His hands gripped her hips. To halt her? Or to pull her nearer?

She held her breath while she waited to find out, her breath coming faster as she remembered the taste of his kisses. The feel of his mouth all over her body.

Maybe her thoughts showed in her eyes, because a moment later, he was kissing her like his life depended on it. Hungrily. Demanding.

And she answered him with her whole body, pressing shamelessly to him, rocking closer still. Her hands worked under his jacket to splay over the broad muscles of his shoulders until he jerked back.

"I'll take care of the fire," he announced, already moving toward the hose she'd laid out when they first began laying the logs in the pit. "You should go inside and warm up."

Switching on the water, he sprayed down the flames so they smoked and hissed.

"I'll wait and warm up with you." She grabbed a bucket of dirt she kept nearby and added that to the pit, smothering the remaining fire.

He'd already made things better with the bonfire and his physical presence and his compassionate ear. Surely if she lost herself in the chemistry of their attraction, she would be able to burn away the rest of the feelings buzzing all through her.

Gavin shut off the hose and took her by the hand, the determined expression on his face sending a thrill of anticipation through her in spite of all the heavy feelings of the day. She needed this. Desperately.

Needed him.

Minutes later, they were in her dark kitchen, kissing their way through the house and bumping into things, unable to let one another go long enough to switch on a light. She toed off her shoes and then tripped on them, all without letting go of Gavin.

"Where is your bedroom?" he asked when he released her lips long enough to lick a path along her neck.

"Left," she murmured, her legs already trembling from that wicked glide of his tongue over her throat. "We're close."

She tried to guide them, but his hands sliding up under her shirt distracted her. Her skin tingled. She backed them into the hallway wall before righting their path.

Maybe his eyes had adjusted then, because he lifted her up and carried her the rest of the way, elbowing closed the door behind them. Her bedside alarm had a blue light around the base, enough to see once they were inside. She peeled off her cardigan and tee with zero finesse, unsteady on her feet.

"Lauryn." His voice halted her briefly, and she paused in unhooking her bra to see his eyes fastened to her body. "Let me."

Awareness stirred in her belly. Lower. But she forced her arms down to her side while he closed the distance between them, his shirt and jacket already discarded. Then she couldn't think anymore because his mouth found her nipple, licking his way around the peak before drawing on it. Her back arched, sensations spiraling to all corners of her body from that hot kiss.

He unhooked her bra and slipped it off her before giving her other breast the same attention. She reached to unfasten his belt and found his hand already there, working the clasp and placket before he stepped out of his pants.

"Do you have a condom?" She had purchased some just in case after their time together at the mountain retreat, but retrieving them from the bathroom would delay what she wanted—needed—most.

"Yes, here. You hold on to it." He passed the packet to her a moment before he picked her up and laid her on the bed.

She was tearing it open when he dragged off her leggings and panties. A moment later, he covered her and she rolled the condom into place. Briefly, their eyes met. Held.

His heart pounded so hard she felt it in her chest. She laid her hand over the place where it thumped, and all the feelings she'd been battling today threatened to come to the surface.

When he edged his way inside her, she welcomed the rush of heat and hunger for him, her body ready for how good he could make her feel. He moved slowly at first, giving her time to savor every inch of him. She nipped his shoulder, her fingernails lightly pressing into his skin.

"You feel too good," he whispered hoarsely in her ear, his hips rocking harder.

Faster.

"You feel better," she whispered back, the promise of her release already balling tight in her midsection. Her spine arched as she pressed herself into him, meeting every thrust.

When he reached between them to apply pressure exactly where she needed it, pleasure unraveled in wave after delicious wave, her body clenching his tight.

Gavin rocked his hips harder. Deeper. His shout vibrated through her as he found his finish.

Fulfillment. Contentment. She breathed them in and out with every breath for long moments afterward, his body a hot weight that she welcomed where he slumped against her. The night had been special in so many ways.

He slid to one side of her, tugging a blanket off the footboard to wrap around them. Cocooning them together. The movement must have dislodged her cat from somewhere along the foot of her bed, Festus mewing softly before leaping to sit on a windowsill.

Gavin stroked a hand over her hair for a few minutes before his fingers slid lower, down her shoulder to the place where her network of scars lay. He traced the lines carefully, outlining each ropey layer. "Are you okay?"

She understood what he was asking. Recalled his concern about indulging their intimacy, so new and untested, on a difficult anniversary day for her.

"I am. And I'm glad you're here." For a moment, she allowed the peaceful feeling she'd experienced by the bonfire to fill her up again, savoring the knowledge that she'd remembered her friend— her family—in a positive way.

But thinking about the family she'd made for herself as a foster child called to mind Gavin's fractured family. She needed to share what her father had told her about the disinheritance, and she wasn't quite sure how to bring it up without causing him pain.

"How about you?" she asked, thinking back to the note he'd tossed into the fire. "Did the letter bring you any closure?"

"I was glad I got a few things off my chest," he admitted, though something about the way he'd phrased it made her think there was a wealth of sentiment behind the simple words.

She wished the room were brighter so she could read

the nuances of his expression more clearly. Stroking her fingertips up his arm, she remained quiet, hoping he'd share more.

"I just wish I understood why my father cut me off." He gave her a speculative look. "One of the reasons I agreed to stay for the bachelor auction was because I thought you might know since you worked with him."

"Me?" Elbowing up higher to face him, indignation chilled her insides. "You wanted to get close to me to find out how much I knew?"

He swallowed hard but met her eyes. "At first, yes."

Disappointment threatened to swallow her whole. All that attraction— had it been a lie?

But Gavin didn't seem to notice how his words gutted her. He rushed to add, "Then I got to know you, and I realized you wouldn't have hid something like that from me if you'd known Duke's reasons."

Small consolation for being doubted. For being… used for his own ends?

She turned that over in her mind, telling herself that her emotions were too raw right now to see the situation clearly. Still, it stung.

Gavin's attention had drifted to the ceiling as he lay beside her, seemingly deep in thought. "Anyway, I knew I wasn't his favorite, but I never knew he resented me to that point where he'd exclude me from everything related to the Kingsley legacy…except the name itself." He gave a harsh laugh. "Clayton should be glad he wasn't saddled with the moniker, when our father planned to rip away everything it stood for."

Shoving aside her own hurts, Lauryn could understand Gavin's pain. Shunning two of his sons hadn't been fair of Duke Kingsley, but she also knew that bitterness and resentment festered worse than any physical wound.

As sad and disillusioned as she felt with her own father, she also knew she would work to forgive him because they were family.

"I asked Dad if he knew anything about the disinheritance when I confronted him about working for Duke," she ventured carefully, hoping the information would at least give him some peace.

"And?" Gavin sat up, his shoulders tense.

Lauryn turned to flick the bedside lamp on low, needing to see him better. Wanting to be diplomatic with what she had to share. "Dad heard Clayton and your father had a huge falling out before Clayton left Silent Spring—"

"That's hardly a secret." Gavin's forehead furrowed as he scowled. "We're still searching for him because he's fallen off the grid."

Placing a hand on his arm, she hoped the touch would gentle a harsh fact. "My father said people heard Clayton threaten to get even with Duke one day when he and you destroyed the legacy he'd built for his other two sons."

Gavin's brows shot up. "That I hadn't heard, though it doesn't surprise me. And the sheriff thinks Duke cut us out to try and protect what he'd worked hard to build." Frowning, Gavin shook his head as he seemed to weigh the possibility of his father cutting him off because he feared the Kingsley legacy would be run into the ground at Gavin's hands. "My own father didn't understand a single damned thing about me if he believed that."

"But doesn't that make you rethink leaving Silent Spring? If your father was only trying to protect his assets—"

"From his own sons?" he interrupted sharply, turning to find his shirt and punching into the sleeves. "No matter his reasons, disinheriting tells the world that either he didn't trust us or he didn't love us. I'm not about to stick around a town where everyone thinks I wasn't worthy of my old man."

Was Gavin leaving now? His abruptness caught her by surprise.

She understood he was upset, but she wasn't sure what to think about an abrupt departure after what they'd just shared. Still, she slid from the bed to find her long cardigan and slipped it on. The gray cashmere covered her like a robe, the soft fabric providing scant comfort when the conversation was an unhappy one.

"Why would anyone think that?" She didn't think the argument about not being "worthy" held any water. Gavin had carved out an identity separate from his father's, and he'd been successful in bull riding and ranching without any Kingsley family assistance. "Duke Kingsley had a mercurial temper, and everyone in his life knew it. Just because he made a bad judgment call with his will doesn't mean you have to turn your back on your brothers. They're your family."

While she spoke, Gavin had finished dressing, although his shirt remained half-buttoned and his jacket lay on the bed between them. She paced circles around her side of the bed, telling herself they weren't arguing. And yet, with the whole bed between them, their tense postures and the anxiety balling in her stomach, the moment felt combustible. Like it could turn into an argument quickly if she wasn't careful.

Was she pushing him away to make it easier when he inevitably left her? She hadn't meant to do that, but here they were. Her heart pounded harder, confusion and her feelings for him twisting into knots.

"Not according to my father, we're not," Gavin reminded her, his eyes dark with the grudge he now bore.

Frustration swelled. "How can you allow him to decide who is important in your life and who isn't? Your brothers love you and want you to remain in town to build the business you agreed to run together."

"Or they could just feel guilty about Duke's decision, and they're offering to cut Clayton and me in so they feel better about themselves." He spread his arms wide, exasperated. "I'm not going to take pity handouts from an estate that was not intended for me. I'm not some charity case for them to swoop in and save."

Her frustration turned to red-hot anger at his words. She threw the blanket back on the bed in a frustrated toss, her other hand clenched tighter where she held her sweater closed.

"Do you see it as a 'pity handout' to offer someone a sense of love and family?" Her pulse hammered an angry tattoo, her blood heating. "Do you think I'm a charity case, too, because my parents gave me a home when they took in an abandoned kid?"

He swiped a hand across his face, which had gone a shade paler. "Lauryn, no. Of course that's not what I meant."

But the dam on the emotions roiling inside her on this day had burst. Yes, she'd found new healing on the anniversary of Jamie's death. That hadn't soothed the new ache of her father's betrayal of her trust or made her feel any better about her parents' marriage. Or the fact that Gavin had only initiated a relationship with her to find out what she knew about Duke's will. Oh, and add to that the fact that Gavin couldn't shake the dust of Silent Spring off his expensive shoes quickly enough, and she had the perfect recipe for stress. Tension. Unease.

And now? The stress ball had exploded into messy shards that scattergun-shot all around her.

"No matter how much you resent your father, Gavin, you were still the indulged son of a Kingsley for the first ten years of your life. You knew luxury and security that most people never experience." She wondered if he could even imagine the kinds of places she'd lived before finding a permanent home with the Hamiltons. "I understand if you want to walk away from the money. But I will never comprehend how you can throw away people who want to call you *brother* and claim you as one of their own."

He rounded the bed to stand closer to her, perhaps to argue the point more, but she didn't think she was in a good position to talk any more about a stance she viewed as stubborn. Arrogant, even. Yes, her perspective might be different from other people's because of how she was raised. Because she'd lost a foster sister in a blink, and she'd never have that piece of her heart and her family back again.

Even the sheriff, for all his flaws, wasn't someone she would give up on without a fight. Just as her dad hadn't given up on her, even when they disagreed. Family mattered.

"Lauryn, please. I never meant to suggest my brothers were expendable. In time, maybe we'll work things out."

She nodded, her mouth tight. "Maybe you will. I hope you have enough time to do that. But since you're going to be leaving after the bachelor auction anyway, maybe it's just as well we move on too."

In her heart, she knew she was the expendable one to him.

And maybe that was the stressor that had been hurting most of all tonight. No matter how amazing their time together had been, Gavin would walk away from her without a backward glance once their expiration date arrived.

He even confirmed it for her when he gave a nod a moment later.

Agreeing with her that moving on would be best.

Soon, she stood alone in her darkened bedroom. As the deeper pain of what had just happened began to sink in, Lauryn realized she had just said goodbye to the man with whom she'd fallen in love. Of course, she'd had to do it since he hadn't wanted her for more than a fling.

She'd even fooled herself at some point that was all she wanted too. But with the pain of losing him spreading to every atom in her body, she began to see how very wrong she had been.

Thirteen

Gavin drove to the Stockyard.

The bar would be closing soon, but he wasn't in need of a drink after his talk with Lauryn that had gone so devastatingly wrong. No, his thoughts were already fractured and pinballing around his mind so fast that his head spun like he'd had a few too many as it was.

What he needed right now was his brother and the reality check that only Levi Kingsley could provide. Well, that and a little company from his dog. Gavin dug his fingers into the thick black fur of Rocco's ruff as the Rottweiler mix sat beside him on the front seat, his lead secured for safety. Gavin had made a stop at the house to see the dog since he'd left the Rotty alone for most of the day. They'd taken a walk together, then Rocco had jumped in the truck cab for this late night errand.

Now, cracking the window of the truck for the dog and assuring Rocco he'd be back out in a few minutes, Gavin parked his truck in the near-empty lot of the bar, close enough to the front that he'd be able to keep an eye on his pet. This wouldn't take long anyhow. He charged across the gravel, up the steps and through the door, wondering why the former hot spot was still so vacant. He should ask Levi about that. See what he could do to help business.

Except the first words out of his mouth when he saw Levi seated at the end of the bar were purely selfish because what weighed on his mind more than anything else was Lauryn.

"Does it seem like I'm turning my back on you and Quinton to pull up stakes here and move to Wyoming?" he blurted, dropping into a seat two down from Levi. He and his brother were the only people in the place except for a couple of regulars sharing a drink at the other end. "Or does it take the pressure off, knowing you don't have to rework the whole estate to try and divvy it up more?"

"Good evening to you too," Levi greeted him dryly, not turning away from his electronic tablet, where he was working on a spreadsheet of some kind.

"Right. Sorry to abandon manners in a time of personal crisis, but I'm in serious need of wise perspective, and you're one of the most grounded guys I know." Raking a hand through his hair, he couldn't believe he'd been in Lauryn's bed just an hour before.

Happier than he could remember being in a long, long time.

Until a simple discussion turned into an argument that he'd been completely unprepared for. How had he misstepped so badly?

Shutting down the tablet screen, Levi turned weary eyes his way. "I wouldn't be so sure about that. Maybe I just play the role of responsible firstborn because that's what was expected of me."

Something in his brother's tone was off. A darkness that he didn't normally associate with Levi. Remembering what Lauryn had said about hoping he'd have time to work things out with his brothers if he left town, a pang shot through him.

"You're right. It's wrong to always expect you to hold things together. It wasn't fair of Dad, and it's not fair of me either." He slid his elbows on the bar and dropped his head into his hands. He didn't want to have any traits in common with Duke Kingsley, but he was beginning to see a selfish streak that he didn't care for. Straightening again, he turned back to his brother. "But maybe that's all the more reason I'd like an answer to my question. Is it selfish of me to leave town? To leave you and Quinton to enjoy the inheritance?"

"Loaded question, brother." Levi reached behind the bar for a large jug of water and a second glass. He topped off his and then poured the second full for Gavin while the jukebox played a sorrowful country song that echoed the bar's dejected atmosphere.

"But considering Lauryn just as good as called me a self-centered ass when she booted me out of her house tonight—" damn, but it hurt to remember the way she'd told him they needed to move on "—could you do me a favor and still answer my question?"

Levi studied him over the rim of his glass for a moment before he set it back on the bar. "Is it selfish to follow your own path? Of course not. Do I wish you could wait until we settle the public relations nightmare Dad created when he severed the family in half? Yeah, Gav. I really do."

The mirror up to his actions was necessary. But that didn't mean he liked what he saw.

Swearing softly, Gavin drained the water glass.

"You've told me that too. I guess I just didn't believe it before because I couldn't imagine why you'd want me hanging around when eventually you'd need to cut me loose." He still didn't quite understand it.

Levi and Quinton had worked their asses off to be where they were today. That their father left them everything he'd worked for as well wasn't their fault. Duke Kingsley had manipulated them all with his power play from the grave intended to divide the family.

A dark scowl descended over his brother's features. "What you don't seem to appreciate is that I literally cannot do this—I don't *want* to do this—without you. If you choose to walk away from the other business interests, it would be one thing. A PR nightmare, but I'd deal with it." Levi waved good-night to one of the regulars who stood up to leave the bar. "It's one thing to break up the business, but I don't want this to break up the family. Don't let this drive a wedge between us."

Gavin recalled how many times he'd turned to his brothers for help and advice. Like tonight. When he'd been out of his head with fear about losing Lauryn, his first move had been to seek out his sibling. Maybe he needed to think more about what he'd be leaving behind if he went through with his plans to relocate. Did he want to alienate Quinton and Levi? Not to mention Clayton, if the guy ever turned up again?

While he mulled over his brother's words, Levi asked, "So you and Lauryn Hamilton?"

Memories of her smile after their glider ride reminded him of how much they'd had together. They'd grown close quickly, but their time had been significant. Meaningful.

She'd let him hold her last night when she was hurt and grieving. He'd been grateful as hell that his presence had comforted her.

"Yeah. Me and Lauryn." He shut his eyes, picturing her face when she'd asked him to leave. "I didn't see it coming, didn't know how different she would be from anyone I've ever dated."

Levi snorted. "With all due respect to your past girlfriends, you should have come to your wise and grounded older brother for some perspective before now, and I would have told you that Lauryn is nothing like the Camille Jorgensens of the world."

He could acknowledge he'd kept relationships superficial in the past. Maybe it had something to do with how complicated relationships had been in his family. His MO in the past had been to cut and run before things got messy. Sort of like he'd been planning to run from his brothers to avoid the aftermath of the disinheritance wrecking ball. For that matter, he'd been dangerously close to running from Lauryn—the best thing to ever happen to him.

Maybe it all looked more obvious in hindsight. Or maybe Levi had a point, and Gavin simply hadn't been ready to date someone like Lauryn before now. Hell, based on the way she'd tossed him out on his ear, maybe he still wasn't ready.

But he realized now without a single doubt that he wanted to be. Because what he felt for any woman before Lauryn couldn't compare with how deep his emotions ran for her already, even though their relationship was new.

It was special.

More than that, actually. He loved Lauryn.

Lauryn, who worked tirelessly to support a cause that mattered to her deeply. Lauryn, who—unlike him—had always strived to make good choices. She'd survived a traumatic past and fashioned a life for herself that was honest and true. Her goodness humbled him. And he wanted to be the kind of man who deserved a woman like that.

"You're right." Scrubbing a hand along his jaw, Gavin let the truth wash over him, infusing him with new purpose. New understanding. "I can't leave Montana because I won't leave Lauryn." Rapping his knuckles on the bar, he got to his feet, knowing he needed to figure out something fast. Make big plans before the bachelor auction. Because Lauryn deserved everything he had to give. "I love her."

A grin stole over Levi's face as he raised his water glass in a silent toast. "I knew I liked that woman."

Gavin was already backing away, a hundred possibilities spinning through his mind for how to show her how much he cared. How he could be a person who deserved her.

Still, he paused to point a finger in Levi's direction, acknowledging his help. "Thank you for this. For everything. I'm going to be a better brother."

"I'm holding you to it," Levi called back, but Gavin was already jogging out the door to his truck.

He had a one-in-a-million woman to win back.

Circling the Studs for Sale event with her tablet in hand, Lauryn ran through her checklist for tasks that needed to be completed before the bachelor auction got underway. She'd clung to her lists like a lifeline for the past two days since things ended with Gavin, relying on nonstop activity to prevent herself from thinking about him.

Regretting words spoken in haste before he left Silent Spring for good.

"Champagne?" A tuxedoed young server stopped in front of her with a tray full of bubbling flutes.

"None for me, thank you." Lauryn waved the server on, glancing around the event inside the Kingsland Ranch Thoroughbred-show arena, temporarily transformed into an elegant black-tie venue.

Of course, considering the state-of-the-art facility built to Duke Kingsley's exacting specifications shortly before his death, it hadn't been difficult to decorate. The pale wood interior had a skylight that ran along the ridged roof, while laminated-timber trusses supported a curved ceiling.

Since the sun had set before the start of the evening event, the skylight didn't help illuminate the arena, but the impressive stars of Big Sky Country were visible through the glass overhead. A popular country band that Gavin had secured for her played on the far end of the arena, the dance floor already filled with two-stepping couples. She saw her friends on the floor. Kendra and Hope danced together, their very different red gowns making them an eye-catching pair. Kendra wore a satin sheath with zero ornamentation, while Hope rocked a fringe-filled flapper-style dress. Lauryn had said hello to them briefly but hadn't had time to visit. She hoped they knew how much she appreciated their support.

Lauryn and her team of volunteers had decorated with red roses in heart-shaped wreaths, while an art gallery from Billings had brought an installation of ironworks sculptures from a Montana artist who worked with recycled horseshoes. The effect of the tall black-iron sculptures and wealth of red-rose wreaths was particularly lovely next to the backdrop of pale wood walls and columns of the arena. White lights and horseshoe table centerpieces completed the look while letting the custom architecture shine.

A familiar male voice sounded behind her. "Looks like your event will be quite a success."

"Dad?" she turned in surprise, seeing her parents dressed in their evening finery. A simple gray suit for him. A pretty purple wrap dress for her mother.

Her parents had RSVP'd—finally—the day before the event. But even then, she hadn't been certain whether or not they would attend. Her shoulders tensed as she faced her father.

Yet it was her mom who spoke first. "You look beautiful, darling." Violet leaned closer to kiss her cheek, and whispered, "Just hear your father out, okay?"

She nodded a bit woodenly, unsure what to expect since she'd wanted to hammer out their opposition to Gavin and her event long before now when she needed to focus on things running smoothly. But when her mom excused herself so that Lauryn and her father could speak privately, she refocused her attention on him. Just to hear him out, as her mom had asked.

Nearby, in the whirl of dancing couples, there were plenty of cowboy boots and Stetsons with tuxes given the Hooves and Hearts theme, the party well underway. It would be time for the auction soon, but she could spare her dad a few minutes.

"Lauryn, I just wanted to say I'm sorry for being so mule-headed about Gavin." Her father's blue eyes met hers. Even in the lowered lighting, she could see the emotions there. Sadness, maybe. Regret, even?

Some of her tension eased at her dad's overture. She knew making an effort wasn't easy.

"He's a better man than you realize," she told him quietly, her own regrets filling her chest, making her ache.

"Maybe you're right. But even if turns out that you aren't, I realized that an old grudge isn't worth losing you. You're too important to me."

Her throat clogged with emotion. The words soothing raw parts inside her. For the moment, the rest of the party disappeared while she looked into the eyes of a man who— she knew without question—had done his best to be a good father the only way he knew how.

"You're important to me too, Dad."

The corners of his mouth lifted. "Our talk made me realize that I've been a damned fool holding onto the past. I love your mother, and I'm lucky to have her." His blue eyes glanced away, searching the party.

Settling on Violet Hamilton where she shared a laugh with a friend near the dessert bar.

Lauryn's heart filled with relief. Gratitude that her dad could recognize what he had in his wife.

"I hope you make sure Mom knows that," she pressed, thinking how much her mother deserved an ardent, devoted partner who valued her.

"I promise I will." The other side of her dad's mouth curled in a full smile now. "And I'm going to make peace with Gavin Kingsley too. He's next on my list tonight."

"Really?" That surprised her more than anything else her father said.

And why did her heart have to go and start beating double time at just the mention of Gavin's name?

"It's never too late to admit a wrong." He settled his hands on Lauryn's shoulders and squeezed. "Are we okay though, you and me?"

"We're really good," she told him, meaning it. "Thank you for coming tonight."

Her dad wrapped her in a bear hug. "I'm so proud of you."

When he left her to seek out Violet again, a swell of contentment filled her. She felt sure her father would heal things. Already, she felt better about where they stood.

If only the rest of her hurts were as easily remedied. Now, the scents of roses and treats from the dessert bar sweetened the air. She only wished she could share her satisfaction in the event with Gavin since he'd helped her with so much of the planning. The reason they had a packed house tonight was because of him. She'd received dozens of last-minute ticket requests during the week of the bachelor social media profiles.

No surprise, the most tickets were purchased online the day his profile ran. Her chest squeezed around a hollow ache at the knowledge that she'd pushed him away with both hands. She'd been scared of what she'd been feeling because falling in love with Gavin had seemed too risky.

Trusting others? Easier said than done after her birth parents had abandoned her, the foster home shuffles and loss of her foster sister. Even the rocky assimilation into her forever family. Stepping outside her comfort zone was hard as hell.

Thinking back on it now, she was all the angrier with herself when she should have been trying to embrace life and live hers to the fullest. Yet when it came to the biggest risk of all, she'd failed to take a chance.

Aggravated and hurt, she needed to return to her checklist before she wound up in tears again. This night was bigger than her feelings, although it wasn't easy to remember when every part of her ached.

As she returned her attention to the tablet, however, Levi Kingsley approached her. He'd been her official host for the evening since Gavin had pulled his support from all things related to the Kingsland Ranch.

"Lauryn, can you spare a moment?" Levi wore his traditional tuxedo with the ease of someone who had been born to wealth and privilege.

Whereas her dad would have rented his clothes for the evening, Lauryn recognized Levi's garb had been custom-tailored. Gavin's would be, too, she knew, though she hadn't seen him yet this evening. Several of the bachelors had opted to wait to make their appearance until the auction, which would begin soon. The auctioneer had already texted that she was taking the stage in five minutes.

"Certainly, I can," Lauryn answered, greeting Levi with a polite smile. "The auction doesn't start for a couple of minutes."

He passed her a white envelope with her name scrawled across the front in a bold, familiar hand. "Gavin asked me to give this to you before the auction."

Her heartbeat stuttered as she stared at the high-quality stationery, curious what Gavin could have to say to her in a note.

She didn't realize that she hadn't reached to take the paper until Levi actively pressed it into her palm.

"I hope you will read it upon receipt, Lauryn." Levi spoke quietly, in a tone meant for her ears alone. "I do believe it's very important to my brother. And, because of that, it's quite important to me as well."

Surprised at his words, when she had thought Levi would be angry with Gavin for leaving Montana and forsaking the business they'd planned together, she didn't know quite how to answer. But it didn't matter because Levi moved away again, leaving her a moment alone before the auction started to open the message.

Jitters swirled in her stomach as she slid a finger under the seal and tore open the envelope. Inside, there were two pieces of paper. One was a handwritten letter. The other a blank check signed by Gavin.

Confused, she ducked behind one of the horseshoe sculptures to gain a little privacy while she read.

You're the only woman in the world who matters to me.

The shocking opening line of the letter made her palm go to her chest. She pressed it against the bodice of her crystal-embellished silk crepe de chine gown, needing a hand there to soothe the erratic pulse that hammered hard in answer.

The idea of a date with anyone else—even for one evening—is something I can't bear when my heart craves you alone. I will cover your bid of any amount, but I'm asking you—no, pleading with you—to win me at the bachelor auction. I promise you, whether you choose to bid on me or not, I will not leave Montana. More importantly, I will never leave you if you opt to give me another chance.

Yours Forever, Gavin

By the time she reached the end of the note, her hand had moved from her pounding heart to her lips, where she needed to stifle a gasp of surprise and emotion.

He wrote almost as if…he loved her too?

Stuffing down the swell of hope at the possibility, Lauryn hurried to the coat check table in the back, where she'd left her purse. She didn't have time to overthink this, not when the time was fast approaching to place her bid for Gavin. Already, the auctioneer was taking the stage, announcing the start of the event and introducing the first bachelor.

After requesting her bag, she tucked the letter and the check inside the beaded silk before handing off her tablet to an event volunteer. She couldn't possibly be responsible for organizing anything else tonight when her thoughts were in a tangle with Gavin Kingsley at the center, her heart racing faster than any Thoroughbred's at a finish line.

She needed girlfriend support to get through the auction before Gavin came on stage.

"Excuse me," she murmured as she made her way through the crowd that had gathered around the stage near the band.

A small runway had been erected in front of the stage so the bachelors could walk closer to the people bidding on them—a blend of men and women since the bachelors had been able to invite bids from whatever gender preference they chose.

"Lauryn," a woman's voice whispered as she neared the stage.

Turning, she found Ellen and Chip Crawford, her former foster parents, arm in arm. Pausing to hug them both, she soaked up the love and support from people who would always be family in her eyes. "I'm so glad you're here. Thank you for coming."

"We wouldn't have missed it for the world," Ellen exclaimed animatedly even though she still kept her voice quiet in deference to the bidding war going on around them for the first bachelor. "And we won't keep you but wanted you to know that Zara is in love with Toffee. I've just been overjoyed to see their bond grow so quickly."

Her throat closed at the lump of emotion. This was why she'd worked so hard to grow Hooves and Hearts.

"Thank you for telling me that," she said once she'd cleared her throat. "You and Zara should come by the stables once I get the equine-therapy piece of the rescue up and running. I'll bet she'd enjoy meeting all the horses."

After agreeing to do just that, Ellen and Chip excused themselves, leaving Lauryn free to move closer to the stage again. She reached her friends, Hope and Kendra, to stand between them while bachelor after bachelor took the stage.

None of them Gavin.

Lauryn knew she'd slated him to go near the end of the line since he promised to start a huge bidding war. The prices women had bandied about on social media were astonishing, but she'd told herself that was just chatter and wouldn't be what she'd really receive in donations to Hooves and Hearts.

And how could she justify spending so much of Gavin's money if she were to outbid them all?

Because yes, she really, really wanted to do just that, and his letter made it clear he wanted that—wanted her—as well.

As another bachelor was awarded to a giddy lady surgeon from Billings for an astronomical price, Kendra leaned closer to observe quietly, "Lauryn, I'm so happy for you. The bids are going to be so great for the rescue."

Hope leaned in from Kendra's other side to add, "Now if only we could get Kendra to bid."

Kendra shook her head, her elegant blond updo sparkling from a spray of crystal flowers woven through the chignon. "I'm off the market, remember? Although, Lauryn, if I could afford it, I'd be bidding, too, even if I decidedly don't want to date anyone."

Squeezing Kendra's hand, Lauryn wanted to reassure her friends. "I'm just glad you're here. That's all the support I need." Biting her lip, she let go of Kendra's hand to reach in her purse. Withdrawing Gavin's letter, she passed it to her friends. "Okay, maybe I could use just a little more support. Tell me what you think I should do about this."

She watched as Kendra's eyes went wide. A moment later, so did Hope's.

"Is it wrong to bid his money?" she asked nervously, wondering what they were thinking. "I don't know if—"

"Are you insane?" Kendra whisper-hissed back at her as she turned to squeeze both of Lauryn's shoulders. "You have to go for it. This is the single most romantic thing I've ever heard of."

Bolstered by her friend's words, she started to smile even before Hope added, "You can't leave a man in love to the single-lady vultures, Lauryn. You have to win him."

Was he? A man in love?

Lauryn's heart curled possessively around the word, longing for it to be true. And winning this bid would offer an amazing first step in giving them time to explore their feelings.

The auctioneer's voice returned to the microphone then, her next announcement the one Lauryn had been waiting for. "And now, for our next bachelor. The one. The only. Your local bull-riding hero and stud expert, Gavin Kingsley."

The clamor that went up from the crowd might have intimidated Lauryn a week ago since it was blatantly obvious there was plenty of competition for Gavin's affections. And yet, as the man she wanted to see most in the world walked out onto the stage in his black bespoke tux, she couldn't doubt for an instant that he wanted only her.

His brown eyes lasered in on her, finding her in the throng and communicating everything she needed to know.

His feelings for her were still there. Focused fully and completely on her. The connection reaching out as tangibly as if he'd gathered her in his arms.

He didn't want to lose her any more than she wanted to lose him.

And the spark between them was more than alive and well. It was a fire that wouldn't go out.

Beside her, her friends were encouraging her as the bidding started, but she wasn't ready to show her hand just yet. Not that she wanted Gavin to wonder if she was going to bid on him. She guessed that he could see right through to her heart the same way she'd read his when he walked down the runway.

But they'd spent hours and hours planning this auction event together, and she wasn't about to let her prize stud go for any less than he deserved. Gavin Kingsley held a worth greater than she'd given him credit for. He was so much more than a handsome bull rider. So much more than a successful rancher.

Everything she needed to know about him she'd seen the day he'd held her through an anxiety attack. And again the night he'd helped her start a memorial blaze for her foster sister.

"Bid soon," Kendra urged her as the crowd quieted for the bidding war between two determined competitors. "They're already higher than any of the other bachelors."

Turning around to scout out the competing bidders, Lauryn recognized Camille Jorgensen as one of them. The other woman was a petite brunette in a beaded blue sari.

The auctioneer waited for a bid to top Camille's latest. "Going once, going—"

Lauryn raised her bidding paddle, her eyes on Gavin, who stood beside the auctioneer. "Ten thousand."

A startled gasp from the crowd told her no one was topping the bid. But all the while, she didn't shift her attention from Gavin.

The man who'd promised he'd never leave her if she gave him another chance. She hoped he could see what her gesture meant, even if she'd been bidding with his money. She wanted to give them both a second chance.

"Going once, going twice, sold to bidder number

twenty-nine!" the auctioneer called before moving on to the evening's final bachelors.

Vaguely, Lauryn felt her friends' hugs and heard their congratulations before she made her way toward the back of the room near the steps to the stage. Angling through the crowd, words of congratulations and even a bit of teasing echoing around her with every step closer. Finally, she reached the golden rope and moved it aside to claim her prize. Claim her man.

Gavin was already waiting for her, his arms outstretched.

Lauryn stepped into them, holding him tight. Breathing in the cedar scent of his aftershave as she tucked her head against his chest. The rest of the arena faded as they stood in the shadows of the fundraiser.

They held one another for a long moment before Gavin edged back to look into her eyes. "I'm so sorry for not seeing everything I had in front of me. I've been so busy being hurt and angry with my father that I didn't see the hurt I was causing my brothers. To you."

His hand cradled her face as he tipped it up to his.

She melted at the contact, appreciating his words even if they weren't necessary any longer. She had seen the truth of them in his eyes when he'd walked out onto that stage earlier. He carried pain and baggage from the past just as she did. But they hadn't let it break them.

And she wasn't going to let it steal their future. "I was hasty and on edge, all too willing to take offense because I was—"

"You were entitled to being on edge." He cupped her shoulders, fingers massaging lightly. "It was the worst-possible day for you."

She shook her head, her heart aching with how close she'd come to ruining things with him forever. "No. The worst-possible day for me is the one where I lose you."

If she'd had any doubts about how he felt about her, they

evaporated now as his shoulders slumped with relief. She hadn't realized how tense he'd still been until that moment.

"Lauryn, I love you, more than I can express. But I want to have the time to find the words to explain how precious you are to me." His hands rubbed up and down her arms, as if he could rub the truth of them into the skin bared by her halter-top dress. "And I'm willing to do whatever it takes to make things work between us. To make things as happy and beautiful as you deserve."

Her heart fluttered. She shivered with the feelings his touch stirred. Awareness, and so much more.

"Then let's start now," she urged, remembering well that forever wasn't always guaranteed. With Gavin at her side, she wanted to keep living her dreams, working to make them come true every single day. "Let's begin our future tonight. I love you, too, and I don't want to wait another day to begin the happiness we *both* deserve."

Gavin wrapped his arms around her again, pulling her against his chest and holding her tight against his crisp lapel. "I don't know how I got so lucky, but I'm not going to question it. I'm just going to make sure you never re-gret choosing me."

Feeling her first and best dream already coming true, Lauryn kissed him with all the love in her heart, taking her sweet time to do it right. Thoroughly.

Lucky for her, they had forever.

* * * * *

THE INHERITANCE TEST

ANNE MARSH

For Lillie (and Pinto and Ava). Your tweets are a very bright, happy light in my week.

Thank you!

One

"Prove you're Masterson material in the next ninety days or you're out."

Declan Masterson had never backed down from a challenge in his life, but this one was a shock.

In the years since his adoptive father J.J. had plucked him and his brother Nash from foster care, dropping them into the exotic world of Hollywood, J.J. had blustered and threatened whenever Declan had failed to live up to the illustrious Masterson standard of a ruthless Hollywood player. In the past, Declan had responded to J.J.'s criticism by going off on another of his wild adventures, but he'd turned over a new, reformed leaf when J.J. had finally named him as his heir apparent.

"You'd better define *out*." He sprawled in his chair, watching J.J. carefully. J.J. looked relaxed in his white shirt with the sleeves rolled up, suit jacket discarded, but underestimating him was like mixing up snakes and celebrities in Hollywood's famous Runyon Canyon. You only made that mistake once.

"Fired," J.J. snapped back. "No longer provisional CEO of Masterson Entertainment. I have an offer to buy this company—and they don't need you."

Much as he pretended it didn't, J.J.'s criticism stung. Declan's jaw tightened involuntarily. He'd spent two years under J.J.'s thumb earning the chance to run the family company, to green-light his own projects and make films that would change people's lives. Despite years learning moviemaking from the ground up—because J.J. would hand him nothing and he earned it or did without—now it could all be taken away.

Because he wasn't, and never had been, a true Masterson.

"I've tripled our revenues," he pointed out. "I'm damned good at what I do. We both know it."

Masterson Entertainment produced films in partnership with other major film studios and was about to ink another multi-film cofinancing deal. While Declan could walk away and start his own film studio—his acting career had earned him millions—he'd have to give up projects he felt passionately about if J.J. followed through on his threat to sell. He'd have to start over from nothing.

He'd vowed he'd never be nothing again.

J.J. pinned him with a glare. "You've made a joke of the Masterson name with your adventures. In the last two years, you've free-climbed the tallest casino in Las Vegas, headlined a Megavalanche bike race in the Alps and dove with great white sharks."

He'd also run the company and, in the year prior to that, made a blockbuster movie that had outperformed its projected revenue at the box office. Those contributions were outweighed by his reputation as the playboy prince of film.

Declan couldn't explain the restlessness that constantly

drove him. He simply had to lose himself in intense, thrilling activities. It was a drive that he'd—mostly—channeled into his career as one of Hollywood's leading action heroes, and now into Masterson Entertainment. But since he could only be on set so much, he also climbed, skied and raced as fast as he could. The more extreme the conditions, the more he loved it. In the past few years he'd earned a reputation as a fierce competitor in the world's top sailing races. And when there wasn't a race or a film or a business deal to be made, yes, there were women.

"Those things would be fine," J.J. continued, since clearly *his* definition of *fine* was the only one that mattered, "in moderation. Instead, you turn everything into a spectacle, with a film crew, ridiculous bets and women. You proposed to an actress by scaling the wall to her hotel balcony. You did this at midnight, in boxer briefs and with a candy ring from a gas station."

Declan grinned. "Harry Winston was closed, so I improvised. You left out the part where she refused and the paparazzi caught the whole thing on camera."

He'd fallen off the respectability wagon rather publicly that night in Beverly Hills, but it had been funny, at least until the photos had surfaced and his impulsivity had been commemorated in the tabloids and on dozens of celebrity gossip websites.

Proposing to Jessie St. Chiles, his costar in his last film, had been an impulse. They'd been friends with benefits, but Declan knew he wasn't marriage material. His own biological father had walked out early and J.J.'s wife had divorced him after just six months of marriage. She'd been long gone before Declan and Nash had arrived at the Malibu mansion. Jessie knew he wasn't actually looking to get married and they'd both had a good laugh.

"When people hear your name, they wonder what ludicrous stunt you'll pull next," J.J. growled.

"Which is very on-brand for us."

J.J.'s face darkened. "It is—for our film talent and our marketing department. But when you were racing in the Alps two months ago, you were off-grid for two weeks. Our cofinancing deal went bad and we lost a ten-picture deal because no one could find the CEO. You've spent more time out of the office than in. No one takes you seriously in the boardroom because the only time we can count on you to show up is for the start of a race. You're no Masterson."

"Not by birth," he agreed. J.J. had adopted him and Nash at the ages of eight and six. J.J.'s own biological son was estranged. Depending on who told the story, Revere had either left the Malibu mansion at seventeen or been kicked out. Either way, he hadn't been heard from since.

J.J. flipped a photograph across the desk. The camera had caught the woman in the picture off guard, her eyes half-closed, lips parted. Late twenty-something with brown hair pulled back in an unremarkable ponytail, she wore a boring, white polo shirt with an embroidered logo. *Martha's Kids.*

"This is the daughter of Bryant Palsgrave, a successful Wall Street investor from one of New England's oldest families. Wealthy. Discreet. Her brother could be a future president."

"Charming," he said dryly, unsure of J.J.'s angle.

That kind of stultifying, quiet lifestyle was a pretty prison. Fortunately, old money families wouldn't have anything to do with someone like him, an actor, recklessly decadent and from a working-class background that J.J.'s adoption could never compensate for. Declan had no problem working his ass off—he'd spent his twenties building his film career, starting as a stuntman and then moving into feature film acting. He'd made a lot of money and been on the cover of magazines, but now he wanted to produce.

Growing up in Malibu, his neighbors had all been in the industry: movie stars, producers, screenwriters, musicians. The gated homes might cost north of seven million dollars, but when your kid went down the street to play, the mantel held an Oscar or Golden Globe. Bodyguards and luxury cars, with paparazzi lurking behind the well-manicured palm trees and dodging the dog walkers to the stars, were the norm. As a working class transplant, Declan had been shocked and then enchanted. He'd yearned to be part of those beautiful people with a magnetism and presence that marked them as members of a powerful Hollywood tribe.

J.J. followed the headshot with a glossier sheet of paper, a press release for a New England boat race that made Declan laugh. The participants were sailing two-person keelboats, just twenty-two feet long with a shallow draft and one mast. He'd raced faster and bigger when he'd been a teenager.

"The race around Martha's Vineyard next month raises funds for charity. One local and one celebrity per boat. The fastest boat wins the million dollar prize for the charity of their choice. Charlotte Palsgrave needs a partner and I owe her father a favor."

"You're joking," he snapped. He raced million-dollar yachts with a full crew in the world's most extreme weather conditions. No way would he partner with a spoiled, local, blue-blooded princess in what amounted to a glorified dinghy.

J.J. leaned forward, steepling his fingers. "You will partner with Charlotte and win this race for her—and you will be the perfect Masterson representative. Charming, well-bred, disciplined. There will be no scandals. You will prove, once and for all, that you are a worthy heir to the Masterson legacy and that I can count on you to be where you're needed. In exchange, I will refuse the buyout offer

I have and will sign Masterson Entertainment over to you. You'll own it, lock, stock and barrel, and you will have sole control."

It was just a race, he told himself, and not even a hard one. One lap around Martha's Vineyard, some photo ops with the blue-blooded princess and he'd be on his way back to Hollywood with the real prize: his inheritance.

"Win this race," J.J. said. "And it's all yours."

Declan didn't know why J.J. had decided to finally back his bid to lead the family company—or why he'd consider selling the precious Masterson film studio. J.J. had a pathological need to be in control. And he loved nothing better than designing a series of challenges for "his boys," challenges that only underscored how unworthy he thought they were of whatever prize he'd dangled before them. Nash had walked away from J.J.'s tests five years ago, immersing himself in his oil and chemical company. Declan had done the same—until two years ago, when he'd given into temptation and returned. The only thing that had made it tolerable was knowing he could see the finish line—a line that J.J. had just moved. Could he still win this? He thought he could—but he'd also learned a thing or two during his years in Hollywood. One of the most important lessons? Always, *always* get the deal in writing.

"Draw up a contract," he said. "Thirty days. In exchange for no bad publicity and one race win, I get Masterson Entertainment."

He wouldn't lose.

Two

Prince Charming and the wallflower, Charlotte Palsgrave told herself. *You know how this story goes.* But truth was she didn't. Not anymore. Anxiety had her wallflower self twisted up in well-deserved knots. She swallowed the boulder-sized lump in her throat because if she cried now where people could see her, her secret would come out. For months she'd dreaded discovery and part of her wanted to stand up and scream the truth. To admit *I'm sorry.* She'd made a disastrous mistake that she regretted with all her heart. This race was her very last chance to fix the damage before it irrevocably hurt other people, so she really, *really* needed Prince Charming to get on board with her make-up plan. If she'd known just how badly off course life could get, she would have planned better.

Invested in a pair of kick-ass glass slippers…

Just in case she'd secretly acquired a fairy godmother, she double-checked her feet. Nope. Her ever-so-practical navy blue sneakers hadn't been magically transformed. She was still on her own. It was times like this that she couldn't quite shut out her father's disapproving voice in her head, a loud, critical voice that she'd never managed to measure up to or please. She'd gotten better at ignoring the voice or even occasionally talking back to it, but that hard-won confidence vanished when she faced a social situation like today's. Not only was she standing at Martha's Vineyard's most exclusive yacht club, but she'd voluntarily agreed to get in a boat in three weeks, race at unspeakable speeds through open ocean off the coast of Massachusetts and do it all in the company of a celebrity Prince Charming, aka Declan Masterson, aka her new nemesis because she desperately needed to win the million-dollar prize and he refused to get onboard with her plans.

Magicking up a pair of glass slippers would have been easier.

Mostly because while she preferred to color neatly within the lines, guided by her master plan and a binder bristling with sticky notes, Declan preferred to careen at full speed in random directions.

Worse, while he looked like a hero on the outside, he was one-hundred-percent nefarious villain on the inside.

She slanted a glance at where he stood, surrounded by an admiring crowd of yachties and media. This was only partly due to his celebrity status as a Hollywood star and acting CEO of a blockbuster film studio—and mostly due to the man's sheer animal chemistry. He channeled rugged today, his wavy blond hair tousled from tugging his fingers through it. Hazel eyes, a stubble-roughened, firm jaw and the man's mouth… Well. It was honestly a blessing that when he opened his mouth what came out had her seeing red, because otherwise she would have stopped and stared because the man was a work of art and she felt a sensual tug when she was close. That was a first for her, that overwhelming awareness of a man, the curiosity about what it would be like to get closer. A whole lot closer.

He must have made some kind of Mephistophelian deal with the devil for that charm he turned on and off at will.

Just be glad that they're taking his *picture and not yours.* The YouTube videos she'd watched on mastering selfie poses seemed entirely inadequate as Declan flashed a killer grin at the nearest lens. *Doesn't matter.* She had zero interest in competing for Miss Photogenic in this beauty pageant. She froze in front of a camera. Her life didn't revolve around pictures and social media and she valued that. She worked behind-the-scenes as the director of the nonprofit Martha's Kids, creating summer camps for foster kids so they could swim and kayak, swap friendship bracelets and enjoy lighthearted fun. Camp had been her own escape from a less-than-idyllic childhood home, so she loved making the magic happen for these kids.

"Charlotte," her golden-haired nemesis called. "Join us."

Her feet moved automatically because the man had his own gravitational pull. Oh, God. She was doomed.

Resist.

She stopped walking and deployed her secret weapon: the truth. "You don't need me over there. Thanks anyways."

Then she smiled because politeness mattered. Declan stared at her thoughtfully. *Great, okay, move right along, big guy.* Most people looked right through her, their gaze skipping over her very ordinary face and the medium-length brown hair she always pulled into a ponytail. She didn't bother with makeup beyond a moisturizer with SPF and her wardrobe consisted of yoga wear and comfortable shoes. She might be dismissed as boring, but she loved herself and felt safe. That was all that mattered.

Okay, so she *had* felt safe, until her ex-fiancé had vanished, taking with him her dreams, along with most of

Martha's Kids' annual operating budget. As a result, she'd pulled strings to enter the race that took place in three weeks since, despite his flaws, her father was a prominent Vineyard local. She'd lucked out with her random partner. Declan's pretty face and celebrity standing would rake in donations during these pre-race events because people fell over themselves to make a man like him happy. Plus, he actually knew how to sail a boat. He was a guaranteed winner and that prize money would make up her budgetary shortfall—*if* she could ever get him to agree to picking Martha's Kids as their charity.

"Come on, darling." He winked, fully aware no woman would deny him. Handsome and hot, yada yada. *Pay no attention*, she told her hormones. "You make my day brighter and we're partners."

She snorted. She preferred to think of their arrangement as a sixty/forty split where she handled decision-making and responsibilities while he looked glamorous and expensive. That division of labor played to both their strengths. "Three weeks until race day. Tick, tick, Hollywood. I'll meet you at the boat for a practice run when you're done posing."

He shook his head and held out a strong, sun-bronzed hand to her. He wore faded board shorts and a white T-shirt that hugged his muscled chest and framed a whole lot of masculine strength. The tousled hair, warm eyes and stubble screamed, *I just rolled out of bed and don't you wonder who was there with me?*

Which she didn't. She went one worse and imagined herself in that bed, possibly a fantasy bed in the luxury hotel where he'd held off terrorists in his last box office hit. He'd had a memorable moment with his leading lady in that movie, one where they'd celebrated being very much not dead by ripping each other's clothes off. Carefully, she looked away from him, aiming her gaze at his feet in case he could tell from her face that she was imagining him naked.

It was just a Prince Charming side effect, one that would pass when she broke free of his orbit.

"One quick picture," she bit out, ignoring his hand. He wouldn't move on to the next agenda item until he was ready, and to win this race, she needed practice—lots of practice and exposure therapy in the measly three weeks before race day. Unlike Declan, who was a world-class racer with wins in exotic locations like Malta, the Route du Rhum in France and all parts of the Caribbean, she had a love-hate relationship with the ocean. While she'd happily admire it from the beach, she'd almost drowned the last time she'd gotten too close.

Declan wiggled the fingers on his outstretched hand. *Ugh.* If he actually crooked a finger at her, she'd give felony murder serious consideration. *Just win the race and save your kids and* then *you can kill him.*

So she hotfooted it across the deck, stopping awkwardly next to him. Even at five foot nine in her bare feet, the man had six inches on her. Declan took charge, effortlessly and with a great deal of charm. He slung a casual arm around her shoulders, tugging her into his side and turning them both to face the photographers. Cameras clicked and then he dropped his arm, stepping away. She didn't mind, she told herself. When someone protested, he shook his head.

"The lady said one." He snagged a white linen shirt from the chair where he'd tossed it and pulled it on over his T-shirt. The expensive Rolex watch he'd won in his last race glinted in the summer sun as he slipped his sunglasses on.

From the crowd of his admirers, a reporter asked the inevitable. "Have you decided which charity to sponsor?"

She opened her mouth, but Declan beat her, flashing

the man a warm smile. "We're committed to an animal charity."

"*We* haven't decided yet," she growled. Not that the media pack paid attention. Nope. They were watching Prince Charming button his shirt. "Martha's Kids is obviously my first choice. We'll be sure to let you know."

Naturally, Declan heard her.

He just wouldn't *listen*. He'd suggested six different animal charities, each more ridiculously specific than the last.

"Let's discuss and revisit." He winked at her again—was it too much to hope his eye got stuck that way?—and set off with a long-legged, way-too-sexy stride.

Darn it. That meant he'd get to their as-yet-unnamed boat first and then he'd take command of the tiller just like he took command of everything.

If she were a braver woman, she'd shove the man sauntering down the dock into the water. One surge of speed plus a quick shoulder check and *boom*, six feet three inches of muscled, sun-kissed, way-too-arrogant male would hit the oil-slicked, briny flotsam bobbing around the boats in the marina. Surely even Declan Masterson's Hollywood good looks couldn't survive that swim unscathed. If she weren't so invested in winning their boat race in three weeks, she'd do it. Maybe. Okay, so almost probably definitely not because she generally believed in being nice and keeping things calm, and nice people didn't push a man into the water and make a scene.

Even if that man totally deserved it.

Future Charlotte moved *dunk Declan Masterson* to the top of the bucket list she'd tackle after she won this race and fixed her mistake.

Everything had all happened so fast: handsome and funny, George Moore had wowed the board of Martha's Kids during his interview six months earlier and afterward he'd been so eager to work with her. She'd handed over the reins of their accounting to him, had failed to double-check him because he'd seemed so perfect. They'd enjoyed a special connection, or so she'd believed. He'd wined and dined her with a series of romantic dates to the Vineyard's flashiest spots.

Caught up in the whirlwind romance and knocked off-balance by the outgoing George's obvious interest in her quieter, shyer self, she hadn't questioned his motivations. It was friendship, attraction, a lightning-bug spark of attraction. After mere weeks, he'd declared his love and suggested they go diamond shopping. Her father had flat-out stated that a man who looked like a Greek god would never be interested in a plain-Jane girl like her. And his totally expected criticism had made her decide that for once she'd dig in her heels and live.

Which had turned out to be a big mistake. *Huge.* Because six months after he'd blown into Martha's Vineyard, George had slipped away without any of the fanfare he loved so much—and he'd cleaned out not only her bank account but Martha's Kids' as well. She'd been thinking *romance* and he—well, he'd thought *smoke screen.* The embezzlement would become public knowledge when the district attorney filed charges shortly. Nothing stayed secret forever. This race was her ticket to repairing the damage George had done because the prize money would refill the foundation's coffers even if it could never erase her guilt.

She concentrated on the sun-warmed planks of the dock stretching away in front of her. Mooring posts jutted up out of the salt water and were decorated with seagulls. Despite the sky's perfect shade of blue, the warmth of the sun didn't work its usual magic on the tension that had the muscles in her shoulders knotting. Breaking into an undignified trot, she caught up with Declan, trying not to think about the ocean that she'd soon be sailing on.

"Charlotte." He slanted her a look she couldn't interpret. "What is your problem?"

"Why do I have to have a problem?"

His eyes danced. "You're clearly upset. Let's fix this."

She shook her head. "Is everything easy for you? No, don't answer. I've got a great idea. How about we stay on schedule and nominate our charity?"

"I've made multiple suggestions. You've shot them all down." He made it sound as if she were the illogical member of their team when the opposite was true.

"Your suggestions were ridiculous," she gritted out.

"So, convince me. Here I am, entirely, completely yours." He threw out his arms. "Why does Martha's Kids matter so much to you?"

Jeez. "Because I direct it? Because those foster kids deserve a summer of cabins, kayaks and crafts? Because *you* want to donate a million dollars of prize money to rescuing guinea pigs, which has to be a joke?"

He lifted one powerful shoulder in a shrug. "Guinea pigs are awesome."

"Not a million dollars' worth of awesome." Giving up on dignity, she speed-walked down the dock. Their two-person boat was at the very end, just to better mess with her head.

Declan's husky chuckle floated after her. *Ugh.* He was never serious. Toeing off her boat shoes, she sidled up to the edge of the dock. And froze. One step down. One big step down, minding the gap and the water—

"Nice try." Warm hands wrapped around her waist, shifting her gently to the side, and she bit back a squeal. Mostly. She was ticklish. Okay, and something else, a sizzle she wasn't willing to admit even to herself as he effortlessly moved her out of his way. Her arm brushed his side.

"Cheater," she hissed.

His mouth brushed her ear. "Takes one to know one."

He couldn't possibly know. No one knew. Not yet.

With another chuckle, he jumped down into the boat. Not for the first time she wished the charitable folks of Martha's Vineyard had belonged to any club other than the yacht club. Golfing, badminton, even birding—why couldn't the prize be for the team who spotted the most herons? Water slapped against the dock, the waves darker blue and deep. At least the answer to her problem ex wasn't platform diving. She didn't have to put her face in. *Count your blessings.*

"One step at a time." Declan held out his hand to help her in. "You want to tell me why you don't like water but you've volunteered for a boat race?"

Even if she had been in the habit of sharing her fears with a complete stranger, she wouldn't have told him the truth. She wasn't sure she could, not after so many years of keeping quiet and pretending that everything was *fine.* So she went on the offensive.

"I'm fine. Why don't you tell me why you're headlining a no-name boat race for charity instead of living your Hollywood best life?"

Three

Charlotte Palsgrave liked to pretend that everything was fine. But Declan was trained to pay attention to his opponent's body language in a fight and right now everything about his new partner screamed *anxious*.

Slightly rude.

And…unexpectedly sexy. Not that he had noticed. Much. The only time Charlotte didn't try to fade into the background was when they fought, and so far, she'd limited even those fights to brief verbal jabs and sideways glances. She didn't like him.

At all.

Insta-hate was a first. Most people focused on the wealth he wore like a shield or the surface excitement of his Hollywood success. They wanted stories about famous people, the inside scoop on the decadent Malibu parties and the vicarious buzz from hearing how he'd get out of a studio car and fans would roar as the cameras went off. They had to actually get to know him to be disappointed by who he was and to realize that he was simply playing the part he'd been cast in. Charlotte, however, had been disdainful from the first. She'd dismissed him as a pretty package that she couldn't be bothered to unwrap.

He was good at shucking off criticism thanks to the constant public scrutiny. If she also felt the desire that ate at him when he saw her, she covered it up well, directing only dislike his way, along with impatience and annoying superiority. He, on the other hand, couldn't keep his mind on the upcoming race. When he was around her, he wanted to kiss the tight line of her mouth, nip at the plush lower lip until she opened up and let him all the way in. She might not like drawing attention to herself and she might not be beautiful in the sparkling way that drew photographers and a crowd of admirers, but she was something, alright. His craving for her was a problem.

"Sit." He handed her a life jacket and pointed to the spot where she could get least in the way, ignoring her muttered *woof.*

While she fumed, flipping through the color-coded binder she clung to like a mooring line, he got them underway for their practice session. Guiding twenty feet of sailboat past slips filled with expensive luxury boats and out into open water was child's play, but he wanted to fine-tune their rig and get some more average headings for their tacks.

He'd met a lot of gorgeous women but Charlotte was different. Entirely too prickly, as well as stubborn and determined to make his life hell, but suddenly he knew what people meant when they said that "beauty was only skin-deep." Objectively, her looks were nothing out of the ordinary—brown hair, brown eyes, too curvy to fit into a sample size. But there was something about her that he liked looking at.

Martha's Vineyard skimmed by, all creamy sand and

expensive beach cottages, as the boat's sails filled and she picked up speed. The familiar beat of wind on canvas and the play of water on the hull was invigorating, but he still couldn't quite believe he was once again dancing to his adoptive father's tune, vying to win his inheritance test. Except...

Charlotte Palsgrave was perfect window dressing.

He thought about that while he took them out into the open water, their little boat skimming over the waves. A feminine inhale, quickly stifled, shifted his attention from the ocean to his companion. She had a death grip on her binder, her eyes fixed unwaveringly on the horizon.

Reaching over, he pried the binder free and tucked it in the waterproof compartment beneath his legs. She promptly transferred her grip to the lifeline by her shoulder. "You okay?"

"Wonderful." She didn't look at him.

He was pretty certain that she'd just as soon tie the anchor to his ankle and drop him overboard in some convenient stretch of water as admit that racing and open ocean made her nervous. As far as he could tell, she made it through their daily practices on sheer determination.

And keeping secrets...

The only thing she didn't keep secret was her dislike of him and he had weeks before he could claim victory and head back to California.

"You're the one who wants to discuss things—here's your opportunity."

"You want to talk *now*?"

"We could stop and swim," he teased.

She winced. "Let's pick our charity. It's Martha's Kids. Not hedgehogs or guinea pigs or whatever other animal you decided needed rescuing."

"Come on, darling," he said. "You need me to agree."

Martha's Kids seemed like a fine organization, especially given his own background as a foster child. The optics were great. But playing J.J.'s inheritance game was boring if necessary and arguing with Charlotte was shaping up to be his one note of excitement.

"You're asking me to be the good guy here," he continued.

"Some of us clearly lean more toward the bad end of the scale," she muttered.

He liked to win, and while he didn't cheat or hurt others to do so, he also went all in on his goals. He left everything out there on the playing field and sometimes he stepped on some toes in the process. So no, he wasn't a *good guy*.

"What can you offer me?" He leaned back, crossing his arms over his chest.

"It's charity." She briefly threw up her hands before seizing the lifeline again. "Why is everything about you, Hollywood? I know you live for attention and adventure, but some of us are trying to do the right thing. Maybe you could try to be different? Just this once?"

He was sick and tired of being told to change because who he was wasn't good enough. Maybe she should try it. He bet she'd hate it every bit as much as he did. In fact—

There was nothing Charlotte hated more than being the center of attention. Her reluctance to put herself forward gave him an idea.

"Since I'll be doing something that runs counter to my nature, it's only fair you do the same."

She looked at him, suspicion painting her face. "Like what?"

"I change—and you change," he said. "If I become a good guy and support Martha's Kids, you stop hiding in the shadows you love so much. You get a makeover. Hollywood-style. Hair, makeup, the works. I'll teach you everything I know about being a star. And when you're the belle of the ball on race night, I'll make sure Martha's Kids gets that million-dollar check. Do we have a deal?"

Declan Masterson could take a long walk off a short pier, and oh look, there was a handy dock at the marina just waiting for the king of Hollywood to take his fashion walk.

"That's a terrible deal. Why would I hand you another opportunity to humiliate me?"

Her nemesis crossed his arms and leaned forward. When he spoke his voice had the whiskey-rough cadence that had made the man famous. "Because you want me to give a million dollars to your charitable foundation."

"I'll earn it," she muttered. "I have to put up with you for an entire month."

"So a month alone with a movie star on the water is a hardship? Do you know how many people would take your place?" His jaw tightened. "You weren't picked for this boat, darling, because you're the director of Martha's Kids. You're here because your dear old dad is on the yacht club board and wants the locals to represent."

"Don't forget how much he likes winning." Her face heated. It wasn't untrue, but at least she'd got the world-champion sailor when the race committee had done the blind draws for partners.

"No one enjoys losing. Not that you would know anything about that, Princess."

Was the guy for real? "I lose all the time, so I can tell you from personal experience that, yes, it sucks and, yes, I prefer to avoid it. I don't know what your problem is, Hollywood. I'm here to raise money for a nonprofit that tries to erase the gap between people who have everything and people who have nothing."

He laughed. "With arts and crafts projects and campfires? Is there a special gold medal for sentimentality?"

She shot to her feet but had to sit back down again hard

when she remembered how close she was to the water. Indignation and boats paired as poorly as Cheetos and white wine—or herself and this Hollywood charmer lounging on this stupidly small boat as if it were a movie set and she was a stand-in. No. Wait. In this metaphor, she was the person who fetched coffee and never got credit for the movie magic.

Although she could see why he was the source of that magic. He took up so much space, his big body relaxed, the wind playing with his hair as he radiated an easy confidence despite the open ocean surrounding them. Nothing knocked him off-balance and he didn't seem to know how unusual that was.

"I'm in this race for the right reasons," she insisted, double-checking the closure on her life jacket.

"And what reasons would those be?" He flashed her a teasing grin.

She revised her push-Declan-Masterson-into-the-water plan, speeding up the timeline. Push now, race later.

"I'm doing this for my kids. Not for you. Not for anyone else. For *them*. This is Jimmy." She whipped out her phone and pulled up a picture. "He likes the cabins because they're quiet and no one got shot last summer. And here's Jay. He doesn't get three meals a day when he's at home and unlimited hot dogs are his idea of heaven." She thumbed to another picture. "And this is Maggie. Like Jimmy and Jay, she's also not a cute little guinea pig. She's a ten-year-old girl who wants one summer to act like she's ten rather than ten-going-on-forty because she has a mother with severe depression who can't always get out of bed."

What she didn't add was that the best apologies came with a make-up plan, and only a million dollars could make up for what George had stolen. No matter how many times she said "I'm sorry" to the staff at Martha's Kids, the board and her kids, those were only words. Important words, but still.

"Charlotte—" He closed his eyes briefly and groaned. Funny how the real-life man was so different from the action heroes he played on the big screen. She liked that made-up man so much more. *He* saw a problem and he jumped in to fix it. "—are you really, truly doing this for the children?"

"Mostly," she said, because she had a no-lying policy, and pride and not disappointing her father had also factored into her decision to participate in the race. Martha's Vineyard was her home and screwing up on her home turf felt a million times worse than if she'd done the same in New York City or Boston—in any place, really, that she could run home from.

The smile spreading across his handsome face spelled trouble. "Still not convinced to be Team Martha's Kids. Are you sure you're not just in this for a shot at me?"

That was—

Her mouth hung open. The man was unbelievable. "Explain to me how your movie star awesomeness is all the motivation I need to be out here in the world's smallest boat on the world's biggest ocean?"

"Second-largest," he corrected. "The Atlantic is the second-largest ocean. You should get your facts straight, Charlotte. Admit that you like me," he crooned. "Just a little. Tell me the truth."

"Oh, my God. No."

"You're such a liar," he said cheerfully. "Completely full of shit. I'm not sure I should like that about you."

"I do not like you. This not some big sexual come-on, you ass." Did no one tell this man *no*? She gave him another irritated glance. Doing something seemed important, so she shuffled her butt down the seat so she could hang on to the side and poke at the steering stick thing at the same time.

The stupid boat didn't change course, though. She tugged on the stick—*tiller*—but it remained locked in place. Declan winked at her. Right. She tried for a better grip but since he wouldn't move out of her way, she had to reach over him, her life jacket bumping against his chest and side.

Whoa. He smelled good. Not that she was deliberately sniffing the man, but it was impossible not to notice. The piney, woodsy scent had to be cologne, but the rest of it—clean and male—was all him. And while she might like that scent far too much, it in no way meant she liked the *man*. How could he look so much like the screen god she might—*might*—have had one or two—or a thousand—fantasies about when the real-life person was such a disappointment?

"Are you sure? About not liking me?" He folded his hands behind his head, leaning helpfully back and out of her way. He also gave the tiller a quick nudge with his knee. Dammit. The boat moved.

"Quite," she bit out. "I'm sure *someone* has told you by now. The Vineyard loves a juicy piece of gossip, and although my relationship ended *slightly* less publicly than your last relationship, it was public enough. My fiancé ran away rather than marry me. I'm on a dating hiatus until my ovaries start sending notice. No one will think we're anything but race partners. You're entirely safe."

He frowned. "He dumped you."

"Quickly and quite publicly." And that wasn't even the worst of it.

His frown deepened. "So we actually have something in common. Do we have a deal? I'll play the good guy and throw my support behind your foundation. And you'll do the makeover."

She didn't trust his smile.

"It'll be fun." He flashed her a grin.

Danger.

"There's nothing wrong with me."

He made a rough noise, more growl than not, and tugged her in front of him. His legs bracketed hers and that put her practically on the man's lap. She started to protest but then he set her hands on the tiller, his closing over hers, moving hers. Show and tell.

"Move left to go right. Right to go left. Keep the changes small and smooth." The smooth wood sliding underneath her hands almost distracted her from the feel of Declan's hands covering hers. "There's nothing wrong with you. But we both need to reinvent our public selves, yeah? People see me and they think Romeo on a balcony. They see you and they remember George the asshole. This race could be a fresh start for both of us."

He unwrapped himself from her and shifted up the boat to balance their weight. Her heart pounded, her face flushing—from the way the boat rocked until he settled, she told herself. And not because watching Declan got her going.

"You really think a makeover will help me support Martha's Kids." She nudged the tiller to the left.

"I do."

"You realize that sounds completely ridiculous, right?"

"People will pay more attention. Some of them will be curious, while others will believe that if you look and act the part, you know what you're doing."

"So you're saying confidence is key." She squinted at him. "My first-grade teacher put that on the wall of our classroom."

"Still true," he said.

He flashed her another smile, this one genuine. The good humor and warmth in his grin had her wanting to agree, so clearly she hadn't fixed her man picker yet. It was all sign-me-up in the face of Declan's charm.

He winked at her, eyes bright with amusement. "Say yes."

Her heart turned over. Did that *flutter* thing.

Not a chance. NO.

There was nothing likable about this man. He was all surface charm and no depth. At least if she forgot that truth, he'd remind her the next time he opened his mouth.

"Do we have a deal?" He gestured toward the tiller and she sighed. Right. They were probably sailing toward Cuba or Madagascar. Since that was more ocean time than she was ready for, she made room for him and he took over. And let's face it, she was grateful for his easy confidence.

Grateful and a little turned on. She'd learn how to do this sailing thing if it killed her, but it had been a long day and there was a cheeseburger calling her name. Pie, too, if the local bakery truck hadn't sold out. When she moaned and he slid her a sideways glance, she shrugged. Pie was the best.

"So," he said. "Normally, I'd interpret that as a yes."

She sighed and he laughed.

"Yes, Declan. We have a deal."

"You want to shake on it? Seal it with a kiss?"

"Are you kidding me?"

He winked. "Just testing you."

"We're done for the day here," she said.

While he laid in a course toward what she hoped was the pier, she retrieved her race binder and put a large check in the box next to *practice new sailing skills* and *nominate a charity*. Then she added a new box for *makeover lessons*. Next to her, Declan laughed. She ignored him. It was okay to be a work in progress.

And sure, the sun would go supernova and it would take a billion years before she actually *finished* working on herself, but still. She was doing that work and her interest in Declan extended no further than the man's impressive sailing skills. She couldn't possibly be interested in anything more. He was a movie star. A professional racer and seeker after adrenaline. And while she fully planned on taking advantage of his racing expertise to cross that finish line first, she was not going to get involved with a shameless charmer.

Never ever again.

Four

Two words had governed Declan's life since the day he'd had to weigh the potential dangers of jumping off a roof with the adrenaline rush of completing a difficult stunt.

Risk.

And *reward.*

Declan had earned his place in Hollywood through hard work, sheer determination and an uncanny ability to judge that risk against its potential payoff. Those efforts had yielded a fortune, star status and now the chance to seal the deal of a lifetime. He might have been adopted rather than born into the Masterson family, but he'd prove that he had what it took to be one of them by passing this last test.

The five-thousand square foot brown-shingled mansion he temporarily called home in Martha's Vineyard was worthy of any New England blue blood family. The interior decorator had chosen a rustic, industrial farmhouse look, both trendy and expensive, and the Atlantic was clearly visible through wide-open French doors. The rolling, green lawns were painstakingly manicured to perfection, billows of hydrangeas and wild grasses surrounding the pool and the cabana. It was all perfectly pleasant, well insulated from the ever-present paparazzi, endlessly serene…and he itched to be anywhere else. He had more than enough money to rent the exclusive compound for the entire summer, or to buy it outright, but it wasn't enough.

Nothing ever was.

Yacht races and heli-skiing, kayaking in the Arctic and cave diving in the Great Blue Hole—none of it held his attention for long.

In the forty-eight hours since his deal with Charlotte, he'd brought in stylists, aestheticians and a walking coach. The makeover team bustled around the far end of the room, waiting for today's reluctant star. Charlotte Palsgrave had been determined to get her pretty, spoiled way about who they sponsored for the charity race. And as the reclusive, quiet daughter of one of the island's oldest families, Princess got what she wanted.

Still, she'd agreed to pay his price. He'd give her that, and when she got the million-dollar check for her beloved children's charity, he'd get the family company. For now all he had was the steady beat of the sun on the water, the wind that had already whipped tiny whitecaps onto the otherwise calm surface. So much peace and quiet. Ridiculously, he still felt like that eight-year-old boy, swept from a California foster home into a life he could never have imagined. He'd been a miscue in the smooth Masterson script, a wrong line, the out-of-place story beat. Taking control of the family company would solve all that.

He'd always been hyperaware of his surroundings, a requirement of his rough childhood, so he was the first to notice the newcomer hovering in the doorway. *Gotcha*, he thought. Charlotte had agreed to come and she was the kind of person who believed a promised made was a promise kept.

At twenty-nine, she was four years younger than him, but she'd grown up in a completely different world. She was a genuine "good girl," quiet and reserved, the daughter of a New England family with deep-rooted connections to the island and a long pedigree he couldn't have cared less about. Taller than average for a woman, even in ballet flats, her brown hair was pulled back in her usual casual ponytail that ended just below her shoulders—which he knew because she toyed with the ends of her hair as she surveyed the room, watching from the sidelines as always. The perfect care with which she approached everything only made him think of messing her up, undoing all that prim tidiness.

She hesitated, clearly unsure what her next step should be. Nothing about her outfit of black yoga pants and a Martha's Kids windbreaker screamed "look at me." She'd be eaten alive in his world, so there was no reason to draw her into this game. If he'd been a better or a nicer man, he'd have allowed her to continue hiding in the shadows she liked so much. He wouldn't drag her front and center in J.J.'s game.

But since being nice wouldn't win the race and J.J.'s challenge, he sprang into action and took the decision out of her hands by striding toward her.

She registered his approach with wary caution. "Declan."

"Princess." He braceleted her wrist with his fingers, tugging her gently forward.

She grimaced. "That's not my name, Hollywood."

"Queenie," he offered. "Buttercup. Dream Girl."

"If I push you overboard after we cross the finish line, no one will blame me."

He grinned at her, delighted. "*Everyone* will blame you. I'm deeply beloved."

This made her groan. "Clearly this *everyone* hasn't heard you go off script."

He ignored the truth of her words. "A new you awaits."

This earned him another groan. "Explain to me how this helps us win the race."

Feminine and warm, the smooth tones of her voice made him think of sliding between the sheets with her, an off-limits activity as he was reformed, at least publicly. And while parading a genuine New England princess around on his arm could only bolster his good-guy image, she didn't like him. She was refined, classy and entirely, completely unimpulsive.

He was her polar opposite.

He captured her hands between his, feeling his mouth curving upward into a grin. They might be opposites at heart, but playing with Charlotte was a definite perk. Despite the princessy, uptight attitude, the woman herself was a delightful surprise package. Beneath her practical clothes she had a sweet, curvy body and legs for days thanks to her above-average height.

He hadn't dated anyone since his disastrous joke of a marriage proposal. Despite myriad opportunities, he'd been strangely reluctant. Casual sex, no matter how adventurous, was somehow no longer enough. The smile faded from his face. He had no intention of changing—only of winning.

"You could trust me," he suggested softly, startling himself.

Brown eyes narrowed. "Not a chance."

Her voice held a definite snap and not a hint of her usual politeness. He wondered if that defensiveness was due to her fiancé—but what man couldn't see the quiet beauty and wry wit she tried so hard to hide?

She tugged against his grip. "Explain the plan to me."

"Winning."

Letting go of her, he set a palm on the small of her back and steered her toward the army of people gathered around racks of clothes and a portable beauty station. As a stylist started pulling a handful of looks, Charlotte shot him a mutinous glare.

She fingered a cashmere sweater. "None of this says 'Martha's Kids.' Who pays for these?"

"I do," he said. "It's a business expense. Think of it as advertising. This is a charity race with social events and networking. Yoga pants aren't the look to go for at the gala ball. If you want people to back you, you need to sell them first."

"This is revenge."

"Really?"

She groaned. "Of course it is. You're not only stuck with me, but you can't give ridiculous amounts of money to a save-the-guinea-pigs rescue foundation."

He bit back a grin. "Most women would be thrilled."

This earned him a sideways look. "So I'm not most women."

That was true.

She said the words lightly, as if it were no big deal. He knew that forced lightness. He'd acted the role too many times himself to not recognize it. Someone had made her feel that different was bad, when in fact it was everything. Perhaps not everything was perfect in her kingdom after all. Before he could give in to the unfamiliar urge to deviate from his game plan—where he turned her into the perfect, public answer to J.J.'s demand that he act exactly like a Masterson—he shooed her toward the room designated as a temporary dressing room.

Nice was a weakness he couldn't afford when he was so close to the finish line.

Ten minutes later, when she still hadn't emerged, he rapped sharply on the closed door. It wasn't, he told himself, that he was eager to hear—and see—what she thought of the new clothes. He was busy and she was a step in his game plan, so the sooner she got on board, the sooner he could wrap this up.

"Come on out, Princess."

The answering rustle on the other side of the door had him thinking of clothes sliding over bare skin.

"My name is not Princess." Her voice radiated irritation as she tugged the door open to frown at him.

Leaning against the frame, he took her in. Dressed-up Charlotte was stunning. White linen pants clung snugly to her hips before flaring down to her ankles and a cropped, black button-up sweater bared a teasing glimpse of her stomach.

"I like this on you." He made a spinning motion with his fingers, laughing at her little growl of frustration.

"This sweater shrank in the wash." She tried to tug the edge of the sweater down and he gently caught her hands with his, his fingertips brushing bare skin. Heat flared through him.

Doing his best to ignore it, he carefully shifted her to one side and then reached around her to rummage through the rack of clothing by the door. She looked amazing, but he didn't want her to feel uncomfortable so he pulled out a white cashmere sweater with brown stripes and a Hermès scarf.

Her own clothes sat neatly folded on the bed, a T-shirt with cheery pink cartoon fish topping the pile.

"Try your shirt," he said. "With mine."

"Are you a stylist now?"

He turned around ostentatiously. "Take. Your. Shirt. Off."

He dangled the T-shirt from his hand and she moved

closer to snatch it. He did his best not to notice the almost brush of her body against his, the warmth of her skin and the subtle feminine scent. Instead he studied the closed door as she shimmied out of the cropped sweater and back into her T-shirt.

"Safe?"

"Enough," she muttered.

He turned back around. She stood there awkwardly, hands fluttering at her sides as if she wasn't quite sure what to do with them. He had some ideas, but he kept them to himself and settled instead for tying the hem of her shirt up into a jaunty knot that stopped at her waist without baring any skin and then holding the new sweater out for her to slip into.

Unexpectedly, part of him wished he was doing this for someone special like a wife, someone he just had to spoil because she was his person and he needed to show her just how special she was in his eyes. That part of him was tired of the Hollywood games. It was one reason why he wanted Masterson Entertainment to be his; finally, he'd be making movies that reflected his vision rather than someone else's. It also meant he'd have a place, a chance to build on the Masterson legacy. He'd belong, once and for all.

The woman standing stiffly in front of him belonged here, in Martha's Vineyard, and most definitely here in the yacht club with its reserved, refined air. Her brisk, no-nonsense walk was endearing in its directness. She set her course and she stuck to it. She'd been all those things in yoga pants; the expensive new clothes couldn't change who she was fundamentally, but they showcased it, like a frame around a picture.

She looked curvy but strong. Tall. Not the kind of female lead he usually played opposite, who was lean and toned, telegraphing sex appeal and a body confidence that announced she knew her worth. Instead, she was more like a treasure chest or a nesting doll—so much hid beneath Charlotte's soft, calm surface.

He got the hell out of the room, leaving her to neatly fold and put away the discarded clothing. He was already sprawled on the enormous sofa when she came back out, but as soon as she stepped into the room, he barked a command to the small army of stylists who descended on her.

She's not for you.

Charlotte had many nightmares, not all limited to nighttime hours: Walking naked into a crowded room. Her teeth falling out like a bad cartoon character. Not being able to replace the money her ex-fiancé had stolen before the theft became public knowledge and her kids lost their magical summer forever because of her bad judgment. Prior to yesterday's makeover session, however, that list had not included pretty clothes, makeup or walking from point A to point B. Her afternoon at Declan's summer mansion yesterday had revealed just how unprepared she was for a life of Hollywood glam.

And as if the time he'd spent transforming her into a very expensive fashion model wasn't awkward enough, he'd added walking lessons. Posing lessons. She had actual homework to stare at herself in the mirror and practice smiling. On *top* of their sailing practice and race prep.

She'd never so much as paddled a kayak since that disastrous day when she'd come closer to drowning than she cared to remember. It still took the better part of her courage—and preferably the world's biggest life jacket rather than the sleek, non-inflatable PFD Declan preferred—to walk down the dock and get into the keelboat. Declan hadn't said anything, but he had to be disappointed. For all his flaws—and he had many—he was an international caliber sailor.

Trying to get out of bed revealed another shortcoming.

Sailing used a disturbing number of muscles she hadn't known she had and she was sore. Since she'd been adamant that she needed to sail and not just sit about decoratively, Declan had reviewed basic sail positions and adjusting for "maximum wind contact."

Her attempts at sail adjustment had left them both soaked by the ocean spray she'd somehow directed straight into the boat. He'd only laughed. She'd like to think that the patience and good humor in his hazel eyes were genuine, but charm was an illusion.

What if she couldn't do it? What if he got fed up with her ignorance and demanded a new partner? He was a Hollywood star and the biggest name participating in the race, so his wishes would be catered to. She groaned. The makeover silliness might be the smallest concession she'd be willing to grant. For Martha's Kids, she'd do almost anything. Not that she'd hop into bed with Declan or try to seduce him into a better mood—she had limits and, frankly, she doubted that sort of strategy worked outside the pages of a book. Plus the man could hardly be hurting for companionship. He was gorgeous.

Her body humming with some very pleasant recollections of just how good-looking her partner was, she finally rolled painfully out of bed and staggered over to the window. Charlotte lived in a guesthouse behind her father's house for a very modest amount of rent. A place of her own would have been great, but her salary as the director of a children's nonprofit was hardly a match for the often exorbitant rent in Martha's Vineyard. She knew she should be grateful for his assistance and most days she was. She loved being able to live here on the island year-round and her father didn't mean to make her feel less than adequate.

She had no idea why her racing partner believed she was a rich girl with unlimited access to the Bank of Dad. Hah. That couldn't have been further from the truth. She worked hard and handouts were on her Over-my-Dead-Body list. Too bad, then, that George hadn't felt the same way.

Declan, on the other hand, seemed as willing as she was to work for what he wanted. Thinking about him was bad because it made her want things, things she'd stupidly believed she shared with George. It was hard to remember that painful lesson about trusting too fast watching Declan. The casual power of his big body and the ease with which he moved around the boat and sent them flying across the water was simply too sexy. What would it feel like to have all that strength and interest focused on her? Despite the differences between them, she couldn't stop thinking about it.

She'd never felt this sort of heat and need for a man before. Certainly not for her ex-fiancé, a thought she set aside for later. She needed to focus on Martha's Kids. But something about Declan had some very erotic thoughts running through her head, and not just because the man was a Hollywood Prince Charming.

Stupid, sexy thoughts.

She had a date with a decidedly *un*sexy grant application and a mountain of paperwork. Declan was a distraction she couldn't afford when all her focus needed to be on her kids and saving their summer camp. This week she should've been paying the deposit on the campground. Planning s'mores and kayak routes. *I'm so sorry, kids.* Throat tight with guilt and anxiety, she turned away from the window.

It didn't matter that when he looked at her, she felt that just maybe he saw something—some*one*—worth looking at. She'd spent her life avoiding attention and now here he was, watching. Staring. *Seeing* her. And that made him dangerous in a way even his Hollywood characters weren't.

Five

The beloved up-island lunch spot of several presidents who enjoyed its chic, laid-back vibe and Modern American cuisine, Bryant Palsgrave's favorite restaurant looked like a white stone cottage tucked into an English country garden: Peaceful. Romantic, even. Normally Charlotte would have at least enjoyed the food, but time spent with her father was challenging, to say the least. She dug into her beet salad, hoping the honey-and-clementine dressing might sweeten her companion's words. Or perhaps her lettuce crunching would drown them out.

As always, their weekly father-daughter lunch had the same agenda: the many ways in which she'd failed to meet his expectations.

Despite retiring five years ago from a successful Wall Street career, her father still favored bespoke three-piece suits and powder blue Hermès ties. She presented him a new one yearly for Father's Day because he liked them and she knew better than to rock that boat. She'd kept the peace since her mother had walked out on them when she was seven. She'd thought a few times about trying to track her mother down and then she'd let the thought go. Shanna Palsgrave's own lack of attempts to contact her daughter spoke volumes.

"Tell me the next steps." He cut into the grilled salmon the server had set before him. "With Martha's Kids."

He'd already checked his watch twice and not, Charlotte knew, because he was tracking his resting heart rate or his steps for the day. She bored him and he had better things to do. "We're planning the annual summer camp."

"You should think bigger."

He made a dissatisfied gesture, his face falling into familiar, disapproving lines. He'd have preferred her to have a high-powered job in New York City, a job that would have afforded her a multi-million-dollar brownstone as well as a summer place. In his world, philanthropy followed a successful career or marriage to a man with political aspirations who could eventually invite his father-in-law to Washington, D.C., social events and the White House. Her older brother had made partner two years ago in a prestigious Boston law firm and was shopping for a Vineyard house to accommodate his own growing family. Their father was convinced he'd sit on the Supreme Court in a few years and Charlotte's more modest aspirations simply didn't register on the family's success scale. She loved peace, quiet and the chance to work with kids who needed her and to make her small difference in the world around her.

And yet her father insisted on reviewing her life plan with her each week, criticizing or dismissing her minor accomplishments because, as he said, he only wanted what was best for her and for Martha's Kids. He didn't understand her reluctance to grow the charity into a national organization hosting summer camps across the country. She hadn't told him about George's theft.

"Martha's Kids doesn't have the budget," she explained yet again through a throat tight with regret. *Which is my fault since George stole it without my noticing until it was too late.* "And our mission is to be a good neighbor and focus on our community."

"You could be so much more if you stopped thinking so small. Why limit yourself to just Martha's Vineyard and Massachusetts? There are foster kids elsewhere."

"I love my work." She murmured a quiet thank-you to the server who discreetly removed her largely untouched salad and replaced it with her entrée.

"Think larger," he snapped.

Translation: don't screw this up. She was actually just the interim director of Martha's Kids, although the board of directors had made it clear that they'd renew her two-year contract if she did well. And she'd had a shot, until George. "Still loving what I do."

That had her father explaining, his voice growing louder, about the greater possibilities for funding and scope if she took Martha's Kids national. He didn't understand there was enough work right there in Martha's Vineyard. He only saw what could be improved upon.

"Not everything has to be bigger or better," she said when he turned his attention back to his salmon. "Maybe Martha's Kids works exactly the size it is?"

She focused on her chicken while he blustered on. She'd spent the morning stalling the program director, who wanted to know when she could start hiring camp counselors for the summer program. The answer was no time soon, although Charlotte had stopped taking her own salary to preserve their remaining funds. The program director was concerned—and not the only person who suspected something had gone badly wrong. Charlotte had to tell them soon.

A stir at the front of the restaurant had her head turning, grateful for a distraction as an outsize wave of whispers spread through the dining room. A moment later, she saw why.

Declan stood in the doorway. Her stupid breath caught because, really, the man was too sexy for her own good. From the looks the other diners sent his way, she wasn't the only one who had noticed. He followed the hostess toward the Palsgrave table with a confident stride.

"Charlotte and I have a sailing date," Declan said, when he'd reached their table.

This was news to her and most definitely not on the schedule tucked inside her race prep binder. They sailed every other day, after she finished at Martha's Kids. The alternate slots were, unfortunately, blocked off for more of Declan's "makeover lessons." She still thought they were a waste of time, but so far she'd had walking lessons, along with some highly entertaining explanations from Declan on how best to pose for the inevitable camera, where he pretended to be either a high-society lady or a successful influencer. He didn't mind laughing at himself, she'd learned.

Declan's eyes brimmed with mischief. "Let's go." He gestured toward the exit as if abandoning her father midsalmon was perfectly reasonable.

"Declan's teaching me how to sail," she said, hoping to defuse the irritation building on her father's face. He hadn't decided yet if the apparent double-booking was simply another example of her incompetence or intentional rudeness on Declan's part.

"It will take more than an afternoon," he said. "You'd still be on the island next year. Our Charlotte's no Kate Middleton."

Ha ha. She opened her mouth to say something—she had no idea what—but Declan crossed his arms over his chest, frowning down at her father, clearly not impressed with the unfavorable comparison to English royalty. Although now that she thought about it, she wasn't at all sure that Kate had even won her last charity race. Ouch.

"Charlotte just has to be Charlotte," Declan said. "She doesn't have to be someone else to win."

Her father ignored this.

"Couldn't hold on to George Moore," he said, in that overloud, jovial voice he used when he was *just joking*. She'd never figured out if he genuinely didn't understand that his jokes hurt, or if he merely pretended ignorance. "Her fiancé," he added, in case no one in Martha's Vineyard had explained Declan's very public abandonment to him. "He ran. Bolted. Couldn't do it anymore.'

By *it*, he meant Charlotte because of course she was the problem. The dumpee was always the one who hadn't been enough.

"His loss." Declan sounded as if he actually meant it. He turned to Charlotte, "Can you finish quickly?"

She decided to live dangerously. "I'll take it with me."

Her father had a rule that you left what you didn't eat—Palsgraves didn't do leftovers—but her chicken was amazing and she was hungry. Plus, she was the Palsgrave who lived on a budget, thanks to the sad state of her checking account. Hunger won out over pride any day. Declan caught the eye of the waiter hovering nearby and her plate was whisked away.

"We should go," she half shouted, hopping to her feet before her father could protest.

Something flashed in Declan's eyes, but he just nodded. Usually this would be where she'd start apologizing, but what could she say? "Sorry that my dad's such an ass"? Plus, she almost thought she was done with that sort of thing: apology things. She tested the thought and realized she wasn't feeling as stressed as she usually would. She felt—okay. Even a little bit happy.

An amused smile played about the corners of Declan's handsome mouth. He saw far more than he let on, and if her father thought he was just a handsome face he was mistaken, even if the odds of his admitting to being less than perfect were low. So instead of wishing for the impossible, she savored the short walk out of the restaurant and the way Declan's hand rested on the small of her back. The gesture was old-fashioned, but she liked the small connection. It told her that he was there with her. For the few moments it took them to walk outside, she let herself enjoy the sensation of someone having her back.

"I won't screw this up," she told him. "I won't lose the race for us."

A luxury sports car waited out front, black, low-slung and expensive. He opened the passenger door for her, tipped the valet as she slid inside, and then went around and got into the driver's seat.

He gave her a look that she couldn't interpret. "This entire race isn't on you, Charlotte."

He put the car into gear with an easy confidence.

"Did I miss something? Am I a good sailor suddenly?"

"You try hard." His voice was rough and low, a sexy rasp that made her think about suggesting they forget about sailing lessons and races. The man gave her goose bumps.

"Trying isn't enough." True story.

"It is for me." He paused. "Tell me something. Would you kick me out of the boat if I made a mistake?"

"Of course not," she said. "But we both know you're not going to do that."

"I make plenty of mistakes."

She shrugged and focused her attention out the window.

Martha's Vineyard in the summer was beautiful. "I'm the novice sailor. You're the one who's going to win this race."

Faster than she would have liked, he was pulling them into a parking spot at the marina. Not that he'd broken any speed limits—despite the obvious speed potential of his car, he was a careful driver and she'd never felt unsafe with him. She got out without waiting for him to come around and open the door, and then they set off down the dock.

Which was surrounded on three sides by water.

In truth, she would have been happier if this was a land race.

Declan shot her an assessing glance and she bared her teeth at him, wondering if *nothing to see here* was a sentiment she should tattoo on her face.

"Do you want to finish eating first?" he asked.

"Nope." She couldn't risk throwing up in front of him. "Let's do this." She eyed the boat, which was at least a great distraction.

She could focus on whether or not the ocean was truly out to get her rather than, say, on the size and heat of Declan's large body so close to hers. She wasn't attracted to him like that. He was a big, well-built guy who was confident in his skin and who had a hidden sweet streak. That wasn't *actually* a basis for attraction.

Wait. It totally was.

She blew out a breath. The need and desire she sometimes felt around Declan didn't mean anything. There weren't any real feelings there, feelings like liking and attachment, intimacy and a commitment that extended further than beating the butts of their fellow racers. He certainly didn't care about her or even value her, while she was using him for his sailing skills. It was good that she could be so practical about all this.

"Your chariot, milady," he teased, gesturing toward the boat. "I'm at your command. Just tell me what you want."

Then he jumped down into the boat, held up his hands to help her in, and, when she insisted on doing it by herself, smiled and busied himself with casting off while she put on her life jacket and wondered if this was a case in which two jackets were better than one.

How far *was* she willing to go to secure Declan's cooperation? The makeover dare was a small price to pay when she would do almost anything short of—

Sleep with him! her body suggested gleefully. *Let's sleep with him! Take one for the team!*

It was good she had boundaries, she decided as she dropped awkwardly into the boat and he got them underway. Otherwise she might have added *sex up the movie star* to the day's checklist.

Six

Declan worked out his frustrations on the ocean, while Charlotte recorded rig tuning observations on their waterproof notepad. She liked working her way down her list and checking stuff off. And she definitely liked knowing what came next. Still, she'd let him drive her out to the marina and she'd gotten on the boat after a little teeth gritting. His favorite part had been when she'd kicked off her ballet flats and rolled up the white cotton pants that snugged her hips.

From her tight expression and the way she fidgeted with the straps on her life jacket, she hadn't magically conquered her fear of deep water yet. He debated asking if she wanted to talk about it, but the look she shot him said *that* topic was off-limits. He also considered introducing the topic of Bryant Palsgrave and grade A asshole, but he was shockingly willing to avoid talking about fathers. His own was a problem, so *glass houses* and all that.

Eventually, when he fell into an easy silence, Charlotte started barking out orders, trying to sail their boat by proxy if not by skill. Cute. He'd managed to keep a straight face while steering them out into open water. Who'd have thought he'd find his prickly, bossy race partner so much fun? But after their rather contentious start, she'd been a good sport about her makeover. And from the stack of beginner sailing books he'd spotted in her tote bag yesterday, she'd tried to learn the basics of sailing.

Not that it mattered because he knew enough about sailing for the both of them. Their two-person keelboat might be smaller and far simpler than the monohulls he'd raced in the world's most exotic locations, but the principles remained the same. On the water was the one place he'd always felt at home—as if he belonged and had nothing to prove.

And after Charlotte had practiced her new sailing skills, he'd taken over, sending the boat flying over the water. For the next two hours he'd switched between running the boat on upwind and downwind legs to get a feel for how she went. The more time they spent on the water, the better race day would go.

Charlotte was a good sport. Other than the ocean itself, nothing seemed to bother her: Not the water that constantly splashed them. Not the salt spray that turned her sleek ponytail into something wilder and larger. Not the sun that was slowly turning her cheeks pink. She moved where he directed, adjusting their placement in the boat to respond to the wind angles.

He'd expected his uptown girl to hate the glorious messiness of sailing. But maybe there was a whole lot more to her than he'd first thought. Maybe she was more than daddy's princess, the rule-following good girl who'd gone from sitting on the volunteer board of a children's charity to stepping in to run the entire organization when the previous director had retired unexpectedly. He knew he wasn't being entirely fair to her. She was a person with many sides, not a cookie cutter, one-dimensional woman.

He watched her from his side of the boat, taking in her quiet enjoyment as she pointed to a pair of seabirds winging past overhead. He couldn't help comparing this smiling, relaxed Charlotte with the contained woman he'd surprised at lunch. His mind replayed those moments—the disapproving looks her father had aimed at Charlotte, at him, at the world.

A short internet search last night had uncovered some mentions of Charlotte's engagement and subsequent un-engagement. Most of it focused on her now ex-fiancé, a man who'd never met a camera he didn't like. It was hard to imagine the reserved Charlotte with such a man, but he'd be the first to admit that photographs couldn't capture everything. It certainly went a long way toward explaining Charlotte's reluctance to put herself forward and made him want to show her what he'd started to see: that she was smart, loyal and had her heart in the right place. Anyone who didn't value those qualities was a fool.

The real question was, why did Declan want to make it up to Charlotte? Why did he care if she'd been hurt?

He was turning that thought over in his head when Charlotte grabbed for a loose line.

"Charlotte," he said in a warning tone. She didn't listen, probably because she did things for herself even when she wasn't sure what she was doing. She pulled on the tail of the line and of course it climbed right up the mast, as lines did.

"Wow." She tilted her head back and squinted up at the halyard. "That was not part of the plan."

He gave her a small smile. "Didn't think it was."

She sighed. "Tell me how I fix this."

Now it was his turn to sigh. "Maybe you let me fix it."

She shook her head. "My mistake. My responsibility."

He adjusted the sails, slowing the boat. "A quick pit stop and we're good."

Moving lightly on his feet, he moved up to the bow and dropped the anchor and chain, then let the chain pay out. The boat swung in a lazy arc, coming about as it slowed to a stop.

She watched him, suspicion all over her pretty face. "Are we stuck here? Because I have to go to work tomorrow, so this doesn't work for me."

"I'll always get you home, Charlotte." He toed off his shoes, following her eyes as they stared at his bare feet. "Ask nicely and I'll give you a strip show."

She rolled her eyes. "What are you really doing?"

He looked at her calmly. "Getting our halyard back."

"You're going up there? I'm sure I can figure this out." She looked at the top of the mast as if it were Everest.

"You don't need to worry about me." She worried about everyone else, as far as he could tell, so adding one more person to that equation was unnecessary.

"Really?" Her voice rose, concerned. "You're just going to climb up there and grab it? What if you fall?"

He locked eyes with her. "I won't. Promise."

The mast was maybe thirty feet. He'd climbed far higher. Hell, he'd fallen farther as a working stuntman. This was easy.

"Stop," she demanded. "I have a firm policy that no one else pays for my mistakes."

She surged to her feet, apparently determined to single-handedly prevent him from going aloft. It wasn't a big boat and Charlotte hadn't quite found her sea legs. He reached out to steady her, and the fact was, he didn't mind pulling her close. Not at all. She felt amazing even if she'd decided to punctuate her claim by stabbing him in the chest with her index finger.

More than amazing, he amended. It was embarrassing how much he liked holding her close like this.

"Charlotte." He kept his voice low. Calm. He'd figured out on day two of their partnership that Charlotte didn't like confrontation or conflict. "I've got this." He rubbed a small circle over her cheek. "So what if you let go? It's just a mistake. A small one. Okay?"

"Sure," she said, sounding uncertain. Damn it. Charlotte wasn't perfect. Fact was, she made mistakes. But so did he. A shocking number of mistakes, if he was honest, with the most recent one being the deal he'd made with J.J. to nail down his ownership of Masterson Entertainment. He'd spent years longing for his old man's recognition and appreciation, but he hadn't appreciated the freedom of not wanting those things. Winning this race had seemed like an easy way to seal his deal with the old man.

Mistake number one.

Mistake number two had been letting J.J. know just how badly he wanted the family company. He'd built that business for two years, developing a roster of new talent, crafting deals, taking chances on a script or two that no one else would green-light. It had just started to pay off and he had a team of guys who needed that work, who'd bet their careers on Declan making good on his promises. And it felt great to know that he had J.J. over a barrel, that the man couldn't renege on their contract as long as Declan won this stupid race. So he'd win, no matter what...

And that had led straight to mistake number three.

J.J. would think Charlotte was perfect.

He didn't like the thought of Charlotte getting drawn into J.J.'s schemes, even if she was getting something she wanted out of their deal—a whole lot of money for her charity. He hardly even registered that he had drawn her closer, gathering her up in his arms, slowly enough—or so he told himself—that she'd had plenty of time to object.

"I can't even with you," she muttered.

She didn't move away, though.

He noticed that. He noticed everything about her, which was an entirely different problem. Water slapped against the side of the boat, rocking them gently. *Very* gently. Charlotte promptly lost her balance, throwing her arms around him.

"I'm blaming you for this," she muttered.

With a head shake, he steadied her. Even through the life jacket, she felt warm and soft in his arms. Of course, she steadied him right back because Charlotte was a big believer in keeping things even.

"Is this okay?" he asked quietly.

She nodded.

"You have to say it."

"You," she whispered, then she pushed up onto her tiptoes, her mouth reaching for his. Good enough.

Her hands came up to cup his face and then she tugged him down toward her. He went willingly, wrapping his hands around her back, steadying her a second time as he braced them both. Slowly, to give her time to change her mind, he erased the space between them and kissed her. Soft. Careful. His mouth asking for something more.

She shifted back when the boat rocked, staring at his mouth, her gaze flying up to hold his. "Yes?"

"Yes."

Tucking her up against him, he kissed her again. She relaxed into him, letting her body rest against his.

"This is just to shut you up," she told him.

His own mouth curved in an answering smile. "Anything you want, Charlotte."

Turned out, what his lady wanted was *more*. She laughed and then she gasped when he kissed her deeper, nipping teasingly at her lower lip. He drank in the sweetly cautious sound, answering with a rougher, hungrier noise of his own, holding nothing back. There wasn't an inch of space between them and he liked that. Wrapping her ponytail around his hand, he lost himself in a kiss that was better than anything he'd ever felt before.

When he finally pulled back, her eyes were closed, a flush of pink on her cheeks and all of her soft and trusting. He held on to her, not ready to let go. And that led to another soft brush of his lips over hers and then *she* kissed *him*. Hot. Sweet. Letting him in more than he'd ever dreamed possible.

"Wow." She bit her lower lip when they finally pulled back and stared at each other. "That was something. It's a good thing we got that out of our systems."

As if. He smoothed her hair back from her face. "We're not done. All you have to do is tell me what you want. Anything you want."

She took a step back and dropped down onto her seat, pulling the band out of her hair and smoothing her hair back into a neat tail. She shook her head, her words coming out less than steady. "Fix the boat, boat master."

He winked. "As my lady wishes."

Anything you want. Charlotte replayed those three dangerous words in her head as Declan did exactly as he'd promised: what she'd asked for. He went up the mast effortlessly, the muscles in his broad back bunching as he climbed. In less than five minutes, he had the AWOL line secured and was making his way back down toward the deck. And her. The way he handled things made her feel safe, the sensation unfamiliar and too tempting, and as much as she hated to admit it, he made her want *things*. Declan-shaped, sexy, forever-sized things.

He secured the line once he had his feet back on the deck and turned to look at her. "You're in the driver's seat."

She absolutely wasn't.

He met her gaze. She wasn't sure he knew how to back down. "You are. You've got this."

She didn't, but she got up to sit at the helm.

"You want to talk about it?" He sat down next to her. "Or you can knock me overboard if you'd rather. Freeze me out the way you do everyone else."

She focused on the tiller. Maybe it was the rudder? She had no idea how people named boat parts, but the words on her list of sailing terms weren't easy to memorize. "I don't freeze people out."

"You do, but it's none of my business," he said slowly. "Not really."

She stared fiercely at a point on the horizon. "I don't have the best track record when it comes to men. I'm sure you've heard the stories by now. There are a ton, all embarrassing. I met this guy when we were both working at Martha's Kids. We dated, a real whirlwind romance, and he asked me to marry him. I said yes. We'd known each other for two months and it seemed so magical. Like a modern-day fairy tale. Here he was, my very own Prince Charming, going down on one knee and promising me forever."

Declan didn't look amused or surprised. He just nudged a line and nodded for her to keep going when it was embarrassing how much she'd already shared. "I'm not one to judge, obviously. You know the stories about my first proposal." His shoulder pressed against hers, warm and steady. "Let's just say that I did not get that right. Tell me what happened next?"

Confessing to Declan was a bad idea. The pictures of his failed proposal were everywhere and of course the locals had been interested when he'd agreed to headline the charity race. But even if he'd come off as impulsive and too playful about something she believed, deep in her heart, should be the decision of a lifetime, the actress's refusal had surprised many people. George's rejection, on the other hand, hadn't been unexpected. At all.

"He changed his mind," she said. "That's the long and the short of it. I wasn't what he wanted. So he broke up with me and left Martha's Vineyard. The end."

"Would you want him back?" The strong, warm shoulder pressed against hers a little more firmly and his hand covered hers on the tiller. "Because someday he'll realize he's made one hell of a mistake and he'll come back."

She looked down at his hand and hers. "That won't happen. Is that what you thought would happen with you and the actress? Or is this a heads-up that you're planning your reunion?"

"No." He shook his head. "I wouldn't be here kissing you if I were waiting for her to change her mind. Sometimes mistakes are just mistakes."

She nodded. "George didn't love me and thinking that he did was my mistake. He was charming. Everyone loved him. It was all so easy. So when he walked away *so easily*, I learned a few things and I won't make that mistake again. You and I—"

"Have a race to win," he said softly. "I get that."

He had no idea just how important winning was. "I can't afford another one-way relationship. So I need to learn how to sail this stupid boat and we need to race."

"And win," he said.

"Yes. Winning is very important. I wish—" What was that saying? If wishes were horses, beggars would ride. She recognized that she was headed into dangerous territory, so she switched directions. "We'd never be a real couple. I'm the boring, quiet local girl who will stay on this island her entire life and I'm good with that."

"And who am I?" he asked, sounding curious.

"You're our Hollywood Prince Charming. A star temporarily visiting. People expect you to be with someone like you. Your real girlfriend would be put together and beautiful, successful and glamorous. You can't force the pieces from two different puzzles together."

"A summer boy." He sounded unhappy.

"We come from two different worlds," she said. "Everyone knows that. And once the race is over, I'll stay here and you'll go back. To Hollywood. To your glamorous life with the, the—"

"The other movie stars and pretty people."

He leaned over and brushed a soft kiss over her mouth, his fingers sinking into her hair to hold her still. And she might have gasped—just a little—in surprise but she certainly didn't want to get away from him. The man was addictive, as was the smell of sun and salt on his skin. Golden, warm and present—three of her favorite adjectives—and she didn't want to let go when he released her.

"But I'm here now," he said, voice husky.

She nodded, because the man made a good point. She'd had a point of hers to make, she thought, floating in a sea of sensual warmth, but then he gave her another kiss and picked her up as if she weighed nothing, settling her on his lap as his arms closed around her. While she tried to remember why she'd wanted to argue, he sent their boat flying over the water.

The wind pushed at them, almost tearing the breath from her mouth even as it stung her eyes. But it felt so good. Sailing—*racing*—had been an unwelcome challenge, an obstacle to overcome, and the only solution she had left to fix her George-sized mistake. This, though… This made her feel alive and had her laughing at nothing in particular.

"Who are we racing?" she yelled into the wind.

"No one," he yelled back. "Everyone. But we're totally winning."

She shook her head. The man was crazy.

"Trust me." He tugged her a little closer, which should have been impossible unless they were naked and he was—she squirmed and he groaned. And then, "Charlotte?"

"Yeah?" she whispered, knowing that somehow he'd hear her despite the wind that whipped away the sound.

"Do you trust me?"

"Enough," she said, leaning back into him. Because it was true that she felt safe with him, safe in a way she never had with anyone, and not just because she was sure he wouldn't capsize them or let her fall overboard.

His mouth brushed over her ear. "Good," he growled. "Hold that thought."

She laughed and he kept his arms around her even as he did something that made the keelboat pick up speed until they were flying over the water, racing that invisible opponent as the wind pushed them toward the harbor.

Seven

Walking the red carpet had never featured on Charlotte's bucket list. While her childhood self had played dress-up, trading shorts and T-shirts for tulle, fake diamonds and three-inch plastic heels, that had been a game. Sometimes she'd been a princess; sometimes a movie star. Once she'd crowned herself the all-powerful ruler of the universe. The real deal was exciting and addictive, frightening and overwhelmingly loud—and that was from the inside of the limo she'd shared with her father.

The ride from the Palsgrave compound to the fancy resort hosting tonight's event had been too short. Their driver pulled into the wide, circular drive, joining a line of luxury town cars and limousines. The Vineyard loved its social events. The front of the hotel had been decorated with lights and swaths of flowers. Spotlights swept the night sky and an actual red carpet led past a phalanx of reporters and then up the marble steps and inside. Cameras flashed and reporters screamed as the occupants of the car preceding theirs got out.

She'd spent her entire life hiding in plain sight and yet here she was, about to walk the red carpet into a celebrity fundraiser. At least she looked every inch the princess she'd pretended to be as a child. A stylist had sent a vintage 1920s flapper dress the color of her favorite peonies. Tier after tier of pink crystal fringe swirled around her when she moved. It was whimsical and almost like walking in ocean spray. Delicate crystal-embellished Louboutin sling-back sandals and a clutch completed the outfit. She was an elegant, playful version of herself. Princess Charlotte.

Yes was a powerful word. She'd said *yes* to George when he'd proposed. *Yes* to the opportunity to crew a race boat. And *yes* to Declan's makeover plan that had upended her quiet life and sent her careening down a rabbit hole like Alice, except she'd landed smack in the middle of Declan's life—his Hollywood life—and not a topsy-turvy wonderland.

If she got out of the car, her life would never be quite the same again. She'd walk inside, holding up her end of the devil's bargain she'd made with Declan, and people would talk. They'd pay more attention than they ever had to Martha's Kids, attention that would make keeping secrets almost impossible. And while she'd always known the truth would come out, she'd wanted to fix the damage first. The limo inched slowly forward. She still had time to back out. Not much time, but enough.

The phone clutched in her hand buzzed and her father frowned as Declan's message flashed across her lock screen. Delayed—meet you inside, Princess. You've got this.

The publicist's original plan had Declan meeting the car to walk her inside. Now, she'd be flying solo since her father wasn't doing the red carpet and would be driven to a side entrance. "Declan's been held up," she said.

Her father shook his head. "He's not really interested in you. Why would he ever choose you?" He gestured outside the window at the hotel lit up like a fairy-tale castle. Even inside the car, she could hear the muted roar of the waiting crowd, a human ocean of people coming and going, rushing in to meet the new arrivals and then chasing out after them. "You're a convenient prop, an accessory. He's a Hollywood star who dates glamorous women." When she made a noncommittal noise, he continued. "There's that sex scandal he was involved in before he came here— the man scaled a balcony naked to propose to a woman he barely knew. He'll never settle down. He'll always be hunting for the next new face. Watch. He'll have moved on by the end of the race and he'll have some movie star or famous model on his arm by then."

What her father meant, she thought, was that a woman like Charlotte couldn't hold a playboy's interest and that Declan's interest in her would fade. That was fine, she told herself. They weren't a couple—they were partners with a common goal. Partners were good. Partners were *better*.

"Perhaps I chose him," she said. Because that was a possibility, too, wasn't it? Declan had a choice, but so did she. She had to choose him, too. Her father shot her a dry look, but she ignored it. Or tried to. Some things were still a work in progress.

The car stopped and someone opened the door. The flash of cameras blinded her. Declan's lessons rushed through her head: Smile. Don't stop for questions. Don't go off script.

She got out of the car and paused as an army of men and women in discreet black suits directed the flow of celebrity traffic and corralled the photographers and curious summer tourists. An honest-to-God red carpet led toward the ballroom, but first she had to make it past the media. The click of their camera lenses sounded like a thousand cicadas chiming in at once.

She reminded herself that she liked cicadas just fine.

Funny, but her pulse still sped up, straight into heart attack territory. Mentally, she drew up a list. Step one: get out of the car. Done! Step two: shut the door. Or did she leave that for the driver? Hadn't Meghan Markle gotten in all sorts of trouble for closing her own door? Next: do a discreet check to make sure her dress wasn't caught up in her panties. Then: Take the first step. Take the next.

Repeat that last one a thousand times and she'd be inside and under cover. It was a great plan.

She managed half of one step before a minder rushed over and started hissing instructions to her. Walking—and stopping—was more complicated than Charlotte had imagined it could be. She told herself that she might not be a Hollywood princess, but that tonight she looked like one. She even had a loaner Prince Charming somewhere and it would be downright rude to keep him waiting. Fun, but rude. She grinned at *that* thought and that was the picture that would run tomorrow, her rueful, laughing, too-real smile as she fast-walked past the people waiting for her and the other stars of tonight's celebrity event. *Welcome to Declan's world*, she thought.

Declan snuck his sports car into the employee parking lot before heading into the hotel through the back entrance. The place was bustling, the event well underway. Glamorous guests dressed in expensive cocktail attire and a fortune in jewelry packed the ballroom and he spotted dozens of famous faces.

A week of pouring rain at a shoot site had forced Masterson Entertainment to rethink the final stunt sequence for a major film, a problem that had compounded when the leading stuntman had been injured and the rain had stopped unexpectedly. A replacement stuntman and fire hoses had saved the shot, but the negotiations had delayed Declan's arrival. He strode through the crowd, acknowledging greetings and looking for Charlotte.

He'd wondered if she'd balk at doing the red carpet alone and ask her driver to take her around back to skip it, but from early reports she'd done well, displaying the same quiet courage she'd shown on the water. He found her at the edge of a small group of guests, smiling politely.

Pink was the perfect color for her. Her hair had been pulled up in a sleek twist on the crown of her head, baring her neck and shoulders in lines that were as elegant and classy as the woman herself. The dress hugged her curves and showcased her long legs, strands of beads twirling out around her when she turned to greet a newcomer. He'd teased her that she was a princess, but tonight she was all queen.

The stylist had originally pulled a classic ivory sheath for her, pretty and soft, and entirely forgettable. But *he* couldn't forget her, and he wanted everyone to see Charlotte the way he saw her, a surprise no one had seen coming.

Snagging a flute of champagne from a waiter, he walked up to her, setting his hand against the small of her back and offering her the champagne.

"You shouldn't have," she said.

He grinned. "You want to make a list of all the reasons, don't you?"

She shook her head, but took the champagne. "Thanks so much."

He eased her away from the group. "How are we playing this?"

"Asking for my advice?"

"You're good at planning," he said lightly. "And we're on the same team."

"True." She cast an assessing gaze around the room. "The rules give us a one-minute head start on race day for every ten thousand dollars in donations we bring in tonight. So we can either pitch the big donors or try to hit as many groups as possible."

"Or we can bring them to us," he said, plucking the champagne flute from her and handing it to a passing waiter.

"With what? A nice hunting call? Here's a tip," she mock-whispered. "People generally run the *other* way when they're asked to hand over their money."

"With a show. Follow my lead." He wrapped his arms around her back and dipped her low. Her hands fisted in the lapels of his tuxedo jacket. She looked surprised. And unsettled. But she didn't look away from him and he couldn't stop looking at her, either, partly because she was stunning and there was nothing between his palms and the smooth, warm skin of her back. Mostly, though, because he wanted her to realize that he wanted nothing more than to peel her out of her dress and show her exactly how she made him feel.

He kissed her lightly, a brief brush of his mouth over hers, there and then gone as he righted her. Then he twirled her in a circle that sent the beads on her dress flying as he reached for her hands, bringing them to his mouth and brushing another kiss over her fingers. "Beautiful, partner."

"Thank you," she whispered, sounding as if she didn't believe him one bit.

A camera shutter clicked softly nearby. She drew a deep breath. The audience made her nervous, as if it somehow changed how he saw her, as if she had to perform to someone else's expectations. He'd meant it when he said she was beautiful.

The photographers called out their names, urging them to turn first in one direction and then another. Together. Arms around each other. Embracing. No one asked for a solo shot—their kiss had done the trick.

"That was ridiculous," she muttered.

"Window dressing," he said. "Watch. Now they'll all come to us because they're curious."

He was right. Guests walked up to them and introduced themselves, smiling and posing for the ever-present photographers. He knew the event's organizers were glad to have his name, his famous face and the movie star power—because that was the point of a fundraiser. Charity wasn't inexpensive and no foundation ever had as much money as it wanted. He liked Martha's Kids' focus on providing kids with a specific summer experience rather than vaguer, loftier goals like *promoting independence* or *developing lifelong skills*.

Charlotte turned out to be shockingly good at steering him toward various groups of guests, although he gave her credit for not just picking the ones with the deepest pockets. The newest couple was a pair of summer residents, one of the many who flocked to the Vineyard during the summer months. She was the CEO of an online yoga start-up, while he managed a hedge fund on Wall Street. Wealthy, but not recognizable celebrities, they were starstruck.

"Declan loves kids." Charlotte directed a smile at the wife's obvious baby bump. "It's why he's passionate about supporting Martha's Kids."

"Kids are great," Declan agreed. "I'm sure we can all agree on that. It's too bad, though, that not all of them have the same opportunities—and that's where Martha's Kids comes in."

Charlotte launched into a charming explanation of her

foundation's summer programs and the kids they served, while the couple smiled and nodded.

"Summer camp is my happiest memory from childhood," Charlotte said.

"I was always the homesick one," the man laughed. "I pestered everyone at home constantly, asking when I could leave."

"Not me." Charlotte shook her head, making her sleek ponytail bounce. "I would have stayed forever if they'd let me."

"Did you go to summer camp growing up?" the husband asked, looking at Declan.

He slid the man a look, but it appeared to be an innocent question. "No. I was in and out of foster care when I was younger," he said. "Summer camp wasn't an option for me, but I would have loved what Martha's Kids offers. Every kid should have the chance for campfires and marshmallows, canoes and arts and crafts. Working in Hollywood, in the industry, as a stuntman was a lot harder and far less safe. You realize this when you're on your first set, at the top of a steep hill and the director's yelling for you to just ride your bike down it as if God's angels will lift you up if you crash."

"Did you?"

"Sure." He lifted one shoulder. "And one of the production assistants patched me up afterward. We got the shot, so it was a good day."

The dad-in-training looked like he might be taking notes for his future baby. "So you started as a stuntman?"

"And then transitioned into acting. Met a lot of people, learned a few things." Which was an understatement. He hadn't wanted to trade in on the Masterson name, wanting to earn his place. "I'd go into an audition in the early days, cocky and sure I had what it took, and then I'd take a good look around the room and see that casting had ordered up a dozen men who looked just like me. Twenty of us like matching roses in a bouquet, all in beat-up jeans and a white Oxford shirt. You learn fast that you're replaceable."

"But you're not replaceable," the guy pointed out.

"Not now." He pulled a face. "I had to work hard to get to that point and I'm not complaining about that. But I learned fast that, at the end of the day, the problems you face on-screen are make-believe. The real problems are what the kids whom Martha's Kids sponsors face. Home-lessness, poverty, parental addiction, hunger—they're overcoming the hard stuff, which is why Charlotte and I are racing. And also because I know I'm damned lucky, like they're lucky, to have her on my team."

He winked at Charlotte, who picked up his story without missing a beat.

"Although he would have been a nightmare to keep safe." She grinned, nudging his shoulder companionably with her own. "This passion of his for climbing and stunts didn't just develop overnight. Imagine an eight-year-old Declan in one of our kayaks."

There was more laughter and then the pair shared a few summer camp hijinks of their own. Declan laughed and smiled. Then he stopped watching their companions and started watching Charlotte. She radiated a genuine and warm interest in their stories, and their audience re-sponded to that, even if she wasn't the loudest or wittiest member of the group.

"Remember," he said when a natural break in the con-versation came. "By donating tonight to the race fund, you're giving a summer camp experience to other kids—and every ten-thousand-dollar donation made to our boat specifically buys us a minute's head start on race day."

"And we'll need that extra time," Charlotte chimed in. "Because I'm better with kayaks than keelboats."

She smiled ruefully, everyone laughed, and then the

couple broke out their phones and brought up the mobile giving app. They took pictures together before he and Charlotte moved toward the next group of people.

"You're good at this." He deftly swapped her warm champagne for a new, chilled glass.

"Keep thinking that," she warned him. "Because here comes trouble."

The man approaching them wasn't Declan's usual brand of trouble, either the movie kind or the paparazzi kind. He was middle-aged and wearing a tuxedo and a broad smile.

"Are you ready?" he asked.

"Always," Declan said. "But specifics would be appreciated."

"To lead off the dancing," the event host said. Charlotte merely nodded pleasantly at the man, unsurprised. His partner had been keeping secrets.

"You've been holding out on me," he said as they followed the host toward the dance floor.

Charlotte's mouth curved upward in a smile. "Consider this payback for every time you've put me on the spot."

"Right." He stared at her mouth. "Tell me what the plan is, please?"

"Can you dance, Hollywood?"

"I'm no Fred Astaire, but I can waltz. Tango. There may have been Irish line dancing on one memorable evening in Dublin."

Her smile deepened. "How about a rumba?"

"Charlotte." The woman standing opposite him laughed. "Revenge is beneath you. Be the bigger person."

"Just follow my lead, *Hollywood*."

She set her left hand on his shoulder and grabbed his right with hers. So far, so good. He hated not being able to just dive in. Hanging back was not how he'd lived his life. The music started, a Latin sound, upbeat and fast with lots of string. He slid his free arm around her back as every eye in the ballroom turned their way.

And just when he was starting to think she'd leave him standing there clueless, she whispered instructions to him. "Make a box. Two steps to the side and then one step forward. Slow, quick, quick. And, Hollywood?"

"Yeah?"

"Wiggle your hips. A lot."

Right. He scanned her face, far too aware of the tiny shifts and tensions in her body that announced her next steps. Dammit. But he loved the amusement lighting up her eyes, the smile on her face. And the bold curve of her mouth was downright beautiful, so stare-worthy that he would have missed a step if he hadn't had excellent reflexes, honed by years of performing dangerous stunts.

"Are you sure you've never done this before?"

"You're my first." He winked and what the hell... He spun her in a circle. And then another. He had no idea what he was doing. Oh, wait, he did. He was taking her up on her dare and he was winning this game.

This earned him a raised eyebrow and then she upped her game, adding spins and a sensual wiggle to her own hips that drove him wild. Desire tightened his body and had him fantasizing about stripping that dress off her and worshipping each delicious curve of her body, because it turned out that his wallflower partner who hated the spotlight could really, really dance. And when she danced with him, she forgot all about their audience. He mirrored her gestures, adding a few embellishments of his own as they danced on.

"We fit together," she said, laughing up at him.

We fit together...

She was right, he realized. Her eyes were heated, happy, as she enjoyed the moment, caught up in this thing between them. She wasn't thinking about their audience or the race. He'd have bet on that. She simply danced with him and it worked.

And losing that rightness scared him more than anything.

The music swelled and other couples joined them, turning the ballroom floor into a sea of twirling bodies. He only had eyes for Charlotte.

"You're beautiful," he said, his grip tightening on her hand as he twirled her. "But you've got to be the hardest worker I know."

Her lips parted. "Wow."

"All true."

And then the steps had them moving apart again and any more conversation wasn't happening. She beamed at him as the music ended, flushed and happy.

She grinned at him. "See? You can dance."

He pulled her up against him and grinned back. "I had an excellent teacher."

And then he lowered his head to hers and kissed her. They'd never discussed kissing, but this felt right, too. She raised up on her toes, fitting herself into his embrace, and kissed him back. She kissed like they'd danced, a slow, slow, quick that took them from an easy awareness to burning passion. A slow tease of his tongue against her closed lips was followed by the slow, teasing way she opened up for him and let him in. The quickening of their breath, the instant heat, the seductive, possessive need that raged through him... He didn't care who was watching them, not when all of him was focused on the sexy woman he held in his arms.

The applause called him back. The event host approached to congratulate them, trailing a photographer.

"That was just for our audience, right?" she asked, stepping back and putting some space between them.

He recognized the wariness in her voice and, dammit,

he shouldn't have kissed her in public. She'd made it clear she wasn't dating anyone, let alone a movie star.

"It was a hell of a show," he agreed.

Except that kiss hadn't been fake.

Not completely.

Eight

Declan had stopped being impressed by wealth long ago. The Palsgrave compound overlooking the ocean barely registered. The night sky, a velvety swirl of stars and clouds, would have been worth a second look, but they weren't alone. Dammit. A photographer waited for their car in the shadows lining the driveway, camera up and ready. Good quality shots earned hundreds of dollars, but a unique picture would net thousands. Word must have got out in the hours since their "kiss."

"We have a photographer doorstepping." He kept his voice low, grateful that the windows of his luxury Mercedes were tinted. "He's waiting for you to come home, hoping to snap us together."

The possibility of a romance between him and Charlotte would have paparazzi bombarding the house. He pulled out his phone and fired off a text to his security service. Charlotte would need protection.

She shrugged. "I'm not that interesting."

He hated her easy dismissal of her own worth. "You are to me."

She pulled her evening wrap around her and picked up her clutch, not waiting for him to charge to the rescue. "Is that the new movie star math? If I'm interesting to you, then I'm interesting to your fan club out there?"

"Something like that," he said. "We need to get inside, Charlotte."

She rolled her eyes. "Since I'm not happy about the prospect of living in your car forever, yes. I do."

Before he could point out that they were partners and it was therefore a question of *we do*, she opened the door. Cameras went off in a blinding flash of light. Charlotte froze, but he was already on it, striding around the car to slam her door shut even as he put himself between her and the paparazzi.

"Come on." He squeezed her fingers gently. *Work with me.* "Let me walk you inside."

The photographers were calling her name now, demanding she look their way. There were two others he hadn't spotted, in the shadows where the security lights didn't reach. They must have parked on the main road and then walked in.

"Charlotte, are you dating Declan?"

"Is there an engagement between you?"

"Are you moving to Los Angeles?"

"Does your former fiancé know you're having an affair with a movie star? Is that why he broke it off?"

"Will you resign from Martha's Kids?"

"When's the baby due?"

"Are you kidding me?" She whirled, clearly intending to set their unwanted company straight, but the first rule he'd learned in Hollywood was *never engage*.

Pulling her into his side, he brushed her ear with his mouth. "Front door or back? What's the fastest way in?"

She gaped and he bit back a curse. She wouldn't like these pictures. The crunch of gravel behind them announced new arrivals. They needed to move.

"You got your shot, man," he said to the nearest photographer, then tugged Charlotte up the front steps, taking her bag from her and fishing out a key. He held it up for her to see. "Yeah?"

She nodded, he got the key in the door, and then they were in. Frankly he'd expected Bryant Palsgrave to have a butler. The man seemed like the type, an impression borne out by the ostentatious entryway. A mahogany staircase with an elaborate wrought iron balustrade swept upward to the second floor. There was marble tile and more marble on the walls. An antique console held a lavish arrangement of white roses and expensively furnished rooms were visible through an archway.

Beside him, Charlotte muttered a curse of her own. Which, for the record, he hadn't heard her do, even after his showboating at the charity event. "How could they say those things?"

"It's their job. They're fishing for a reaction because reactions sell. You in a pretty dress?" He shrugged. "They snapped that at the charity event. Now they're looking for me stripping you out of the dress or a kiss. Something that will make people look."

"So they make up a baby? And a ring?"

"Yeah," he said. Did it make sense? No.

It didn't have to.

He stood there longer than he should have, trying to not think about those things. With Charlotte of all people.

She wasn't for him.

He wasn't the kind of man who did forever and he certainly hadn't seen any examples of what a good marriage might look like. J.J. had already been divorced when he'd adopted Declan and Nash and he'd never remarried.

Declan's own parents had split up before Declan's birth and Nash had a different father. He'd grown up poor and then he'd worked like hell for his place with the Mastersons. A fancy house like this one?

He didn't belong.

Which didn't stop him from remembering how that angry, resentful eight-year-old boy had felt when he'd been swept away from the latest in a long series of foster homes and dropped into J.J. Masterson's Malibu mansion. He'd worked hard to earn a place there and he'd succeeded. Almost.

Good times. Even now, years later, he still had plenty of resentment, resentment that made him restless and eager to get the hell out of Bryant Palsgrave's stifling mansion and back to his own home in the Santa Monica Mountains. He breathed better outdoors and Hollywood was a short drive away by California standards.

Charlotte shifted and he looked at her. Right. It wasn't her fault that her father was a pretentious ass and it was *definitely* Declan's fault that she was now trapped in her own home by paparazzi.

"Away from the windows." He nudged her gently.

She snorted but started walking. "This isn't one of your movies. Girls like me don't go out with guys like you."

"What's wrong with me?" He'd bet she had a list.

A long, rank-ordered list.

He followed her into a palatial living room with massive wood beam ceilings and a sea of white furniture. A sheepskin rug had been layered over a vintage Persian rug in front of a brick fireplace and French doors looked out onto a pool, a manicured expanse of lawn and the Atlantic Ocean. It was hard to imagine anyone actually sitting in here. It looked like a movie set, something he was an expert on.

Charlotte sank down onto the closest sofa and tugged

off her heels with a groan. "You're so Hollywood. And I'm not."

That wasn't a bad thing. Sinking down onto his haunches before her, he rocked back onto his heels and caught her foot in his hand, then rubbed the arch. "You've got a chip on your shoulder about the whole movie star thing, don't you? There's no reason why we couldn't be together." So what if they came from different backgrounds? And so what if he had a high-profile job while she stuck firmly to behind-the-scenes work?

"If we're talking about sex," he continued. "Because that's just fun and not a fairy tale or a country song. I wouldn't fit into your pretty life here either, not for long."

She sighed and collapsed backward on the sofa. "Is that what you think? That sex is just fun?"

He tugged gently on her big toe. "If you haven't been having fun in bed, there's your problem."

This earned him a glare. "I can have fun."

Not exactly what he'd said, but okay.

He switched to her other foot. "We should talk more about how fun sex is because right now, all those photographers outside think we're having sex."

She groaned. "We're going to have to disappoint your fan club. No baby, no engagement, no public sex."

He grinned. "So just sex in private? Because I feel the need to point out that we seem to be totally alone right now."

She tugged her foot free and stood up. "Opportunist much?"

He wasn't much of a gentleman, but he got to his feet, because she was in a dress and…she deserved all of his respect. "They'll keep trying to find a romance between us. It's a good story. They'll run with it."

"It's both ridiculous and untrue."

"It's good press," he countered. "We'll get plenty of positive coverage. Donors like happy love stories."

J.J. would like it, too, as long as Declan kept things G-rated and stuck to the fairy-tale script. A Hollywood movie star who raised money for children and fell in love with an unassuming local girl? That was story gold, and he hated that he recognized that truth even if he had no intention of acting on it. He wasn't that much of a bastard.

"We're not pretending to be in love to hoodwink people into supporting us."

"Let them take their photos and speculate that we're a real couple," he argued. "We don't confirm or deny. Eventually, they'll lose interest."

"When I'm dumped for the second time," she pointed out. "Still not seeing how this is a win for me."

"Just for a little while."

"Nope," she said. "No, not a chance. Been there, done that, didn't even get a lousy T-shirt."

"Well if all it takes is a T-shirt," he said, "that can be arranged."

She had to kill him. Bury his big, beautiful body somewhere no one would ever find him. *The movie star? Nope. Got no idea where he went.* Ugh.

She strode over to the French doors trying not to think about what he'd suggested—either the sex or the fake relationship.

"Right," he said, following her. "We can try to find some other way to sort this out, but they'll run the kiss from tonight's event, plus what they snapped outside your place. I took you home and they'll fill in the blanks after that."

The entire Vineyard would be convinced that she'd fallen in love with another handsome guy. Half the locals would plan her fairy-tale wedding, while the other half would predict she'd crash and burn.

Again.

Just months ago she'd been sure George was her person and he'd taught her a very public lesson about trusting too fast. Ever since, she'd tried to fix the destruction he'd left behind him because she was the only one who deserved to get hurt. She wasn't proud of keeping silent about all the ways he'd betrayed her, but the district attorney had asked her to keep silent while they investigated. Plus, it didn't make her a person she was proud to be and that was the truth.

She wanted to tell Declan to leave now—to walk away from her and Martha's Vineyard. But that would mean abandoning the charity boat race. Losing her chance to make Martha's Kids whole. Being dumped publicly a second time because of course she and Declan couldn't possibly be a real couple. They'd list the ways she'd been lacking. Even now she couldn't think about George without a deep, sickening feeling of humiliation. She did *not* want to do that again, but—

The bastard sensed her weakening because he said, "We can't go back in time, sweetheart, but this can work to our advantage. It won't be all bad. We'll race and then we'll go our separate ways. Things will calm down."

"Have you really thought this through? Because while you'll get to put an entire country between yourself and the breakup, I'm the one who has to stay here and explain to people I see every day. It will be very, very bad."

"We don't have to break up publicly. We can just—drift."

She snorted. *Was he delirious?*

"Think about it," he suggested. "For now, let me walk you back to your place. You're in the guesthouse, right?"

"What do you think is going to happen to me?"

He met her eyes with a level gaze. "The paparazzi could scale the wall. They could find some way in before my team gets here."

"I don't need a babysitter or a bodyguard."

"I know you think that," he said calmly. "But I have more experience with this lifestyle and I want your life to change as little as possible. My team is discreet. They'll stay out of sight unless someone gets in your face."

Lovely. Now she felt ungrateful. And yet... "This wouldn't have happened if you hadn't decided I needed a makeover. And then kissed me. In public."

"It would have happened. Because I've never met anyone like you and the degree of attraction between us isn't something I know how to manage. You're gorgeous. I want to put my hands all over you, and sooner or later, someone would have caught me doing exactly that."

Charlotte stared at him, speechless as he opened the door for her. That wasn't her usual end-of-date conversation. She replayed it in her head as she stepped through the door and headed for the guesthouse tucked between the main house and the ocean. Surrounded by boxwoods in antiqued urns, billowing pampas grass and lavender, the dark rectangle of the pool reflected back the lights of the house.

She made a shooing motion with her fingers. "You can go. White knight rescue duty done for tonight."

He grinned. "You don't want to kiss me good night? Or tell me that was a great speech?"

She sighed. "I thought the whole point was to make the stories go away?"

"This is a photographer-free zone," he said. "It could be our last chance."

The man had a point, but she didn't want to kiss him. Much. Plus didn't photographers have long-range lenses and sniper-worthy covert hiding skills? Years ago she'd toured Althorp House in England. An excited guide had recounted the grand romance between nineteen-year-old Lady Di and the Prince of Wales, noting that the room with the piano had been the only one the photographers couldn't see into. Lady Diana Spencer had spent a lot of time there. It had seemed unbearably sad to know that an entire estate was outside the door but she was trapped in a single room.

Declan put a finger beneath her chin, nudging it up. "So are we good?"

"Absolutely," she lied.

He frowned. "We're not."

"So fix it," she challenged. "If you think there's a problem."

He studied her for a moment. "There's definitely a problem. You think I only want to kiss you because everyone thinks we're in a relationship."

"Yes!"

No. She bumped her forehead against his warm, muscled chest. The real problem was that she'd already used up her mistake allowance for the year—possibly the century. Declan was nothing but risk, a charming, bad boy actor even if he was turning out to be unexpectedly thoughtful. They'd race in a week and then part ways. She wouldn't see him again, not this all-too-real man who looked at her with concern on his gorgeous face.

"So I like the way you kiss. Sue me."

He gave her a heated look, laughed…and didn't kiss her. "I've got an idea. Maybe you don't guess what I want. Maybe I tell you."

There was a serious note in his voice that she hadn't heard before.

"What would you tell me?"

Wrapping a hand around the back of her neck, he tucked her against his larger body. Her arms went around his back. He felt so good. Safe. He felt like everything she'd been missing.

"Might be easier to show you," he said roughly. A new, delicious kind of silence stretched out between them. This was the last moment of *before* because, whatever came next, things would change. For better, for worse. For pleasure.

His head lowered toward hers. "Please?"

She nodded. "Yes."

And then he erased the very small space between them and kissed her. Gently. Slowly. As if he wanted this to last for so much longer than a kiss ever could.

She kissed him back, moaning when he deepened their kiss. He made a rough sound, his fingers sliding into her hair. They kissed until they had to break apart for air. She sucked in one breath, then a second, staring at him, wide-eyed.

His own gaze was heated and far from calm. "Christ, you make me want."

"Declan," she whispered, the sound swallowed up by his mouth as he kissed her again.

Guilt and panic flooded her because it was one thing to race with this man, to fight and to sail with him. She could even let him dress her up and dance her around the floor at a Vineyard social event. Those things were easy. It was entirely different to kiss at her front door, to feel as if for this handful of moments he saw her and no one else. This was too real. Too much.

She'd rushed into a relationship too fast with George. Maybe if she'd gone slower, insisted that they take their time, she'd have seen the truth. Sooner. Maybe even from the beginning. George hadn't loved her and she—well, she'd loved the *idea* of him more than the man.

But then she wasn't thinking because Declan braced an arm by her head, leaned in and kissed her more, and her brain stopped functioning. She could only feel. *Oh, God.* He made her feel so much. His mouth, his big body pressed up against hers, the addictive warmth of him...

At some point they must have come up for air again because she opened her eyes and Declan was leaning into her, one arm still caging her in place, one hand cupping her face. His thumb stroked her cheek. He tasted like ocean, outdoors and male, and he made her want things. She was off-kilter, off-balance.

Freaking out.

She couldn't do this again. Handsome Prince Charmings didn't fall for the plain-Jane wallflowers—they faked it to conceal an ulterior agenda.

"There aren't any photographers here," she said, then ducked under his arm. "There's no need to pretend."

"You really think that was fake?"

She sighed. "You and me... We're a bad idea. Even if you kiss like a god and I really like it."

Like you.

"But?" His eyes narrowed.

"But I can't do this. I can't be someone I'm not."

He tugged her back. "I don't need you to be different."

"Makeover?" she prompted.

"That was a game," he growled. "Icing on a cupcake."

His words were lovely, even if she wasn't sure that she could believe them. Did she have a trust problem? Yes, yes she did.

He didn't look away. "I'm not George."

She opened her door. "I know that."

"And you're not Jessie," he said gently.

"So?"

"We're Declan and Charlotte."

She really, really needed to go. "I'm not ready for that," she said and went inside and closed the door behind her.

Nine

Charlotte still wasn't ready the next morning. Thanks to Declan's stylist, she had a brand-new, luxury wardrobe of sustainable cashmere and strict orders to never, ever leave the house in yoga pants again. The stylist had left a tag on one item and Charlotte had just about hyperventilated. Even if brands donated their clothing in exchange for the publicity, she directed a nonprofit and those were crazy prices.

As she came around the house, she mentally reviewed her Saturday to-do list. With the addition of the race events and practices to her usual work week, she was behind. And with no coffee or coffee creamer left in her kitchen, she had zero chance of catching up, so she was a woman on a mission when a man stepped away from the side of the house and blocked her path.

"Ms. Palsgrave." He followed this with a tip of his chin. He wore a dark suit and tie, and although his size put him in lumberjack or football territory, he also seemed qualified to be a club bouncer or a former SEAL.

She smiled her most reliable, I'm-a-trustworthy-person smile at him. "Are you a court bailiff? Because if you are, I already shared everything I know with the district attorney."

"Not what this is about." The man's professional expression didn't waver. "Mr. Masterson sent me."

She stared at him.

"I'm security, Ms. Palsgrave. I'm Ryan."

"I really don't need a bodyguard."

He fell into step beside her. "Have you been out front this morning?"

"What's going on?" When she stopped, he stopped with her.

"Mr. Masterson said he explained that in light of the paparazzi already outside your house last night, he expected there to be more this morning."

She eyeballed her new companion suspiciously. "Was he right, Ryan? One-hundred-percent, no asterisks right? Because if so, I have complaints."

This earned her a bark of laughter from Ryan. "He usually is, ma'am. I'd like to review the situation with you and run some options if you intend to leave the property today."

"Ryan." She waved her empty travel mug at him. "I'm not a prisoner in my own house. All I want is coffee. I promise that I am supremely boring and anyone who is out there will lose interest fast."

Ryan tapped his phone screen and brought up a series of photos from in front of the house. She counted one, two, six—no, make that *seven* guys in jeans and T-shirts with expensive-looking camera gear. They were all staring at the front door with far more interest than it merited.

"Coffee," she said. "It's what makes the world go round."

Okay. So it was really the trifecta of coffee, chocolate and doughnuts, but a man with Ryan's build probably didn't acknowledge the existence of sugar.

Ryan tapped something into his phone and hers buzzed. What kind of coffee do you want? Declan asked.

She ignored the warmth spreading through her and concentrated on her righteous indignation. "Did you tattle on me?"

"My job is to keep you safe."

Uh-huh. Because she was just surrounded by vicious predators. And also because she was a delicate flower who needed protection. Since that wasn't a battle she could win, she settled for tormenting her celebrity faux boyfriend. A good man would know how his girlfriend takes her coffee.

The text she received back said, I can buy one of everything, but then it'll take twice as long. Ryan says you're desperate and to come and save him.

As if. She snorted, eying her new nemesis, who hadn't budged from where he blocked her easy access to the outside world.

"You should let him bring you coffee," Ryan said. "Mr. Masterson has done this before. He knows how to handle the press."

"*Mr. Masterson* got caught scaling a balcony in his boxer briefs. How does that make him an expert?"

Ryan shrugged. "It makes him an expert on what not to do. And I wasn't working that night."

Right. "Were you working last night?"

"No, ma'am."

"What kind of coffee do you want then?"

After Ryan had been convinced to place a coffee order, she texted Declan back with their requests. She wasn't stupid enough to turn down free caffeine delivery, even if she was stupid enough to kiss the man in a very public place.

She received another text that announced, Be there in ten.

And then, proving once again that Declan had mind-reading powers, he sent a picture. Of Gitty's bakery truck.

I'll kiss you again if you bring a half dozen, she texted.

Not that she really planned to trade her virtue for muffins, but Gitty's baked goods were amazing. She and Gitty had been friends since childhood and Gitty's muffins had only gotten better with time.

"Come on back," she said to Ryan. "We'll wait by the pool."

As soon as she sat down, however, he disappeared back into the shadows. Not that there were many shadows as it was morning, but the man had mad skills. While she waited for Declan, she got on the internet. Last night's event had drawn lots of coverage, with multiple celebrity gossip sites running pieces on the "clinch" between her and Declan. There were photos, too—photos in which she almost didn't recognize herself, so his celebrity makeover lessons must have stuck more than she'd thought.

In one shot they were laughing and the lighting somehow made them seem as if they stood in a golden spotlight. The beads of her dress had caught on his arm and the expression on her face—

She looked dazed. Swept off her feet. Drunk on the man holding her in his arms. Was there a twelve-step program for people with addictions to handsome charmers?

"I should have pushed him overboard when I had the chance," she said to herself. Ryan wisely remained silent.

Her email inbox overflowed with messages from people she hadn't talked to in years, asking if it was true that she was dating the movie star Declan Masterson. Some wanted introductions, while others pitched scripts. Her fifth-grade teacher had acting aspirations.

A buzz of sound rose up from the front of the house. People shouting and calling things, among them Declan's name. She tried not to listen to the questions too hard because they were all variants on last night's horribly embarrassing interrogation. A few long minutes later, her father's housekeeper showed Declan out to the pool. He held a cardboard tray of coffees in one hand and a bakery box in the other.

He passed her a coffee, then offered her the box. She tore it open because, as last night's pictures proved, she'd already misplaced her dignity. Gitty's muffins were the ambrosia of breakfast baked goods and Declan had been true to his word. He'd brought her six muffins—and a caramel brownie.

"I'm considering accepting his apology," she told the muffins. "Even if you brought your evil twin, Mr. Brownie, with you." She picked a muffin out and bit in. Oh, God. Had she moaned out loud?

Declan laughed. She totally had.

"Why a brownie?" she asked around a mouthful of muffin.

"Muffins are just cake masquerading as a health food." He smiled wickedly. "So why not just eat cake?"

She looked in the box. "But you brought me muffins and a brownie."

He held up a paper bag she hadn't spotted, probably because he'd kept it hidden. "I'm saving the cake to bribe you with."

He handed a coffee to Ryan and then sat down opposite her, hands wrapped around his own cup.

"So," he said.

Her stomach dropped. Was the press coverage that bad that he felt the need to ease into it?

Or did he just feel guilty because he'd been the one to dip her into that clinch and he was the movie star? "How bad is it really, on a scale of one to catastrophic?"

"It depends on how you look at it. And I do mean you. Not me, not Ryan, not your dad or anyone else. The story is great for the race. It gets eyes on our race cause, people are donating and it's reading as romantic."

"The story being how your famous self swept a local girl off her feet in a whirlwind Hollywood romance?"

He winced. "Yeah. That part. Honestly, they'd like it even better if one of us was royalty and had a castle."

"Can't help you there," she said. "We're short on castles in New England."

He eyed her cautiously. "It will mean attention. The reporters will run what they can and dig into your life. It's not as if you've done anything newsworthy or embarrassing, so the digging won't get them far. At the end of the day, we're just two people who shared a dance and maybe a little more. They'll run the pictures from last night on a loop while they try to get something more interesting. As long as we both keep our clothes on and don't do anything stupid—"

"Like climb a balcony naked," Ryan interjected.

"—it will be fine," he finished.

She had a feeling that her having dated a soon-to-be-indicted embezzler probably wasn't going to fly under the radar. Should she break the district attorney's demand for secrecy and tell Declan? Not yet, she decided. Not until after she'd made a phone call and asked if she could.

"Actors and actresses date outside the industry," Ryan offered. "It's actually not uncommon at all. People like who they like and as long as you two don't do anything new to draw attention, things will calm down."

She studied him. "How do people live with that kind of scrutiny? And I mean, how do they really live with it? Can you even go out and buy toilet paper like a normal person?"

Declan shrugged. "It's one of the price tags on getting the chance to do a job I love and that matters to a whole lot of people. Plus, it doesn't always happen overnight like this. You sort of get eased into it and don't realize it's happening until you make a midnight run to the convenience store and get snapped in your pajamas. Ryan's the best and he knows how to shut things down when interest in my girlfriend gets out of hand."

"Fake girlfriend," she said. "And how much does Ryan cost?"

"That doesn't sound like a no." He nodded to Ryan and the bodyguard strolled away. Apparently like all men they spoke a secret language. "And I've got the cost covered. Don't worry about it, okay?"

"I'm new in this fishbowl. Be gentle."

He grinned. "I can do that."

She was *not* going to think about that. "But is it always this bad?"

"Not usually," he admitted. "But there's an upside." He held out his phone so she could see it. The race organizers had set up a set of cutesy thermometers, one for each boat. As donations came in, the thermometers filled. Declan and Charlotte's thermometer was completely full now, when she knew for a fact that it had only been half-full yesterday afternoon. Last night's kiss-and-flirt strategy had borne fruit.

"Tell me what you want to do," Declan said. "I know it's a lot to ask, living with paparazzi. If you want to pull the plug, we can."

"You'd quit the race?"

His eyes held hers. "If that's what you want, yes. I'll quit. It's your call. I can put out a statement. We can find you a new partner."

"Why did you agree to participate?"

"J.J. asked me to do it," he said. "It mattered a whole lot to him and making him happy had some upsides for me."

Right. She sucked in a breath. "I don't want you to disappoint him."

"Just tell me what you want," he said again.

That would be a very long list. "I can't pretend I'm going to like having all those people watching us, thinking they get to weigh in on what we're doing. But I'm thinking it's time I stopped explaining so much. Even if I like playing by the rules and having a plan, I think there could be a time to not do those things."

"Fortunately," he said, "I'm an expert in operating without a plan."

"Right."

He shrugged. "So maybe you should just go with your gut. Fly by the seat of your pants. Live life planless."

"And be your fake girlfriend and race partner?"

"Yeah." He was smiling at her again, and damn but he was hard to resist. "And my first official act as your fake boyfriend is to invite you on a picnic. Date me, Charlotte."

Charlotte's life was neat and predictable, with no room for tall, handsome movie stars who got mobbed by paparazzi and who kissed indiscriminately at public events. *Get used to it; you can't take back kisses and it's just a lunch with a guy who's practically a business partner!*

"Food," he coaxed. "Even better than muffins."

That was an outright lie, although she'd bet that the movie star version of lunch did not involve her beloved—and budget-friendly/spill-proof—PB&J. She looked back at her not-boyfriend and wondered how well she could pretend that she was comfortable with his luxury lifestyle. *It's not weird; it's just lunch and you can get through it. Free food!*

"Lunch with my hot fake boyfriend? Of course, we'll have to actually leave the house and I'm apparently under house arrest."

"All I'm hearing is *hot* and *arrest*," he said lazily.

She rolled her eyes at him. "Don't tell me. Your favorite fantasy costume is the naughty cop."

He mimed zipping his lips, which was a problem because the man's mouth was dangerous, open or shut. She'd learned last night what he could do with those lips of his when he wanted.

"Come on." He got up and held out his hand. "Brave the horde out front with me and I'll feed you. Put something in your stomach besides sugar and caffeine."

"Those are the most important food groups." She had a horrifying revelation. "You're not one of those California healthy living advocates are you? Because that's grounds for an immediate breakup."

The bastard actually laughed.

"I do whatever the part requires."

She waved a hand. "But does it ever require doughnuts? What's the point of being a star if you can't eat what you want?"

He laughed more, so of course she followed him, and leaving her own house was even more of a production than she'd imagined. The photographers had multiplied like bunnies, but without the cute factor. These were jostling, shouting, downright rude rabbits.

Declan's mouth brushed her ear. "Say nothing."

No problem. Given that she had goose bumps from just that little touch, she was fine with taking a perpetual vow of silence. Declan guided her past the paparazzi, directing a polite smile and a "no comment" at the yellers. Better yet, Ryan somehow turned himself into a human wall, deftly inserting himself between the cameras and the two of them. In less time than she'd thought possible, Declan was handing her into his sports car. She took a deep breath and yanked the door closed.

"Good to go?" he asked her, sliding into the driver's seat.

"Yes," she said. "I'm also fine with fleeing, running away and driving like a maniac."

She decided not to think about getting back into the house. Somehow, it was hard to worry when she was riding shotgun with Declan, probably because the crazy wild chemistry between the two of them was a greedy thing that left no room for other feelings.

Declan seemed to know where he was headed, so she just enjoyed the ride and the scenery, both inside the car and out. He radiated strength and she amused herself by making a little mental list of all the things to admire about him: A pair of powerful forearms bared by the shirt he'd rolled up above his elbows. His thighs in those damn blue jeans. And—she might have leaned forward *just* a little— the pair of black, beat-up work boots he wore. He'd flashed her a smile at that one, but it was worth it because her list also included his sense of humor, his willingness to listen and his insistence on looking out for the people who came into his life, even if they were temporary additions.

After he'd made a quick pit stop to pick up a picnic basket, a covert exchange behind one of the Vineyard's fanciest hotels that had her looking over her shoulder for spies or hit men, he took her to a private beach. She knew it was private because a half dozen signs and a security guard said so. Feeling a bit like a trespasser, she slid him a glance as they were waved in.

He grinned. "Called in a favor."

"Right," she said lightly. "Because you're best friends with the rock star owner?"

"Producer owner. We've worked together."

Great. He knew movie producers and rock stars. She loved her life. She did. But moments like this just reinforced that in his world he was a on a first-name basis with famous movers and shakers, while she might peep at them for five seconds in the local coffee shop.

The private beach was a creamy stretch of sand squeezed between the ocean and sand dunes. Other than four white Adirondack chairs lined up to take in the view, there was nothing but sand, the tide washing in and some impressive bluffs at the far end.

She immediately kicked off her sandals and pointed to his feet. "Take them off."

"Woman, you keep trying to get me naked."

She laughed. "You're wearing far too much clothing for the beach."

"You know you could just ask me to undress? For you, the answer would be yes." He toed his boots off and tossed them onto a chair, holding his hand out for her own sandals which he set more carefully next to his.

"So what's the beach plan?" And then when she gave him a sideways glance, he shook his head. "You know you have one. We'll work you up to going fully planless in baby steps."

"Walk first," she said. "Then we eat all the food."

"Got it," he said and tugged her down the beach.

After a few minutes, she repossessed her hand. She assumed it was automatic on his part, but her glamorous new haircut was in no way windproof and she had hair in her mouth and her eyes—possibly up her nose, too. She twisted her hair up, securing it with a hair tie she'd had the forethought to stash on her wrist.

And not an elegant twist or a fancy chignon. Nope, she wound it like spaghetti on a fork and let the ends flap free. It was at-home, sweats-and-a-T-shirt hair, but Declan just tucked an errant end under the tie and smiled. "Pretty."

The casual gesture made her feel shockingly good.

They wandered down the beach, poking at interesting piles of driftwood and letting the chilly surf foam around their ankles. She picked through the shells mounded at the hide tide line, slipping a particularly pretty scallop and a pearly moon shell into her pocket. Heat tingled through her when he threaded his fingers through hers as they made the return walk back up the beach.

A black SUV that she assumed belonged to Ryan was parked next to Declan's sports car, but the bodyguard himself was out of sight—probably not far though.

She and Declan spread out a plaid blanket on the sand and he grabbed the picnic basket.

"Let's start with dessert. Just in case we get interrupted."

He shot her a lazy grin. "By paparazzi?"

"Sure." She tugged at the basket he was holding. He had promised to feed her, after all. "Or an alien space invasion, the apocalypse, whatever. Give."

This earned her a laugh, but he set the basket down and flipped open the lid. Then he pulled out a huge, chocolate-filled plastic clamshell. "A backward meal? I like it. But be warned—I know the secret to winning your heart now."

"You started it," she said. "When you brought cake for breakfast."

Okay, so Declan had actually only handed over the six muffins and their brownie best friend, but he'd claimed to have cake.

It turned out that *cake* actually meant *cupcake*, but she could work with that, especially when he handed her a plastic fork. He'd planned well for a man who claimed to hate planning.

Ignoring the teasing glint in his eyes, she dug in. And moaned. He laughed. "What? I have sunshine, the ocean and delicious cake. What more could a girl want?"

He rolled over onto his stomach and rested his chin on his arms, watching her. "I have an idea."

She pointed the fork at him. "Nope. No sex talk."

"Who, me?"

Yeah, him. He was such a problem. She wished that the breeze that kept the summer air from getting too hot would do something for her libido. She ate her cupcake and tried to figure out a solution to her Declan Masterson-sized problem.

The source of all that heat rummaged in the picnic basket, pulling out his finds: Cold lobster rolls with thick chunks of pink-and-white lobster in white rolls. Plump strawberries. And Boston cream pie cupcakes, because her movie star not-boyfriend definitely knew his way to a woman's heart. She tried to find something to be irritated about but, really, he'd gotten everything exactly right. After he'd made her a plate and then served himself, they lounged on the blanket and he told her stories about the film industry.

"How did you get into acting? No. Wait." She made a face. "That has to be a question you've answered hundreds of times."

"I've never told you."

"Was it something you always wanted to do?"

"I liked the stunts," he said. "Never met a dare I wouldn't take. I was that kid who jumped off roofs and rode his bike down the crazy hill while standing on his head."

"Did you really do that?"

"Jumped off the roof at my elementary school, jumped out of my bedroom window twice, jumped out of the belfry at church…"

She stared at him. "How are you not dead?"

"Excellent reflexes. Sheer luck," he said promptly. "Although the belfry thing did not go well. I thought I could rappel down the outside hanging on to a bell rope, but it turns out the bells were all on some kind of automated system and a computer rang them. I'm sure you're shocked to hear that everyone thought I was a natural fit for the whole stuntman thing. Which was convenient, since J.J., my father, owned a production company. He was very popular on career day at school because he specialized in blowing things up."

Turned out, Declan was good company. He asked questions about her own work and then told more stories about stunts gone wrong and ridiculous director demands. He also had plenty to say about actors who thought—wrongly—that they could do their own stunts without any training. He was far more self-deprecating and aware than she'd given him credit for. She found herself blushing more than once because he'd been places and met people, accomplishing things that most people only dreamed about.

"Why are we even here having a picnic?"

"I'm feeding you." He passed her the last cupcake, proving he was at least a gentleman.

"But *why*?"

Laughter danced in his eyes. "Maybe I like taking care of you. Maybe we were both hungry and you'd eventually need to eat something and yet there you were, trapped by paparazzi and it was all my fault. Are you always this suspicious?"

"I'm never suspicious and that's a problem."

"So you trust me completely?"

"No. I don't trust you at all, but I'm terrible at remembering to question what people tell me. I don't fact-check. Why would I go around assuming everyone is lying to me until proven otherwise?"

She threw up her hands. Unfortunately she was still holding a cupcake, so instead of making a point, all she accomplished was painting a streak of frosting down her cheek.

"See? I'm a mess. All the makeover lessons in the world are not going to turn me into a glamorous Hollywood swan."

"Charlotte," he groaned, swiping his big, warm fingers

over the frosting tattoo she'd given herself. "You're wearing your cupcake."

His thumb swept over the corner of her mouth.

She froze. Was he—

"You're a perfect mess," he said and it didn't sound like a complaint. At all.

Then he pulled her into his big, warm body and kissed her.

Ten

There was kissing and then there was *kissing*, the kind that made a woman forget where she was and all the reasons that kissing a man back might be a bad idea. Sensation zigzagged through her body, warming her belly and other parts of her. He coaxed greedy sounds from her mouth as her hands tangled in his hair, Charlotte holding him close because this was amazing and she wanted more. She tasted frosting and the sea, sunlight and something warm and male that was all Declan. She didn't hold back either, which was part of that trusting-too-much-and-too-fast problem that she had, but how could she resist? Everywhere they touched, there was heat—and they were touching *everywhere*. It was crazy how much he wanted her, and that was before she pushed him back onto the blanket and he rolled her on top of him.

Flashing her a happy grin, he wiped the rest of the frosting off her cheek with his thumb. She laughed—and kissed him again.

Her heart raced because if he was this good at kissing, what else was he good at? And how could anything feel better? Kissing Declan was like a scene from one of his movies, and yet she knew this was really, really happening. Her knee pressed against sun-warmed sand where she'd slipped off their blanket, but her other knee was tucked against his hip. With all of him stretched out beneath her, she could feel his interest—and he had a whole lot of interest going on.

"I want you." He said it straight out, tipping her chin up so he could see her eyes. He didn't hesitate.

"I want you, too." Truth. Her voice caught in her throat as he adjusted their fit together, bringing her flush against him. She could move away, she knew. He wasn't holding her any tighter than she wanted—and that was another problem.

"Are you sure?" he asked and she came back to reality faster than she would have liked. The kissing was so perfect, as was the holding and the way he fit her against him.

"You mean right *here*?" The sand was warm and they were allegedly alone, except possibly for the invisible Ryan, but sex with a movie star on a beach might be too adventurous for her. *Sex with Declan*, her libido teased. *You know you want to.* Her brain, however, refused to turn off any longer. *You're on a beach! Sand! Paparazzi! Public witnesses!*

"Just kissing today," he said. His thumb rubbed the corner of his own mouth and came away with icing he must have kissed off of her. The heated look in his hazel eyes said he didn't mind. He licked his thumb.

"That sounds like a good plan." She tried to straighten up, to shift herself off him to a safer distance.

His warm hands tugged her back down, sliding up her back and beneath the cashmere cardigan. Calloused fingers skimmed up the line of her spine and then back down again, tracing patterns on her lower back.

"You feel so amazing here." He drew a small circle and she shivered. "And here."

His fingers moved upward, exploring the curve of her waist with lazy intensity. When he drew his fingers slowly upward, he rolled their bodies again so that he came down over her, bracing an arm beside her head. The pressure of his body on hers made her arch upward, had her making space for him between her legs because that felt even better than his kisses. She wrapped her legs around his hips as he bent toward her again, his mouth tasting the sensitive skin of her throat. With him holding her right back, she got lost in his kiss.

When he pulled back with a rough sound of pleasure, she stared up at him. "Wow."

"Yeah," he said. "Definitely wow. Too wow. We're not doing anything you aren't ready to do."

"Believe me," she said, "I like doing this with you. Consider me one-hundred-percent on board with this kissing plan." But what if it wasn't as good for him as it was for her? She should ask, shouldn't she? "But what do you want to do?"

"Everything, Charlotte. I want to do everything with you."

Everything sounded amazing.

Everything sounded perfect.

She breathed out and tried to marshal her thoughts. Her eyes got a little starstruck looking at him. Kissing Declan was crazy. A magical kind of crazy. No one had ever made her feel this way, and pretending to love him would be far too easy.

"But we don't have to do this fast," he said.

That was the worst plan she'd ever heard… Every inch

of her—and quite a few inches of him—were voting *hard*, *fast* and *right now*.

"We can take our time," he added. "And Charlotte, I'm going to need a *lot* of time to appreciate you right."

She laughed. "I'm not that complicated—plus you're clearly on the right track."

He sat up, gently depositing her on the blanket beside him. "I'd like to get this right, even if right now I feel like eating you up and racing right through all the talking and getting to know you stages. Going to bed with you will be amazing."

Will be—not *would be*.

She could tell from the way his eyes darkened that he was thinking about it—imagining the two of them in a bed, starting with kissing and ending with all the delicious, dirty things the two of them could imagine. But he was right that some things shouldn't be rushed. Plus, they'd both rushed into their last relationships and she couldn't bear to repeat that mistake.

"You're good at this," she said.

"You certainly make me want to be." He brushed a light kiss over her mouth. "Come on. Let's get you back to town."

"Race prep," she agreed. "We need to win this thing next week."

He tugged her carefully to her feet. "You bet."

Somehow, though, she felt as if she'd lost.

Eleven

Charlotte sat in the *Cupcake* and tried not to think about the ways today could go wrong. The little boat that Declan had christened after last week's kiss flew across the water, the start line well behind them. *Think positively.* They had a ten-minute head start thanks to their fundraising efforts, so they'd not only started at the favored end of the line upwind but they'd avoided getting stuck in a pack of boats. They had a written game plan for how to sail the racecourse and she'd memorized the sailing instructions provided by the yacht club—and stashed her race binder in the aft storage locker just in case she needed a refresher. Her one job was to monitor the VHF radio on the race channel. Both she and Declan were wearing non-inflatable racing PFDs over their sailing kits so even if she did fall overboard, she'd float. And the man himself had one hand on the tiller and the other doing… Well, she didn't know what he was doing because she still hadn't mastered the finer points of sailing.

She tightened her death grip on the boat as it surged forward and the race start line swung back into view as Declan tacked them into the wind and *Cupcake* shot ahead. The rapid change of direction made her stomach lurch. But knowing that nineteen other boats and sets of racers waited behind them for the starting horn, she welcomed every drop of speed Declan could coax from their boat— especially since they had nine hours of sailing in front of them. The race course would take them around Martha's Vineyard and the first boat to cross the finish line won. Winner takes all—there was no prize for second. Thanks to the dark clouds piling up on the horizon there almost hadn't been a race today. The ocean was equally unset-tled, waves slapping harder and harder at *Cupcake*'s sides.

Her brain unhelpfully flashed her back to that other summer day, the one where the ocean had done its best to kill her. She'd been splashing around in the shallow water when another kid had dared her to race out to a moor-ing buoy and back. Once she'd got to the buoy, tapping the white ball enthusiastically, she'd discovered she was alone. A quick squint back toward shore had revealed a mostly empty patch of beach as everyone had been lured elsewhere, likely by the promise of s'mores and hot dogs because they'd been on a picnic and those things were fun.

By the time she'd shoved off the buoy and headed back toward shore, she'd been tired—and caught off guard when she'd ended up in a riptide. And possibly she'd panicked and tried to compensate by kicking harder for the beach. Maybe she would have remembered in time that you had to swim diagonally to get out of a rip current, that there was no brute-forcing your way through it, but she hadn't.

So no, she didn't love being out on the ocean. She loved the Vineyard, loved the dunes and the rugged shoreline. Dry land was awesome and it was home, even if a rather terrifying amount of ocean surrounded it.

Declan watched her calmly. "Are you doing okay?"

The man saw too much. His job here was to be the pretty face and muscle, a job at which he excelled. He wore dark cargo shorts in some kind of quick-dry material that hugged his thighs, a sailing jacket with the race logo and a high-tech T-shirt that stretched deliciously taut over his powerful chest and shoulders. Sunglasses hid his eyes, but she knew amusement sparkled in them. Amusement—and something else. She hadn't decided yet if that *something else* was affection or caring or just good, old-fashioned lust.

"Just fine," she lied.

His lips twitched. "I can go faster."

"Wasn't that the plan?"

"Didn't know if it was in the binder." A smile teased his mouth.

"Planning is important," she said. For instance, in addition to the PFD cinched around her waist, she'd dressed in multiple race-crew-approved quick-dry layers because her internet research and their practice sessions had taught her that sailing was wet and not infrequently cold. She probably looked like a sausage, but at least she was a room-temperature sausage.

"Sure is." He adjusted something, and dear God, they were, indeed, moving faster. "Ride's going to be less smooth, though."

"The goal here is to win. You do know that, right?"

"I do," he agreed. "Just thought you might like to work up to it."

It being the mind-numbingly, terrifying speed that the *Cupcake* achieved under his command. When she finally opened her eyes, Charlotte couldn't quite drag a full breath into her petrified lungs. Wind tore at her mouth and nose.

Okay, so she still had some oxygen, but how Declan could laugh as if this was his idea of a good time, she had no idea. Two hours later, she remained clueless. She'd spent the time shifting from one side of the boat to the other at his calm orders. Once she caught sight of sails behind them, but for the most part they were alone on the ocean. Declan was, she grudgingly admitted to herself, good at this. She was coming to think they'd win and then they'd—

She didn't know what came next, other than somehow weathering the storm that would break when George's felonious behavior emerged. People would blame her, rightly. She'd been all in favor of hiring him and then she'd dated him. Agreed to marry him. Trusted him too fast and too much. Hopefully the prize money would alleviate the worst of the hurt for her kids.

She used the next hour to sketch out a mental plan. She'd deposit the check, there would be revelations and then, well, she wasn't *quite* ready to watch Declan sail out of her life. The man might be irritating and arrogant, but he was also dependable and rock steady. Not everything was a race with him and part of her was disappointed that they hadn't gotten as far as bed yet. Okay. So she knew exactly which parts those were—some very good, very fun parts of her anatomy—but her head and her heart liked how he wanted to take them slow and not rush things.

By the time they'd dodged the ferries that kept Martha's Vineyard connected to the nearby islands, the wind was pushing them along and the channel currents ran fast enough in the sound to have Declan keeping a very watchful eye out. Maybe, she thought as she shifted yet again at Declan's low command, she might just take a chance—a small, manageable, not too publicly risky chance—and ask him to do something with her after the race. Not a date. Like… Okay, so exactly like a date. A chance to explore a normal relationship with a man she liked and found attractive. Could you have a normal relationship with a movie star? What would they do if they weren't bickering or engaged in a little bit of semi-friendly competition?

The clouds piling up on the horizon now were green tinged and the air had a heavy, expectant feel, not least because fog had started settling between them and the shore, hiding her view of dry land. She'd memorized the map as if knowing the landmarks and the depth soundings would help when she no longer knew where she was. The ocean needed street signs.

"Are we still ahead of everyone?" she asked. They'd only had a ten-minute lead and Declan wasn't omnipotent, no matter what his online fan club believed.

"Not what I'm currently worried about," he said.

"Maybe you could tell me this story has a happy ending."

He gave her a look. "We're going to be just fine."

At the sound of the calm assurance in her voice, she shook her head. "Are you lying to me? Because I've heard that tone before and it always means that I should expect something to go epically wrong."

"No shit," he said.

"Are we okay?"

His voice gentled. "Okay, so the ending will be fine. I promise. The middle may get wet and rough."

She waited for full-on panic to strike, but something about Declan had her pressing pause on her anxiety. And she might not have been big on trust—or trusting her own abilities to get herself out of a sticky situation—but he just calmly did the next thing. And then the next. She managed to take the yellow rain slicker he passed her without visibly freaking out.

"Find the local weather broadcast." He nodded toward the VHF radio. She wished it was a magic teleporter and not basically a walkie-talkie connecting them to the yacht club and the Coast Guard, but, well, she'd make do. She fiddled with the radio, found the right channel and listened in disbelief. The sort of storm they were predicting sounded both sudden and apocalyptic. She switched back to the race channel, checking for new transmissions from the race committee. Sure enough, they were warning the competitors to tune in to the weather channel.

"Don't they call these things off if the weather is bad?"

He nodded. "Sure, but I've sailed through worse."

She narrowed her eyes. "That doesn't help." And then, because it was like inching past an accident on the highway where she'd try not to look but her eyes would go there anyhow, she had to know. "Like what?"

"Hurricane-force winds. Frostbite race on the Chesapeake Bay that turned out colder than four layers of fleece could handle. Wall of water hit the boat once and we heeled over until I was kissing the sea."

"You know what?" she said. "Forget I asked."

"Right," he said. "But you're overlooking one key point."

"What would that be?"

"I was on each of those boats and now I'm right here."

"So you're a bad luck charm!" She threw up her hands. "I should throw you overboard like they did that guy in the Bible."

"*Good* luck," he corrected. "Or, more accurately, lots of practice and experience. I've done this before and I've got this. I've got you. Okay?"

"I'm not really okay about any of this," she said honestly.

"Trust me?"

She'd certainly tried not to. Her trust track record was a series of crashes, wipeouts and epic fails, so his ask was a big one, one she'd been fighting for a while now. She met his gaze and he smiled, the corners of his mouth tipping up as if there was something even remotely happy about their current situation. And yet… Of course he would take care of her when no one else had her back. Because that's who he was.

She tightened her grasp on the edge of the boat just in case. "Okay."

When the thunderstorm started she was still saying *okay*, but the word was a substitute for the F-freaking-bombs she wanted to drop and had a much higher pitch than normal. No amount of bad weather sailing videos on YouTube had prepared her for the reality of a small keel-boat in the middle of a thunderstorm and she was starting to have serious doubts. The *Cupcake* rose and fell, her prow slapping hard against the water and sending spray everywhere. The whitecaps had whitecaps, for crying out loud, and the increasingly stronger gusts of wind made her feel like they were headed nowhere fast.

"Charlotte?"

"Yeah?"

She tried to find a silver lining. Maybe that the lightning hadn't struck them? She counted that as a win. It made the hail that was bouncing down seem downright benevolent. And hey, the hail was merely pea-sized and not the golf ball–sized monstrosities that dented up the Vineyard's cars and roofs indiscriminately. This was totally manageable, even if it felt like she was being attacked by a swarm of icy killer bees.

"You know I won't let anything bad happen to you, right? I'm still right here with you." He gave her a small smile, which was totally inappropriate, in her opinion. If ever there was a moment to panic, now was the time.

"Are you God?" She stabbed a finger in the direction of the purple-and-green clouds—which were no longer on the horizon but somehow overhead and simultaneously all around them.

"You'll be okay," he repeated.

She groaned. "I'd feel better if we were having this conversation on dry land."

"Yeah," he said. "Me, too."

Well. Crap.

A new gust of wind jarred the *Cupcake*. The radio squawked feebly. The race officials had apparently misjudged the rapidity with which the storm would hit. They'd expected the racers to be around the island, heading into the final stretch before bad weather struck, but that seemed less and less likely.

"Since I'm still working on my trust issues," she asked, "how anxious should I be right now? On a scale of one to ten?"

He adjusted the sails some more. "I've run worse races."

"But those were bigger boats, right? With an entire crew of people who actually knew what they were doing?"

"You know what you're doing," he said. "You've got one job right now."

"Right," she shuddered, grateful for her water-resistant layers. "This is where you tell me it's to trust you. That's not working for me, although it's a cute line."

"The worst race ever, we had lightning strikes landing all around us and each time I touched the tiller, I got a shock."

"Did you let go?"

He gave her a level look. "I held on when I had to."

The thunderstorm/apocalyptic avalanche of rain wasn't letting up, though. Even she could tell that. After another eternity of minutes, he turned them toward the island. "We can make a run for shore or we can try to speed up and outrun the weather. I'm voting for shore."

"Did they call the race off?"

"Not yet."

"But—"

"It's just a race," he said. "And while they'll likely call it soon, I'd feel better if we played it safer now."

She couldn't help but notice that *safer* didn't seem to mean *slower*. Or *calmer*, *less nauseating*, or any one of a dozen other words she would have preferred to use to describe their situation. Instead, he sent them flying faster and faster over the water, driving the *Cupcake* toward the island.

The boat dove sharply and she lurched sideways, off-balance. Her feet slid on the water-slick deck and her view shifted abruptly from Declan's concerned face to the water, and suddenly she was staring at the waves. Which were far too close.

Declan cursed, barking out an order to hold on. *Too late*, she thought, *but a really good idea.*

The boat pitched again and then she was sliding fast, fast, fast toward the edge and going over. At first all she could see was water. She'd sworn to make no more choices she would live to regret, but that promise didn't cover this situation. God, she was going to drown for real this time. If she'd known that dying was the plan, she'd have gone for it with Declan, spent less time working and more time doing other things.

Living, for instance…

She went under, the wave closing over her head, and she panicked, unsure which way was up. The PFD wasn't enough. It felt like she'd been jammed inside an enormous washing machine and God had pushed the button for the Rinse cycle. Her heart pounded and her lungs shrieked in warning as her oxygen supplies dwindled faster than she'd have thought possible, making her regret all the time she'd spent on board talking rather than breathing.

She was going to drown.

There was no other option.

A powerful arm hooked around her waist and pulled

her inexorably upward, or at least in the same direction as the body attached to the arm. She let it happen.

"Charlotte!"

She choked on the water in her throat. Salt water stung her eyes. God, she needed to breathe. To get out of the freaking water. "Where is the boat?" she wheezed out, sucking in air.

Declan pulled her to him as another wave closed over them.

"Breathe in and hold," he ordered. "Close your eyes."

She did exactly that, clutching his arm as the relentless water crashed over and over them. *Don't breathe in. Don't drown.*

He pulled them both back up to the surface, angling her until her back pressed against his chest and he was between them and the next wave.

"This is what we're going to do." He turned them and then he locked an arm around her chest, towing her with him as he swam in long, powerful strokes.

"Swim for the boat?" she asked hopefully. She looked, but she couldn't see the boat. For all she knew it was just on the other side of the waves battering them.

"We're going to swim for shore. The boat's flipped by now and righting it will be exhausting with just the two of us."

"Fantastic. And shouldn't we stay with it? In fact, why didn't you stay with it?" She tried to look over Declan's shoulder, but he was too big. And there was just water, water and more water because apparently she'd fallen overboard into the nightmare version of the *Ancient Mariner*.

He grunted and surged forward in the water. "You went overboard."

"And? We didn't both have to drown."

He groaned. "Are you trying to convince me to ditch

you in the middle of the ocean, Charlotte? Because it's not going to work. I promised you I'd stick with you. Yeah?"

She expected him to point out that it was her fault they were alone in the middle of a very pissed off ocean, but he didn't, possibly because they were—okay, so mostly *he* was—swimming for their lives. Recriminations would come later. She started kicking her feet. "Okay."

"Great. Charlotte?" And then when she nodded, and might have whimpered just a little, he said, "Your job here is to hang on to me. You don't let go. I don't let go."

"That's it?"

He swam for a long moment. "Here's the plan. No more talking. Save your breath for when I've got you ashore and then let me have it. Yell. Cry. Whatever it is you want to say, I'll listen."

"So shut up and swim?"

"That's the plan."

It was one thing to fall off the boat, an involuntary action, one that she couldn't stop once started. It was another thing entirely to keep swimming. The waves never stopped battering them and she lost count of the number of times water closed over her head. *Don't stop swimming. Kick your feet. Declan's not worried.*

Not that she really knew what he was thinking.

She felt better assuming and he talked to her, despite the *no more talking* part of their plan. He told her that they were getting close, that she had this, that he could see the shore and a Four Seasons hotel. She might have called him out as a liar on that last one, but instead she swam and she tried to do her part, blocking out the regrets that beat at her. Imminent death had a way of making a girl think about what she hadn't got around to doing. She wished she'd taken a chance on Declan. Taken a shot at *them*.

When her arms and legs flagged, he growled in her ear, "Don't quit on me, Charlotte."

"Not—" she sucked in sea water, coughed it out "—princess? No cute but annoying pet name?"

"You keep trying until we get to shore, I'll call you whatever you want."

True to his word, he didn't let go.

Twelve

Declan had never believed that life emulated the movies or that the intensely physical stunts he'd mastered for that work had practical applications. Today, though, he drew on all that training and then some, pushing his body through the waves, pulling Charlotte with him. It was the hardest thing he'd ever done and not because of the twenty-minute swim in grueling conditions. Keeping Charlotte safe was more important than anything. He'd promised her, and he wouldn't be the next person to break a promise made to her.

Charlotte was clearly terrified. She hated deep water, hated being forced to depend on him to get her to shore. He got that. She made him feel vulnerable, too. Because for once it wasn't enough to be the strongest or the fastest, the most disciplined or fearless. He could shoot a gun, drive at near-suicidal speeds, fall from almost any height and work an explosion. What he didn't know how to handle was Charlotte.

She wasn't fearless, but she fought. She let him take

the lead, but then she played an amazing best supporting actress.

When his knees hit solid ground, he told himself he felt
nothing but relief. He'd hoped for some elation and, even
better, for the next step in this not-plan to reveal itself to
him. Instead, the sickening fear that he'd failed Charlotte
almost kept him there on his knees. There were so many
things he should have handled differently, from not calling
the race sooner to relying on the race committee for historical weather analysis. The sudden storm had blindsided
him. And then she'd gone overboard and he'd abandoned
the standard protocol of trying to bring the boat around to
pull her out and just gone straight after her.

He staggered upright, setting her down beside him but
keeping an arm wrapped around her. The cold pebbled
her exposed skin.

"Just a few more steps," he lied.

She gave him a look. "And then there's a heated SUV
waiting to whisk us off to a luxury hotel for a spa day?"

Okay, so she understood more than he wished she
did. Rather than answer, he tugged her toward the beach,
moving swiftly through the surf that swirled around their
knees. The rain had finally started to ease up, but now they
were out of the water, cold would be a big factor.

"You got any idea where we are?"

"Lost. Shipwrecked. Auditioning for a really bad TV
reality show?"

She was trying to put a good face on things. He admired
that about her, although he wished like hell that she'd been
wrong on the first two counts. The narrow strip of beach
hadn't come with a convenient street sign. He'd also have
taken a parking lot, or any sign of civilization at all. Instead
he got wet sand bordered on one side by the still angry
ocean and a marshy inlet on the other. He saw reeds and
grass bending in the wind, a bedraggled lot of seabirds

hauling ass overhead and more rain. What he didn't see were lights, human habitation or a solution. His current best option was a rather stunted tree fifty feet up the beach.

He drew her up the sand toward the tree because something was always better than nothing. His years in the foster care system had drummed that lesson into him. They had the clothes on their backs. They hadn't been blown off course to Canada or Cuba. And—he patted the dry bag clipped to his cargo shorts—he still had his wallet and his cell phone in its waterproof phone case. Unfortunately, when he pulled it out, he didn't have service.

"Hey," he said, gently tugging her underneath the tree. It had gray bark that made him think of elephants or seals and the branches offered some protection from the rain. She sank onto the sand and he bent down to look her in the face. "Stay here a moment for me, okay?"

"You want to define *a moment*?"

At some point they needed to talk about why she thought people either wouldn't choose to stick around—her ex-fiancé came to mind—or wouldn't come back for her, but now wasn't that time.

"I promise I'll come back, but you're cold and tired and I can do this quicker on my own, which is better for both of us. You've fallen off a boat, swum for your life, and that SUV didn't get the memo or it would be here, so let me take care of this, okay? Let me take care of you, Charlotte."

"You did all those things, too," she said, but she sat down on the sand where he indicated, wrapping her arms around her knees. She'd lost her sailing shoes and crew cap during their swim, but the rest of her was still covered in layers of quick-dry fabric. "I'm okay. Are you okay?"

"Yeah." He pressed his mouth against her cheek, not liking the way she shivered or the paleness of her skin. She was tapped out. "Hang on for me."

"Go." She waved a hand. "Find us a rescue party."

He considered her for a moment, then draped his own, larger sailing jacket around her. "As you wish."

After the longest ten minutes in the history of time, Declan jogged back. Charlotte was happy to see him, as her already low tough girl reserves were frozen through and through. She hadn't even started to process what losing the race would mean.

"You still okay?" he asked. She didn't know what he expected would have changed, but she warmed at the concern in his voice. Given her current state as a sea salt–flavored human popsicle, she'd take that warmth.

"Okay enough," she said grimly. "And—thank you." She grimaced. "For coming after me. For sticking with me."

"Jesus, Charlotte." He stared at her. "You need to work on your expectations."

Sure. She'd do that later—after she'd warmed up all the way and could forget just how close she'd come to dying. *Again.* Since she preferred not to think about near death, she made a give-it-up gesture.

He sighed. "You want the good news or the bad news?"

For the record, she *never* wanted bad news.

She looked around them but, nope, no Four Seasons had miraculously sprouted while he'd been gone. She also didn't see a car or any other sign of a rescue party. "The bad news is that we're still lost and shipwrecked. Oh, and we're out a million bucks, so perhaps we should start hunting for buried treasure."

A smile lit up his face. "Yeah, but that's also familiar news. The good news is that I found us something better than a tree."

"Hey," she said, patting the tree trunk. "Don't malign him. He's doing the best he can."

"You want a lift?" He patted his back. "Hop on."

She shoved to her feet, shaking her head. Of course she wouldn't let him carry her. He'd already dragged her butt to shore, so she needed to pull some weight here. "I've got this. Where are we going?"

He gave her an assessing look, then nodded slowly. "Not far."

He tucked her into his side, putting himself between her and the wind that blew off the ocean and straight through her wet clothes. A hundred yards up the beach, he cut away from the shore and through the dunes to where a weathered set of wooden steps cut through the sand. The thunderstorm was moving off, but so was the daylight.

The weathered house perched at the top of the steps. *Shack* might have been a more accurate description as it looked as beat up by the elements as she felt, with shingles peeling off the roof and a wide, wraparound porch full of ancient rattan deck chairs that listed suspiciously eastward and downward. She spotted no lights and, more disappointingly, no cars. They were still on their own.

Declan tugged her up the steps and straight to the front door, where he proceeded to bang hard enough to make the frame shiver and shake. She wasn't surprised when no one answered. The Vineyard was dotted with summer places, owners coming and going as life and their work schedules permitted.

"You might want to turn your back," he suggested. "If you're squeamish about felony B and E."

Beggars, choosers and all that. Shrugging, she swiped a large decorative conch from its place of honor and handed it to him. "Here you go."

He raised an eyebrow but took the conch shell, which had either come from the granddaddy of all sea snails or been manufactured in China, and broke them in with a quick, hard blow to the doorknob.

Gathering the remnants of her energy, she followed him

inside gratefully. The first floor was all one room, with windows looking out at the ocean on one end and a massive stone fireplace on the other. A large, L-shaped sofa and several mismatched armchairs were grouped in front of the fireplace. It was homey and unpretentious, furnished with finds from flea markets and attics. She wasn't quite sure what the protocol was when you'd been shipwrecked and stranded on an absent homeowner's beach.

Declan held up a palm and moved swiftly up the stairs to the second floor. Normally she would have protested his easy assurance that she'd follow his lead and stay when told to stay, but she wasn't sure her legs would carry her up the stairs. She could hear him calling out a greeting, just in case the homeowner had somehow slept through their felonious entry. Sleeping sounded like a good plan. The best ever plan, in fact. She staggered toward the sofa, debating planting on it, wet clothes and all. There were no light switches and the air held a damp chill, even though it was summer. It was just their luck to have found a cabin with no heat or electricity.

Declan returned with an armful of blankets before she could summon the energy to lie down. "Strip."

"Don't I get dinner first?"

He grinned and tossed her a packet of dried fruit and a handful of granola bars. "Ask and ye shall receive. Strip. I'll build a fire."

Getting out of her wet clothes suddenly seemed like the best idea ever, so she peeled off her sailing leggings and the sodden scuba hoodie while he gave her his back to give her some privacy and built a roaring fire faster than she would have thought possible. When he turned back around, looking pleased as warmth started to wash over the room, she could barely hold in her sigh of pleasure.

Just admiring the scenery, she told herself. Who knew that what she really got turned on by was a guy who knew how to scavenge for groceries and build a fire? Looking wouldn't hurt her.

And then when he busted her, she pretended it was the fire that had caught her interest. "Impressive, Hollywood."

"Lots of practice," he said. "My brother and I lit a lot of stuff on fire when we were teenagers."

Casually, he stepped behind the sofa and stripped off his own clothes. She would have liked to see more, but the sofa back was high and he had to work to get the wet cargo shorts and T-shirt off. She caught a flash of some kind of thinner undergarment before she remembered she wasn't looking.

"If you came over here and lent a hand, you'd get a better look," he said. "I'm not the shy one."

"Cute," she said, tempted. But getting them both warm, dry and fed was more important right now. Plus, her blanket toga wasn't exactly sexy lingerie. She padded into the kitchen that was tucked away in the back, trying to ignore the wet *squelch* as he took it all off, and rummaged around for two mugs and some water from an ancient plastic five-gallon jug.

When she came back, he'd wrapped a blanket around his hips and legs and had a second draped over his shoulders. It should have made him look ridiculous. Instead he looked ridiculously hot. Her libido promptly decided that they should hold a naked, sexy celebration of life.

Tamping down that thought, she shoved one mug at him. "Here."

He took it and patted the sofa cushion beside him. "I saved you a spot."

Instead of teasing her further, though, he handed her a granola bar and pulled his phone out of his dry bag, holding it up for her to see. No signal. They were good and stuck. Ignoring his invitation, she paced back and forth, ate her granola bar and failed to come up with a plan.

Imagine that.

Right now all she had was a list of disasters: a lost race, a wrecked boat and no way to fix the hole that George had put in Martha's Kids' budget. How could she not freak out?

"Hey." Warm fingers braceleted her wrist, slowing her. "Come and sit with me, Charlotte."

She let him pull her down onto the sofa and up against his side. She liked sitting with him. Being next to him. Okay, so she just liked him. A lot. And since thinking about that just freaked her out, she returned to her first topic. "No one knows where we are. We lost the boat. We lost the race. We just committed felony B and E. As days go, this one sucks."

"It could be worse," he said.

"How... No. Wait." She slapped a hand over his mouth. "Don't tell me how it could be worse. That's need-to-know information only."

He pressed a kiss against her palm and gently shifted her hand away from his mouth. "Let's make a list, Charlotte. Next steps. What we'll do tomorrow."

She stared at him. And lied her ass off. "You may be used to catastrophes and disasters, but this is my first time."

"I'll be gentle," he said solemnly. "What's the first thing we need to do after we fall off the boat and into the ocean?"

"Get to shore." She gave him a look. "Find help. Take the world's longest nap."

"We've done the first one," he said. "And now we're helping ourselves. We've found shelter. We've got a fire. And hey, I've even made us dinner."

"Sure," she said, "but since no one knows we're here, we're also stranded."

"But we've got six things crossed off." He mimed striking through a line.

"Thank you again," she blurted out. Was it smooth? No. But it was one-hundred-percent heartfelt.

"I was happy to help."

"I—" She had no idea how to explain. And did she really want to?

"Don't like water. Yeah. Believe me." He scrubbed a hand over his still damp hair. "I get that. I know you don't like to talk about things, but maybe you should talk about this one?"

It was possible that he was right.

She stared up at him, assessing her chances of getting out of this with her dignity—and her heart—intact. Not only was she far too close to his spectacular chest but, just possibly, she'd used up all of her luck on the whole falling-overboard-and-not-drowning thing. "Okay. So first of all, I suck at thank-yous, but I owe you this one. Thank you for jumping in after me." She paused. "It was a stupid thing to do and you could have still won the race."

"You wanted me to sail on and leave you there?" He sounded incredulous.

"Well, I was more thinking you could have fished me out before you sailed on. One-handed? Like a knight leaning down from his horse?"

He looked down, angling his face until he could see hers. "I told you I wouldn't leave you. I made you a promise."

"Well. Thank you. Again." She paused. "Wow, this is awkward."

"Do you know many people who would leave someone alone in the water? I'm asking for a friend here."

Was *she* his friend?

"It happens," she said carefully. "And as I'm an adult, I'm trying hard not to judge those people, okay?"

"Not okay," he said. "Not ever. Also, Charlotte?"

"Yeah?"

"It will never happen on my watch and never to you."

As promises went, it was a doozy.

"I knew you liked me, Movie Star."

"Charlotte." The way he said her name, rough and intense, melted something cold inside her. "Did something like this happen before?"

Thirteen

Charlotte opened her mouth. Closed it.

Declan knew that look. He'd seen it on his own face before he'd learned to hide it. It was the look of someone who'd been left. He hated that for her.

"I got left a lot as a kid," he said quietly. "My biological dad left first, before I was born, so my mom always had work to go to—errands, a second or a third job. She'd leave Nash and me alone in the apartment with food in the fridge and a list of things we weren't to do or touch. It took longer and longer for her to come back, though, so eventually I'd break the rules. In hindsight, she likely tried the best she could, but I was a kid and being alone was scary. I thought it was something I'd done wrong."

"Was that when you went into foster care?"

"Yeah. And then a couple of years later, she died in a car accident. J.J. adopted me eighteen months after that."

"That had to have been hard," she said softly.

He didn't like talking about those days. He'd been vulnerable then and now he wasn't. Except that for Charlotte he might make a tiny exception. "I learned a lot in the years between my first home and J.J.'s. Mostly how to be tough and to stand up for myself. I got into a lot of fights and figured out that I liked the adrenaline rush. I liked it even more when I realized that fighting could be strategic, that it had a rhythm, a choreography of sorts. It all prepared me for the stunt work that led to my career, so I'm not complaining."

"I'm glad it had a silver lining for you, but I'm sorry, too." Her mouth quirked up ruefully. "And I know that isn't the right thing to say, but yeah, that's me. Queen of the conflicting emotions and poor phrasing."

He pulled her closer. "J.J. was… Well, J.J. was his own kind of challenge. He chose to bring me home and then he spent a lot of time after that laying out the ways in which I'd turned out to be a poor choice. And when he got mad or criticized, I'd throw myself into my next adventure since I'd already disappointed him. I'm guessing your childhood wasn't picture-perfect."

She wiggled back an inch and stared at him. "Wait. Was your sharing a clever trick to make me share? Because I'm going to need more details if we're trading life stories."

He let out a low laugh. "Busted. But Charlotte, please tell me?"

"I was at a beach party," she said quietly. "The adults were up on the bluff. It was a pretty important event. There were some people my father wanted to do business with and he'd warned me about staying out of the way. So I went down to the beach with the other kids and we horsed around in the surf. Nothing too out of control—it was all perfectly safe."

He had some thoughts about the safety of unsupervised kids on a beach, but he kept them to himself.

"One of the other girls dared me to race her out to the

mooring buoy and back," she continued. "I agreed. I was always a bit shy and this girl was super cool. So there she was talking to me and actually asking me to do something with her. No way I'd refuse plus I was an awesome swimmer and I was totally going to kick her butt. We got in the water and someone called the start of our race and I really went for it. I didn't realize until I tapped the buoy that I was out there alone."

"She turned back?"

She shook her head. "She never swam at all. She was laughing on the beach with her friends. I never found out if the dare was a joke or if someone she was actually friends with had distracted her and she forgot about me. They went back up on the bluff and then I had to swim back alone. There was a rip current and I was too tired and inexperienced to get myself out of it. Eventually one of the other parents did a head count and figured out I was missing. When they spotted me out in the water, they called the local rescue team who retrieved me. My father was pissed off that I'd caused such a commotion."

"That was a rough day," he said. "There's no excuse—"

"But there's a silver lining to my story," she said.

He stared at her. "What?"

She frowned. "Well, I learned that I hate the ocean, suck at racing and don't care for front-page coverage in the local newspaper. Which pretty much makes us opposites."

They were opposites if she meant that he loved the ocean, won every race he entered and had millions of social media impressions. None of that was the important stuff, however. Today had gone wrong in more ways than she knew. In losing today's race, Declan had lost J.J.'s test. No more CEO, no more Masterson Entertainment. He set that thought aside for later, pulling Charlotte closer. The storm that had wrecked them had moved off, the rain slowing. He could head out, find help. And yet—

She twisted in his arms and looked at him. "Thank you for coming after me."

"We discussed this," he said roughly. "No thanks necessary."

He would have said something more but her new position had her straddling his thighs. And then she rose up on her knees, his legs between hers, and things lit up faster than the sky during the storm.

"Declan?" She leaned down, bracing her hands on his shoulders.

"Yeah?" he asked, intending to suggest a getting-rescued plan. Instead his arms went around her back, sliding beneath her blanket and across bare skin. The heat of her set him on fire, filled him with a new purpose and sense of connection.

"I want this chance."

And then she leaned down, set her mouth on his and kissed the hell out of him.

A chance to do something new.
To do something. To go for what she wanted...

She kissed Declan because they'd almost died and because time was precious. She wasn't going to waste it, not when the man she wanted was here, they were both naked and they were trapped together. If that wasn't a sign from the universe, she didn't know what was. So she kissed him, sinking into the heat and the desire, the rightness and sense of belonging she tried to share with him, with her mouth and her hands cupping his face so that she could have her way with him. A groan tore from him when her tongue found his and she might have made a few answering sounds of her own.

She was breathless, as was he, when he pulled back, locking his gaze on hers. "When you want to stop, say stop," he said. "I won't take advantage of you."

While she appreciated him putting the control in her hands, she needed to make one thing clear. "You're not taking advantage. And the key word here is *if*. If I want to stop, I'll say it."

He nodded, his hands tightening on her back. "That's another promise, Charlotte."

The man and his promises were killing her.

"So you want to kiss me," he continued.

Warmth pooled in her belly. Declan was always in motion, always doing something. Now he was waiting.

For her to make up her mind.

To choose him.

He reached up and tucked her hair behind her ear. "Is that all you want to do?"

"It's the first thing on my list," she said. "But it's a long list and there may be crying if you don't have a condom."

"Yes," he said roughly. "In my wallet and thank God for dry bags."

"So prepared." She laughed and trailed her fingers over his face, the roughness of the stubble that covered the hard line of his jaw making her shiver. He was strength and heat in a delicious package and—

He drew her mouth back to his. Bracing her arms on either side of his head, she sank into his hold. A hand cupped the back of her head, strong fingers threading through her hair. And then he kissed her, a kiss that started out gentle, his teeth nipping softly at her lower lip, and then deepened as his tongue swept inside her mouth.

She'd never felt this kind of desire. She wasn't a casual kisser, hadn't dated much and didn't jump into a relationship feetfirst—or heart first. But this man made her burn and ache for something more, as if he was the happy ending she'd dreamed about. True intimacy took trust and she didn't trust easily. In fact, she didn't trust at all, and that had her holding back rather than letting go.

George had been a mistake. He'd charmed and flirted his way into her life, and then when he'd told her he wanted more, that he wanted *forever*, she hadn't seriously considered whether or not she could give him that—if she even *wanted* to give him that. And while she'd been hurt and humiliated when he'd left her, she'd also, on some level, expected it.

People didn't stay. People *left*.

But, her heart protested, *Declan is different. He came* after *you*.

And the truth was, he had. Every single time it counted, he'd come after her.

"Still a yes," she said against his mouth. "And also please, thank you and hurry up."

"Yeah," he said roughly. "Me, too."

That one word said it all, didn't it? He slid a big, strong hand through her hair, pulling her back so he could kiss her some more. *Yes* to this moment. *Yes* to this night. *Yes* to the two of them and exploring whatever that could mean.

At some point during all of the kissing, when their hands had both wandered south, he turned them both, tucking her beneath him on the couch. She tilted her face back up to his, letting him see exactly how much he made her feel. "You make me crazy."

"Good," he growled. "Because the feeling is mutual and it's also crazy new. This isn't a one-night thing for me and I don't want to watch you walk away from me in the morning—but I also don't know what you're feeling or what you want."

She laughed against his mouth. "We want the same things."

She knew that because he was hard against her and no way was he close enough. She slipped her hands around his back, tugging him nearer. "Make love with me?"

He groaned against her mouth. "This wasn't exactly how I imagined our first time together."

Laughter and heat bubbled through her body. "Did you actually make a plan for it?"

"I've had a few fantasies, Charlotte. I want you, but I imagined showing you how special you are by doing this somewhere better."

"I'm safe, we've got a fire, we're both here," she said. "That sounds perfect to me."

"Yeah?"

And then his mouth was gliding over hers again, kissing her softer and then deeper as he teased her lower lip, her cheek, then the curve of her throat as he loved his way down her body.

The blanket fell away and Declan smiled, a wicked, sexy grin at the sight of her bare body. "Beautiful." His hands stroked over her body, learning what made her sigh, what made her giggle, the touches that made her whimper and whisper his namc before making some noisy demands of her own.

"Beautiful here, too." He touched her lower, his fingers trailing slowly over the soft skin of her thighs and then between them with a care and skill that had her whole world focusing on him, breathy sounds escaping her mouth. He made her want and want and want.

"Declan," she murmured, wrapping her legs around his, rocking into his touch. She was close and she needed him inside her. "I'm—"

"Beautiful," he whispered, his mouth chasing the teasing touch of his fingers. He found her bare breast, kissing and sucking as his fingers slid into her and she forgot to hold back and just held on to him. And when he moved lower still, his mouth replacing his fingers, she got completely lost in the erotic tension, her soft, breathy sounds mingling with his rougher, hoarser murmurs.

"Are we still good?" he asked when he'd explored every inch of her with his hands and she'd said, "Yes, more," and "Oh, God," and "Now?" more times than she'd ever expected. And then she'd come apart for him, fireworks exploding behind her eyes.

Her body quivered, wanting all of him, ready to do it again.

"Can you be better?" The man did like a challenge, after all.

He grinned at her. "Better. Or very, very bad depending on what's on that list of yours."

And then he pressed her down, using his mouth and his fingers to show her all the ways a woman like her could enjoy a man like him. A long, long time later when she'd come for him a second time and was floating in a sea of pleasure, warm and boneless, she heard the sound of a condom packet being opened and then he moved back up her body and came into her, proving that she was no more done with him than he was with her.

Fourteen

Later, as they lay there, tangled up together, Charlotte wondered how she was supposed to put herself back together. The rain was stopping, the steady drumming on the roof easing up, and she could hear the ocean again, the waves pounding on the shore. There were a million things they should do, but mostly she never wanted to move again. Who knew sex could be so amazing?

Declan's quiet "Be right back" sounded promising. She watched through half-closed eyes as he got up and dealt with the condom and the fire before returning to scoop her up on top of him. She curled into him gratefully because part of her was still cold.

"Why weren't we doing that sooner?" she asked.

He gave a rough laugh and pulled her closer still, until his chin rested on her head and his hands were locked on the small of her back. "If we'd done this any sooner, we wouldn't have been out there on the water. I'd have spirited you away to my castle tower and locked us in."

"That sounds rather grim. I'm not sure castle towers figure prominently on my fantasy list."

"My private tropical island then," he said. "And feel free to tell me more about this fantasy list of yours."

There was a note in his voice she couldn't quite make out. "Do you actually have one of those?"

"A castle? No." He traced her cheek with a calloused hand. "But I'll get one if that's what you want."

"Just you will do," she said.

That's a big ask. She shoved away the unwelcome thought. She had tonight, didn't she? And she'd promised herself that she wouldn't waste chances, not anymore.

"You can have all of me, Charlotte."

"Really? All of you?" she asked. Certain parts of him were making it clear that all of him was ready to repeat what they'd just done.

"You bet," he said and then he kissed her and one thing lead to some very pleasurable other things so that the fire was dying down again before they'd finished.

Charlotte drifted off eventually, or possibly she fell asleep, because one moment she was wrapped up in the very sexy Declan as he pressed kisses against her hair, which had to be a Medusa-worthy tangle of salty waves, and the next the room had that not-quite-dark light it got when the sun was almost ready to start making its morning appearance. And Declan was still holding her.

The fire had gone out altogether, but she was plenty hot, possibly because she was being held against Declan and there was a whole lot of bare, warm skin to enjoy. One arm kept her close, while the other was tucked beneath his head. She admired the downright gorgeous line of his deliciously scruffy, morning-after jaw before she realized that he was awake and watching her right back.

Oh, God.

They'd slept together. She turned that thought over in

her head: the boating disaster, the terrifying swim to shore, his insistence that nothing would hurt her while he was there and then the far more personal turn things between them had taken. The kissing. The naked touching. The sex. The amazing, mind-blowing, best-ever sex.

That was going to be a problem.

And also? He was still watching her.

"Hey," he said finally.

She stared at him some more.

"You look like you have something to say."

She was sure she did. She was equally sure that it would take days—weeks—for her to form a coherent thought. "What?"

"Are you okay?" he asked.

"I don't know what to do here," she admitted. "And honestly, this doesn't seem like your usual scene."

"Holding a beautiful woman? Or holding you specifically?"

Her breath caught. "That might be too much honesty."

"Because holding you is really working for me," he said.

Her heart nearly stopped. She was starting to realize that he saw her as more than an island fling and she couldn't bear the thought that she'd get her hopes up and then he'd leave and it would all turn out to be a misunderstanding or a mistake.

Charlotte looked nervous. This was not a look Declan was okay with, especially when he was holding her and they'd just had the most amazing sex of his life. *More than that*, he thought. His brain tried out a brand-new pair of words: *making love*. When he'd first been matched up with her for the race, he'd been irritated. And attracted. And yeah, he realized, eager to score points with J.J. with his makeover dare.

Charlotte still didn't know about that deal with J.J.

When he'd dared her to do the makeover, she'd believed he was an arrogant Hollywood know-it-all who'd decided to torment her for his own reasons. And sure, he'd had reasons. Plus, her irritation had amused him, making him mad on her behalf that the people in her world routinely overlooked her because she wasn't splashy or putting herself out there. He'd unintentionally misled her about his reasons for racing, and truth was, as he'd gotten to know her, he'd lost sight of how J.J. would see it: that Declan had found himself the perfect cure for his rakish, playboy reputation.

The flushed woman in his arms, warm and completely undone and open, wasn't Instagram ready or perfect in any of the ways Hollywood prized, but her eyes, full of affection—and possibly something more—met his and he knew he was on the verge of something amazing if he just reached for it. They fit together and he loved it. She felt like she might just possibly be the most important adventure of his life, and yet he hadn't been as open with her as she had been with him. If she'd been just a casual hookup, the J.J. deception wouldn't have mattered.

But it wasn't casual. Not on his part, not any more.

He tried to imagine how that conversation would go. *I've mentioned J.J.? And how he's a bit of a controlling bastard? Funny story, but he offered me a once-in-a-lifetime deal. If I pass his test, he'll hand over the family company to me. I have to prove I'm reformed, respectable material by winning a high-stakes philanthropic race in Martha's Vineyard.*

And oh yeah, we lost that race. Badly.

They'd have to have the conversation, he knew, but not here. Or now. If it went badly, she couldn't leave, at least not safely, and he'd never do anything to make her feel unsafe or threatened.

This was too important, even if he wasn't sure yet what *this* was.

He moved his hands over her, soothing, tucking her in closer, making sure she was as happy as he could make her. And also to distract her, because he was certain she was already thinking and planning.

Sure enough, she looked at him and grimaced.

"At least you didn't get caught scaling a balcony naked this time."

"If I'd known it would be like this, I'd have been outside your room every night."

"I live on the ground floor." She laughed, clearly thinking she'd deflected his interest in having a serious conversation. And truth was, he didn't want to talk about what had happened. He didn't do emotions and he certainly was no expert in opening up. But even he knew that what they'd just shared was more than amazing sex, and he wanted it to happen again.

He wanted it to happen with her.

"This is nothing like that," he said.

"Good," she said. There was an awkward pause.

While she hopefully thought about what he'd said, he leaned up on one arm so he could check out her face. Mostly, he wanted to make sure that she was still okay, at least physically. Falling off a boat could be really bad. She could have hit her head or an arm, injured herself and not noticed it. He'd seen stuntmen take a blow and keep right on working for hours and hours until the adrenaline wore off and their bodies gave out. He never wanted to see Charlotte get hurt.

Leaning over her, he brushed his hands over her face, then down her body, relieved to find nothing wrong. "You sure you're okay?"

This time her amused laughter was genuine. "Yes, doctor. Or was that a comment on your bedroom skills?"

"Hey. If I didn't get it right, we can keep practicing." Nudging her chin up with his thumb, he kissed her.

Fifteen

It wasn't the sun pouring through the windows that woke Charlotte up. It was the banging on the front door. The banging—and the voices. She and Declan had fallen back asleep in a cocoon of firelit darkness and the warmth of their bodies, a sweetly private space that had terrified and amazed her.

She liked Declan. That thought was the first that swam up to the surface. Possibly more than *liked*, a little voice whispered. *You got naked with him; you had sex and you opened up in* all *the ways. That's the* other *L word.* Her heart decided this was a good moment to start banging around inside her chest, as if it had something to contribute to the conversation. Or maybe that was whoever was outside the house. The house they'd *broken into.* She shoved that thought aside for later. Apparently orgasms did wonders for her anxiety because she couldn't remember the last time she'd felt so relaxed. Kissing. Touching. Out-of-this-world sex. Those were good things, but she loved non-sex time with Declan just as much. After all, they'd only had sex for a handful of the hours she'd spent with him. Sex would have been simpler.

Easier to maintain her distance.

Which was non-existent at the moment.

She was wrapped up in his arms, one of his legs thrown over hers. This position was vying for her favorite Declan position (although he'd certainly shown her a few new favorites last night) as her face was pressed against his chest. His heart beat beneath her cheek, solid and steady. And just in case she hadn't paid enough attention to his chest last night, she brushed a few bonus kisses over the smooth, sun-bronzed skin. She might have licked him. Just once. Okay, twice.

The real problem was that she wanted to do it all again. And then again and again. He held her as if she were precious and he was completely bare. The blanket slipped off one hard, muscled shoulder and of course she couldn't help looking at him. He was something so unfamiliar, someone she liked—*loved,* her traitorous heart whispered. *This isn't a simple case of the likes.* And maybe, just maybe, he had the same kind of curiosity about her and they could see where this went. She was turning that thought over in her head when the banging sound started up again.

That was bad.

Or good? Had they been found already? Declan cursed, tightening his arms around her and shifting her off and onto the couch. He tugged a blanket around her even as he got up.

"We've got company," he said, cursing some more. "The rescue party's here."

While she hadn't expected to wake up to the first day of forever with Declan, she also hadn't imagined that they'd be rousted by a large search party. Somehow, when she'd imagined a rescue, she'd imagined a much smaller—and less curious—number of people.

Declan tugged on his cargo shorts and strode over to the door. Despite their drenching in the ocean and rough swim to shore, he looked amazing. She drank in the muscled perfection of his chest, the strong line of his back as he turned, and the tousled mane of hair. And oh, God, if he was wearing just a pair of shorts, she was naked.

He yanked the door open, blocking the doorway with his body. She had a bad feeling that it was too little, too late. After a brief consultation with whoever was out there, he shifted his attention to her.

"We've been rescued. Brace yourself." Then he turned back around to what sounded like a hundred people and said, "Charlotte needs a moment."

He shut the door and crossed the floor toward her, a small smile tugging at the corners of his mouth.

"This is totally your fault," she said. "I'm not the one who got me naked."

He gathered her clothes from where he'd laid them out to dry and she pulled her leggings and T-shirt on under the cover of the blanket, blessing the quick-dry fabric for living up to it marketing promises. The noise level outside grew. While she donned what armor she could, Declan swiped his T-shirt from the chairback where he'd left it.

"Am I decent?"

"Yeah." He gave her a quick check. "Charlotte—"

"Because," she interrupted, "I've learned enough about social media to know that I do not want to go out there with my butt hanging out."

He put a finger on her lips. "I'll take care of this."

"Hey," she said. "We're partners."

"Not a dictatorship," he agreed. "Partners. And as the expert partner on scandals, I'm warning you that things are going to get a little rough out there, but I'm not going anywhere. Got it?"

"O-okay." It took her two tries to get the word out.

He nodded and then gently pulled her outside and onto the porch. Jeez. She tried to smooth her hair back, to pretend that nothing had happened when everything had changed. People in various uniforms milled around the house and there were even more members of the press. She tipped her head back and, yep—that was a helicopter circling overhead. People greeted Declan by name, offering coffee and jackets, EMTs and assistance. Ryan popped up, moving fast, and the two of them were halfway to him when she spotted the *Cupcake* washed up on the beach below them.

Oh. My. God.

Their poor *Cupcake* was in pieces. She lay on her side in the surf, the mast snapped off and the sails dragging in the water. Panic squeezed her chest, the truth hitting her. The race was lost and she wasn't going to win the money that Martha's Kids needed to stay afloat itself. All she would be able to do was say "I'm sorry" a billion times.

Declan squeezed her fingers. "I'll be right back."

She scanned the crowd while he walked away to exchange a few low, terse words with Ryan. There was no one she really knew, although she could put a few names to some faces as it wasn't a huge island. The search and rescue team went down to the beach to salvage the boat or whatever it was that people did with shipwrecks. Was there AAA for the boating world? She was still trying to figure it out when Declan handed her a cup of coffee, slipped a pair of shoes he'd magicked up onto her bare feet and shepherded her toward the helicopter that had landed some distance away on an open, grassy expanse.

The press, which had been pushed back down the driveway, started yelling out questions again, asking what had happened.

He barely paused, keeping her tucked into his side. "Bad luck and the storm. You can't win them all."

"How do you feel about losing the race when you were was so far out ahead?"

"What do you want to say about the rumors circulating that you're dead? And that the Academy is planning a tribute?"

"Charlotte! Can you describe Declan's heroism for us? Did he save your life last night? What was it like being stranded with Declan overnight?"

Everyone turned to stare at her. Why hadn't someone invented an invisibility cloak? Cameras clicked as she scrambled into the helicopter. She'd never ridden in one before, but desperate times called for desperate measures.

"For God's sake," Declan muttered. "Next they're going to ask if we've sold the movie rights."

"Can we just go home already?" she asked.

"On it," he said. "I'll take you anywhere you want to go."

Charlotte's usual life called for minivans or beat-up SUVs, so the helicopter was perhaps one new thing too many. Declan's playful exchange with the reporters replayed in her head. Last night he'd said he saw them together, but he'd given no hint of that to the reporters. Since her options were limited, however, she let Declan settle a pair of headphones on her. Moments later the private pilot had them airborne, Martha's Vineyard falling away from them. *Lifestyles of the rich and famous*, she thought hysterically.

After a brief flight, the pilot swung them back over the ocean and toward Edgartown. All too soon they were settling down on the concrete helipad behind the house. A late-model BMW was parked next to Declan's sports car, along with at least a dozen other cars. The pilot killed the engine, and after the blades had stopped spinning, Declan came around to help her out.

"Hi," he said, wrapping his hands around her waist and swinging her out. She grabbed his shoulders, suddenly off-balance. "We really need to talk."

She slid her hands off his shoulders. "Right now?"

All she wanted was more coffee, a hot shower and a bed, because she was pretty sure she didn't want to deal with messing up Martha's Kids' second chance yesterday. Plus, she looked about as bad as anyone would after nearly drowning, going without hot water for twenty-four hours and spending the better part of the night making love instead of sleeping.

"There's a lot of interest in what happened yesterday. TV coverage, social media, that sort of thing. People want to talk to us, hear what happened. We've sort of come back from the dead. At least that's how the headlines read."

"Everyone thought we were *dead*?"

He nodded. "And now we've been resurrected."

He wrapped an arm around her shoulders and started toward the house. There was a crowd of people pressed up against some kind of barricade at the end of his driveway. A roar went up when they spotted Declan.

A mound of flowers, stuffed animals and glass candles had been piled up against the barricade. She'd known that Declan was a star, but she hadn't realized until now what that really meant. Lots and lots of other people thought they lo—*liked*—him, too.

"Is that what you wanted to talk about?"

"Not really." He steered her toward the door and then stopped, bracing an arm by her head and leaning in. She rested her forehead on his chest, numb with exhaustion. "But there are lots of people in there. J.J.'s doing media."

"What? Why?"

Declan's mouth brushed hers. "Because he's a Hollywood mogul and this is great exposure. Because he's an ass. And probably also because he is my father and he thought I was dead."

"So he's giving interviews?"

"Some people like to talk."

Great. She was going to meet J.J. wearing yesterday's salt-soaked sailing kit. She was just grateful that she couldn't see what her hair looked like. And yet somehow Declan managed to look rugged and handsome, like a victorious Viking seafarer home from conquest.

Paparazzi called their names, asking Declan how they were.

Declan didn't slow. "Right now, I need to get the woman I love inside, warm and dry. That's my only priority."

She froze. *Love?*

He tugged her inside while the reporters yelled and cameras went off. Inside turned out to be equally chaotic. Doors were thrown wide, people with headsets rushing in and out and rattling off brief, incomprehensible details to each other. The living room had been turned into a temporary television studio.

A tall, broad-shouldered man in his late fifties strode toward them. His dark hair was streaked with silver, the waves ruthlessly tamed. He wore an open-necked white dress shirt tucked into tailored suit pants and a Rolex glinted on his wrist. He had the same aura of command as Declan, but with a harder, more predatory edge.

"Introduce us," he said to Declan.

Declan just looked at him. "Charlotte, meet my father, J.J. Masterson."

"Mr. Masterson."

"Call me J.J., Charlotte." J.J.'s hand engulfed hers in a

firm, quick grip. "You're even lovelier than your pictures. Tell me my son took good care of you last night."

Not sure what to say, she stuck to the truth. "He did."

J.J. nodded. "He knows the right thing to do on the water."

Declan stared back at his father and they engaged in a silent conversation, exchanging tense looks.

"Not well enough," J.J. said with a nod, as if he'd just had the last word in that silent conversation. He winked at her. "But we'll fix that. There's an entire team to take care of you. You're a prize and Declan here knows that."

Charlotte felt the breath catch in her throat. "Pretty sure I cost him the prize."

J.J. looked at her. "Not yet, darling. Not yet."

What?

Then he turned to Declan. "Good job, son."

"Not now," Declan growled. "We're not getting into this right now."

J.J. waved a hand and walked away with someone who wanted to run a media schedule by him. Charlotte thought she recognized an online reporter from a popular morning show, along with a woman she'd seen on prime time at night. She was too tired to sort it out.

"What you said out there," she said. "Right before we came in?"

"That the only thing I need to do right now is take care of the woman I love?"

"Yeah, that," she said faintly.

Declan just watched her.

"You love me?"

"Yes." He brushed a kiss over her forehead.

She inhaled, legs quivery with exhaustion. "You love me."

"You don't have to say anything right now." He winced. "Or at all. But whenever you do want to say something, I want to listen. Right now, though, I want to get you some-where you can lie down and be quiet. If that plan's okay with you."

"I love you, too," she whispered.

Sixteen

"You think a free meal is worth all this effort?"

Charlotte jumped, pressing her palms against the windows lining the hotel ballroom. The glass was pleasantly cool despite the decidedly midsummer temperature outside. The sun had barely gone down, but it was dark enough to see the man reflected in the window behind her. *Declan.* Her tuxedo-wearing, smiling Prince Charming. Her heart did some much less startled, sexier jumping.

"Definitely not." She tilted her head back, resting it against his shoulder. "But we're pretending that we're not sore losers, right?"

"Speak for yourself." He caged her in his arms, pressing a kiss against the top of her head.

The man in the reflection was extraordinarily handsome in his designer tuxedo, the black jacket stretched across powerful shoulders. He belonged in this room of politicians and celebrities, wealthy Vineyard residents and donors, who had come together to celebrate the winners of the charity race. Surprisingly to her, the woman standing with him looked as if she fit, too.

Charlotte fit.

Almost, impossibly so, or at least with this one, wonderful man. His stylist had pulled a dark rose tuxedo jacket for her with a low-necked white bodysuit that scooped her breasts up and then up some more. The matching floor-length pencil skirt hugged her curves and set off a pair of Christian Louboutin sandals in a glossy red that echoed the cherry-colored lips the makeup artist had given her and the Edwardian rubies surrounded by clusters of old mine-cut diamonds that dangled from her ears. She looked good, she decided. Better than good. Despite everything, she looked—happy.

Or at least, happy enough.

She was trying to decide if Declan regretted their loss when he smiled down at her. Okay. So definitely probably almost certainly teasing. After their disastrous end to the race three days ago, Charlotte suspected that almost everyone would have excused them from tonight's awards banquet. Most of the other racers had been forced to abandon the race, although none in quite such a spectacular fashion. In the end, the winner had been the last boat to start and had managed to wait until the worst of the sudden storm had blown through before leisurely sailing to the finish line entirely alone. It was the classic Tortoise and the Hare story. No one had expected a member of the local Coast Guard and an international dressage competitor to win. Declan had come in for more than his share of good-natured teasing.

And far too many people had spent the evening staring at her and Declan, speculating about what had happened in that beach house. She told herself that words were, well, just words. She'd ignore them and get on with her life. She'd almost managed to stay off the internet this morning and avoid reading the latest article on how Declan had bravely plunged overboard after her and brought her nearly lifeless body to shore.

Awkward.

But she'd congratulated the winners and tried to pretend that she was merely politely disappointed to have not landed the grand prize for Martha's Kids. The orchestra hired for the night launched into a waltz.

"One last chance to play Cinderella," she said.

He pulled her a little closer, giving his head a little shake. "You'll always be my queen."

She laughed. "Cheesy, much? Also I'm almost certain that you accused me of being a princess. Have I been promoted?"

He groaned. "You're not going to let me live that down, are you?"

"No." She grinned up at him.

"I was wrong." He nipped her ear gently, smiling. "You're far more than just a princess."

"Ruler of the universe, that's me." She smiled back at him.

For a hopeful moment, she thought he'd be content to flirt or dance. Instead, he exhaled roughly and his smile turned rueful. "Charlotte?"

"Are you going to ask me questions I don't want to answer?"

"Probably."

But he didn't ask, not right away. Instead he held her, letting her hide behind his broad chest from the billion people crowding the ballroom—all of whom were staring at them or talking about *how heroic Declan was* and *what do you think* really *happened that night*? She wondered what they would think and say if they knew about George's sticky fingers. After a minute, she took a breath and stepped out of his hold to stand next to him.

He slanted a careful glance at her. "Answer me this. Are you okay?"

"Can you be more specific?"

"Charlotte," he growled.

"You already said that," she whispered. His presence beside her felt so good, forming a sort of human shield even though she knew that she could stand up for herself. But no matter how safe and protected and, oh man, so wonderful—white knight Declan was, this side-by-side thing was even better.

"I'm waiting," he murmured. He took her hand casually, running his thumb over her knuckles.

"We lost." She shrugged as if it were no big deal, as if she weren't...overwhelmed by losing that one last chance. Overwhelmed with guilt and remorse, regrets and what-ifs.

"Spectacularly," he agreed.

"So there's no million-dollar donation for Martha's Kids. We could have used that money."

He nodded once. "For your summer camps. So Maggie can be a kid and Jay can eat himself full for once."

She loved that he'd really listened to her, and she warned herself not to get any rash ideas about confessing. She needed to keep the truth to herself so she didn't make things worse, because the district attorney hadn't given her the green light to talk about the case and because maybe, if they found George fast enough, there would be some money left. It was about trying—and failing—to protect her summer kids, keeping them safe from the mistakes the adults in their lives made.

But this was *Declan*. Keeping secrets from him felt wrong. She weighed silence against sharing, and knew that she couldn't keep this from him, not if they were going to have any kind of a real relationship. She had to trust him with everything, including the not-so-pretty parts of her life.

"We have a budget problem," she admitted. "I mean, there's never enough money when you're a nonprofit, right? That prize money would have been... Well. Let's just say this Cinderella is going to have a lot of work to do when she gets home from the ball. Because—"

She stared at him, willing the words to come out of her mouth. To tell him the entire truth. *Because my ex-fiancé stole everything. Because I trusted when I should have been asking questions. I'm so, so sorry. And—*

And she had no idea what to do next.

"Charlotte?" He ran his fingers along her jaw. "It's okay. Whatever it is, it's okay."

It so wasn't, but apparently she was going to chicken out. "Let's not talk about it, okay? Not tonight. It was just a race and a crazy idea of mine." *Like the crazy idea of us.* But he'd said he loved her.

He squeezed her hand gently. "Isn't that what Prince Charming is for? Fixing all of his ladylove's problems?"

"News flash. You're not a prince, Hollywood." She brushed a kiss over his mouth. "Can we leave?"

"Sure." He let out a low laugh. "I think we've done enough in the name of good sportsmanship."

She laughed, but then he was dancing them out, right across the ballroom floor in a sweeping, ridiculously romantic not-quite-a-waltz. She knew exactly how Cinderella felt, dancing on borrowed time.

The valet brought Declan's car around and she slid gratefully inside, leaning her head back against the buttery leather. A moment later, he joined her and got them on the road.

His right hand brushed her cheek briefly. "Come back with me?"

Her insides clenched. Her driver was one dead sexy man.

"Let's do my place," she said, needing the comfort of home and the familiar.

Tonight there were fewer paparazzi waiting out front, some of the furor over their dramatic capsizing and rescue having waned. They slipped past the photographers and Declan exchanged a few low words with Ryan before joining her inside her cottage. He looked large and very male in the small space.

Before she could forget, she pulled off the earrings and held them out to him. "You'd better take these back before I lose them, too."

He gave her a look. "They deserve a good home." He curled her fingers around the fistful of diamonds and rubies. "You keep them."

She groaned. She had no idea how much vintage Edwardian jewelry cost, but these earrings weren't roses or even a half dozen of Gitty's muffins. "I can't."

She set them carefully on the coffee table. Then she kicked off her gorgeous sandals, groaning. "How can something so beautiful hurt so bad?"

"Absolutely no idea." His small half smile said that maybe he did know.

She hated to see him sad.

"We need a do-over on this week," she said, holding out her hands to him. "Dance with me."

He raised an eyebrow but he took her hands, mock-dancing her around the room while she hummed her favorite waltz. And if it might, just possibly, have starred a yellow dress and the prince of beasts, sue her. Everyone deserved a fantasy. Which reminded her...

She wound her arms around Declan's neck, tugging his face down to hers so she could breathe him in, then pressed her mouth to his where he tasted of champagne and something sweeter, wilder and all Declan. It turned out she had a serious Declan addiction.

"Are we still dancing?" he asked, but he wrapped his arms around her and swung her in one last, crazy slow circle. She tightened her grip on him but he set her on her feet, his hands sliding up her back and then down. He pulled her closer until she could feel the heat and strength of him through the tuxedo.

Which was bone-meltingly lovely, but not enough. She fisted the front of his dress shirt, dragging him nearer still. Her nipples tightened from the contact. "That's a no on the waltzing, but I have another idea, Hollywood."

"Found a use for Prince Charming after all?" he asked, voice hoarse, when they finally broke apart after another kiss.

"You bet. Think he takes orders?"

"He's willing to try. Always." He leaned into her, his lips finding hers again. "But he can be a screwup."

She rocked her hips against him, making him groan. "I hope there's a dirty pun in there."

He smiled. "I'm all yours."

"For right now."

His smile deepened. "It will always be right now."

"Good plan," she said breathlessly. "The absolute best of plans."

He nodded. "You want me to bring you your binder so you can immortalize it?"

"Declan." She ran her fingers along his jaw. "I'm pretty sure we sank that binder. Along with our boat."

The *Cupcake* had washed up on shore, so maybe someone had salvaged the binder, but she wasn't thinking straight, at least not about itemized plans and next steps. She blamed Declan for that. The heated look in his eyes didn't make her want to plan, or think about what would happen tomorrow or next. All she cared about was *right now*—and Declan.

"We'll figure it out," he promised hoarsely.

"Promise?"

And as if he'd read her mind, he made a very male sound and picked her up. Her cottage was so small that a few strides had them in her even tinier bedroom, a room that seemed a thousand times smaller now that it was full of Declan, or maybe that was just the too-big feelings squeezing her chest, her ribs, her heart...

"Yeah," he said. "Promise."

"So beautiful," Declan whispered, making short work of Charlotte's clothes and his own. This was his favorite side of her, the one that was bare and open, trusting him to make her feel good. And then when she made that cute little snort of disbelief that she made far too often, he gently placed his palm over her mouth. "The clothes and the fancy makeup are pretty, but they're like a picture frame for what I really want to look at. You don't need them, Char." His voice was whiskey-rough and strained as he rolled her on top of him, stroking her body with his hands as he drew sensual patterns over her skin.

"Don't lie to me," she said fiercely, straddling him. "Don't ever lie to me, not about this, not about us."

"Won't," he gritted out, running his hands up her soft thighs, tracing each curve with clever fingers. She was such a giver, so warm and open, her body heating for him where they touched, the rounded globes of her breasts meriting more kisses, the tight tips demanding his attention, and then his mouth explored the sun-kissed slopes and the paler skin that had been hidden beneath her swimsuit tops. She gasped out his name, her body welcoming him, moving restlessly as she gripped his shoulders and held on. It was...everything.

He lost himself in her, forgetting the race and where they were, the world camped outside this small, private place for the two of them. The brush of her skin on his sent pleasure shooting through him, her hands stroking him, her mouth pressing kisses against his throat, his shoulder. He loved that she trusted him to give her this, heat and desire racing through his body as she touched him and he loved each part of her that he could.

"Charlotte."

She stared down at him, dazed. "We really don't need to have a conversation right now."

"Is this okay?"

He gripped her hips gently, his thumbs stroking over the sensitive skin and moving down to where she was slick and wet.

"Don't you dare stop," she whispered. And then, "Please, Declan."

She leaned down into him and he kissed her, his fingers never stopping until the rhythm of her breathing changed, her body tensing. He found a condom and then he was inside her, guiding her hips in a new, harder rhythm that made them both groan, half words and rough pleas falling from their mouths.

Their next kiss wasn't as sweet as their last kiss had been. It was hungry and open, things Declan usually didn't share with anyone because he hated being vulnerable. But Charlotte cupped his face with her hands, her breath coming in short gasps as she kissed him back, her hips rocking on him, and if she could do it, he wanted to as well. She was trusting and open, sweet and so goddamned giving that he just *knew*. No matter what happened with Masterson Entertainment, with his father and the work projects he'd thought mattered so much, he'd already won when this woman chose him to make love to her—to be her partner in every sense of the word.

Her face pressed against his throat even as she let out a few of the sexiest whimpers he'd ever heard. "Can you finish this, please?" she asked, sounding desperate. "Now, Declan. Right now. Please."

So he did, giving her what they both needed because he was hers right now and, quite possibly, forever.

Seventeen

The day was shaping up to be a Martha's Vineyard classic, full of sunshine and bright blue sky. The weather had been picture-perfect in the two weeks since the race, as if to make things up to her. Unfortunately, even if Charlotte had had a free minute to step outside and enjoy it, paparazzi had parked across the street from Martha's Kids. Earlier today, when she'd stepped outside with her PB&J, hoping to eat down by the water, they'd pounced. Ryan had convinced them to back off, but lesson learned. Free time now meant inside time. Preferably in-bed time.

With Declan.

She loved the time they spent in bed. A lot. Declan was always in motion, running, racing, putting his body through its paces because the man loved challenges. And even though the Vineyard got its share of famous visitors, the summer tourists stared when they were out and about, asking to take selfies with him or for an autograph. Public Declan was charming, but the private man was hers

alone. He laughed easily, his eyes full of warmth as he
sprawled like the king of the cats, listening to her talk.
Nothing threw him. He was calm, sure of the next step to
take but careful not to force his opinions on her. And the
way he was always touching her… She loved that, too.
He'd sling an arm around her, give her shoulder a gentle
squeeze when he came back into a room where she was
and stroke her hair. She'd never been a touchy-feely person but she loved how he touched her. Her face flushed as
she remembered just how much she loved it. They'd kept
each other up far too late last night.

Five minutes ago, she'd been looking forward to the
end of a long day trying to make their nonexistent budget
work when she'd got a phone call from the district attorney's office. Never, she reminded herself, make the mistake of thinking a day couldn't get worse.

Because it could.

The district attorney's office had what they needed to
press charges against George Moore even if they hadn't
yet found the bastard. It had been a lengthy process. She'd
turned over copies of the foundation's bookkeeping re-
cords and then had made herself available to answer their
questions. Finally, the DA had *sufficient evidence to take
to a grand jury.* She'd known for months, of course, that
George was a lying, stealing weasel, but now it would
officially be public knowledge. She no longer needed to
keep silent and there would be an epic PR storm when the
news broke.

She wasn't sure what to do next, which was a first. She
always had a plan and finishing the letter of resignation
that she'd drafted when she'd first realized what George
had done seemed like it should be number one on her to-do
list. It was just that she'd stupidly thought she'd have more
time, that she could find a solution to the damage. Instead,
she'd failed. She suspected that failure was about to make

it onto national television thanks to her not-so-fake-now relationship with Declan.

A tap on her office door had her looking up. Declan stood there, sun-bronzed and relaxed. Her heart skipped a beat.

After the crazy finish to their race, they'd done round after round of media interviews. There had been photographs and invitations to appear on several television programs, all of which she'd begged off. He'd done them, though, and she'd watched, marveling at his ease in front of the cameras. And at that thought, she winced a little. Despite his makeover lessons and the designer clothes, she was still Charlotte. She didn't fit into his Hollywood lifestyle and couldn't imagine life lived in that fishbowl. And she'd tried—because this thing between her and Declan wasn't just sex or even the friendship that she'd come to value so highly. It was both of those things, as well as the fact that her heart had gotten involved as well and the end of the summer was coming closer and closer.

Today was the first time since the winners' banquet that Declan hadn't had a scheduled appearance and she'd planned to catch up on work before heading out to watch the fireworks at Oak Bluffs with him. It had been his idea that they go out tonight and she didn't have the heart to tell him that she would have preferred to spend it alone with him rather than in a crowd. She didn't know when he had to head back to Hollywood and his film studio, but she doubted they had much more time together and she didn't want to waste it in public. Her heart seized at the relaxed smile playing around the corners of his mouth.

"Are you okay?"

"A bad phone call," she said. "But nothing unexpected."

He leaned down, capturing her mouth in a kiss. Because she'd driven to work, he followed her back to her place in his car. And then, when he followed her inside and she tried to get changed because she wasn't watching fireworks in business casual, thank you very much, one thing led to another and it was close to sunset before they got out of bed and on the road.

The fireworks at Oak Bluffs were legendary and the night was clear and perfect. Visitors and year-round residents crowded the grassy expanse, picnicking around a white bandstand lit up and decorated in bunting. A brass band cranked out Sousa tunes. Declan grabbed their supplies from his car and then threaded his fingers through hers, drawing her through the crowd and to the bandstand.

Proving he got her more than anyone else ever had, he'd stocked their picnic basket with lobster rolls and root beer in glass bottles. And true to form, they'd started their picnic with dessert first: cupcakes from Gitty's bakery truck. Afterward, he tugged her onto his lap. Fortunately it was growing dark, although she spotted at least one cell phone turned their way. Maybe she'd get lucky and a former president or a rap star would show up.

As the band wrapped up their next-to-last number, he shifted her off his lap. "I need you to do something for me." He smiled at her. "Think you can do that?"

She had some very pleasurable memories of the last time he'd ask that particular question. "Does it involve my holding very, very still while you have your wicked way with me? Because there are far too many people here for that to work. Only one of us is comfortable with performing in public."

He groaned. "You're killing me. And no. Not yet. Give me five minutes more here and remember that I love you."

She still got a fizzing sensation when he said those three words to her. It was surreal. More than once over the past year she'd wondered, mostly when she'd been hiding in her bed, what was so wrong with her that no one stuck around. Her father hadn't noticed when she disappeared. The man she thought she'd loved and had promised to marry had seen her as a means to money. No one had wanted her for *her*. No one had wanted to stay. She'd promised herself she wouldn't whine and that she'd get on with her life—and then Declan had crashed into it.

"I love you right back," she said.

He dropped a quick kiss on her mouth and then stood, tugging her up with him. "That's a promise. Don't forget."

The music stopped and then the band started again, but it wasn't the usual 1812 Overture that always ended the fireworks show. Train's "Marry Me" filled the air as Declan dropped to one knee in front of her, smiling up into her eyes. "Will you?"

She had no idea what script he was reading from or what her line was. There was a roaring sound in her ears, a foggy sensation creeping over her. Her face flushed as everyone around them turned to watch them.

"What?"

"Marry me." He wrapped his fingers around hers. "Charlotte, will you marry me?"

She smiled back automatically. This was… *Yes*, her heart screamed. Her brain thought… Well, it had derailed because the last month had been amazing, maybe the best of her life. Declan was a great guy who believed in her and who'd stuck with her through some hard moments. She was working, trying to make a difference for her foster kids, and for the first time in what felt like forever she was one-hundred-percent in charge of her own life…except for those late-night visits with Declan, because the man was deliciously bossy in bed and made the best suggestions about how he could please her.

That was amazing.

It was love.

A game changer.

She didn't know what this was, although it sure seemed like the game had changed. Again.

People around them were whispering, a sea of cell phones capturing their moment. *Did she say yes yet? Did he get down on one knee? Can you see the ring?*

She stared back at them, suddenly wishing she was anywhere else, and realized her teammates from Martha's Kids were in the crowd. None of them had mentioned that *they* were planning on attending tonight's fireworks. And there was…her father? Now that she looked, the entire Vineyard seemed to have packed itself onto the lawn—and none of them were watching the sky for fireworks.

They were all staring at Charlotte and Declan.

Declan, who was holding out a small, open velvet box with the hand that wasn't wrapped around hers.

She reached for it automatically. It was a diamond ring, an absolutely beautiful ring. A gift and a promise. The kind of sparkle that all the best dreams had.

"Say yes?" her dream man asked, looking up at her.

Her mouth wanted to blurt out "yes" and get right on with the business of happily ever after, while her heart helpfully offered a list of all the reasons that was the best-ever plan. One: he was so strong and sure of himself. Two: he fought for what he believed in and she loved that that included her. Three: he kept his promises and he didn't let go. Or was that four? And five… He was a charmer who had fought his way to the top and who now wanted to share his life with her. He gently rubbed her fingers, waiting patiently.

"Declan," she whispered. A camera shutter clicked somewhere.

"I love you," he said, his eyes serious. "Marry me. Yes?"

She nodded. He slid the ring on to her finger.

The crowd whooped and the band burst into a new song,

an ad-hoc wedding march. She'd had no idea a brass band could do that.

Fireworks exploded overhead spelling out: SHE SAID... YES.

At least someone had added the ellipsis, as if there had been a chance she would say no. Would they have sky-written a refusal? She choked back a hysterical giggle, but Declan was on his feet, wrapping his arms around her and swinging her in a dizzying circle as he whooped. All he had time to do was plant a brief, hot kiss on her mouth before their audience moved in to congratulate them.

Later, after they'd spoken with what had to be almost every person on the island, she found herself face-to-face with J.J., Declan's father. He fit easily into the Vineyard's celebrity crowd with his expensive haircut and tailored pants, his white dress shirt rolled up to reveal tanned forearms. Money was just the polish, she realized, as he held out his hands to her. The man radiated power and authority, a confidence stemming from years as a Hollywood power player.

"Welcome to the family." He pulled her in for a brief hug.

Charlotte wasn't a fan of casual hugging with people she didn't know well, but it was easier to embrace him quickly and then step back than to refuse. She'd have a lifetime to get to know him. Her heart started beating hard and fast again, pounding out an *oh God*, *oh God*, *oh God* rhythm with each frantic pulse.

"You're absolutely perfect," her future father-in-law announced. "I approve." She didn't think he was looking for her agreement, so she smiled and leaned into Declan, not sure what to think. Perfection wasn't her strongest selling point.

"Well, thank God for your approval," Declan said dryly.

"You chose the better prize," his father continued.

"Sure, you lost the boat race and we'll get around to discussing that later, but this lady right here? She's everything I'd expect from a Masterson bride-to-be."

Charlotte had no idea what he was trying to convey to Declan. What, exactly, was she perfect *for*? She felt as if she'd stumbled into a conversation that had started long before she'd arrived. Maybe Declan's dad was just weird or lived in the nineteenth century when parental approval was actually a thing. Maybe J.J. needed to feel like he was the center of attention. She didn't need to have the conversation now, not when she was getting married—*married*—to the man she loved. Suddenly the whole evening was too overwhelming.

"Can we get out of here?" she asked Declan, leaning more heavily on him.

"Anything you want," he said firmly, the smile fading from his face. "Always."

Eighteen

The large, decadently chocolate muffin on Charlotte's desk looked lonely. It needed a muffin best friend or two—or possibly a cast of friends like a TV sitcom, because she planned to eat her sorrows. She held her hand out. "Muffin me."

A new muffin landed in her outstretched hand. Bran, from the grainy texture. "Are you kidding me?"

"Friends don't let friends muffin alone," Gitty said. "Plus, there's only one chocolate muffin left and my day has sucked."

Gitty gave her a small smile. Brown curls bobbing, gray eyes warm with sympathy, she waved a plastic knife at the chocolate muffin she held in her other hand. "But I'm willing to be convinced to go halfsies if it's an emergency."

Uh-oh. Sharing—the sad details of her day or the muffin—was not part of today's plan.

"Waiting for a life update," Gitty prompted.

Charlotte took a bite of muffin. Unfortunately, no

amount of delicious sugar and chocolate chips could help her. "There are reporters outside. I'm never leaving the building again."

"Like one of those medieval nuns who live in a cloister?"

Charlotte had no idea if it was a thing or not, but it sounded good to her. "I'm going to give it my best shot. I'm pretty sure you can get everything delivered these days."

"You may need to dig a moat," Gitty offered. "There are a lot of reporters. Also, they like muffins and I charged them double."

Timma, the Martha's Kids' staffer who had volunteered to do reconnaissance behind enemy lines, popped her head in the door, knocking on the frame as she did so. "Six reporters out front."

"Crap," Charlotte said. "Okay. Company meeting in here, please."

Three minutes later, she, Gitty and the three staff members were crammed into her tiny office.

"Why are there reporters out front?" Thea asked. Barely five feet tall, fifty-something Thea ran their office like a benevolent dictator. Not only was she a spreadsheet whiz, but she always crocheted something for each office birthday. She also had an uncanny knack for ferreting out secrets.

Charlotte looked at her.

"Okay, so we all know," Thea admitted. "But we figured you'd rather tell us and we'd rather to hear the George details from you anyhow. Go straight to the source."

Charlotte fiddled with her muffin and tried not to angry cry. Timma reached over and stole a bite of muffin.

"George didn't quit," she said. "He emptied my bank account, then he emptied Martha's Kids'. Our summer camp budget is currently ten dollars. We're broke because of the chief financial officer I hired. I'd hoped that the charity boat race would refill our coffers. I failed you all and I'm deeply sorry." *Hope is not a strategy*, her father's voice announced in her head. *Thanks, Dad. I'm aware of that.*

Timma choked on the muffin. Thea cursed. And Mimi just looked like she might be plotting murder. Charlotte had never loved them more.

Gitty raised her hand. "Do you think George came here deliberately to meet you?"

What did it say about her that that hadn't occurred to her? She'd just assumed he'd romanced her to gain her trust after realizing she was the director. "So my entire relationship was a hunting expedition?"

"I think you should consider the possibility." Gitty handed Charlotte another muffin. "Banana chocolate chip, so it counts as a serving of fruit."

Gitty had a wide-eyed look of wholesomeness that was totally at odds with her lack of a filter and boisterous enthusiasm for life. Gitty didn't stop at one muffin if she was still hungry and wanted a second, and during their middle school days she'd taught Charlotte how to drink out of a glass soda bottle without getting her tongue stuck, shared her hot pockets and called out the playground bully, who had decided Charlotte's old-fashioned name begged for some ugly nicknames.

"So what happens now?" Thea asked.

"I don't know exactly," Charlotte said honestly. "But I'm on it. I'll keep you all in the loop. I do know that the district attorney is filing charges and law enforcement is officially looking for George so they can arrest him."

Timma frowned. "Will he have to give back the money?"

"If he still has it, yes." Charlotte paused. "But I'm guessing he didn't take it just to have it."

That was the cue for everyone to start talking at once, discussing George's potential shopping list. Thea voted for real estate because every evil villain needed a private, gated estate, while Timma wondered if he'd invested in cryptocurrency. Gitty was sure he must have a secret gambling problem.

Charlotte knew he had a character problem.

She, on the other hand, had a PR problem. After Charlotte's team had left, with Charlotte's repeated promises that she was doing everything she could to fix the problem and that their jobs were secure, she and Gitty scrolled through the social media postings. The big Hollywood gossip sites had run the story about how the famous movie star's brand-new fiancée was facing a career-ending audit as to why and how her previous fiancé had run off with almost a million dollars. There were the not-unexpected speculations: that Charlotte was in on it and just waiting for her chance to relocate to Belize or Fiji; that a broken-hearted Declan had fled to his Hollywood mansion and the arms of not one but three of his former costars; that he'd broken it off between Charlotte and him because loving her plain-Jane self was a clever PR move to whitewash his dented reputation.

"So you broke up with George—and congratulations on that, by the way," Gitty said. "And then you upgraded and dated a movie star."

"George left me," she pointed out.

"Details. You would have dumped him when you confirmed he was an ethics-less asshole. But since you didn't tell your team here about George's actions, I have to ask. Did you tell Declan? Or is he finding out right now?"

Charlotte looked out of the window to where Gitty was pointing and tried not to panic. Because she was right. Declan had just pulled up and the reporters were all over him—and no, she hadn't told him. She'd wanted to fix her mess before confessing.

"I just found out two months ago and then I had a

chance to make up the shortfall if I won the charity boat race and I took it."

"So that's a *no* on sharing with him." Gitty patted her hand. "But honey, the thing is—people share with their friends. Their family. The ones they love. And if Declan is all of that for you, why couldn't you tell him?"

Someone knocked on the door, saving her from yet another non-confession.

"I'd bet the last muffin that's your Prince Charming rushing to the rescue," Gitty said and nudged her. "I'd recommend letting him in."

Since that seemed like as good a plan as any, Charlotte got up and went to the front door to let Declan in. He didn't look happy.

"Why didn't you call me?" he asked.

Charlotte had no idea where to start, but Gitty didn't have that problem.

Staring intently at her phone, she said, "Because she was busy freaking out. And also, isn't this at least fifty percent your fault?"

Charlotte had no idea what Gitty was talking about, but she appreciated the support. Mostly. She did not, however, want an audience for this conversation with Declan.

Ignoring Gitty, Declan met her gaze. "I'm not George Moore."

"Neither is she," Gitty said, undeterred.

Charlotte froze and tried to get her mouth to work. She had to say something because this was her conversation to have, her and Declan. It didn't matter how much she hated confrontation or confession, particularly when she was the one in the wrong.

Gitty didn't look up from her phone, but she didn't hold back, either. "Uh-huh. You had to know this was coming. You let those people out here get their morning-after pictures. You let Charlotte walk into this. No one would be staking out the parking lot if you weren't a freaking Hollywood star."

"If I'd known that embezzlement charges were about to come out, I would have handled this differently."

"Right," said Gitty slowly. "But would you have skipped the proposal altogether?"

Declan and Charlotte both turned to stare at her. "What?"

Gitty held out her phone. Charlotte took it, heart sinking as she scrolled down the screen. Unflattering morning-after pictures of her post–boat wreck? Check. Additional morning-after picture of her not so sneakily leaving Declan's place? Check. Pictures of him leaving *her* place? Yep. Worse than the speculation about their sex life, though, was the newest headline.

Hollywood Bad Boy Signs Good Guy Contract?

She had to read the story twice before the truth started to sink in. According to "reliable sources," Declan had made a deal with J.J., a bargain where he traded his good behavior and rehabilitated public image for the family film company. The gossip site suggested that the well-timed, highly public proposal to a wholesome, plain-Jane local girl had been intended to seal that deal and paper over a night of debauched, post-wreck sex. *You chose the better prize,* J.J.'s voice echoed in her head. *She's everything I'd expect from a Masterson bride-to-be.*

She put the phone down and looked at Declan, who said the three words that killed a relationship faster than anything.

"I can explain," he said.

She really wished he would.

He'd said she was perfect, but maybe she should have asked him for a list of reasons why. Hurt twisted her stomach into a hard knot and slammed her stupid, hopeful heart into her ribs as tears smarted her eyes.

"These are angry tears," she told him. "I cry when I'm mad."

"Charlotte, look at me."

She did, because apparently she *could* make a greater fool out of herself. He met her gaze, the expression on his face pitying.

"Oh my God," she said. "It's all true, isn't it?"

"For fuck's sake," he growled. "You can't think I proposed to get a film studio."

"That would be a dowry first," Gitty said. She stood up, grabbed her phone and headed toward the door. "Right. I'm leaving now."

Charlotte waited until she was sure that Gitty had let herself out and the door had closed behind her. Given the way her life was going, she didn't want to risk a reporter sneaking in and accidentally-on-purpose overhearing their conversation.

"Did you actually have a contract with your dad about inheriting Masterson Entertainment?" The media lied. Exaggerated. She knew that.

He scrubbed a hand over his head. "Yes, J.J. and I had a deal in place before I came to Martha's Vineyard. You don't have to worry about it. It's over and done with and it was between him and me."

"We did this too fast." She felt numb, which was probably a good thing. "The engagement was a mistake."

We were a mistake.

He wasn't who he'd said he was. Or rather, his reasons for pursuing her weren't what he'd claimed. She'd thought he wanted her for herself, but instead she'd been a means of sealing a deal with his father.

"Charlotte, please listen to me."

"Maybe you should tell me what you were thinking. Why this made sense to you."

She grabbed her tote bag and started shoving things into it. Her laptop. A random stack of papers from the desktop. The muffins.

"You were never window dressing, Charlotte."

On that point, she agreed with him. "Well I don't look like window dressing, now do I?"

Or wait, maybe she did? She scrolled through the article again. A *good guy* contract. J.J. had made it perfectly clear—in writing, no less—that Declan needed to rehabilitate his public image. And what better way to do that than by falling in love and serving up a fairy-tale wedding? She wasn't going to do this a second time.

She yanked at his ring on her finger. "Take this back."

"I can explain," he said again.

Handsome, charming George hadn't bothered with explanations. He had been, she'd realized too late, the center of his own world and she'd merely been a useful appliance, propping up his public image and making it easier for him to do whatever he wanted. And while Declan had only stolen her heart, she couldn't do it again. She wouldn't be the window dressing for someone else's life so that that someone else could live his dream life.

She held out the ring. "I won't live in a fishbowl and I won't be a convenient choice."

Declan locked eyes with her. "Believe me, there's nothing convenient about you. Talk to me."

That hurt. "I won't be the cheat sheet on your inheritance test."

"So that's it? One piece of bad press and you're done with us?"

"No," she said. "One hard piece of truth and I'm done with us. It's not what they wrote, although it hurt to read. It's that it's the truth, Declan. You made a deal with your dad and you never shared that with me. You had so many chances to say, 'Hey, my old man will turn over the family company to me if I turn over a new leaf.' You should have told me."

"And you should have told me about George, about the problems at Martha's Kids."

She set the ring down on the desk. "I didn't want you to think I was anything less than perfect."

"Right," he said. "How's that working out for you? Ready to admit that you need help and to let someone get close to you?"

She looked at him. "If I am, that someone won't be you."

Then she turned and walked out of the room.

Nineteen

*Don't let someone who isn't worth your love make you
forget how much you're worth.*

If he can walk away from you, let him walk.

Forget what's gone.

Or who.

Charlotte glared at her phone. She'd discovered in a
late-night, ice-cream-fueled binge internet session that Declan was back in California and that people actually made
breakup apps. Since anti-dating seemed like a smart plan,
she'd downloaded one that flooded her screen with inspi-
rational quotes at suspiciously opportune moments, as if it
could telepathically sense her weakness, which would have
been a neat trick for a bunch of bits and bytes or whatever
it was software apps were made of.

Of course, *she* was the one who'd done the breaking
up—at least, the hostile-word-exchange part—but still.
She was *broken up*, if that was a word. Or a thing. The
ache in her chest whenever she thought about Declan was

painful. She prodded at it like a sore tooth, trying to see if everything was miraculously better. And... Nope.

Declan had still come to Martha's Vineyard fully intending to swap a race win for a CEO and owner role at Masterson Entertainment. If he'd been up-front about what he had riding on the race outcome, she'd have done things differently—or at least been better prepared and less shocked.

You weren't one-hundred-percent honest either, were you?

She shoved her phone into her desk drawer and shifted her glare to her laptop screen where she'd just finished revising her resignation letter. And then she hit the Send button.

Two seconds later Thea barreled into her office. Wow. Even for Thea, that was fast. "What did you do?"

"I resigned," she said. "I'm sorry. What I did just isn't fixable."

"You're just going to leave us?" Thea wanted to know.

"I let down our kids. I don't deserve to stay."

The ache in her chest got worse. Her head, clearly jealous of the attention, decided to throb along. Ignoring Thea's protestation, she grabbed her box of things and went outside. Now that the paparazzi had given up on her and Declan, she could walk unimpeded to her car. Her Kate Middleton moment was over. She could go to the grocery store in her pajamas and only the cashier and her fellow shoppers would know—not random people in North Dakota or Timbuktu. She'd made the mistake of reading the online comments once and people were harsh when they didn't say it to your face.

The sound of someone laying on a horn drew Charlotte's attention across the street. Right. It was Monday, so it was Muffin Monday and that meant Gitty's bakery truck. At one o'clock in the afternoon, the breakfast pastry crowd had dwindled and the afternoon cookie line hadn't yet formed.

"Did someone die?" Gitty yelled.

She shoved the box of crap into her car and marched across the street. "Do you think I have a problem asking people for help?"

"Do you want an honest answer or are you going to shoot the messenger?"

Charlotte narrowed her eyes. "Okay. So I'm hearing a *yes*. Except why won't you just come out and say it?"

Gitty sighed. "I promised I'd work on my filter, but what the heck. I'll start tomorrow. You hate asking for help. Remember when you got trapped in the bathroom in the fourth grade and you wouldn't admit it for hours? We all thought you had food poisoning but you were trying and failing to figure out how to take the door off its hinges."

"I'm sorry. I could—"

"Don't say 'fix it,'" Gitty said softly. "You don't have to fix everything. You can't—no one could—and as your friend, I'm not okay with what that does to you."

"I can't fix this," she admitted. "No matter how much I want to. Martha's Kids is out of money. We can't fund the summer camps. Raising those funds was my responsibility, so I've resigned."

Gitty nodded. "And did you ask the board what they thought was best for Martha's Kids? Maybe you could try asking them for help?"

She hadn't. She thought about that while Gitty made her a coffee and popped a leftover muffin into a paper bag for her. She'd tried to handle everything on her own. She'd insisted on it, because if you fixed the thing fast enough, you didn't even have to confess that you'd been the one to break it in the first place.

"I should have brought the budget issues to their attention," she admitted.

Gitty nodded. "And?"

"And—" She stopped because, really, she didn't know what the next step was. She looked at Gitty, who also shrugged.

"And then there would have been a bunch of smart, caring people brainstorming solutions," Gitty said. "And maybe one would have worked. Maybe you would still be broke. But there would have been an apology followed by a conversation."

There probably would also have been yelling, finger-pointing and…forgiveness.

"I made another mistake, but this one I can fix." She had to un-quit.

Gitty flashed her a thumbs-up. "You've got this."

Charlotte wasn't as sure, but she was going to try. Oh, boy. She was going to try. Turning around, she marched back inside Martha's Kids and into her former office. Hopefully still her office, she told herself. And then she fired off a second email, taking back the first one, since as they ran a summer camp and not a multinational IT company, no one had figured out yet how to shut down her email or change the locks.

"We have a budget problem," she told Thea when Thea stuck her head in the door a few minutes later. "And could you schedule a board meeting for as soon as possible? I need to explain the situation to them and pitch some possible solutions." She sucked in a breath and looked at Thea. "But I need help to do that. I need your help."

Thea smiled. "On it, boss lady."

Charlotte knocked on the front door of the house, keeping a wary eye on the bushes and driveway. No paparazzi jumped out to snap her, which she put in the *win* column. She could only imagine the stories they'd have spun. She didn't miss the unwelcome attention. But she did miss…

Declan.

She was done with pretending to be perfect, pretending that she had her shit together and that she took full responsibility for what she got wrong. She just wanted to let go.

And go to Declan.

Her father actually opened his own front door. He looked around the driveway, then turned and walked into the house. She followed him to his study.

"You moved out," he said, sitting down behind the big desk. He had the same look on his face that he'd had when the election results came in and his candidate had lost.

She had. Turned out, it was hard to draw boundaries with her father when she walked past him every day. "I did."

"So now you'll pay rent when you're lucky to still have a job at all. You got it all wrong there, Charlotte. You didn't have the experience or the charisma to handle a man like George Moore. He rolled you and your board."

The zing of shame in her stomach was familiar. Ignoring it was not, but she tried. "I didn't," she admitted. "I—"

But her father was on a roll. "You're too trusting. Naive. You had a good thing with that actor and then what happened? He made you look like a fool, too."

"George did that stuff," she said even though he was still talking and not listening. "Not me. I interviewed him. I voted to hire him. Clearly I did not make sure we had a good process in place or he wouldn't have been able to make off with the money he did. And yeah, he cleaned me out, too. I trusted him. That was my mistake. But I'm not responsible for his stealing or for his leaving because he was too much of a cowardly shit to own up to his mistakes."

It was a good speech, one she might have practiced before coming over, but it was wasted. Her father talked over the whole thing, commenting on Declan's shortcomings and her failure to keep him in line. "You were looking better. Today you're windblown and your nose is red. I don't understand why you can't make an effort. It's not that hard."

Translation: her makeover had worn off, although she'd kept the cashmere.

"I've done what I could to help you," her father continued. "You wanted to participate in this race and I got you a partner who all but guaranteed a win: handsome, athletic, knew how to win a crowd and how to sail a boat. You could have taken Martha's Kids to the next level with the prize."

"You picked Declan as my partner," she said numbly. "I thought it was random."

"His father owed me a favor," he said. "I made a quick call, reminded him of that."

It was nice that her father had wanted her to win. Except that he'd wanted her to win because he thought she was a failure at her job. He thought she needed to *take Martha's Kids to the next level* despite her repeated explanations that the organization's size was a choice and not a mistake. Like he always had, he'd ignored her.

"I have to go," she said. "No, I want to go. I've said what I needed to and this isn't a conversation. This is you telling me—*again*—that I've disappointed you. I know that, but it's going to have to be okay because I can't fix it. I *won't* fix it. Oh and FYI, I'm canceling on our next lunch date."

As her father blustered on, she left the room.

This wasn't a movie. There wasn't a script and a next line. Declan had said she refused to let other people help, that she insisted on fixing things that weren't her mistakes. He'd been right. She couldn't do this on her own. Fixing what wasn't right in her foster kids' lives would take more than one person, no matter how much that person cared. It took a team. An island's worth.

Declan had also said that he held on when he had to,

even when it was hard and it hurt and letting go would have been the safer option.

She'd done the opposite.

She'd let go.

Of him, of her life, of the things she couldn't control. And instead she'd held on far too tightly to all the wrong things: The pride that had her hating to ask for help. The ugliness of her father's emotional abuse. The hurtfulness of George's betrayal.

It hurt her, holding on so tightly. She opened the front door and went outside. It would be nice if she could let go of all of those things that were so bad for her as easily as she'd stepped over her father's threshold, but she had to accept that it wouldn't be easy. She'd have to do it one step at a time and sometimes she might go backward instead of forward. She'd watched Declan throw himself into life, the race, their relationship, willing to take the risk even if it meant possibly crash-landing. He'd given it everything.

While she'd held back, afraid of losing.

Twenty

Declan had jumped off buildings and bridges. He'd launched himself from planes and mountainsides with explosions licking at his heels. It wasn't all that often that he hesitated and he'd built a reputation in Hollywood for his ability to do whatever it took to make a scene happen. Even when Charlotte had disappeared over the side of the *Cupcake*, he'd known exactly what to do next: follow her, hold onto her, bring her safely to shore. Being strong enough, fast enough, well-trained enough—that had been, well, *enough*.

Now he had no clue what came next.

His agent was still angry about the quickie engagement and breakup. He'd been rooting for the perfect fairy-tale ending to Declan and Charlotte's story and then Charlotte had returned his ring. Hell, she'd kicked him out without considering the optics or what people would say. She'd called him out for making their relationship be about other people and for putting his career first—for that goddamned stupid contract he'd signed with J.J., which hadn't been about being his own boss or being the CEO of a successful company. Part of him was still the kid who'd been left in the foster care system by his parents and then adopted. And adopted meant that someone could take it back. Could take his life away and tell him to go.

Bottom line? He was afraid of being left so he made sure he was the one who left first, and if he couldn't do that? He made a game out of the relationship he'd been seeking, so it was all fun and nothing that could actually hurt him.

He'd thought he'd be fine, that he'd get over his feelings for Charlotte, that he'd go back to California and immerse himself in Masterson Entertainment and everything would be fine.

He wasn't fine. The media coverage after their breakup had been as bad as his publicist had predicted. Articles had speculated about his relationship with Charlotte. Nothing nice had been said and the pictures had been worse. All sorts of people had also come forward, too, from previously unknown members of the biological family to Vineyard residents who, it turned out, had plenty to say about Charlotte and her ex-fiancé.

And then there had been today's new development: a picture of George being escorted off a plane from the Bahamas in handcuffs. From what he'd heard, Charlotte's ex wanted to make a deal to avoid the consequences of his actions as much as possible and had shared in great detail what he'd done at Martha's Kids and how. The *how* concentrated on Charlotte's gullibility and her falling for George's charm, which turned her big heart and openness to trusting people into a fatal flaw rather than further evidence that she was an amazing person.

What pissed Declan off most, however, was that the impending demise of Martha's Kids was a footnote in the media coverage. The disappointed kids who wouldn't get their summer camp experience, the people in Charlotte's office who counted on their paycheck from the foundation, all of Charlotte's plans—those were collateral damage. Since that was just about the only thing he could fix, he'd made an anonymous donation yesterday.

But that was just money, which he had plenty of. He was across the fucking country from her when he needed to be there by her side. Or, since she'd sent him away in no uncertain terms, he needed to be on the island. Down the street. Anywhere he could do something for her. If George made her cry or worry one second more than he already had, Declan had plans of his own and he was implementing step one today.

He'd made the journey from his Santa Monica house to Hollywood in record time. They had two films in post-production and a new shoot starting on-site this week for one of his particular projects, so there should have been questions aimed his way. Most of the people on the lot, however, detoured out of his way once they got a good look at him. He knew he looked grim as he stormed inside.

"J.J.?" he demanded of the young guy parked at the receptionist's desk.

"Conference room. I'll let him know you're here, Mr. Masterson." The receptionist stood up, discreetly trying to block Declan's path, but Declan was around him and down the hall before he'd finished speaking.

He'd spent plenty of time in that conference room. He'd hammered out contracts, argued the pros and cons of projects and fought for Masterson Entertainment repeatedly. Today J.J. sat in his usual spot at the head of the long table. He didn't look surprised to see Declan, although Nash's presence on his right-hand side was unexpected. Nash didn't often leave his chemistry lab, even though he'd already earned a fortune from his research. He nodded at his brother, who nodded back.

J.J. said nothing.

Classic power move.

Declan didn't know what he'd hoped his adoptive father would say, but it wouldn't have been the kind of stuff movie fathers said about how they were proud no matter what the kid did. J.J. prized winning. And sure enough, that was where the man started when he decided the silence had stretched on long enough.

"You lost," J.J. said, not bothering with a greeting. "Sell me on why I should still make you my heir and not take the buyout offer I have."

Nash leaned forward like a hunting dog scenting his target. "So the media coverage is actually true? You were stupid enough to sign a contract with him?"

He reminded himself that he loved his brother. "I was, but that's not on today's agenda."

Nash gave him a level look. "Are there slides for this agenda? Speaker notes? I was told this was a family lunch and I'm feeling unprepared."

J.J. cleared his throat and they both looked at him. Declan had been on the receiving end of J.J.'s disapproving looks before, but this was the last time. He might be an ass, but he wasn't too proud to learn from the smart people in his life. Charlotte had made the decision to stand up for what she believed in. She'd put her shoulders back and walked into a ballroom as if she were royalty and that woman hadn't been half as brave as the woman who'd told him to get lost. She made him want to be a better man. Well, that and she just made his world better.

"Declan did sign a contract with me," J.J. said for Nash's benefit. "We made a deal. He'd get Masterson Entertainment if he could prove that he was Masterson material."

"You gave him an inheritance test," Nash scowled. He

didn't seem to mind that he hadn't been invited to take the test or that J.J. had effectively disinherited him.

"You did rehabilitate your image some," J.J. said to Declan, ignoring Nash entirely. As if what Declan cared about was how people talked about him. There was only one person who mattered. Okay. Two. Nash—and now Charlotte. "Getting yourself engaged to a genuine New England princess was clever, although you seem to have lost yet another fiancée."

"Asking Charlotte to marry me was the smartest thing I've ever done," he interrupted. "And she's a goddamned queen."

"Have you told her that?" Nash asked.

Declan hadn't. And since that was *also* something he could fix, he pulled out his phone and texted Charlotte. I'm an ass and I miss you. He hadn't stared at his phone waiting for a woman to respond since, well, ever, so this was a first for him. And while he hadn't really expected a handful of words to magically fix everything he'd screwed up, he was still disappointed when she didn't text him back.

He held up a palm when J.J. opened his mouth and started to talk. There was nothing he could say that mattered. "We need to get a couple of things straight. First, I'm done here. I quit. No more tests. I'm starting my own film studio, so heads up that Masterson Entertainment has a new competitor and we intend to kick your ass. Second…" He shook his head. "No, wait. That covers it. I'm out."

Then he turned around and got himself the hell away from J.J. No more contests, no more manipulation. Probably shouldn't have thrown down the gauntlet quite so obviously at J.J., but he was trying to change, not become a completely different person. He was competitive; he went after what he wanted. And even though he had more money than one man could spend thanks to his career, he couldn't sit around doing nothing. And that included doing nothing about Charlotte. He needed her back.

But after the very public nature of their courtship on Martha's Vineyard, he knew he needed to be cautious. Charlotte hated being the center of attention, although he hoped to convince her that she might like being the center of one particular person's attention. His.

Nash followed him out of the conference room, catching up with him as he entered the stairwell. "What were you thinking back there?"

He took the stairs two at a time. "I thought it was clear. If J.J. still wants a Masterson to run the family company, you can be the new CEO and future owner. Or he can hunt down Revere. I'll send a congratulatory fruit basket if that makes things clearer."

His brother grimaced. Of course, that was pretty much Nash's resting face. Nash was grumpy, surly and watched Declan's back with the ferocity of a dragon, albeit a very well-dressed, very wealthy dragon. "You're really going to walk away from all this because of Charlotte."

"Yeah." Declan shoved the door at the bottom of the stairwell open and headed for the front door. People spotted the two of them and rethought approaching them. Thunder and lightning. That's what people called them. Nash was the large, dark and glowering brother, while he was the brighter, hotter brother.

"Holy shit," his brother said. "You really do love her."

"I do." He leveled a look at his brother.

Who wasn't deterred.

Nash sped up and got to Declan's car first, crossing his arms over his chest he leaned back on it. "So you went to sail in this big charity race because J.J. was all hot about the Jessie St. Chiles thing. I'm not sure why you thought proposing bare-ass naked and with a dollar's worth of fake bling was going to work, but that's a problem for a different day. So you go, you race, you partner with Charlotte and then next we hear, you've been discovered naked and in bed with her after being shipwrecked in a storm. You propose, she says yes and the tabloids go nuts. Did you borrow this plot from one of your movies?"

Declan snorted because it did sound kind of like a script. "The wreck was an accident."

"And the naked part?"

"None of your business."

His brother laughed. "So the two of you hooked up and then, somewhere along the line, you developed feelings for her, but meanwhile J.J. realized he had a use for her after all because she's a lovely girl who doesn't run around starting naked-picture scandals. You proposed. She said yes. So what went wrong and why are you back here blowing up your life?"

"In exchange for letting her choose the charity we would donate to if we won, she agreed to makeover lessons."

Nash rolled his eyes. "Would you say that Charlotte is bright, attractive, funny with a side of determined? Feel free to fill in the blanks here with your favorite words."

"She's sexy, yeah. Curious. Willing to try new things even when it pushes her way out of her comfort zone. She doesn't like to be the center of attention, so people overlook her. Their loss." He shrugged. "But she's a hell of a woman."

Nash stared at him. "And just to be clear, you told this really amazing person that she needed to *change*? And you somehow thought this would endear you to her?"

He winced. "I was thinking of it more as a dare."

"Dare someone to say something dirty to the person on their left or to eat a banana without hands. Sneak into the next-door mansion and skinny dip in the pool. Take the family helicopter on a joyride. Don't dare someone to be a completely different person, especially if you like the original version."

They'd done all those things and more as teenage boys.

"I made that deal with J.J.," he admitted.

"The one where you proved you'd turned over a wholesome new leaf?" Nash snorted. "Christ, he has this whole vision of what we should be. You'd think he'd have figured out by now that people aren't made to order. He got what he got."

"Yeah. Well. J.J. and I signed a contract and part of the deal was that I'd do the race and rehabilitate my public image. Try to look like a real Masterson.

Nash looked at him. "We are Mastersons."

"J.J.'s still looking for the proof of that."

"Let him." Nash ran a hand over the scruff on his face. "Still doesn't change what we are and I still don't see how that caused you to piss all over your relationship with Charlotte."

"J.J. likes Charlotte. He said she was perfect wife material, that he'd be willing to overlook the race loss and stick to the terms of our deal since I'd *landed her*."

"Yeah. There's a whole lot wrong there."

"And Charlotte found out. She wasn't happy about it. She asked me to leave. I left."

His brother gave him an assessing look. "We've concluded that you're an idiot, right?"

"Pretty much."

"So let's fix this." Nash spread his arms. "Assuming, based on your behavior in there, that fixing this is your number one priority. Go back. Tell her whatever you need to make this work."

Declan swore. "Can you be more specific?"

"No."

"Great. That's really helpful. What exactly are your relationship credentials?"

Nash shrugged. "I am a doctor."

Nash was one of the smartest, most analytical people Declan knew. He was not, however, a people person. In any way. Declan had always been the one who could connect easily with others. Problem was, those had been surface connections. Between living in the public eye and the constant need to travel for work, he hadn't stuck around in one place for long—certainly not long enough to meet a woman and fall in love.

"You have a PhD in chemistry," he pointed out.

"Yeah, which makes me a chemistry expert," his brother said smugly. "Although if you're having chemistry problems, I don't want to know. She said yes once, though, so that's something."

"Yeah, but then she took it back."

Nash laughed. "You have to learn to close. Remember that cupcake stand we had?"

"We made two hundred bucks." They'd loaded up on dollar-store cake mixes and set up shop in front of J.J.'s Malibu mansion. Declan's job had been to charm everyone into stopping for a closer look, which he'd done. Gardeners, delivery guys, two dog walkers, a rock star and a well-known director. Once he'd delivered them to Nash, Nash had sold the hell out of their cupcakes. His brother was a ruthless negotiator.

"Charlotte seems nice," Nash said.

"She's not interested in the Hollywood lifestyle," Declan said. "Mansions, luxury cars and designer clothes, red carpet time—those things aren't exactly on her bucket list."

Nash leaned forward. "Nothing wrong with those things, but yeah. I get it. She wants something more than icing."

"What the fuck is it with you and the food metaphors?"

Nash groaned. "I *fucking* missed lunch because of your temper tantrum back there. So what does she love? And put some thought into it, okay? Don't just blurt out whatever comes into your head first."

Declan thought, and while he was thinking a taco truck pulled into the Masterson parking lot. He slid his brother—who was tucking his phone back into his pocket—a glance.

"Everyone should have the taco lady on speed dial," his brother said virtuously.

"Martha's Vineyard, her foster kids, cupcakes. Those are definitely at the top of Charlotte's *like* list."

Nash headed toward the taco truck. "You putting yourself on that list?"

"I screwed up. What if I go back and just screw it up some more?"

Nash sighed and placed his order with the beaming lady manning the taco truck. "You realize I get paid five hundred dollars an hour to consult, right?"

Declan pulled his wallet out and slapped a hundred-dollar bill into his brother's hand. Nash promptly tucked it into the tip jar on the taco truck counter. "Waiting for my advice."

"So here's my suggestion. Do the work to figure out how you make your life fit into hers. The whole cross-country thing is hard. The interest in your personal life is unfortunate because she seemed like the kind of woman who wants to reserve the right to go grab a cup of coffee in her yoga pants, yeah? But then you go there and you actually have a conversation with her. Tell her you still love her and that you want a chance. Ask her what it'll take for her to give you that chance. Then do that."

"That's a pretty simple plan."

"It's authentic." Nash paused. "Also, I'd suggest groveling. Bring her a present that's personal, too, one that shows you've been paying attention to her and that you've got her back. And whatever you do, don't make her feel as if you think that she can't handle her own shit. Just make sure she understands that your goal is to be real with her—and be with her."

Doing those things might actually help. He slid his brother a glance. "How did you get so smart?"

Nash flashed him a rare smile. "Didn't say it worked. This is a working hypothesis only. Go prove it."

Twenty-One

Step one in Charlotte's change-her-life plan: conquer her fear of the ocean. Since the plan also called for accepting her limitations and loving herself as is, the steps were more like baby steps…and had her sitting in a kayak. There was no storm today and no rip current, so she felt optimistic. Or possibly that was because someone had made a large anonymous donation to Martha's Kids. Since the donation had been made on behalf of the "Guinea Pig Appreciation Society," she wasn't entirely clueless about the money's source. Declan had come through for her kids.

The teenager who'd rented her the kayak stared at her dubiously. He was ankle-deep in the water—and all of two feet away from her. "You want a push?"

"No, thanks," she said. "I'm good."

She liked being able to see the bottom. Each time the wave pushed her kayak onto the shore, she nudged it back out to sea with a careful prod of her paddle.

"Seriously," the teenager said. "Happy to help."

She ignored him because she had thirty minutes left on her one-hour rental and she estimated that was just enough time to make it to the end of the beach and back. And also, because while she was trying to ask for help when she needed it, this situation definitely didn't count. By the time she made the return trip, her face was pink from the sun and her nonexistent core muscles had quit in protest, but she'd done it. And if she felt sad and a little teary, she'd blame that on the bag of M&M's she'd mainlined in the beach parking lot for courage. Unfortunately, it explained why her stomach hurt but not her heart.

She made an ungraceful exit from the kayak, once again grateful that her paparazzi days were behind her. But hey, she was voluntarily in the ocean up to her ankles, so she counted that as a win, and it had been hours—half a day, even—since she'd thought about Declan. She'd moved on from compulsively stalking him on the internet and wondering what he was doing and if she'd really, really screwed up this time.

She dragged the kayak up the sand toward the rental kiosk, feeling kick-ass, if tired. A Hollywood action hero with muscles would almost have been a welcome sight. She would've totally asked him to do the heavy lifting. Instead, she panted and heaved and got the stupid, bright yellow kayak back to its jaded teenage protector, who turned out to be mostly interested in finding out if she really knew Declan Masterson and was the dude coming back any time soon?

She had to admit that she didn't know.

But it was…unlikely.

She shoved that thought out of her head and walked back to her car, pretending her calf muscles didn't ache almost as badly as her heart. Although her hair was twisted up on top of her head, she might have been wearing one of the fancy T-shirts Declan had picked out for her, which was a thousand times better than wearing the shirt she'd stolen from him.

She still wasn't ready to call him, though, or even to text him. *She'd* broken up with him, so she owed him an apology. She had a draft written on her phone. She sort of, completely and impossibly wanted to see him.

And touch him. Hold him. Have him back in her life in all the ways. If wishes were horses, she'd have a large herd.

But sending him on his way had been the right thing to do. She'd thought about it and she stuck by that decision. It wasn't her job to fix Declan and it was okay to have boundaries. Boundaries like not accepting half-truths or being anyone's convenience. Boundaries were good. She'd worked on setting a few with her father.

Funny how she'd had to lose the men she loved in order to learn that lesson. Moving on from the past was surprisingly difficult, but she was taking it one day at a time. *Look at me*, she thought. She'd almost made it an entire day without thinking about him. It was as if her brain had one of those clocks. *It has been one day since the last accidental thought of he-who-shall-not-be-named.*

There was someone leaning against her car—a large, male someone with scruff on his jawline and a small frown on his handsome face. He looked like safety. He looked like home.

And just like that, the Declan Masterson clock reset. *Zero days without a lost time accident.* She sighed.

"Summer camp is on after all because a really big fan of guinea pigs made a huge donation."

The frown turned into a small smile. "That's great."

Right. "You wouldn't know anything about that donation?"

He just looked at her. "It can be from whoever you want it to be from."

"A *million* dollars?"

Warm hazel eyes held hers. "Worth every penny."

"Why?" She inhaled. Exhaled. Reminded herself that people breathed successfully every day.

"I love you."

As reasons went, that one was undoubtedly the best and she really needed to hear him say it again. She tested the words in her head. *I love you.* And look at that: the sky didn't fall, a monster wave didn't swamp the beach and everything seemed perfectly normal. Except—

"You just came back to say that you love me?"

"Yes." And then he paused. "Well, mostly. I needed to tell you that I failed the inheritance test."

"Okay," she said cautiously.

"In fact," he said, "it might be more accurate to say I tore it up and walked out on the examiner." She was no J.J. expert, but she had a gut feeling that Declan's dad had not been happy with that move.

She hesitated. "Declan."

He waited for her to say something more, but she was running on empty.

He solved that problem for her by opening his arms. "Can I hold you?"

"That sounds like a good plan." She squeezed her eyes shut to keep the tears where they belonged and stepped forward. Blindly. But it was all good because Declan had never, ever not held on to her even when she was doing stupid things like falling overboard.

His arms closed around her. "I missed this. I missed you, Charlotte."

"We still wouldn't work."

She felt his mouth brush her hair and when she cracked an eye, he was smiling ruefully.

"Nash said I should make a speech here. He recommended sonnets. But here's the thing. I love you. There aren't any strings attached to that. No expectations. No pretty words. But I would like to spend time with you. Do you think you could make space for me in your life?"

"You want in on my life?" she said softly, opening her eyes because she had to see his face.

"Yeah." He smiled at her. "In your life. In your heart. Whatever you've got for me, I'll take."

"I'm a little short on trust right now," she admitted. "I have a hard time believing Prince Charming is as good as he looks. Or that he's not going to get back on that white horse of his and ride away, with my heart and the good silver in his saddlebags. I'm..." She didn't know how to explain, but she knew she had to try. "I'm a work in progress and I don't know if I want a fairy tale anyhow. I'm going to screw up. I'll never be perfect and I'm working on being okay with that. I'm not sure I'll ever be good at asking for help."

"I don't want you to be anyone other than you," he said. "And I'm not perfect, either."

There were a million things she should be asking him. Or telling him. Starting with all the reasons why they shouldn't rush into a relationship—*again*—and ending with, well, she didn't know what.

Because face-to-face with Declan, she didn't want to think about endings. *Or that he's still a Prince Charming and you* know *you shouldn't trust those...*

"You haven't asked me why I'm not perfect," he said. "But I'll give you a hint. I told you that I would always hold on, even if it hurt—and then I didn't. You told me to leave and I did. I'd like to prove to you that I'll never let go of you again. You're not window dressing. You're so much more than that."

"Really?"

"Yeah." Cupping her face, he lifted it to his. "I made a plan to get you back. Do you want to see it?" he asked. "I know how you love lists."

What she loved was him.

"Only if you really mean it," she said. "I can't—I don't…"

"It's a heartfelt plan," he said and then he reached into the back pocket of his jeans and pulled out an honest-to-God list.

The list had been rolled up like a scroll and stuck through a ring. *Their* ring. She unrolled the list with trembling fingers. Declan had written in a bold, decisive scrawl:

1. *Tell Charlotte I love her.*
2. *Tell Charlotte I love her.*
3. *Tell Charlotte I love her.*
4. *Buy a house in Martha's Vineyard with a tower. Or at least a turret.*
5. *Love Charlotte forever.*

"I repeated the most important part," he said. "So there's a lot of duplication in my plan because there's only one thing that matters: if I love you and you love me. I have the first part covered, but the second half is all yours. That's what makes this a partnership."

She blinked away tears.

"Just so you know, crying was not part of my plan," he said, his voice full of concern.

"It means your plan is working. And I'm happy."

"And—" he prompted.

"And I love you, too."

* * * * *

COMING SOON!

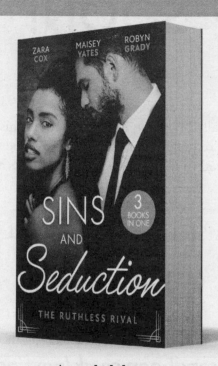

MILLS & BOON

THE HEART OF ROMANCE

A ROMANCE FOR EVERY READER

MODERN
Prepare to be swept off your feet by sophisticated, sexy and seductive heroes, in some of the world's most glamourous and romantic locations, where power and passion collide.

HISTORICAL
Escape with historical heroes from time gone by. Whether your passion for wicked Regency Rakes, muscled Vikings or rugged Highlanders, away the romance of the past.

MEDICAL
Set your pulse racing with dedicated, delectable doctors in the high-pressure world of medicine, where emotions run high and passion, comfort love are the best medicine.

True Love
Celebrate true love with tender stories of heartfelt romance, from the rush of falling in love to the joy a new baby can bring, and a focus on the emotional heart of a relationship.

Desire
Indulge in secrets and scandal, intense drama and plenty of sizzling hot action with powerful and passionate heroes who have it all: wealth, status good looks…everything but the right woman.

HEROES
Experience all the excitement of a gripping thriller, with an intense romance at its heart. Resourceful, true-to-life women and strong, fearless face danger and desire - a killer combination!

To see which titles are coming soon, please visit

millsandboon.co.uk/nextmonth

LET'S TALK
Romance

For exclusive extracts, competitions
and special offers, find us online:

[f] facebook.com/millsandboon

[t] @MillsandBoon

[o] @MillsandBoonUK

Get in touch on 01413 063232

For all the latest titles coming soon, visit
millsandboon.co.uk/nextmonth